The Harrow Quartet

By

Beatrice Fairbanks Cayzer

MURDER FOR MUNITIONS

MODELS MURDERED IN MILAN

MADRID's MOCKING MURDERS

MEXICO's MOVIELAND MURDERS

The

Harrow

Quartet

B.F. Cayzer

Copyright © 2011 by B.F. Cayzer.

ISBN: Softcover   978-1-4500-5661-8

All rights reserved. No part of this book may be reproduced or transmitted in any form or by any means, electronic or mechanical, including photocopying, recording, or by any information storage and retrieval system, without permission in writing from the copyright owner.

This book was printed in the United States of America.

To order additional copies of this book, contact:
Xlibris Corporation
1-888-795-4274
www.Xlibris.com
Orders@Xlibris.com

Contents

Murder for Munitions 9

Models Murdered in Milan 109

Madrid's Mocking Murders 191

Mexico's Movieland Murders 285

I dedicate these books to S.A.S. Prince Albert II of Monaco, whose probing mind has developed from oceanography, to the environment and to embrace outer space.

Beatrice Fairbanks Cayzer

Frontispiece from an oil painting by French Impressionist Jean de Botton

Murder for Munitions

Characters in Murder For Munitions

Rick Harrow, British trainer of racehorses who travels the world to locate the best bloodstock available for sale
Hillary aka Happy Harrow, his jockey wife and mother of three
Sven Jensen, a mysterious self-proclaimed Norwegian who is traveling the world to find the best polo ponies
Stinky Ollert, a successful Florida businessman originally interested in reining horses, but latterly wanted polo ponies
Fran Purcell, opera and Rap singer who wants to win a derby and instructs Rick to travel until he finds a future derby winner
Sir Arthur Snodgrass, Fran's M.P. fiancé, who is tricky
Dolores aka Lola Snodgrass, who has an ongoing incestuous affair with her brother
Jeremy Grace, the future Earl Cabrach, a former member of Britain's M-15, a neighbor of the Harrows
Ellie Grace, Jeremy's cousin and Happy's close friend
"Ben," a Saudi prince who wants Rick to train racehorses for him and makes 'an offer he can't refuse' to Hal Murphy
Hal Murphy, Rick's richest owner who wants more racehorses
Clara Murphy, his wife who wants a divorce
Ali, Egyptian self-vaunted millionaire who bids on racehorses
Fatima, Ali's much put-upon traditionalist Muslim wife
Harry Bloom, said to be a high executive of McDonald's
Mafalda, an ex-courtesan who zeroes in on divorcé Hal
An anonymous racegoer who much resembles Sven Jensen
Señor Puyana, a Colombian racehorse owner who is down on his luck, and desperate enough to sell his truly great horse

Chapter 1

"I want you to buy a horse that will win the derby for me." Those were the orders I received from one of my richest owners, the rap singer Fran Purcell. I was seated at my desk in the former tack room of our racing stables on an autumn evening feeling the first cold snap of the coming winter. I'd only just returned from a very long trip to Tokyo and Hong Kong, where I'd won a race at Happy Valley during the time when the 2008 Equestrian Olympics were held there

That trip was followed by another one. Last week, to Florida. I felt exhausted from both trips, but I'd had to act on Fran's orders to inspect a colt for sale in Ocala. That colt had proved a total No-hoper, but the trip had given my wife Happy the chance to solve a murder mystery.

I'd been the prime suspect, so that trip had turned out to be a blessing. I'm a British racehorse trainer based near Epsom, where the English Derby has been run for over two hundred years.

My name is Rick Harrow: I'm forty-three-years old. I've worked for Fran Purcell for three of those years, which added to the weight of encroaching middle age. With a young wife of twenty-four, and three small children, I couldn't give in to the luxury of feeling sorry about what I do for a living.

I have wonderful back-up in the glorious, sexy shape of my darling wife, Hillary aka Happy, who is a licensed apprentice jockey. She'd just recently won a race in Tokyo, with considerable acclaim.

But, buy a derby winner for Fran? She'd done her research, all right. She'd added: "I know that Peter Nelson bought SNOW KNIGHT for only five thousand pounds, and he won the Epsom Derby. I know that Ed Benjamin told Bill Wightman to buy CANONERO II, and, when that horse's front leg seemed gimpy, Benjamin sold him to a Venezuelan for peanuts, and CANONERO II won the Kentucky Derby. Raymond Guest, while he was the US Ambassador to Ireland, won the Irish Derby with SIR IVOR and the

English Derby too. All three horses cost the minimum you can expect to pay for any fucking winner."

Fran's use of four-letter words had not improved even if she HAD learned to do her research when buying horses. My wife, born in the back country of Kentucky hills, used appalling language too, but her courageous loving heart shone above those ain'ts and double negatives.

From Happy there was never a four-letter word. In any case the sublime sex we have took me into another sphere in life as if we rose toward the heavens like the lovers in a Chagall painting.

Fran had another unattractive side to her personality: she was miserly.

When she'd accompanied Hal Murphy to Melbourne, she's flown Tourist. Again, when she went to Hong Kong: Tourist. In Saratoga, for the races, she'd stayed in an American version of a Bed & Breakfast instead of a hotel, although escorted by her constant admirer, Sir Arthur Snodgrass.

With her order to buy a derby winner came a repeat of what she'd said when I was sent to Ocala: "You can take your wife, but I'm not paying the fares for those three kids of yours and the nanny. I'm sending you to Colombia to judge a frigging wonder colt I've been offered. No kids!"

Yes, even though my two little daughters were both under two and would have gone free.

I hadn't dared to bring them along. But I resolved to make an exception for our little Timmy, going on four, who'd been kidnapped a year earlier and I hadn't been parted from him ever since. For Timmy, I was prepared to pay his half-price ticket, and did. Dorothy and Irish, our infant daughters were left at home in Epsom with wonderful Amah. whom we'd accumulated in Hong Kong and for whom I'd been able to make arrangements for her to be admitted to the UK as an asylum seeker because she'd left her village in China during troubles there.

Of course we all three traveled Tourist. Fran wouldn't pay for Happy or me to go Business Class, which I would have much preferred. We flew from Heathrow on British Airways to Miami, and there we boarded a DC-8 belonging to AVIANCA, for Bogota, Colombia's capital.

We were crushed uncomfortably in narrow seats. I sat with Timmy. Happy was given a seat across the aisle, next to the most beautiful man I'd ever seen. Honestly. No sarcasm intended. He was BEAUTIFUL. In England, we're known for our good-looking guys. And occasionally I'd see one that you could almost describe as beautiful.

Among the homosexual crowd there were good-lookers, but usually their looks were enhanced: the blonds had used peroxide. Plastic surgery was responsible for full lips and square chins.

The man seated next to Happy was that ultra rare exception, a truly gorgeous male. He had the type of nose and cheeks displayed on Nazi posters of Hitler youth. His very full head of hair was so light blond the color could only be compared to sunshine. Tall, with broad shoulders not enhanced by a tailor's expertise, he had excellent posture and yet a certain grace. I looked at his hands: his fingers were as long as a pianist's. His clothes were well-cut and looked expensive.

What was this paradigm doing in Tourist? I figured him for an actor coming to Colombia as a contrast for the dark Colombians. But he could talk without a script. All the way across the Caribbean he'd been chatting non-stop with my Happy.

I didn't like it, but what could I do when Timmy was acting up and I had to try to control him?

Timmy solved that. He started to yell: "I want to sit next to Mummy. It's no fun being with Daddy."

No fun? We'd played video games on my lap-top, and watched a Disney movie. Timmy yelled louder: "I want to sit next to my Mummy."

Surprise! With a courtly bow, the gorgeous man relinquished his seat, giving it to Timmy, and then came to sit next to me.

"How do you do? I'm Olav Jensen," he said in a deep baritone voice, slightly accented with Scandinavian vowels. "And I know you are Rick, the lovely Hillary's husband."

Worse, he turned out NOT to be an actor: he was on the same mission as I was. He was coming to Colombia to buy horses, except that he was on the look-out for polo ponies.

"Thanks for giving up your seat, for Timmy," I said. "Would you like a drink?

"Double scotch." He had two of those. When the stewardess came to our seats to offer a meal, he asked for an extra one if there were any left over. I paid for three glasses of wine for him, and he countered by inviting Happy and me for dinner that night after we'd checked into our hotels.

He spoke with his mouth full: "I'm staying at the Tequendama. I've never been to Bogota before, and don't know anything about the hotels there. I was told it was built in the 1950s or 60s by an American company. I'll take my chances."

"Where are you going to go to find the polo ponies you want?" I asked.

"At the Polo Club. There's sure to be some spoiled son of a polo player who was given a pony by an over-expectant father. The son will sell it off cheap. Happens all the time. Sons don't always want to play polo because Daddy does."

I nodded. Don't I know? My Timmy has no interest in racehorses. He seems to resent them because I spend so much of my time with them. Poor Timmy: he wasn't enjoying this trip. He'd had three changes of clothes:

Epsom was freezing, Miami was staggeringly hot, and now he was outfitted for cold Bogota, perched high in the Andes at an altitude of 8.600 feet.

Sven asked: "And you? Where are you going for the horse you want? Be careful going out into the countryside. I guess you know that kidnapping is Colombia's second most lucrative business."

I swallowed hard. It was not in me to tell this stranger that my son had been kidnapped in Kentucky and my wife abducted in Dubai, and that I most certainly didn't want to round that out by being a third victim. I mumbled: "Fran Purcell is the owner who has sent me here. She made the arrangements. I'm to drive out of Bogota to an hacienda and meet a Señor Puyana, who is supposed to have an exceptional colt."

"Those two names intrigue me. I have followed Fran Purcell's career from opera to rap. I wish she'd kept to opera, she was magnificent in DON GIOVANNI. But then I realize she must earn $200,000 a year doing rap and would get much less as an opera singer. And is this Puyana related to the famous harpsichordist?"

So Sven Jensen was more than just a horsetrader: he knew his musicians.

I said: "I remember a Rafael Puyana who was the son of a beer tycoon, but who preferred playing ancient musical instruments to running the family's breweries. It would be interesting to learn if the Puyana I'm to meet has any precious harpsichords lying around."

Our DC-8 was hit by turbulence. The plane dived a thousand feet, then climbed above clouds to pass the peeks of mountains that bordered the savannah surrounding Bogota. From watching the Magdalena River snake through forests, we now looked down on this vast plain where skyscrapers intermingled with red tile-roofed huts. Majestically situated on one of its highest peaks was a religious sanctuary that gave luster to the scene.

While Sven stared out at Bogota's vast plain, I got a good look behind his ears to check out whether he'd had plastic surgery. He had. All that incredible beauty WAS the result of a surgeon's knife.

Because Fran Purcell had made our living arrangements, we found ourselves at a down-market hotel. Happy took that in her stride, as she does so many things. One advantage of the hotel was that it could provide babysitters, and we were able to park Timmy while we went to dinner with Sven.

The Hotel Tequendama was built in a modernistic style popular in the 1950s. It provided a rather incongruous comparison to a graceful colonial-era chapel next door, Capilla San Diego.

Sven had reserved a table in a cafeteria. Not elegant. Nervous, Happy had unpacked her best dress for this dinner and could just as well have arrived in jeans.

"Welcome!" Sven handed menus to us. "Everything's good here. But I particularly like the coffee ice cream for dessert. The last time I stayed here I heard that when this hotel opened and the Bogotanos tasted coffee ice cream for the first time, it created a riot with people storming the place."

I listened with great interest. This reminded me of a scene in GODFATHER II, where the Godfather hears his elder brother Fredo reveal he was a liar. Fredo had forgot that he'd pretended not to have been with another gangster before, and stupidly let slip that he had been. Sven made a similar mistake too: he'd distinctly told me he hadn't been to Bogota before. Why would he bother to lie?

The answer came quickly. "Mrs. Harrow—may I call you Hillary—would you accompany me to the polo club and help me select a pony?"

Was that his game? He was a flirt, trying to seduce my wife?

Happy looked pleased, and flattered. "Sho 'nuf. Ah'd LOVE to accompany y'all. But tomorrow, Ah's goin' t'take Timmy on the cable car ride up thet mountain to the sanc-tu-ary."

"Fine. We'll go to the polo club the day after tomorrow."

Those arrangements suited me. I planned to leave Bogota by the day after tomorrow.

I didn't. The following morning I had my hired car drop off Happy with Tim at the cable car station and I went straight to the Puyana hacienda. It was a perilous drive. We left the plain, dropped several hundred feet into a canyon populated with prehistoric-looking giant ferns, then soared up another road to reach what seemed to be a French manoir. Instead of the usual thatch-topped gateway, this estate greeted visitors with huge columns leading up the drive. The house itself was in disrepair, with paint peeling and loose tiles leaving gaping holes in the roof.

Instead of a uniformed butler, a surly peasant woman in an ankle length skirt and dirty blouse opened the door. She hadn't combed her hair, and it fell to one side as if pushed there by a pillow. She had broken teeth, and her hands were coated in flour.

She pointed past an empty hall to another closed door. I opened it to enter a large room. There were no furnishings, no lamps, no pictures, no rugs. A stooped, balding, very thin man came to offer me a handshake.

"Shall we go straight to the stables and see my colt?" he asked, without any offer of a drink.

The stables were as run down as the house. But the colt was superb.

I ran my hands down his legs to feel for heat. They were sound. I looked into his eyes to find honesty. I found honesty, plus intelligence. "May I ride him?"

"He accepts the saddle." A saddle and bridle were provided. I did my usual, and once in that saddle I felt there was plenty of horse beneath me.

After I dismounted, thoroughly convinced this colt was a winner, I asked: "Have you all his proper papers?"

"Yes. My cousins have always imported their horses from England and if any were born here they were immediately registered. I followed suit. You can race him with no problem."

"What's the asking price?"

"The price is a firm price. I will not haggle. As you have surely noticed, my home is in a bad way. There is a mortgage I cannot pay. The estate will be foreclosed. This colt is my only hope. I want four million dollars."

Not good news. Knowing Fran as I did, I was fairly certain she would never pay that amount. Why had she sent me here? Hadn't she talked price earlier? I thanked Senor Puyana for showing me his colt and told him I'd let him know what I could do.

He walked me to the chauffeured car. "Don't stop if any bandits appear on the road." No goodbye.

We did see two dangerous-looking types when we skirted that canyon again. But my experienced driver revved his engine and we drove past them so fast they had to jump to the side of the road.

When I returned to our bedroom, Happy was still touring with Tim. I telephoned Fran, and was told: "Bloody well forget the deal. Get your ass back to England, to take care of my horses there."

I made one other telephone call. I rang my Canadian owner, generous Hal Murphy, who had been outstandingly kind when Happy was abducted and Tim kidnapped, anteing up most of the necessary. I said: "Hal, I've seen a winner today. The breeder wants $4 million."

Hal said immediately: "Buy him. I'll have my bank wire the money tomorrow."

Had I made a mistake? Now we would be spending another day in Bogota.

When Happy returned she was gung-ho for her trip to the polo club with Sven. She talked about him incessantly. I told her about those telltale surgical scars behind his ears. "Who-all cares? Ah knows ladies what made thesselves prettier with thet plastic surger-y. Why not a man?"

I was hoping for good sex when we went to bed. No such luck. Happy was on a tack talking about Sven. She started by saying: "Y'all knows how Ah loves stories. This Sven, he told me an ugly one but one Ah cain't fo'get. All the way across thet Caribbean Sea while Ah sat next t'him, he told me about a Colombian lady, Clara Rojas, what got released by Terrorists after six years in the jungle. A Terrorist had done raped her three years ago. Pregnant, she had her baby by Caesarian with no one to do the job but a nurse who used a kitchen knife. When that nurse done pulled the baby out, she broke his arm. Later that baby got malaria, and real bad worms: leishmaniasis, caused by a jungle parasite. Even the Terrorists felt sorry for thet baby. The mother called him Emmanuel, and let the Terrorists take him away from her to save his life. He went to a family what had five other chillun, but the baby got so sick the gov-ern-ment had to take him away and bring him here to Bogota. Emmanuel's almost the same age as our Tim. Po' little fellow,: by the time he was two he still couldn't walk. His grandmother used her DNA to prove this little boy was her daughter's child. Now the mother got released from them Terrorists, and just a few months ago got reuni-ted with Emmanuel. Some story. Sad. Ah can't think o' nothin' else."

I remembered reading about Clara Rojas and Emmanuel in several newspapers. I'd said nothing about them to Happy, because of her own suffering during HER abduction, and then Timmy's kidnapping. I'd have kept my mouth shut now, except Happy said something I couldn't accept.

She said: "Sven don't think bad about them Terrorists. Says as how they're like our own George Washington, fightin' a revolution fo' their freedom."

I growled: "George Washington didn't sell poison to financé his fight. Some of his soldiers had no shoes, but they didn't sell their souls. These Terrorists make peasants grow coca leaves and then they have their labs process them into saleable cocaine." No contest. Happy would believe what she wanted to believe. But, just moments before she DID initiate lovemaking, she said:

"Ah's reservin' mah o-pin-ion of Mr. Sven Jensen."

Chapter 2

Happy left with Sven Jensen for the Bogota Polo Club early the next morning. I had to wait until nine a.m. for the local banks to open. Hal's order for the $4 million demanded by Puyana was not going to be had easily.

I had no option but to let Happy go off alone with Sven.

As I don't speak Spanish, I couldn't hope to go to the banks without an interpreter. Our down-market hotel didn't offer a business center. I needed to go to Sven's hotel, The Tequendama, to locate an interpreter.

She was adorable. Her name: Carmen Vasquez. She had dimples in both cheeks and an airy manner coupled with sparks from eyes that twinkled. She had a brownish complexion, straight black hair and the shape of her eyelids suggested there was Mongolian blood somewhere in her background.

"I studied at Oxford," she told me shyly, but with a trace of pride. "You'll know how old I am if I tell you I was there at the same time as Benazir Bhutto. What a wonderful woman! Headed our debating society, and the Oxford Union. Isn't it terrible the way she was assassinated last December?"

She talked non-stop, probably to prove she was worth her salary. To accentuate her Colombian nationality she had draped the local cape, the ruana, over her shoulders. "Aren't you cold, in your summer suit?" she asked with marked consideration.

"No. I'm fine. My base is at Epsom, and as you no doubt know, it's a lot colder there than in Bogota." But I appreciated that she had shown a caring attitude.

She took me to the Banco de Colombia, where it turned out that the manager spoke English and I could have done without an interpreter. I was glad to have her along, nevertheless.

The negotiation was tiresome. I had only my own identification: nothing of Hal Murphy's. Yes, he'd received the FAX from Hal regarding the $4 million. No, the bank could not authorize a payment without more paperwork.

Thanks to the miracle of FAX and e-mail, I soon had the necessary. That was one hurdle covered. Next I had to find a vet wlling to travel to the Puyana hacienda.

"Too dangerous," three vets declared. A fourth said: "I don't like the road. Many ambushes on it. But if you can get an armored car, I'll come."

I was going to need an armored car to take the $4 million in any case. But before I negotiated for that, I went to the Minister of the Interior, Carlos Holguin, to ask for his help acquiring the all-important export license.

Carmen proved invaluable with all these hiccups. Finally, in our armored car complete with vet we arrived back at the tired pillars leading to the Puyana house.

He pointed out a colt in the far field. He did NOT offer to accompany me down the muddied grass.

Carmen whispered: "Maybe he has only the one pair of good shoes. I remember two poverty-stricken well-born sisters who could only appear one at a time, exchanging the one dress they owned for each appearance."

I walked down to the field with the vet. Fortunately I'd bought a basket of raw carrots acquired in the Hotel Tequendama's kitchen, again with Carmen's help. I needed those carrots, NOT for my prospective purchase but because he was now accompanied by a fearsome stallion.

This horse, a boarder with Mr. Puyana, reared high and like a boxer baring his fists he warned me with his hooves he would brain me. He roared as if there was a mare in season he wanted to cover.

Taught by Happy's example how to handle various difficult horses, I laid a path of carrots to the next field and wooed the stallion into it, where I promptly closed an intervening gate. The colt was very upset at losing his friend. He acted up like Timmy when HE didn't get his way. The vet calmed him, took samples of blood and manure and hurried back up to the main house.

I delayed. I had to ascertain positively that this colt was not a ringer. I was reminded only too well of how a ringer had been offered to me in Dubai for Hal. I could not take a chance of that happening here: not with $4 million involved.

This colt had the same three white socks and a star on his forehead as the one I wanted to buy for Hal. But we trainers all knew how easy THAT is to paint on. I'd brought a magnifying glass with me to inspect the tattoo on his lower lip to assure myself that they were the same numbers as I'd seen before.

They were. I placed the halter I'd brought around his neck, and he followed me politely enough to the horsebox readied beside the armored car. Packed inside, with the vet standing sentinel to be sure he wouldn't be switched at the last moment for a ringer, I made my way into Senor Puyana's study and faced him down.

"You get your money when the colt is safely on the cargo plane. You can accompany us and I'll pay you at the airport."

Carmen, who'd been beside me all this time, drew close to Senor Puyana, and with great gentleness she spoke comforting words to him in Spanish, to explain that there was no desire on my part to insult him, but that a previous bad experience had necessitated these ploys.

The drive to the Bogota airport was anything but jolly. I might have been following a hearse. We had a scare in the canyon, when a group of bandits passed us by on horseback, but they had other prey in mind and ignored our convoy.

I inspected the facilities on the cargo plane. They were adequate. Polo ponies were a frequent export and this plane was fitted properly for transporting horses. I paid Senor Puyana, who scuttled away like a starving dog that had found a bone.

It was a wrench to part from Carmen at the Hotel Tequendama. Those dancing dimples had caused my important bits to rise beyond my control. But Happy's lovemaking the previous night kept me from offering anything untoward. Luckily, because Happy and Sven arrived at the hotel at the same time as we did.

No chance for asking for a spare room! And had Happy been propositioned by Sven during their day at the Polo Club? It didn't look like it: Happy had her quixotic expression curling those delicious lips.

Sven didn't offer dinner. We were dismissed.

Back at our own hotel, with its second-rate meal, I questioned Happy about her day.

"Glor-i-ous!" She gulped down her dinner like it was ambrosia. "Ah got t'ride all the ponies he wanted t'buy. Mo'e than thet, Ah was asked to do figure-eights with them, to test their a-bi-li-ity to turn at command. Ah loved thet!"

"Yes, darling. Of course you would."

Happy struggled to keep from laughing. "Ah's felt like Ah was in them there Ol-y-mpics back in Hong Kong. Where we saw what y'all called dressage. Ah tells y'all, when Ah cain't keep my jockey license no mo'e, Ah's goin' t'have me a dressage school."

"Did Sven make a pass at you?"

"Yeah man. But Ah told him like Ah loves mah husband. He didn't insist-like. He were too busy. Suckin' up t'some weirdo. A man what gave me the creeps. If'n Ah was a castin' director fo' a crime movie, Ah'd hire him fo' a killer."

"A Colombian?"

"Don't rightly know. But they spoke in Spanish. Sven says he knows lots of languages. Says he knows everythin' about everybody. Even me! When we was sittin' in the airplane he pulled out his lap-top and googled my name. Sho 'nuf, it came up thet Ah'd won a race in To-ky-o last month."

"Anything else?"

"Yeah." Dear Happy modestly stared at her shoes: "On Google it said like Ah was a sleuth what had trapped three murderahs."

"Interesting. I imagine THAT was when he decided to play a considerate gentleman and exchanged seats so he wouldn't sit beside you. Very interesting. But then, why his invitation to dinner? Why invite you to the Polo Club?"

"Dinner? He needed to know how to expo't them ponies, and he knew y'all had learned them ropes. Polo Club? He needed someone exper-i-enced t'test them polo ponies. He don't know nothin' about hosses. He would've bought one what were lame if Ah hadn't rode him."

"I didn't figure him for a proper horseman. Didn't walk like one. Didn't talk like one. Why the polo ponies? What else brought him to Colombia?"

"Don't rightly know. It's connected somehow WITH ponies. But he told me somethin' Ah thinks might int-er-est y'all. He said your Senor Puyana lost all his money playin' poker. He's a bad-luck gambler."

We finished our revolting arroz con pollo and went upstairs to our bedroom. Happy wanted to dismiss the babysitter early from the adjoining room because she'd clocked up a lot of pesos that day. Timmy was contentedly asleep as a kitten.

But there was not to be any delicious sex. Happy got back on to the heart-wrenching subject of Clara Rojas, and the woman's six years held in captivity by one of Colombia's revolutionary armies: the FARC. "Thet little Emmanuel's so cuddly. He cain't stop huggin' his mother. Ah told Sven what y'all said about George Washington's soldiers not sellin' their souls like them FARC men what trade in cocaine. He insists like they got a right t'fight."

"Cocaine. I wonder if there's a way to smuggle coke in the polo ponies. I heard from my interpreter that many surreptitious ways of hiding coke have been tried. Coke packed in with the flowers that are a big Colombian export. Coke packed in condoms and then swallowed by carriers called 'mules.' But, ponies? They have to be examined by vets, before they can be exported. No way would a pony swallow a condom. Any surgical incision would be probed. How, then?"

"Gelding them." Happy stated flatly. "Ah sho' noticed thet all them ponies had been gelded."

"You would," I laughed, "you and your very special libido."

"T'ain't no laughin' matter t'them ponies. They'll nevuh have the fun o' bein' stallions. Po'r ponies! But think about thet. Cocaine COULD be packed into their empty scrotums."

I did think about that.

Chapter 3

We didn't meet any interesting personality on our return flight to Miami. Happy slept most of the way on the plane, and I was left to deal with Timmy. I calmed him, keeping him from running up and down the aisle, by promising that our first stop in Miami would be to a McDonald's, HIS eatery.

In fact, Hal Murphy was waiting for us at the airport and HIS idea of a fine restaurant was decidedly *not* McDonald's. Yet that kindly roughneck deferred to Timmy's clamored wishes and we ended up at the McDonald's closest to the airport.

"What did you think of your new colt?" I asked, after we were settled in a booth and Happy was helping Tim to rustle around the freebie toys.

"Looks good. But $4 million?"

"Could be worth every penny. Fran Purcell had ordered me down to Colombia to look at the colt as a future derby winner. When she balked at that price, I gave you first chance at acquiring him."

"My precious wife, Clara, she thinks the colt could come up trumps. Even has a name for him: Hal's Comet!"

I nodded. That was certainly better than most of the other names Hal had chosen by himself: starting with MIGHTY MORON.

Happy brought Tim to our table, loaded with plastic toys from McDonald's give-away basket. "Where's HAL'S COMET now? Did y'all find good grazin' fo' him? Ah worries he might not take to livin' in a stable. He's been loose in a field, with a boardin' stallion."

Hal nodded. "Yes, so Rick advised me. I've sent him up to the Delray Training Center. Rick, you'd better get up there fast, because I hear my colt's refusing to eat. Even refusing water. In this heat, he'll die."

I agreed I should take myself up to Delray, soonest. But, I asked: "What about Happy, and Tim?"

"Rented a nice condo for all of you in West Palm Beach, at the Wellington Polo Club. Good security. I checked out a nursery school for Tim. Easy commute for you to Delray on the Sunshine Turnpike."

No arguing that. I knew about Hal's rented premises for his employees, and I'd enjoyed superlative quarters as his trainer in Hong Kong, Tokyo, Saratoga and Lexington.

Happy didn't look too pleased. She'd also enjoyed the luxuries of our earlier premises. What was bothering her?

She was quick to tell me after we'd said goodbye to Hal and were in a rental Hummer heading for West Palm Beach.

"Sho' don't like the idea of livin' in thet there polo club place. Sven lives nearby."

"Sven."

"Yeah man. Told me he leased him a big house and a $2 million barn. And he's on a private air club's grounds what allows members t'keep a private plane. Members share the runway, keep their planes parked by their houses. Ah asks myself what does a man in polo need a plane for? Them's club planes are too small fo' transportin' hosses."

"You don't have to see Sven."

"Ah sho' hopes not."

Chapter 4

But she did.

Sven had a prominent box in the newly built stands. We were invited to the grand opening of the new owner's facilities, and as luck would have it—our box was smack next to Sven's.

There was to be no polo: too early in the season. But the new facilities were being given a trial run. On the field was a show of a renowned breed of horses that only recently had been awarded a place to compete in the Olympics. Called Reining horses, they would be termed "quarter horses" under other conditions. I'd seen them on the "herradura" trails in Colombia, where they could handle the vertical mountains with their hooves firmly wedged in stones planted in mud. I'd admired their steady pace on flat surfaces, where by neither cantering nor galloping they permitted a rider to stay in the saddle for hours on end. Reining seemed to me to be a Western version of dressage. It could demonstrate the willingness and ability that a horse needs to work cattle. I'd been to the National Reining Breeders' classic in Oklahoma and become quite interested in reining horses.

Sven noticed Happy's exalted expression as she caught sight of these horses' unique abilities. He called to her, his voice sultry and provocative: "Hillary, you should come to the Reining trials with me sometime."

Happy ignored him, but she continued to follow the Reining horses' stylish show.

Sven tried again: "Hillary, did you notice how differently kitted out their riders are? They wear casual clothes, and farmers' hats."

This time, Happy tossed him a quick answer: "Ah's more in-terested in hosses whut dance."

Sven took that as an invitation. "The Lippizaner horses from Vienna will be performing tomorrow night at the Kravis Center. I'll buy tickets."

Now I intervened: "Not a bad idea. **BUT** *I'll buy the tickets. We'll all three go.*"

At eight o'clock the following evening there were four of us as a party for the Lippizaner show. Sven brought along a rough toughie, who looked like the villain in an old-fshioned Western. His name was Stinky Olsen. Because he stank. Overweight, he had a very pronounced case of under-arm odor.

Even the familiar horsy smell given off by the Lippizaners could not blot out Stinky's stink.

Stinky was interested in buying Reining horses from Colombia. His ticket for this show had been paid for by Sven, who seemed only too eager to go back to Bogota on a buying spree.

Stinky gargled in his baritone: "I've got the hang of it now: buying, and shipping horses from Colombia."

Sven contradicted him: "Stinky, you need an expert like me to go to Colombia for you."

Stinky shouted over the music that cued the Lippizaners' movements: "I want bargains."

"Not many of those left in Colombia. The good horses, the really valuable *Caballos de paso* cost in six figures, and more. Why, when I went to Medellin on this last trip, I saw a parade of *CABALLOS DE PASO*. They were magnificent: their pelts gleaming from oil. They had their ears pricked. Their eyes shone with intelligence."

Medellin? I caught that city's name. Why had Sven not mentioned to me that he'd gone to Medellin?

Stinky made a sour face. His lips took a dive. "It takes more than a short trip to learn all the ins and outs of the business surrounding Reining horses. You got to test for worms, bad ones you never even heard of in the USA. You got to watch out that the owner doesn't have an enemy who might poison the horse."

Sven showed his glistening teeth as he boasted: "I guarantee I'll get you bargains. BARGAINS are my middle name. And you'll get a horse that shows off you have power and money. See those Lippizaners on the stage? You'll get a horse that can copy some of the Lippizaner crossed leg movements."

This was one tacky evening. The only plus was that Sven was too determined to make a deal with Stinky for any hanky-panky attempts where Happy was concerned. His perfectly polished boots remained under his chair: no footsie business with Happy's open-toed sandals.

I cut the evening short when the Lippizaners stopped doing their dance routine.

Later, playfully, I said to Happy in the privacy of our Hummer: "Darling, I'm so excited by those great horses, I'm going to be the best lover you ever had."

"Sho nuf. Since y'all's the only ONE Ah've had."

Never boast. Never tempt fate.

That night, when we were on top of the bedcovers, I experienced my first encounter with the dreaded ED.

Chapter 5

The next morning I got worse news than that I might have recurring ED. A call from one of the Delray Training Center's vets warned me that Hal's $4 million colt was in imminent danger of dying.

Happy listened in on that warning. "Sho 'nuf, we all's got to go to Delray right now." She packed our three children into the Hummer, still in their pajamas. Happy, who may be the world's worst cook, has always maintained a spotless home. But this morning she left the dirty dishes in the sink and the urine-stained sheets on our "chilluns'" beds. But she did remember to bring a basket of carrots for HAL's Comet.

He was one very sorry-looking horse. Worse than sorry-looking. Dying had not been too severe a description. For three days he had refused water and food. According to some experts, he **should** be dead by now.

Happy smelled the water that had been offered. "Disgustin'," she squawked: "Ah wouldn't drink it, no way. More chlorine in it than Ah never smelled befo'e. And he don't like this Amer-i-can feed. **We-alls got to find a field where he can eat good grass.**"

We did. HAL'S COMET **did** nibble at the grass. After Happy poured bottled Evian water into a bucket, he drank that. He ate the carrots. But still his head hung low and his eyes were dimmed.

Happy said: "He want a friend. He HAD a friend, you told me in that field of Senor Puyana's, a ret-ir-ed racehoss."

I got on the blower to Hal and requested he give permission for one of his older horses stabled at the Delray Center to go into the field with HAL'S COMET.

He agreed readily, although I hadn't described the truly desperate state his colt had fallen into.

Happy and I were hanging around the fence enclosing those two horses when Stinky suddenly appeared.

"Those three kids yours?" he asked, pointing to my "chillun" who were crawling all over the adjoining field. Timmy was playing baby, and leading his sisters on his knees.

"Yes, mine," I spoke shortly. I hadn't any fond feelings for Stinky. I was wishing he'd go away.

He didn't.

Stinky wanted an audience. "I've been thinking of expanding my equine holdings. Reining's great. But I don't see why I can't play polo. A few lessons, and I'd be fine."

I wondered what he'd smell like after an afternoon of heavily-competed polo. I growled: "Why not ask Sven to buy you a few ponies?"

"No thanks. I examined them horses he brought last week. Good enough, maybe. But I want better than just good enough. I might want to breed polo ponies. His ponies were entire, all right. I tested the scrotums in case he lied. Entire, yeah. But the quality weren't that great. They'd had drugs."

"Drugs?" I asked.

"Sure, what you think: second-class ponies like that would offer such outstanding form? So many of them hosses what come from Colombia have been fed drugs. Maybe cocaine: that comes pretty cheap there."

Was he giving me a hint?

Who's to know? After those remarks Stinky took himself to another field to get a new audience from anxious owners watching their sick filly.

"Drugs!" Happy's voice was exploding like a firecracker. "Good God: you reckon we got us a coke-head?"

Now we both examined HAL'S COMET with renewed interest. And, although I hate to admit this: but Stinky HAD BEEN giving us a hint. HAL'S COMET perked up when we called over a Colombian groom who just *happened* to have ready a dose of white powder.

"We can't allow Hal's horse to be ruined:" I moaned, when the groom took enough money off us to go get lost.

"Little by little we'll cure him of add-ic-tion," Happy said loud and clear.

How? **NOT by offering smaller and smaller doses. We made HAL'S COMET go cold-turkey. Happy managed to give him so much loving care that soon he began to act like a normal colt.**

Happy and I moved to Delray. Among other reasons, Happy was suffering toothaches. "Ah's been to them fancy dentists in Wellington," she complained: "all them dentists wanted to do was to cap mah teeth or make me have implants: at $15,000! Ah's found me a good dentist in Lake Worth what charges $100 a fillin': and mah mouth's about cured."

We didn't miss Wellington, with its $2 million barns. I'd worried that Happy might get ideas from the fancy horse owners there who spent $15,000 on a dress, although most of those women never combed their hair and lived in jeans.

"I noticed an awful disparity between rich and poor, in Wellington," I remarked when we were visiting a much-improved HAL'S COMET. The grooms are near starving while the owners have private jets and—"

"Yeah man, and Ah saw a $65 million estate bein' sold. Called WINDSOME FARM. Thet ad were in a national ma-ga-zine. Said how the estate had 40 acres of field. It has an Olympic Dressage ring, two show-jumping and training rings, four lakes. They got them 72 stalls fo' hosses, and 4 formation stables. Wow! But this mornin' Ah found a nice cottage fo' sale in Lake Worth for $65,000. Some difference."

"Are you suggesting we buy it and settle here? You know I can't. In fact, my darling, we'd best get back to England fastest or I'll lose my owners there."

"Ah's ready to go to Epsom. But only if y'all convince Hal we must bring this hoss with us. Ah cain't leave him behind t'become a coke-head agin."

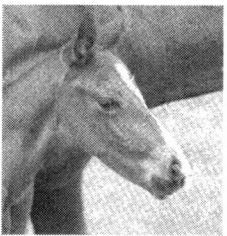

Chapter 6

Gold-hearted Hal was easily convinced. My little family and I were on a BA plane for Heathrow within a week. HAL'S COMET followed and was in England only one day after our arrival. Bur my little family was growing.

Happy had morning sickness. "Ah's pregnant agin," she told me wonderingly: "but Ah's been careful t'take a blue pill every day."

"And WHERE did you buy the last batch of blue pills? *Colombia?*"

"Yeah man. Why? They make them different there?"

"I don't think those pills are made there at all. But show me the bottle. I'm ready to bet they are past their sell-by date."

They were. The date: February 2006!

Happy grinned. "Don't y'all fret. We'll welcome this one same as t'others."

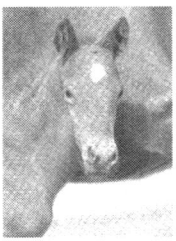

Chapter 7

I love England in the autumn. There's a lot to be said for those famous opening words: "Breathes there a man with soul so dead who never to himself has said: this is my own, my native land." Autumn in my Epsom garden means the tart perfume of burning leaves, the reddening ivy on the barn walls, the golden chrysanthemums. Overhead arc pheasants from a nearby shoot, safe over my land, and the kwaking of ducks in my pond. Yearling foals are nearing their two-year-old seasons and begin to look like racehorses. Wonderful!

Happy had worse morning sickness and fainting spells, but cast aside any worries thanks to her memories of the same when she was pregnant with our other three tots. At Epsom, she found her own satisfaction with England: her friendship with our neighbor Ellie, now nearing the term of *her* pregnancy, the opening of a preschool for Timmy, and her new-found interest in dressage which she learned more about on Google.

Ellie Grace looked enormous with her eight months' pregnancy. I'd been accustomed to seeing her in hacking jacket and tight jodhpurs; it was a shock to discover that she had heavy legs that now matched her tummy.

The one blot on my return to Epsom was my difficult relationship with Fran Purcell: now one of my most important owners. Her ghastly use of four letter words had worsened. She had no compunction for raining them down like hail.

"You really are a cunt," she said in my over-heated office. I was sweating from the upturned thermostat, another unpleasant trait she had: fiddling with other people's thermostats. Too hot or too cold to suit most of us. Now I noticed half-moons of sweat staining my flannel shirt. She continued, spit flailing me from her over active tongue. "You were so busy shagging your wife you never looked for that derby horse I wanted. No! You bastard, instead you went and bought FOR HAL MURPHY the horse **I'd found out about.**"

No answer to that.

In lieu of words, I pointed out the Puyana foal grazing in a nearby field. Even a non-professional owner who made her money as a singer could gauge how sickly the poor colt was.

"THAT pathetic turd cost $4 million?" She demanded hoarsely. "I'd have killed you if you'd spent my money on that sad lump of shit."

"Yes, I don't doubt that you would have. Poor young colt: he's called HAL'S COMET. He has a lot of improving to do before he can hope to earn that name. We're doing the best we can to add condition. He's taken to Spiller's horse nuts, so at least he isn't starving himself. Took to our Epsom tap water too."

"Where are you going to find a derby winner for me?"

"How about I try in Ireland?

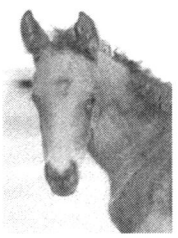

Chapter 8

I wasn't to go to Ireland. Not for Fran, not quite yet.

One Sunday morning when Happy and I were sipping coffee seated on our bumwarmer enjoying an early fire in our hearth, we heard Fran's Daimler chugging up our drive, its motor complaining from lack of maintenance. **Miserly Fran kept her cars in bad repair until they broke down like starved athletes.**

Fran burst into our little cottage with reddened eyes streaming with tears.

To me, she said: "You'll have to cut down on expenses. I'm having a fucking time of it trying to pay bills."

I'm a sucker for a weeping woman. I tried to comfort her. When she sat down next to me I put an arm around her heaving shoulders. She yanked it away.

Happy tried patting her hands. Fran lunged off the bumwarmer. In her hoarse contralto she said: "It's these damn teenage girls who fuck up my album sales. First there was Charlotte Church. Now that she's a frigging mother and playing the householder, I've got Taylor Swift to worry about. All of eighteen, and nominated for Best New Artist Grammy in all genres. Won the CMA Horizon award. Now she's setting records for that damned OUR SONG she wrote—can you believe this—in Ninth Grade. For weeks it's been Number One on the country charts. Just when I've switched to country."

"Ah's got mornin' sickness," Happy moaned, and fled to our downstairs bathroom.

"And I need to take a line," Fran announced, following her to the loo.

Bad news. I'd believed that Fran had quit drugs after she became engaged to Sir Arthur Snodgrass.

When Fran emerged, jumpy from coke but ready for a chat, I said: "When would you want me to travel? I could go to Ireland after Ascot's *Queen Elizabeth II Stakes* in October."

"Shit, no! Forget that. You told me yourself the prices in Ireland had gone through the fucking roof with Coolmore bidding $15 million for a colt."

"That figure was reached in Miami, not Ireland," I said sotto voce. No good arguing with Fran Purcell.

I needed to expand the stable. With no new owners it was imperative that I acquire more horses for the owners I already have.

Happy emerged from the bathroom. Her face had that glorious luminescent quality prefacing the months of a big belly. If I could love her more, it would be during these early months of pregnancy.

She said: "Why not Russia? Ah hears like there's bargains in racehosses there."

"No bargains in Russia for anything. Too much oil money floating around," Fran snapped. She strode to the liquor tray and poured a large double from the whisky bottle. At ten a.m.!

Loyal Happy insisted on her theme: "Russia's got it some real fine hosses. Ah hears like them hosses come de-scen-ded from winners what was taken from Germany after the Second World War. Great blood lines."

I nodded enthusiastically. I thought: "Leave this to Happy."

She won the day.

Fran opened her checkbook. "Not a farthing over one million," she spat, **but signed a check for that amount.**

When Fran's tired Daimler struggled up our drive returning Fran to London, Happy told me the truth behind Fran's outburst.

"Fran's got a real reason fo' her miseries. Y'all must have noticed how Sir Arthur kept postponin' the weddin' and ain't even given her a ring."

"Yes. I have."

"Sho 'nuf. Ain't got nothin' to do with sales of her albums. They's doin' just fine. No. She done found out thet Sir Arthur Snodgrass *snogs* his sister. Yeah man, thet ugly Lola. Seems like they been doin' thet since she was ten and he eleven. No stoppin' them now."

"Dolores Snodgrass! Incest?"

"Yeah man. Like in the Bible when Lot snogs his daughters to re-pop-u-late the land. Po' Fran bought her a $15,000 weddin' dress from thet Miz Emmanuel what made the weddin' gown fo' Princess Di all them years ago. But when Sir Arthur told her by telephone not to plan on wearin' a ti-a-ra at the weddin' because she ain't the daughter of a peer, Fran went to his apartment and charged into his bedroom where she found him inside his sister. Both hog naked. And at it."

"Nasty. But none of our business."

I went to our local travel agent and made inquiries for a quick trip to Russia. I wasn't thinking about Miami, and Florida.

On my return from the travel agent's I was sitting in my office in our stables when Happy tore into the room waving a newspaper cutting.

"Read this! Our babysitter sent it to me.*" She whistled.* "Headline says LOCAL WELLINGTON SPORTSMAN DIES IN MIAMI ACCIDENT. Article tells about Sven's pal, Stinky. Seems like he went to meet him in Miami's tallest buildin' and fell down an el-eva-tor shaft by mistake. Didn't see a sign what read *out of order.* Nothin' wrong with Stinky's eyes, as Ah recollects."

I dialed Sven's West Palm Beach telephone number. I got that always-annoying *THIS NUMBER HAS BEEN DISCONNECTED*. I wasn't to know any details about Stinky's death from Sven until by surprise I met him again in Moscow at the horse sales there.

Sven looked very different. He'd altered his hairstyle: now his golden locks weren't combed back from his forehead Twenties-style, they'd been chopped and stood up like a clothes brush.

He seemed shorter and fatter in his cheap Russian-made suit. Tasteless yellow lace-up shoes were as ugly as the flowered red tie he had knotted Prince of Wales style. This military haircut and the down market clothes didn't become him.

Happy took the change badly. "What happened to Mr. Beautiful?" she gulped.

Wasting no time, I approached Sven near the sales ring where the horses for sale were being paraded. "Sven, tell me what happened to Stinky." I gave no hello, glad to see you, or other polite opener.

He turned on politeness like tap water. "Welcome to Russia, to both of you darling Harrows. How wonderful to see you here. Stinky? Poor old chap, he fell down an elevator shaft."

"We read that in the PALM BEACH POST. Our babysitter sent us a clipping. It said further that he'd gone to Miami to meet *you.*"

"That's absolutely correct. Not a convenient truth. We'd agreed to arrange to buy some quarter horses from a Colombian gentleman, visiting Miami. Stinky thought the price too high, stormed out of the man's office and into a blazing sunset which temporarily blinded him. He didn't see the sign that warned the elevator was out of order."

Very quietly, Happy remarked: "Ah seems to recall thet Stinky wore sunglasses."

"True. He'd removed them to read the contract for those quarter horses."

"Sven, did you buy those horses? You can't have had time to go to Colombia to check them out."

"You're wrong. I did go to Colombia. To Medellin, and I didn't like the horses. Beautiful animals, with their manes and tails so carefully braided, but without the steady pace I look for in quarter horses."

He was lying.

But I had to let it go because at that moment a very fine filly entered the sales ring. Happy prodded my elbow. I looked up the filly's credentials in our catalogue: pure bred with English blood dating back to the 1930s. I waited until her price reached $900,000 and then made my bid.

"$950,000," I heard bid behind me. I twisted like a dancer to stare into the brown black eyes of a curious brown-skinned man wearing a fez.

Carefully, not going too fast, I raised my bid: "$975,000."

On the big board where simultaneously all relevant currencies were posted, I read the equivalent in pounds, yen, euros, and pesos. The Russian price wasn't posted. It was called out by the auctioneer. But as I don't speak Russian nor am I able to read the Cyrillic alphabet, I waited for the next numbers in dollars.

They came all too soon. The man in the red fez sang out: "One million."

Fran's top offer! What to do? I didn't want to antagonize one of my principal owners by counteracting her orders. But this filly promised to be too good to miss. In my mind's eye I could already see her winning the fillies' derby: The Oaks.

Happy made the decision for me: she called out, "One million and a quarter." Leaning towards me she whispered: "Hal Murphy would take the filly if Fran won't pay the difference."

We got the filly.

The brown-skinned man in his red fez astounded me by coming to us with congratulations. In perfect Oxfordian English he roared: "Well done. You bested me fair and square. At Rugby, my old school, we were always taught to give credit where credit was due. And as the Duke of Wellington said about another school when giving credit for besting Napoleon at Waterloo: 'the battle was won on the playing fields of Eton.'"

Not quite the right quote, but from this mysterious gentleman, it was welcome.

"Thank you."

"May I introduce myself? My name is Ali Mahmoud, I'm Egyptian, not Russian."

I could have guessed that! "Sorry I took the filly from you. Actually, my owner's orders were to go to one million. I've taken a gamble to go higher."

"You train for Hal Murphy," he stated quite rightly. "I remember that odyssey when your wife was abducted in Dubai, and Murphy came up with the money to buy the horse that prompted that outrage."

I nodded. This was not a subject I discuss with strangers. Painful, and ultimately it could be dangerous.

Happy was easier about her ordeal. "Ah's gone back to Dubai since. Ah's got no hard feelin' toward the Emirate."

The Egyptian's next few words were as welcome as rain in a desert. "How would you like to train for me, Mr. Harrow? As you've passed the figure given by your owner, we could come to a happy meeting of minds. I will hire you and take over the filly at $1,250,000."

Overly conscientious, I countered: "I thought you wouldn't go over one million!"

"With you for this filly's trainer, I will make a point of finding the extra cash."

We shook hands on that deal. God knows I need new owners. I knew I could easily lose miserly Fran by having gone over the million mark. Ali Mahmoud left us, hurrying away to find his wife. I continued to study our catalogue and eventually did buy a colt for Fran at just under one million.

I felt relieved not to have to beg Hal for help. He'd been consistently generous, but I didn't want to add a straw that might break that camel's back: and $1,250,000 was no straw!

Sven had disappeared during the bidding. We found him again at our hotel's bar. How did he know where we were staying? I recalled he'd told Happy he made it his business to know everything about every body. To my astonishment and unease, Sven was at the bar with Ali Mahmoud and a gorgeous Egyptian woman.

She was one very emancipated Egyptian. No burqa for her, not even the thin chiffon headscarf adopted by many Muslim women such as the much revered late Benazir Bhutto. Not only was this lady perched at the bar, but she was downing a very large whisky, totally forbidden for both sexes of Muslims.

"Meet my girlfriend: Mafalda," sang out Ali. There was visible pride in his deep voice. But where was the wife he'd gone to find?

Happy warmed to the woman immediately. "Mah name's Hillary. But just call me Happy." Perching at the bar, she called to the barman, pointing to Mafalda's drink. "Give me the same."

What a conundrum! Happy had hated the Turkish mistress shown off by Hassan, when that woman had flirted so outrageously. She'd kept her feelings to herself when I'd strayed for a one-night stand with Mr. Kotski's Irina, but she'd never have warmed to that ex-KGB operative. Why invite friendship with this Egyptian hoori? Was Happy anticipating I might fall for the woman and preempting any repeat of the one-night stand mistake by fencing Mafalda into a corral? Clever little Happy, if that was her aim.

The evening wore on dangerously. I felt as if I was on the edge of a cliff. The fact that I can't read or write in Russian was a bummer. Ali and Sven went into long diatribes in Russian. When I couldn't even order dinner from the menu brought by a slovenly maitre d' in a frayed dirty shirt, I felt like a foreign exchange student newly arrived at a Russian language school.

Happy wasn't deterred at all by her lack of foreign language skills. She simply followed Mafalda's lead in ordering dinner and the local wines to accompany it. Mafalda's knowledge of English must have been learned in the beds of various lovers. Like a woman who can only speak kitchen words learned from her cook, Mafalda used "love" and "fuck" plentifully.

It was "love this cous cous" or "fuck the vodka." Like Fran, she gave with a liberal sprinkling of four letter words: the only decent one being "love" which she used inappropriately.

By the time a baklava dessert appeared, I was very ready to take my wife to bed. As she well knew I much enjoyed making love in new hotel rooms. But tonight Happy was not sharing my lust. She was too much intrigued by Mafalda to follow me upstairs.

What saved the night for me was the unexpected arrival of Ali's wife. Her late appearance deflated Mafalda as if she'd been a carnival balloon pricked by a nail.

Ali was well able to handle the situation. No doubt he'd had plenty of experience fending off trouble between his wife and his various mistresses.

"Ah, how delightful. Here is my lovely wife, Fatima. How late you are, my dear."

He put Fatima on the defensive.

But apparently she was accustomed to that ploy, and knew well how to handle it. "Kind husband, I could not join you while you were drinking alcohol in a bar. But now that you have moved into the dining room, I'm so pleased to be with you. Enchante. And who are these charming people?"

We were introduced. Happy warmed to this lady too. Not glamorous, not even pretty, Fatima wore a long gown that hid her arms and legs, a head scarf and heavy jewelry. She'd arrived accompanied by a bodyguard, but he melted into the woodwork as soon as she was seated beside her husband.

She spoke English with a French accent, as if she'd learned it in a French school. I noticed she had bad breath, and guessed that her teeth were rotting.

Fatima could have been a leper for all I cared. She'd broken up the party, caused Mafalda to scuttle away like a cockroach and encouraged Happy to make a move to come upstairs with me by prodding her: "Ma chere, you will want to accompany your handsome husband to go to bed, I'm certain. It's so late."

With little ceremony she ate off Ali's plate, cleaning it, and then took his arm and dragged him out of the restaurant, leaving Sven to pay the bill.

Now there were two bodyguards: his and hers, when Ali's bodyguard came out of the woodwork with Fatima's. They dwarfed Sven, who seemed to have shrunk. His Apollo god figure, reminiscent of those painted on ancient Greek vases, seemed insignificant next to these two six foot eighters. Where did Ali find these bodyguards? I imagined they must be ex-basketball players. Becoming bodyguards would be the logical graveyard for ex-basketball players.

Ali and Fatima walked us to the lobby's bank of elevators. "I'll sign the papers tomorrow morning to become an owner in your stable," he said.

"Who's your present trainer?"

"Francois Debarge. I doubt you've ever heard of him. And I haven't had a horse with him for years. He won't be surprised that I've moved on."

Moved *up*. I knew of Francois Debarge: a minor French trainer who ran horses at minor racecourses such as at Cagnes Sur Mer. I'd won races at Royal Ascot, Melbourne, Churchill Downs and Santa Anita to mention a few. Ali was certainly improving his stature in the racing community.

Or was I slipping a notch taking on an owner such as Ali?

Happy's radiant face told me that she felt confident I'd done the right thing.

Ali's parting words were: "I hope you'll visit us in Egypt during your off-season. But *in* season I'd like to see my filly perform at Deauville, Milan, and Bonn as well as at English racecourses."

Big order. It was my opinion that a two-year-old should be raced lightly. And his filly was still a yearling with two months ahead of her before she entered her racing life.

I bowed to Fatima and Ali, and remained non-committal. I pushed Happy into the first elevator that opened its doors.

In our lumpy Russian bed I was very careful with my lovemaking to not jar the bun growing in Happy's oven. She seemed satisfied, purring throughout like a kitten until shrieking with pleasure at her orgasm.

With the time difference between London and Moscow, it was still early evening on our bodies' time clocks. Now, instead of rolling over to go to sleep, Happy wanted a story.

For years I'd been turned into a male Scheherezade, telling her stories to keep our marriage glorious. Tonight was to be no exception.

"Ah wants a real cheerful earful," she cooed.

"You know how our FEATHERS has enriched the dear Ainsleys. Bought for a pittance, FEATHERS was syndicated for six million. Now the Ainsleys no longer look towards dreary retirement years on a military pension. With not enough heat in the winter and no air-conditioning come summer. They can afford anything their hearts desire, within limits. Having FEATHERS end his racing career on such a high to become a highly desirable stallion has changed their lives. For them it was like winning a lottery. Well, I recall a similar situation that enriched an air stewardess who dreamed of owning a winning horse."

"A po' girl like me?"

"I don't know *how* poor. She and her husband had saved up to buy a new car but decided to try for her dream and asked a friend to pick out a racehorse. He did. AND WHAT A GREAT RACEHORSE. They called him SEATTLE SLEW. I may be wrong but I think he cost only $16,000. Price of a car. He went to Billy Turner's barn. Won race after race, and finally became one of the three winners in his decade to win the Triple Crown. In fact he even beat another of that era's greatest horses: AFFIRMED. Peterson trained SEATTLE SLEW during his fourth season and then that wonder horse went to stud, where he threw huge massive progeny. Including many a winner. Good story."

Happy smiled contentedly, making her mouth curve upward in that delicious crescent moon-on-its-back that I so adore.

I should have gone right to sleep. I didn't. There was a niggling idea worrying me: I was wondering what Sven was doing at the Moscow sales of racehorses. He wasn't *into* racehorses. Had he come to trap Ali into something sinister?

Chapter 9

Before leaving Moscow I thought that Happy and I should check out its racecourse. Out of season, of course, but still the facilities should be on show.

It's called the Hippodrome. Listed as the largest race course in Russia, I was walked through its stands that can hold ten thousand racing enthusiasts.

"I'm cold. I want to go eat," Timmy whined. He was with us always now, because daily I dreaded another kidnapping experience for him.

"We'll go to McDonald's," I told him, and Timmy brightened like a flower after it sucks up dew.

"McDonald's, here in Russia?" Happy queried, doubtful but her voice reflected that she felt relieved. We both knew that on our travels with us our Timmy wouldn't eat anything that didn't come from a McDonald's.

Our taxi driver knew the exact location of Moscow's finest. And to tell the truth, this Cotswold Brit enjoyed his Big Mac as much as Timmy did. I'd detested the tough meat in our hotel's restaurant.

Timmy found that the give-away toys were very different from those in Miami, Lexington, and London. There, the toys were tiny and plastic. Here we were offered wooden dolls the size of a hand, or trucks the size of your foot.

"Remind me, I wants t'buy one o' them peasant dolls what holds another and another inside it. Dorothy will love that. Ah ain't got nothin' yet fo' Irish: maybe a wooly hat fo' winter. Ah saw some baby hats in Bogota Ah thought fo' Irish, but the shops was closed when we-all returned from our cable car ride."

"Darlng, I didn't want to sound negative at the time, but—my God—I was anxious for you and Timmy when you took that cable car up to the Monserrate Sanctuary."

"Why? Did you think the cable would go bust?"

"That, yes. It's been known to happen. But also my Bogota translator, Carmen, told me about a pair of Brits, husband and wife tourists, who thought it would be fun to walk all the way up to the sanctuary. They were both mugged and stripped of ALL their clothes, underpants and shoes: the lot. And it's cold at 9,000 feet."

"Don't sound like much fun to me."

"You bet! And to cap it all, some overly conscientious policeman arrested them for being naked in public: or worse, that they were about to have kinky sex."

"Hmmm. Have you heard from Carmen?"

"One e-mail. Nothing special. Just said her plan to go to Medellin had gone down the tube because there was some volcano spewing lava nearby."

"'Curioser and curioser,' as Alice said in thet wonderland book. Curious, Ah thinks, 'cause Sven claimed he'd gone to Medellin. Ah thinks he couldn't have done much testing o' quarter hosses with a volcano eruptin' nearby."

"Darling, we needn't concern ourselves further with Mr. Beautiful. I doubt we'll ever meet up with him again."

"Ah hopes we does. Ah's got plans fo' Mr. Beautiful. Ah's been thinkin' about thet there *incest, what* the Snodgrass brother and sister git up to. Ain't nothin' like what Lot had with his two daughters. Accordin' to mah Bible, thet Lot was used by his daughters so as to preserve their family line. But thet ain't what the Snodgrass brother and sister had in mind, no man! Just liked havin' sex. Fran Purcell won't git t'have her weddin' long as them two keep havin' sex. What Ah plans t'do is to sick Mr. Beautiful on thet Lola. What y'all wants t'bet she leaves off havin' sex with her brother 'n goes for Sven?"

I didn't take that bet. Happy may be in need of a lot more elocution lessons, but there's nothing faulty about her judgement of human nature.

Personally, I put all thought of Sven out of my mind. I met with Ali to sign the relevant papers where he became one of my owners, and arranged to have his $1,250,000 filly shipped to my stables in Epsom.

Before leaving Russia, I decided to fly to St. Petersburg to test a colt Ali wanted to buy there.

What a mess I got into! With no knowledge of the Russian language and unable to decipher the Cyrillic alphabet, I got totally lost with Timmy in Moscow's airport for domestic flights. This was a very different place from the slick international one. There were no signs in English, French or any other language I'd ever come across: including Serbian, which I'd failed to learn while I was posted near Sarajevo during the Bosnia War.

Scanning the boards that probably listed flights and the gates for them, I saw a wall clock that must have dated from Czarist times that showed I was about to miss our plane. Giving up catching the flight, as a lost cause, I wandered to where a babushka sat at a bridge table loaded with miscellaneous items I usually associated with charity parties that featured a White Elephant sale. Arguing in perfect Russian with the old woman was an American, his nationality proclaimed by the garish tie he wore with a Valentine's Day motif of red hearts and the words *kiss me*. While I observed him he pulled out a wad of US dollars and packed into a McDonald's Big Mac bag the only old icon available at that table.

I asked him: "Do you know where I could find the gate for the St. Petersburg flight?"

"Sure *do*. Just follow me, I'm catching that one too." With no apparent hurry, he led us through a maze of narrow aisles and we made the gate with two minutes to spare. No trouble from Timmy: once he'd taken in that Big Mac McDonald's's bag, he followed this stranger as if he were the Pied Piper of Hamlin.

The stranger arranged for us to share a row of three seats together. "I'm Harry Bloom," he announced, his eyes twinkling and his mouth in a steady upward curve. I countered: "Rick Harrow."

I gave him a once-over. He had the largest shoes I'd ever seen: more appropriate for a clown in a circus. His hands were like a mechanical digger's.

Timmy stayed quiet while he opened the conversation. "I've been in Russia since the 1980s, working for McDonald's. What you doing here?"

"I train racehorses. A new owner wants me to check out a colt at a farm near St. Petersburg."

"Got a driver? You'll need an honest taxi driver, or a limo."

"I thought we could take a bus. The farm is near a big village."

"Are you crazy? You'll end up in Siberia. If I have the time, I'll drive you. I love the Russian countryside."

"And what do you do for McDonald's that gives you free time?"

"I've been with McDonald's ever since I was a professional choir boy whose voice changed and had no way to support my mother. Started emptying used trays at the McDonald's in Toronto. Worked my way up. Spoke Russian because my parents had emigrated from St. Petersburg: got sent here. I get plenty of free time, which I usually devote to promoting the McDonald's' charity for sick children: the Ronald McDonald Charity."

"There's a McDonald's' in St. Petersburg?"

"You must be kidding! Of course there is. We have forty-three McDonald's in Russia. We serve one million customers a day. We got one hundred thousand customers the first week when we opened our first McDonald's in Moscow. We served 12,000 Big Macs, 24,000 meat patties, 70,000 apple pies."

Timmy spoke up. "You talk too much. I'm hungry. When do I get to go to McDonald's and eat?"

Oh, oh. I'd hoped Timmy had fallen asleep. When we'd settled in our seats I'd tried to pull down the shade over the window next to me, but the shade came away in my hand. This was one old plane in poor condition. With the light in his eyes, Timmy had stayed awake, listening to every word. I remembered his tasteless remark in Hong Kong, when he'd remarked on how the Chinese had slitty eyes. Now it was a demand for McDonald's food at our plane's thirty thousand feet altitude.

Miracle! Harry Bloom pulled out a tired Big Mac from a pocket. This was probably the one that had been housed in that bag he was using for his newly acquired icon.

Timmy grabbed it. But before he took the first bite, he stated: "No toy! Where's my toy?"

Amiably, Harry explained: "You get a toy with a 'happy meal.' Sorry."

While Timmy munched at the Big Mac, I changed the subject trying to ease over Timmy's rudeness. "Tell me about the Ronald McDonald Charity."

"For every kind of sick kid. Cancer, blind, lame, you name it we pay to try to fix it. You'll visit us someday, Dick."

"My name's Rick." Any excuse not to go into Timmy's kidnapping story.

I shut up. It was too painful for me to speak about my own sick kid, who had a mental problem that needed anger management after his week-long ordeal during his kidnapping.

Harry Bloom opened the Russian in-flight magazine and read it easily. I was the one who fell asleep.

We were landing when I heard Harry's voice. He was pointing to roofs in the city spread below. "That is the point where the Nazis were held from entering the city. One million Russians died to hold the Nazis."

I nodded. I knew about the siege here, it had been described in detail during my military training to take part in the Bosnia War.

Harry Bloom had a company car and driver waiting. He offered to give us a ride to our hotel. Along the way he pointed out the city's sights, gave us the names of the churchs with their onion-shaped domes, and lauded the beauty of the mansions that had once belonged to the Czar's cousins.

"Tomorrow, when I drive you into the country, I can show you where the Grand Dukes built their summer homes: palaces like the Galitzines' had, or the Czar's own bolt hole, that featured hidden water sprays that doused his unwary guests. Too bad he didn't go there with his family and escape to FINLAND, just across the gulf."

"McDonald's!" Timmy sang out, pointing to its yellow and red sign.

"Okay," Harry got the message. "We'll stop and buy you a 'happy meal' before I drop you at your hotel."

Nice man. No nastiness after Timmy's rudeness.

I had a Big Mac too. It tasted just the same as all the others I'd downed around the world, escorting Timmy.

"Try our fries," Harry said. "We brought Idaho potatoes here as samples for the farmers to give us the larger spuds we needed for our signature long fries."

I did. But I was hoping Harry would ease up on the promotion bit when we'd have our drive the following day.

Our down market hotel was crummy. I sat on my bed's faded spread and wished Happy was there with me to give me the joys we shared in new hotel rooms, crummy or fancy. I telephoned our room in Moscow, but Happy was out.

Where? With Sven? I wasn't to know.

Chapter 10

As often happens in my life, when I think of a person suddenly they appear. Sven was at the horse sales, with a gluttonous expression in his beautiful eyes. He was leaning, gracefully of course, on a rail next to Ali and Fatima. At least I guessed the woman was Fatima, since I couldn't be sure who was under the burqa.

"Dick, come join some friends of mine," Harry boomed, and made a move toward Ali and Sven.

"I'm Rick," I corrected him again.

Harry, friends with Egyptian Ali and Norwegian Sven? I could understand that he'd have ample occasion to visit other countries in his role with McDonald's, but it *did* seem a coincidence, and I hardly believe in coincidences.

One glance at the colt I'd come to judge told me he was no thoroughbred, no matter what forged papers he had. A biting wind had come up. It was very cold, and I felt concerned for Timmy who had clothes suitable for Epsom but not northern Russia.

"I think I should make my way back to our hotel," I said. "Timmy's shivering."

"Yes, Dick. And I'll drive you." Whatever interest he had in going to a horse sale seemed to have vanished. I didn't correct him again. It was "Dick," not "Rick" all the way to the city.

On the way, he stopped beside a small beach. "Dick, let's look at the water," he said, inexplicably. I followed, and having sore feet from tight boots, I dipped my feet in the icy waves.

"*Dick, don't do that!*" Harry shouted as if I was about to run into a leper colony. "That water's polluted. Maybe with nuclear runoffs." Gruffly, he scooped up my boots and we led Timmy to the car.

45

Harry left me at my hotel, with a "Goodbye, Dick. Look you up when I'm in England." I thought, "Well, you won't find me if you look for a Richard, instead of Rick."

I bathed and fed Timmy, and hoped he'd go to sleep. No such luck. He'd slept in the car and was adamant about accompanying me downstairs. I buckled and together we went to the restaurant off the lobby.

Oh, no! Sven, Ali, his wife and mistress were all together at a large table for six. "We're saving places for you and your som," Ali called.

No escape, I joined them, trying not to go overboard in trying to ingratiate myself with Ali. But why were they at such a down-market hotel? Surely, Ali could afford better, when he so comfortably bid up to $1,250.000 for his filly.

We ordered steaks, which were over-cooked, greasy and too salty. Timmy had a milk shake, that had no comparison to McDonald's.

Timmy whined: "Need to go potty."

I excused us, and went to the Men's Room. No sooner had I closed the door when I heard an enormous explosion.

Debris hit the door of the Men's Room. And then I heard the screams.

"A bomb! That woman in the burqa, a terrorist. Had a bomb!"

I waited for another blast. There was none. Cautiously I opened the door. In the far corner of the lobby, where the bar was situated, there was human litter. Legs, arms, and half a man. Another man had his intestines on the floor.

Shielding Timmy from that sight, I hurried him to the elevator and took him up to our room. Now he *was* sleepy. I tucked him into his cot, and hurried back downstairs to see how I could be of help. Not a trained medic, I wouldn't attempt to move anyone badly injured, but I figured I could do some good for the walking wounded.

The sirens of ambulances approaching was some solace. I found a woman covered in blood who was like a shell-shocked soldier from the trenches. It was not her blood. When I wiped her clean I found that she was not injured, but still needed medical assistance for the shock.

Sven, Ali and his two women were in a safe corner in the restaurant opposite the bar. No blood there.

Ali, shaking, said to me: "I thank Allah for Fatima's fanaticism that she won't go to a bar."

I said, "How can we be of help to these people?"

Sven grumbled: "By leaving the medics to it. This isn't our problem."

"Hold on. These are people who've been hit. Surely we—"

The beauty of his face and figure did not extend to Sven's choices. "The hell with them. I say let's get into my car and get the hell out of here." He led Ali and the two women to the entrance to the hotel's garage.

I looked around the lobby at the carnage, and wondered: "Why *this* very insignificant hotel? *Who* was supposed to be in the bar? Who was the target? Who was the misguided woman: a terrorist, or some other fanatic? *Why* had she strapped on a vest sewn with explosives and hidden it under her burqa to offer her life and be blown to bits? What can I do to help?"

Abandoned by my friends, I spent an hour cleaning bloodied arms and legs. I helped wipe blood from a man's face only to find he'd lost an eye.

Finally, dismissed by the medics, I went upstairs, where my bedside telephone was jingling.

On the blower was a very distressed Happy, penitant she'd remained in Moscow to go shopping. "You're all right? A lady in the restaurant downstairs interpreted the TV news for me. *Your hotel! And Timmy?"*

"He saw nothing. He's asleep. And I'm okay, Darling."

"Dorothy's got the sniffles. Amah wants us back to handle it. We gotta go."

"Tomorrow morning, Darling. First plane out of Moscow for London."

Chapter 11

You'd think we'd had our fill of traveling. No, as soon as Dorothy was cured of her cold, that had developed into bronchitis, we were on a plane for Cairo.

Ali had summoned us.

Think he'd intruded enough into our lives with his incessant e-mails regarding his filly? Think again. Now he demanded a face to face meeting where I must detail how often she ate, pooped, exercised. The lot! Not an easy new owner: our Ali.

Cairo seemed an odd place to spend Christmas, but with Dorothy's chest not showing signs of improvement, I thought the warmer weather would do her good.

On arrival, I found everything very different from what I'd expected. First of all, there were so many *people. Mostly men, and men wearing the long-skirted djellabah.* No car to meet us. No friendly face. No one offered to help Happy with her mountain of baby's luggage.

We managed to find a tired-looking taxi with a driver who could read the address of our destination: Ali's house. The driver pointed out a few sights: "Authentic ancient statue. Fake obelisk with President Mubarak face carved instead of pharaoh. Road to Gazira, where in World War II many British officer play polo at club there."

When we arrived at Ali's house I was in for a surprise. It was small, it had no garden, and only one visible servant. Grumpy, and with a martyr's expression, the maid led us to a downstairs room overlooking an indoor patio. No Ali, no Fatima.

What caused me to feel I *was* in Cairo was the burst of Muezzin calls to prayer from at least half a dozen mosques near the house. From our one window I could see clumps of men pulling out prayer rugs, kneeling on the street or sidewalk and lowering heads to ground.

Happy looked concerned when she learned that we were to share our bedroom with the three "chillun". "Ah thinks thet Timmy will catch Dorothy's germ," she whispered.

One bedroom for the five of us? I wasn't worried about germs. What clobbered me was the prospect of *no sex*.

It was at least two years ago that Happy and I had decided never to have sex in front of Timmy after we'd discovered him staring at us in rapt attention when we made love one late night.

It occurred to me that we could take a room at a "six to eight' hotel where men brought their mistresses for sex before going home to dinner with their wives. But how crummy that would be!

Ali's appearance drove all other thoughts from my mind. I SAW A HEAVY, DJELLABAH-GOWNED MAN MARCH INTO THE PATIO. He lay down on a pile of rugs, set up a hookah and proceeded to smoke. He drew his smoke by a long tube through a vase of water. The smell was decidedly unpleasant. Hadn't the maid told him we'd arrived?

He certainly looked very different from the man in a navy business suit with whom I'd dealt in Russia.

Without his tarboosh, I could see that he had a mop of greasy hair that needed cutting. Instead of lace-up shoes, he wore curled toe slippers. Had we moved into a scene from a movie about Arabian nights?

Finally, the maid appeared and, scowling, announced our presence. He didn't leave his pile of rugs. Holding the pipe of his hookah, he simply called to me and told me to come out into the patio.

I did. Ali fired at me the same questions he'd e-mailed. "Is she eating well? At grass, or is she in a stable with hay? What kind of water? Did a vet check her out for worms?"

All standard questions. Already answered. What stunned me was his last query: "How much could I get for her in England if I were to sell her now?"

I didn't answer that right away. And I was glad that Happy had remained in our room caring for the children and had not heard Ali, because she'd grown very fond of the filly.

Sell her? Oh, no!

Cautiously, *sotto voce*, I said: "Probably not as much as you paid. Any buyer would worry she'd developed a problem, and that's why she was being sold. Dicey leg, or a breathing difficulty. Swallowing her tongue: that sort of thing."

"So!"

"My advice, if you insist on what I believe is an extremely promising filly, is to race her as a two-year-old, and then—if she wins—you'll get your price or better."

"And if she doesn't win, she'll be worth far less. But YOU will have got your training fees. Which, frankly, I cannot afford to pay."

Not afford! But he'd paid that $1,250.000 without a blink. And the check had cleared. The money had been paid—fair and square—to the filly's former owner. I wouldn't have shipped her to Britain if that hadn't been the case.

We negotiated past sun-down, which at this latitude was later than in Epsom. But Happy, apparently hungry with no lunch except the paltry in-flight nibbles provided by Air Egypt, came into the patio carrying Irish and followed by Timmy and tottering Dorothy.

Timmy made the demand for her: "We need dinner."

Ali laughed at Timmy's outspoken style. He had a silly laugh, almost like a young girl's. "My wife, Fatima, she doesn't cook. And Hala, our maid, she had too much to do today preparing five beds. She does everything else here too, cleans, launders, washes up and cleans my car. But when Fatima returns, I'll drive all of us to a restaurant."

Before Timmy could make any worse complaint, Fatima arrived. She took Happy and the "chillun" into her bedroom, removed her naquib, and surprised Happy by revealing a truly gorgeous body.

When Fatima and Happy returned to the patio, Ali languidly removed himself from his rugs and hookah, started up the car outside and drove us to a very down-market restaurant.

The food was ghastly. There was no children's menu. Timmy kept asking to go to McDonald's. Our infant girls ate from glass jars of babyfood brought from England.

It was far from a glorious evening. Back in the patio, Ali invited us to go rooftop. "Cooler up there. As you no doubt noticed, I don't have air-conditioning. Don't like the noise."

Peaceful, but not much cooler, the rooftop area was blighted by smog. You couldn't see the nearest Muezzin tower. We were given sunloungers in lieu of chairs. Mint tea was served by a much harassed Hala, who had been brought doggy bags of scraps from the restaurant for *her* dinner.

"Ah'd like to do some tourin' tomorrow," Happy said. "What do y'all suggest?"

"Go see the pyramids," Fatima put forward.

"Yeah man!"

I said: "Take Timmy. I'll stay here with the girls. Timmy could remember seeing them later in life. It won't mean much to toddlers."

What I really had in mind was to iron out the finances surrounding Ali's filly.

Ali, perhaps foreseeing we'd need more time to discuss those finances, said: "You should go to see Memphis the following day. Memphis, my favorite destination. I'll arrange a car. You can take Hala, she'd enjoy the ride and help with the children."

Enjoy the ride? With three disgruntled, hungry children? Poor Hala: as if she didn't have enough on her plate. But who was I to complain!

Later, in the so-called privacy of our crowded bedroom, Happy explained about Hala's position in the household. "Can y'all believe this? Fatima told me they have only three bedrooms in this house. Ali's mother were alive when they bought it, and she had ourn bedroom. That left two. Fatima decided she'd rather have a maid than a child, so—bingo—they got Hala."

The following evening, after a harrowing day of changing diapers and attempting to bathe our two girls, I felt immensely relieved to turn their care back to Happy. *She*'d had a glorious day.

"Them py-ra-mids is somethin' else. Much bigger than Ah'd imagined. The stones, huge. How did them slaves ever manage to put them in place? And guess who were there to ride a camel? Sven Jensen!"

"Sven?"

"Yeah man. We seen them py-ra-mids together. Then he told me there was a place nearby where you can ride a camel for ten bucks. We both rode them. Not Timmy, he said they smelled too bad."

The next day was equally joyful for Happy. Returning to our bedroom, she excelled in descriptions of the Memphis statues, bazaar and drive. "The only bad part was when we passed a canal and saw the carcass of a dead dog. Awful."

More awful was what we found when we went into the patio. Fatima was leaning over Ali, who had slipped from the rugs. He was lying on the tiles, crumpled. Dead.

"Help me," Fatima groaned. "He's not breathing."

"We should call a doctor." I didn't elaborate that a doctor would be needed in any case to sign the death certificate.

At least the telephone was working. Her doctor came promptly. He removed a thick piece of meat from Ali's throat. "He choked to death. On a piece of pork."

A half-eaten pork pie lay scattered near Ali on the tiles.

Pork? Ali, a Muslim, had died eating pork? When pork is a forbidden food for Muslims!

Happy surprised me by examining the piece of pork removed from Ali's throat. She also examined the pie.

While Fatima and Hala began making that North African tongue lullating suitable for mourning, I used the telephone to dial the Cairo Hilton and book us into two rooms. I also dialed for a taxi. We were out of Ali's house in ten minutes.

As we drove away, I noticed that Ali's mistress, Mafalda, was arriving. Instead of a chic Parisian dress, she was blanketed in a traditional naquib.

What a delight it was to unpack in an air-conditioned room. Later, the concierge told us how to find a McDonald's and we all five had good meals. But whom did we find eating *his* dinner there? None other than my Moscow airport acquaintance: Harry Bloom. The same, who had driven me around the environs of St. Petersburg, yet had missed the bombing at my hotel.

But I wasn't to give much notice to that. I wanted to return quickly to our hotel, where Happy was pleased to see that Christmas decorations had been strung in the lobby, which was now fitted with a huge evergreen tree ornamented with blinking lights. When she admired the Christmas décor to the concierge, he told her she could take the children to a Christmas party at the British Council where there would be more decorations. "Ah knows we's in a Muslim country," she told him, "but Ah sho' misses them Christmas doin's."

I hurried her upstairs, helped her to put the "chillun" to bed. Finally I had the joy of making blissful love to my wife in our own bedroom.

Chapter 12

The following morning I was on the blower to Hal Murphy in Canada.

"Any interest in buying a truly fine filly?" I asked him, after politely inquring after Clara's health.

"How much?" Businessman Hal always went for the jugular.

"$1,250,000."

"Canadian dollars or American?"

"USA. Worth every penny."

"Rick, I'll take your word for it. Where do I wire the money?"

"Barclay's main branch, Cairo."

"Has this filly got a name?"

"No. You'll have the privilege of choosing one." Ouch, I admire everything about Hal Murphy, except for the awful names he gives his horseflesh.

"And where did you find this filly? I see you're phoning from Cairo."

"Yes, but she has Russian papers. Best English and German breeding, I might add. And she's already in my stables at Epsom."

"Russian? How about Ninotchka?"

"Hmmm. I'd prefer Elizabeth The Great."

"You've got it. Have Tom photograph Elizabeth The Great and FAX the photo to me."

Dear, wonderful, Hal. He always came up with the money in time of need. Now I could comfortably telephone Fatima, give her the condolences I'd reserved, and tell her the good news: that the filly had been sold and she wouldn't even have to pay for stabling.

There would still be complicated paper work to deal with. I hadn't thought she'd have wanted to run the filly In the Estate Of, even if she could afford to, which I much doubted, considering the size of her house and car.

I guessed that right. Once she stopped weeping, Fatima was quick to say: "Please sell that filly. She didn't really belong to Ali. He let his bank account be used to process the payment. But we couldn't have afforded the training fees, and anyway, I know nothing about horses. Can you get the entire price paid? I owe every cent. I may be a bankrupt in any case."

Mafalda got on the blower. I'd never understood Ali's extraordinary *ménage a trois* with her as the *troisième*. Seeing her wrapped in a naquib, totally Fundamentalist, I'd been even more mystified by Mafalda. She said bitterly: "Ali asked you to sell the filly, planning to pocket the money and leave Egypt. But where he could possibly have gone to escape, I've no idea."

Our bedroom was fitted with an extra earpiece for the telephone. Happy had listened to every word. When we concluded our threesome conversation, Happy said with wonder in her soft voice: "What y'all make o' thet? Ali, escape? Escape from what, from who?"

"From being murdered, I don't doubt. He was throttled. Possibly sedated with a substance added to his hookah. Then fingers closed his windpipe. Left no suspicion of murder."

"Ah thinks the same as y'all. Particular-like thet sedated. Ah smelled chloroform on thet piece o' pork."

"Now I'm wondering if Stinky's fall down that elevator shaft in Miami was an accident."

"Yeah man, same here. Then there was thet bombin' o' yourn hotel in St. Pet-ers-burg. Ties in."

"Happy, my darling. I think we should get home soon as possible. Perhaps I'd better send you on ahead. I still have paperwork to do to complete the filly's transfer of ownership."

"Rick, Ah's not scared o' nobody. Or nothin', except losin' y'all. And Ah's not plannin' t'leave Egypt befo'e Ah's done all my tourin'. The tourin' was won-der-ful so far. Ah seen in the lobby some brochures fo' Luxor, 'n Karnak. While y'all deals with the filly's papers, Ah's goin' t'take a boat up the Nile."

Happy left the next day with Timmy. Again I had the two infant girls to care for, but I'd begun to enjoy that job. I was getting quite adept at changing diapers and feeding them out of jars of babyfood. They liked being with me, and we began to bond together, our own threesome.

The telephone calls from hotels where she overnighted brought alive Happy's "tourin'" for me. She liked Karnak the best, with its rows of huge statues of long-gone Pharoahs. There was one hiccup: Timmy developed Nile tummy.

"We's got t'get home, soon." Happy had a pleading tone of voice I'd rarely heard before. She sounded as distraught as when Dorothy was discovered to be in a breech position during that difficult childbirth in Dubai.

I hurried through the paperwork on the filly's sale, brought forward the dates on our return tickets for Heathrow, and with Happy's mountain of baby luggage made our way through the suffocating Cairo traffic to its airport. My most poignant vignette of Egypt was of Timmy holding his sore tummy with both hands, tears streaming down his dusty face, saying: "When do we go to McDonald's?"

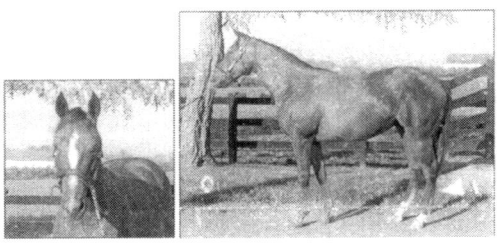

Chapter 13

Elizabeth the Great was sick too. When I hurriedly checked on our string, I found that our new arrival had lost much of the condition brought from Moscow. Her bones stretched her skin, she had a runny nose, and her eyes seemed glazed. What to do? $1,250,000 of Hal's good money on the hoof, and she could have a fatal case of: what? I couldn't even guess.

Our vet, Dr. Jack, had a fair notion. He dosed her for worms and within a day she began to perk up, eat, and move around her stall.

Happy, accompanied by a restored-to-form Timmy, spent time with Elizabeth The Great in that stall. "She needs a friend," she declared. "Just like Feathers did."

I bought a goat from a neighboring farmer and placed the goat in Elizabeth The Great's stall. Both females, they bonded immediately. Her stall took on a distinctive goat odor, but that was worth it when I looked into Elizabeth The Great's large glistening eyes and understood how pleased she was.

What a menagerie in my stables! A retired racehorse for Hal's Comet, kittens for Feathers, and now a goat.

Epsom didn't disappoint Happy as regarded Christmas decorations. The High Street was strung with colored lights. Each shop vied to produce a window with the most original Christmas theme. I didn't want to string lights around our cottage, but in the end I bowed to Happy's wishes and installed lines of blinking snowflakes: tacky, but Happy liked them.

From other years the village children knew we'd distribute Christmas treats and they came in their bright outfits to collect them. Carol singers got paid. We bought candied apples, and a yule log.

When I remembered our unpleasant Christmas morning last year in Miami, when I'd been accused of murdering a boy's father, how relieved I felt to be back in merry olde England.

The stable lads liked their gifts and the Virginia ham dinner provided. Happy loved the Ascot hat I'd bought for next spring. Timmy complained his toys were for babies, but our girls reveled in their silly baubles.

Our Epsom weather improved. We began to enjoy a false Indian summer that so often comes to England to fool us into thinking the worst was over.

In lieu of Christmas cards from them, I received two belated letters that astounded me: they were from my odd traveling acquaintances, Harry Bloom and Sven Jensen.

I burst into Happy's bedroom waving the letters. "I've heard from Sven Jensen, and from Harry Bloom. They're both coming to London for New Year's. What do you think? Should I invite them down here? Both hinted they wanted to come."

"Don't know as Ah'd want *both*. Ah supposes y'all must invite thet Harry, since he drove y'all into the countryside when y'all went to St. Pet-ers-burg. But, Sven? Depends. It depends if'n Ah can get Lola to come too. Got plans fo' them two."

Happy got on the blower to invite Dolores Snodgrass to our cottage.

Success! Dolores, Sir Arthur Snodgrass and Fran Purcell all arrived on Boxing Day. Happy managed to snare Sven Jensen to come that same day.

Talk about marriages made in Heaven: the minute Mr. Beautiful saw Dolores Snodgrass cross our threshold, he went for her like a hammer to a nail.

I thought: that's one hammer that may well turn into a boomerang.

"Lola, meet Sven Jensen. He's Norwegian. We all met in South Amer-ica. He buys quarter hosses." Happy made it very clear that she wanted these two to get together. She had no opposition from either of them. They came on like two armies aiming for the same frontier.

Surreptitiously, I watched Arthur's facial expression. For a man who was engaged to one woman in the room but had been sleeping with his sister, Arthur played dumb. Not a wrinkle around his pursed mouth betrayed him.

Five of us ate the leftovers of the huge Virginia ham that Happy had found at Harrods for our Christmas holiday. Sven Jensen didn't touch it. Why? Was he secretly Muslim, or maybe Jewish?

Within weeks we found out a lot about Sven Jensen. Thanks to Dolores Snodgrass, who had exchanged Mr. Beautiful for her brother in bed, we learned what *she*'d learned during their pillowtalk.

Fran Purcell had been the first to unmask that Sven was not Norwegian, as he'd claimed. "Fuck it, Sven has never even heard of Grieg. When I asked him if he preferred Grieg to Bach, he asked me if they were famous boxers. He didn't know that Grieg was the bloody father of Norwegian music."

But it was Lola, from their pillowtalk, who gave us the biggest news: Sven was a Checheynien, from that rebellious part of Russia that wants to be its own nation. And, yes, he *was* a Muslim. Blond and blue-eyed, thanks to his Russian mother, Muslim because his father belonged to a Muslim tribe in Chechenya. His classic features were strictly the work of a plastic surgeon.

In the chic ladies' loo at Annabel's, where Sir Arthur Snodgrass had been kept on as a member by its new owner, Lola had whispered: "I think that Sven has a brother. Maybe, his *twin*. *Mysterious guy*. Sven wouldn't tell me his name. Definitely not Jensen. He's a big man in some business. Sven wouldn't tell *what* business, not that either. Sven does little jobs for him. Nothing to do with buying quarter horses."

"Sho 'nuf. Ah'd guessed thet the quarter hoss story was a cover. He don't know nothin' about hosses."

Annabel's famous ladies loo attendant hovered for her tips. Happy clammed up, but when next she was alone with Lola at Harrods, again in a loo, she asked: "Any new take on Sven's business?"

"None. He's a wonderful lover. For such a beautiful man, there's nothing pansy about him. He's tender with me, and delicious, but I can't get him to talk about his business."

Lola started making her wedding plans within days of meeting Sven. And he went along with them in every detail. He swore he'd never been married before. Another cause of amazement, considering his fabulous looks. He claimed he'd been too busy to have had another serious relationship.

The dead of winter appeared to be his quiet time, and he booked the Chelsea Town Hall for his marriage. There was to be no religious ceremony: their mutual *beliefs* were too far apart.

Lola was determined to be married before her brother. She wanted to preempt his wedding to Fran. It was not difficult to provide a contrast. Fran had ordered a wedding gown from Miss Emmanuel, who'd designed the late Princess of Wales's famous dress. But Diana's wedding had taken place twenty-six years earlier, and Fran's gown was to have a slim skirt and short veil, more in fashion nine years into the new Millennium. Lola didn't wear a dress: she chose to be married in a suit and hat. "I can wear them next June at Royal Ascot," she laughed. Sven did provide huge arrangements of flowers for the reception at Claridge's, and a horse-drawn carriage to drive the newlyweds to its banqueting room entrance.

If he felt bitter about the marriage, Sir Arthur Snodgrass kept his opinion to himself and turned up trumps to pay for a really smashing reception. There were fully laden dishes of real food, not just appetizers, the best champagne, and a five tier wedding cake. This generosity was primarily to impress his constituents, who had been represented at this family wedding by the prominent contributors to his political cache.

Lola and Sven went on a secret destination for their honeymoon.

I was damned sure it wouldn't include Chechenya.

The mysterious brother didn't show for the wedding. In fact, there were no guests from Sven's roster of friends other than myself and Happy.

When the newlyweds returned to London, Lola needed to find a place for them to live because formerly she'd always shared with her brother. It had become necessary for Lola to find a job. I remembered how Sven had travelled Tourist to Colombia, and had stayed in down-market hotels there and in Moscow. Sven had no visible means of support, although on occasion he could prove generous, as when he picked up hefty bills at Annabel's and Claridge's.

That marriage seemed to be holding together, once Lola found a job as Girl Friday to Fran. We all knew that Fran could be stingy, but as her own wedding day approached, Fran was overwhelmed with all the fancy details her wedding planner proposed.

Snodgrass weddings were beginning to become a moot point with me. Even though most of my horses had grown their winter coats and were rarely exercising, I had plenty to do at my stables.

Elizabeth The Great was very forward, and improving daily. But Hal's Comet gave constant worries. He developed a foot abscess. We had our farrier try poultices, and then new shoes. The abscess grew worse. I brought in a superior vet, he got rid of the abscess, but then our colt went off his feed.

Happy had the answer. She discovered that the broken-down race horse, that was the companion for Hal's Comet's, was dying. Although Hal's Comet hooves were sound, his heart was sore. "We got t'find him another friend," Happy declared.

She went to one of the sorriest places in our town of horseracing buffs: the "knacker's." That was the end of all sad stories in the equine world, where former race horses might be butchered humanely. When an owner "rode to hounds" he or she might stipulate that his meat be saved for the hounds of their hunt. Otherwise, in most cases the meat was shipped to France. This was a topic that was "out of bounds" for most owners, they simply could not envision such a prospect for a beloved animal that had carried great hopes at a racecourse. Those same owners would perhaps pay for a year at grass for their retired animal, but when unexpected vet bills arrived with farrier or hoof paring bills, the horse would be sent to the knacker's.

Happy arrived well in time to save the animal she fancied.

She negotiated a fair price, well below what he could be expected to get for hide, glue and meat, then she personally boxed the horse and brought him home. Called Rex Magnus, this was one very unusual horse. I'd seen horses with all types of personalities: those with anger, or timidity, or cruelty. But this horse had a supremely rare facet to his character: he had a sense of humor.

One warm spring day where sun dappled through the trees' new leaves that were uncurling in the shape of shrimps, I watched Rex Magnus in his field accompanied by Hal's Comet and six of my finest runners. Rex Magnus was busily knawing, nibbling and then chomping on the rope that held a gate dividing my field from a neighbor's. When the rope gave way, Rex Magnus merrily led all seven of his friends into the neighbor's field and then stood mildly at the open gate, laughing at me.

When Hal's Comet watched his Colombian pal coughing out his lungs, I knew I had no option but to put down that old fellow. Not only was he suffering badly, but I feared that his infection could spread throughout my yard.

Thanks to Happy's foresight, Hal's Comet survived the loss of that friend by bonding with Rex Magnus. Early, at dawn, before morning stables, I could look out into their field and see that those two horses had their necks entwined like lovers.

Chapter 14

All my plans for Anchor's final year of racing came to naught when a totally unheralded offer arrived from a Saudi prince to buy him from Hal Murphy.

In gangster parlance, he made Hal an offer he couldn't refuse.

The good news was that this prince, whose name was Mohammed ben Saud, "call me Ben," wanted to leave Anchor in my stable. However he had no intention of standing him as a stallion to be syndicated. Ben paid out his millions for Anchor with the intention of racing him in weight for age competitions for as long as the horse could run.

"Do you recall that great old winner Nijinksy's Secret? Won races right up until he was nine," Ben growled at me. He never simply spoke: it was growl, or nothing. "A Mrs. Jim McDougald bought him when he was thought to be through, and then had five good years out of him."

Ben's English was precise, and perfectly modulated. He'd graduated from Eton, but after a year at Sandhurst, he'd returned to Saudi Arabia. He had impeccable manners, with the exception of his disgruntled way of speaking.

The only time I saw Ben act with implied rudeness was when he met Sven Jensen. Sven and Lola had come to my stables accompanied by Fran and Sir Arthur Snodgrass. He was not only snubbed by Ben, but the prince also told me to ask Sven to leave my grounds.

His Highness had *really shown more than dislike.*

What a quandary! I needed this wealthy Saudi prince. He was already the owner of one of my steadiest winners, and was talking about buying yearlings for me to train in 2010. But I'd never thrown anybody off my property.

Happy solved the problem. "Ah wants t'go up to London," she declared loudly. "Sven and Lola, please drive me there. My old car's safety belt hurts my swollen belly. I saw y'all got a new Jag, why not run me up to town?"

Five months into her pregnancy, it was true that our car had ceased to be popular with my darling wife. Happy cannily left with Lola and Sven. And that was to be the last time for both women that they would see Sven in 2009.

When Happy had returned to Epsom, and we were comforting ourselves at our hearth on our bum-warmer, refugees from a typically-for-March drop in temperature, my dear wife received a frantic telephone call from Lola.

"Sven never came home today. He went out before lunch. I waited until two to eat. He never let me know where he was. And when dinner was getting cold by nine tonight, he called from Heathrow to say sorry but not to expect him to come around for months."

"Y'all knows where he went?"

"No. And he didn't take his Sven Jensen passport with him. He must be traveling under another name. Oh, I always knew there was another name. The one from Chechenya. Which I suppose would be *my* real name, Mrs. *What?* Now, I can't go back to live with Arthur; not when he's about to marry Fran. I don't know what to do!"

"Stay put. My ole' Pappy always said: time cures everythin'! And, *I* say give him those few months for him to do whatever he needs to do."

"Can I come down to stay with you and Rick?"

"Sho can. We'll expect y'all in the mornin'."

Ben had left that same day. There was no reason to put off Lola. But another unexpected arrival showed up: Harry Bloom. He brought *his* problems with him too.

In our cozy kitchen, he told us: "I may soon be out of a job. And that may be the end of my chances to see the rest of the world's great stone antiquities. I'd set my heart on collecting my own photos of them."

Happy, who'd agreed to have Harry in our home because of her Kentucky custom of returning favors and she hadn't forgotten he'd driven me into the countryside near St. Petersburg. Now she perked up and asked with exceptional interest: "An-ti-qui-ties?"

"I know you like seeing them too," Bloom boomed. "I recall how your eyes glowed when you mentioned the Great Pyramid's stones."

"Yeah man! Sho 'nuf," Happy's facial expression was like a child's on Christmas morning about to see her presents.

"If you have a computer, I'll show you what's on Google's list of antiquities."

There was no holding Happy. She marched Bloom through the mud down our lane to my office in our stables. Bloom turned on my computer with professional aplomb: I didn't like it. Was this the real reason he'd come to visit us?

When my computer had booted up, Bloom—like a magician waving his wand at a children's party, and thanks to Google now produced a series of extraordinary pictures. We saw Mexico's Aztec temples, the Mayan ruins of Yucatan, the Parthenon and Acropolis in Greece, the huge heads of Easter Island, and the temple carved out of Petra's famous pink sandstone.

"Rick! Look at thet!" Happy gave a squeal similar to what I hear when she has an orgasm. "We could go to Petra when we're at Dubai for the races next week!"

Oh, oh. It seemed that Happy had developed a bad case of "tourin'."

Harry Bloom smirked. "Yes. I'll be at the Dubai races, too. We can fly to Jordan together. I've always felt disappointed that you didn't come along to Ethiopia to ancient Axum, when I saw how thrilled you were to be at Karnak."

What's this all about? Why, Happy? Karnak, they'd been together at Karnak! Five months pregnant with a huge belly, much bigger than with her last two babies. Her skin had gone lumpy like a fallow field. Her hair was stringy. Surely, Bloom wasn't making a play for my Happy?

She said: "We could take y'all to see Stone Hedge. Ain't thet far from here."

Bloom resisted that offer. "No thanks, I'm saving that experience for the summer solstice."

He had to content himself with a short sidetrip up the hill to Epsom's Derby track, where races had been run for well over two hundred years since Lord Derby first made his famous bet.

"Nice," he commented about the racecourse. "But personally, I'm much more interested in seeing where Assyrian horses competed in chariot races in the time of Nebuchadnezzar."

All this talk of far away archeological treats was undermining my confidence as a provider for Happy. I knew I couldn't afford to send her on expensive trips. We were facing hard times at my stables, with only one new owner and the ever-present threat of losing temperamental Fran Purcell. I knew it could take only one bad race for her to transfer her horses to another trainer.

Nevertheless, when the Dubai races brought us to the Middle East again, I gave Happy the tickets for a return flight to Amman, Jordan. From there she drove overland to see Petra. From her glowing report of it on her joining me in Dubai, it was worth every farthing. "Ah arrived at the narrow entrance from the valley to see Petra's temple just at sundown. The color pink cain't really describe what Ah seen: it was like a light scarlet. Go'geous!"

Dubai's hideous ultra-modern hotels and office buildings could hardly please her with their contrasting architecture. But Happy had discarded her distaste for it two seasons ago, after her horrific abduction that had ended with her near-death experience giving birth to Dorothy in its hospital for jockeys. Dorothy had traveled in the birth canal back-first and was in a breech position that called for a caesarian at that hospital designed to treat jockeys' broken collarbones.

"Ah declare, but it's as hot here in Dubai as on the Fo'th of July," she complained, unpacking in our narrow room. "Or is it because Ah's pregnant again Ah feels the heat so bad?"

She turned up the air-conditioning to its max, but complained again in the bar downstairs, where overcrowding by Europeans had thrown off the architects' schemes for this space to be occupied by Muslims who don't drink alcohol and therefore eschew going into bars.

"Lawdy, if it ain't Mafalda, all done up in one of her old man-trap get-ups!" Happy strode across the bar room to greet Mafalda. "Last time we seen y'all, Ah thought y'all gone Fundamentalist."

"Fundamentalist," that was a big word for a girl from the Kentucky hills. But, Happy had grown accustomed to Muslim terms during her latest forays into the Middle East.

Mafalda was standing at the bar, wearing a tight black jersey dress, low-cut at the breasts but with a skirt that barely covered her venus mount.

I didn't *want* to feel horny; but, it was difficult not to, after staring at her prominent nipples. I was reminded that I'D READ SOMEWHERE HOW A CHINAMAN HAD RECOMMENDED THAT PRIOR TO MAKING LOVE A MAN SHOULD CARESS A NIPPLE TWO HUNDRED TIMES. I knew that wouldn't work with my darling Happy, who'd have an orgasm after the first tickle of a nipple.

I followed Happy to the bar. "Hello Mafalda," I said. "What brings you to Dubai?" I made no mention of her transformation back into the garb of an international playgirl.

"I read in the newspaper that Elizabeth The Great is having her first outing here. I was in Moscow when Ali bid for her, remember? I think I should represent him when she runs here."

A thin excuse. But seeing how Happy looked very uncomfortable with Mafalda seated beside her, I took my darling wife's arm and left the bar without saying more.

With our breakfast tray came a letter from Clara Murphy for Happy.

My darling wife propped herself on our king size bed like a Buddha to read the very long letter on Hal's best notepaper. From what Happy interrupted her reading to tell me, I reckoned that would be the last time that Clara would use Murphy notepaper.

Happy asked me: "Shall Ah read the whole letter to y'all, or just give them highlights?"

"Highlights."

"She writes me that the reason we haven't heard from her is that she's been gettin' a di-vorce from Hal."

"I knew about the divorce."

"Yeah man, but did y'all guess the *why?* Clara says here she ain't never had a or-gasm with Hal. Never in all them thirty years t'gether. Then she met a banker. They had a weekend at Chateau Frontenac. And—wow—what a or-gasm she had! Now she wants to be an in-depen-dant woman, maybe stay with the banker maybe not. Says she's sorry she won't be goin' racin' no more, she really loved Hal's hosses, but thet she has a new life now. Feels like a woman *should.*"

"I'll bet that banker ends up with the money Hal pays Clara for a settlement."

"Sho 'nuf. Thet won't be no surprise. Clara leavin' for a life with or-gasms, thet ain't no surprise neither. My Mammy had such a friend. Woman with six chillun, who left our hills with a travelin' salesman, because he done give her a or-gasm."

I went to the bed, leaned over, and kissed my darling wife on her swollen belly. "Thank God *we* don't have that problem!"

"Sho 'nuf. But, if Ah breaks my back ridin' in races, will you love me still? And then Ah'll have no or-gasms. Would y'all stay faithful to me?"

"Of course I would," I lied. Happy knew I was lying. Hadn't she discovered that I'd had an illicit love affair with Irina, and another with Lois? "But it might be a great idea for you to turn in your apprentice jockey license, and learn dressage. For a mother of four, that would be safer."

If I thought that would be the end of any sex talk between Happy and me, how wrong I was!

Sex talk was to rear its head non-stop the next few days.

Hal Murphy arrived in Dubai the same day as his ex-wife's letter. I met him at the incredible airport, that would look more appropriate for a base on Mars. Although this was my third season of racing in Dubai, I could not accustom myself to its beyond-belief crazy architecture.

Hal looked terrible. From an unusually alert, outspoken tough guy he'd deteriorated into a shadow. He had developed a round-shouldered stoop. He walked dragging a sore foot. He let his head drop like a wilted flower deprived of water.

"I miss my Clara something awful," he said, once we'd gone through Customs and it had been shown that he had no drugs or handguns in his possession.

I noticed that even his breath was bad, as if he hadn't bothered to brush his teeth. I said: "You've got a wonderful new lady in your life, Hal. Wait until you see your Elizabeth The Great."

We drove directly to the stables for visiting racehorses. This area was full of poignant memories for me. It was here that I found Happy, who had ridden away from her abductors although nine months pregnant. It was here that her water broke and we had to rush her to the nearby jockeys' hospital, where Dorothy refused to be born until Happy suffered through a Caesarian. The stables were immaculate, well-lit, air-conditioned and favored with all the latest mod cons.

When Elizabeth The Great was duly led out into the yard to show her off, Hal *did revive somewhat.* "She's truly gorgeous," he said in his new, trembling voice. "But is she fast?"

"Faster than most of what I've got in our yard. But will she beat the other early two-year-old fillies here? Only her race will tell us."

I could see that Hal sorely needed a stiff drink. After we returned Elizabeth The Great to her stall and Hal had fed her an apple and a carrot, we headed to my hotel. For once, Hal had booked into the same down market place his secretary had chosen for Happy and me. "I don't want to feel too lonely. And why would I want the penthouse in that absurd tower?" he groaned, pointing to the famous hotel that leans like the Tower of Pisa.

There was one table left in a quiet corner of the bar available to foreigners, non-Muslims, who ordered alcoholic drinks. I had a print-out of Elizabeth The Great's fantastic breeding, and was pointing out the names of some of her progenitors, when a woman blotted out the light from a ceiling chandelier above our table.

The woman was Mafalda. Her sultry perfume told me that before I looked up to meet her eyes. "Aren't you going to introduce me to your friend?" she demanded. Without an invite, she sat down on the third chair, pulled it closer to Hal's so that their thighs touched, and she made a play for him.

Hal was so immersed in misery, he barely acknowledged the introduction. But slowly, an incredible change began to take place. He sat up straight. A deep flush of blood rose to his face. He turned toward Mafalda, and said: "I hope you won't think me too forward, madam, for leaving my thigh against yours, but it does feel good."

The old outspoken Hal had returned, and in full voice. I guessed that Mafalda's throbbing thigh had done its work and he now had an erection. I couldn't resist looking down at the crotch of his trousers. Yes, there *was a decided bulge there.*

Good for Hal!

He was struggling to regain his former strong voice: "You say, madam, that you were actually at the Moscow sales when Elizabeth The Great was auctioned?"

"Yes. Very much so. I encouraged Ali to bid against Rick. That filly *is* so beautiful."

I know, and Mafalda knows I know, that she knows nothing about equine flesh. Her knowledge of flesh was strictly for humans.

And men, in particular.

Trying to give Mafalda what used to be known as *the bum's rush*, I invited Hal to go into dinner, excluding Mafalda from the invitation. But she'd done her work well, and Hal wouldn't hear of excluding Mafalda.

"Lovely lady, you must join us."

Mafalda knew her craft, she'd been honing it for years. Giving Hal a flutter of her fake eyelashes, Mafalda demurred in the sweet tones of a virgin who wasn't ready to deliver her hymen.

"Why don't I join you later? *Perhaps we could have a nightcap?*"

"Great idea! Meet you at ten, at this very table. Until then, lovely lady."

Mafalda swept away in a cheap replica of Guerlain's Shalimar. Old Hal could hardly walk to the restaurant, he had such a pronounced erection. He used his lucky race hat to cover the prominent bulge.

At the dinner table, where every accessory was in tune with the over-the-top décor, Hal roared at me in the strong voice he'd so recently regained. "She's gorgeous." He brushed aside the ten inch serving plate and it smashed on the floor. In tune with his ever generous ways, he pulled out a ten pound note and placed it on the table to pay for the broken plate. "My God, am I lucky. First, the filly's a real beauty. And now I've met me a real woman. Rick, I haven't felt like this in years! I'm enjoying a hard on, like I had when I was a teenager."

What to say to that? Nothing. I simply nodded like a fellow conspirator. But warning bells were ringing. In my experience, Mafalda was anything but lucky to the man in her life, what with Muslim Ali having died murdered with a piece of pork added artfully into his throat.

Happy joined us for dinner. That put an end to talk of his hard on. Hal turned into the tough racing man who expected the investments he'd made in horseflesh to deliver results on race tracks.

Happy joined us with a frown on her face. "Ah reckons y'all could be very pleased with yourn hosses, Mr. Murphy, Hal. But Ah's got some naggin' worry. Ain't to do with the hosses. Ah's worried that somebody's goin' t'be murdered. And Ah sho' don't want that someone to be my Rick."

"Calm yourself, Hillary," Hal Murphy didn't want the subject of his horses to be interrupted. Yet both he and I realized that Happy generally knew what she was talking about where murders were concerned.

Lightly, I put in my two cents. "Happy, darling. I'm no coward. And I'm not getting the shivers. But what on earth makes you come up with a remark like that?"

"Ah seen thet Harry Bloom in the lobby, here. Same man what Ah seen in Cairo, Memphis and Karnak when Ali was done murdered in Egypt. And didn't y'all tell me he'd dropped you off at yourn ho-tel just befo'e a suicide bomber did dirty?"

"Harry Bloom. Yes."

Hal asked: "What do you *know* about this Harry Bloom?"

"Nothing that I've verified." I looked down at my fingernails. They needed a cleaning after I'd helped out at the stables. "He told me he was an executive with McDonald's, and as such travels the world for them. Also, he helps publicize their charity for sick and injured children: The Ronald McDonald Charity."

Hal pondered a while. When he spoke it was with his old authorative voice. "I'll get my PR department to offer funds for that charity. I'd like to anyway: sort of thing I like to benefit. But I'll have my people put in a query about this Harry Bloom, same time."

With the races beginning next day, and Elizabeth The Great entered for the top one for early two-year-old fillies, the three of us concentrated on her.

We weren't to be sidetracked by anyone or anything: not even Mafalda joining us for breakfast to continue her siege of Harry. She stayed as close as a postage stamp, with either her arm through his or an invited thigh causing the same effect as yesterday.

It was one of Dubai's least sweltering days. Happy wore an Ascot hat to match the blue of her maternity dress. I wore a business suit, which was in line with many of the Muslims who eschewed their flowing garments and roped headdresses for Saville Row single-breasted suits.

Even for breakfast Hal wore the wrong outfit, an orange blazer over checkered pants. But it didn't matter *what* he wore: at the races: as the owner of the fantastically successful Elizabeth The Great, winner by five lengths of her contest, he could have shown up in bathing trunks for all it would have mattered.

Strange how many times when I'm on a high, some awful tragedy comes to knock me off that cloud nine.

We had just left the winners' circle when a steward came up to me with a message that I was required on the telephone.

It was an official of the US Embassy on the blower. He wanted to know if I was a friend of a certain Harry Bloom.

"Why?" I asked, although I'd already guessed what was coming.

"He was found murdered this morning. Lying on the beach, his jugular slit. We are trying to reach his closest of kin, but there is no mention of anyone in his passport. We *did* however find a letter addressed to you." His tone of voice was unpleasant. I wondered if this was one of those same striped pants guys who'd been so unhelpful here in Dubai when Happy had been abducted.

Now was I a suspect in Harry Bloom's murder? Murder?

The same thought had caused Happy's ivory forehead to wrinkle. In her concerned tone, she whispered: "Harry gave me his cell phone number when he invited me to go to Ethiopia with him. Before I turned down his offer, he gave it to me to get in touch. Maybe them embassy folk could check out the cell phone provider and get the address where his monthly bills was sent."

My wonderful wife! Why hadn't I thought of that? I left Hal and Happy to toast Elizabeth The Great's win and rushed to the embassy with this useful suggestion. The striped pants character who interviewed me adopted Happy's idea as his own, probably to win brownie points toward his pension. I was dismissed, made to feel unworthy.

When I returned to our hotel I found Hal Murphy at the checkout desk. He was paying his bill.

"Hal! Where you going? We've still got Hal's Comet running tomorrow!"

"Fuck it! Think I don't know? But I don't want to embarrass Mafalda by asking her to my suite in this hotel. I've leased a seaside cottage where we can have some privacy."

"Where?" My hackles were rising. Damn Mafalda. As if *anything* could embarrass that bitch. But with a murderer loose who favored seaside beaches, I had my own reasons to discourage Hal's plan. Hal, my one true and loyal steadfast owner! I couldn't afford to lose him to a murderer, or even to a loathsome kidnapper of the type who'd abducted my Happy here two years ago.

"A honeymoon cottage," Hal added, wearing a shy smirk suitable for a small boy caught masterbating: "I'm keeping the address a secret. If things don't work out, I'll invite you over to help console me in double Jack Daniels. Shit, but I hope that won't happen. See you at the races, Rick."

Dismissed, I went to find Happy in our room. She was in our kingsize bed, but no hope of any sex for us there because she was frowning over a pad and pencil.

"Ah's been tryin' to remember all them places Harry Bloom talked about what we should go to for to see an-ti-quities." She licked the tip of the pencil. Bad habit, I wished she'd lick my 'pencil' instead, but that had never happened in our six years of marriage. My sexy adorable wife was steadfastly loyal to the MISSIONARY POSITION.

"Oh? I recall that when you were in Karnak he tried to get you to go to Ethiopia."

"Yeah man, to see some old columns and ob-e-lisks. Older than the Queen of Sheba's palace there."

"And wasn't there some talk of Nigeria, to see those amazing sculptures made from the *cire perdu* process?"

"Don't know about no fancy French names. Harry said like there were ancient bronze heads made in a place called Benin as good as the first Greeks made. But Benin was at the very bottom of where camel traders went in somethin' he called 'the sub-sahara region.'"

"But he didn't invite you to go there?"

"Nope. He did say like I might want to go to Sri Lanka to see Hindu carvings or East Timor where there's a huge ancient Buddha." Happy completed her scribblings. With a sweet smile, she patted the pillow next to hers and said: "Ah ain't no Mafalda, but Ah still thinks Ah can pleasure my man!"

The lovemaking was so perfect we almost missed the first race the following afternoon.

Lucky us that we *did* make that first race. Because Sir Arthur Snodgrass, with two disgruntled women, was holding out for our arrival to make a fuss. His lonely sister, drooping without her Sven, and the Baronet's fiancée Fran were both giving him a bad time, which he transferred to us.

"Not on, letting the three of us arrive at the airport with no one there to meet us," he boomed in his best House of Commons debate voice. "I won't have Fran treated in that fashion."

"Apologies, apologies," I murmured. I could hardly tell the truth and give as the excuse that I was making love to my wife mid-day after a long night of the same, when indeed I *had* been advised those three were arriving and expecting to be met.

It was impossible in this alcohol-free grandstand to offer them drinks to soothe their ruffled feathers, but my darling Happy came to my rescue.

"Y'all are in-vited to dinner by us tonight. Eight o'clock at ourn hotel. And we have a royal highness coming, you might enjoy knowing."

Pennypincher Fran had booked into our downmarket hotel. Sir Arthur Snodgrass had taken a suite there. Happy whispered to me: "Ah sho hope he don't intend sharin' them rooms with Lola. We managed to separate them befo'e and we don't want them sleepin' together no mo'e." To Fran, Happy said in her loudest voice: "Ah guess as y'all will be sharin' with Sir Arthur. Save y'all a packet if y'all does thet. Y'all won't like what-all these ho-tels charge. Lola can use the single room."

Problem solved.

Our dinner party went well at first. Ben looked very much the prince now that he'd adopted Arab clothing. He arrived with four bodyguards: no slack in caring for their Muslim princes, even in a Muslim country.

Only Lola, who definitely had not forgotten the prince's rude treatment of her Sven, was in an irascible mood.

Nasty.

I hadn't seen that side of Lola before. She was as sweet as sugarcane with her brother, and with Sven. Now she spit like a cobra. "I don't care if you *are a royal highness. **I'd like to see you dead.**"*

Happy weighed in, as she so often does when I have a problem with an owner. "Ah feels very honored to be here with y'all, Highness. Tell me, do you have any wonderful an-ti-quities in Saudi Arabia?"

Lola flounced off, leaving us with her empty chair at the table. The Saudi prince relaxed, and stroked his oily mustache. "We have al-Hajar ul-Aswad, The Black Stone, in Mecca. Over one million pilgrims visit it every year. They earn the title of *haj*."

"Is Angkor Wat in your country?"

"No, Mrs. Harrow. That's in Cambodia. But over one million visitors go see it every year, too. It's very far from here."

"So maybe thet's why Ah wasn't invited to go there." Happy had her quixotic expression tugging at the corners of that delicious mouth.

I felt intrigued. I'd seen that quixotic expression before and I knew damned well that it often presaged a break-through in one of our mysteries Angkor Wat! That had been in dire trouble during the era of Pol Pot, when terrorists might have destroyed it. Why had Happy chosen to pinpoint that place? I always listened more acutely when Happy played dumb.

She explored further. "Tell me, Your Highness, do y'all have a terrorist problem in your country? Ah noticed that y'all have four bodyguards with y'all at all times."

"In Saudi Arabia, true we've had a few bombings. But not in the part my father gave to me to rule. The four bodyguards? In another era they would have been the elite of my palace guard, they accompany me to give me the proper prestige more than anything."

I recalled that Ali and Fatima had hired his and her bodyguards in Russia. But there had been no evidence of any security at their home in Cairo. No need for prestige there! That could hardly have been the case in their down market house. I listened further.

His Royal Highness, to give Ben his correct title, had much more to say.

"Mrs. Harrow, I pride myself that I'm a benevolent ruler. My people have no reasons to want me dead. I built a state of the art hospital for them, and roads from each village to access the highway to it. If a student shows aptitude for biology, I pay his expenses to send him to Imperial College in London. We have a tradition of honoring poets: so if I have a promising poet among my tribesmen, I send him—or her!—to Oxford. Sick children? I book them into the St. Jude Hospital in America. Their older relatives I send to the Mayo Clinic in Minnesota. For eye diseases, of which we are plagued with in my lands, I send them to the Muirfield in London. Cancer? To the Pasteur in Paris. All paid for, straight out of my pocket."

"What about using little boys as jockeys in camel races?"

"Never! Anyone who tried setting up such a barbarous venture would have his hands chopped off." Ben didn't even have the grace to blush after making *that* booboo. *Hands chopped off? Oh, my!*

I thought it was time I offered him a drink. I well knew he couldn't be seen publicly downing alcohol, so I invited him to our room where I kept scotch and bourbon.

A mistake!

Timmy was wide awake there, harassing the unsuspecting babysitter.

"When do we go to McDonald's?" he turned his fury on me. "You haven't taken me where I can eat!"

Ben tried pacifying Timmy. This was his first introduction to my boy, and he hadn't known what he was getting into.

"Who are you?" Timmy demanded, without any prefix of Highness, or Royal Highness.

Ben proved an able adversary. "McDonald's? What a great idea you've given me, little young man. That's just what I need in my principality. A McDonald's. But I'm afraid you'll have to wait a while for it to be up and going."

Timmy pressed on. No offer of a future McDonald's was going to pacify my boy. "I'm hungry. I want to go there right now."

"How about I fly you to where I know there *is* one? I have a private jet."

Not good enough! Not for my Timmy.

Happy adeptly ended this confrontation by handing Timmy a usually-forbidden packet of M & M chocolates. She followed this ploy by serving doubles from a bottle of scotch to each of us, including the beleaguered babysitter. Happy said in her spritely tone, "Highness, ain't it true that in 1996 seventeen Americans were killed during an attack by terrorists on the Khobar Tower in Saudi Arabia?"

"Yes. True enough. But that wasn't in my principality."

"Isn't there a Saudi Hezbollah that was behind that truck bombing?"

"Yes, but we don't have a problem with Hezbollah in my principality."

Happy insisted sending a double punch. "The USA'd put a bounty of $25 million on thet terrorist Mughniyeh. But when he was on board a commercial flight thet stopped in Saudi Arabia, Saudi officials refused to arrest him and allowed him to leave the country. And when he was finally killed last year, there were Saudis in his funeral procession yelling for vengeance."

"Yes. But, not Saudis from my principality." The prince ended his series of broken-record responses by downing what remained in his glass and leaving the room.

I escorted him back to his bodyguards, and then returned to hug Happy. In the privacy of our bedroom, after paying and dispatching the babysitter, I murmured: "I hope we haven't lost Ben as an owner, but by God—my darling—you certainly put a fire in his pants. Will we ever forget his threat to the organizers of camel races to *'cut off their hands'?"*

Fran Purcell could be as difficult as the most crushing of British owners, but her threats stopped short of "cutting off hands."

With Fran, it was always a case of "cutting off the money."

Seated downstairs in the lobby's mangy lunch room, Fran started in again about how she was heading for economic ruin. "My producer won't try out any of the newest songs. It's all shitty tripe, what I sing. Now there's this fuck-up about my contract in Las Vegas. And I know Cher got a three-year contract at Caesars Palace after Celine Dion's act ended there. She's sixty-one years old, but gets a three-year contract and I couldn't even get booked in for a one-night performance. When I'm still in my twenties. Rick, you can't expect me to buy any more horses!"

I said nothing.

Sir Arthur Snodgrass said the wrong thing. "But my precious one, remember that Cher is the only entertainer to ever had a hit song in every one of the last five decades."

"Thanks a fucking lot," Fran gulped down her coffee, burning her tongue. She dipped a finger into the butter—which was meant to serve all five of us—and coated her tongue with it.

Unexpectedly, Happy changed the subject. "Fran, do you remember that strange Mr. Kotsky who used to have a horse in our stable?"

"Fuck all, of course I do. He stole that Soviet name I wanted for my horse. Son of a bitch. What ever happened to him?"

"He went into a witness protection program. Most terrified man Ah's ever seen. He were fearin' he'd be poisoned with the same nuclear radiation substance what killed thet other British based Russian, Litvinenko."

"That's old news."

"Ah thought of Kotsky this mornin' when Ah read thet another British based Russian done got murdered: a man who became Georgian after thet region broke from the Soviets. He was the richest man Georgia ever had, and when he died in February this year, some of his friends claimed they'd heard a tape where an official in his country's Interior Ministry asked a Chechen warlord to murder him in England. Someone did, and Ah's wonderin' about this Chechen man. The Chechens seemed to breed terrorists. Ah's become interested in them."

"Stick to what you fuck know about, Happy: racehorses."

"Sho 'nuf. Ah knows of a real good bargain might be comin' up. Hal Murphy's turnin' his sights on a woman. Maybe y'all can get that filly you always wanted. Get her away from him."

I gave Happy a warning tap under the table.

She shut up.

Lola took over the conversation. Near to weeping, she moaned: "I've been hoping that Sven might show up for the races."

I said: "Sorry, Lola. Not much chance of that. Sven was looking at polo ponies. Not thoroughbreds."

"But you saw him in Moscow, at the sales. For racehorses."

No comment. I wasn't going to tell Lola that Sven could well be a suspect in Harry Bloom's murder, and if so he certainly wouldn't be showing himself at the races here. I recalled my own horrific experience in a Dubai jail when I was suspected of being an accomplice in Happy's abduction. Sven wouldn't let himself in for anything like that.

And where was Hal on this day of all days when his old favorite Anchor would be running in the prince's colors? I still didn't have the address of his seaside cottage.

Hal *did* show up to watch his former star win his race. Anchor behaved impeccably. Thank God for that: now that I knew our prince believed in chopping off hands, I didn't want to lose mine by losing races for him.

Ben had arranged for us to have a celebration in private. A real fountain had been set up in a private room of Dubai's most famous hotel, and red wine flowed like blood from that fountain. Fresh caviar, brought from the not-so-far Caspian Sea, was the best I've ever tasted. For those of us who prefer champagne with our caviar, that was flowing from a fanciful motorized pitcher. The only people without a glass of wine in hand were the prince's four bodyguards. I wondered if they were Fundamentalists, or merely didn't drink while on duty.

Mafalda certainly wasn't displaying any Fundamentalist leanings. She downed as much champagne as did Harry, making each goblet serve as a loving cup.

Harry was truly in love. Or lust. His eyes glowed like a midschooler on Valentine's Day whose girlfriend had given him a condom.

How to warn him off Mafalda? I feared it was too late to attempt that ploy, and resolved to use this celebration for a word of warning.

By midnight, Hal Murphy was beyond all help. Blotto, he invited all present to his seaside cottage for more drinks. As if we needed them!

"But I own this house," Ben smirked when we drove up to Hal's door. While Mafalda showed us through rooms decorated in either Louis XV, or Jacobean English, or American minimalist styling, Ben showed off what he knew. "Several of us bought into this complex, But none of us ever lived here: not for a single day."

"Highness, why ever not?" Happy asked, quite impressed with the furnishings.

"Totally unsafe. Not because the houses are built on land reclaimed from the seabed. No, not at all. It's because of the palm tree design, where frond-like branches stretch out in such a way that each peninsula is surrounded on three sides by beaches. We could be attacked by revolutionaries in overwhelming numbers arriving by boats."

"Oh!" I digested that information.

Hal's party was no fun. When the host or hostess is drunk, a party always falls flat. With Hal at a piano trying to lure Fran to sing to Mafalda, this party was a disaster.

Fran pouted, and spat out: "I don't sing at private parties. Anyway, I'm too expensive. I get $1 million for a personal appearance."

"I'll give you $1,000, and you'll damn well sing. Instead of the words SWEET ADELINE, you should warble SWEET MAFALDA. Lawrence Olivier once told Noel Coward he wouldn't appear in a show for $200, and Noel Coward told him he would. Well, I'm bloody well telling *you* to sing. Now!"

"And I'm telling you to bugger off." Fran flounced to the front door, threw her drink in its glass to the marble floor, and stalked to her limousine. Sir Arthur and Lola dutifully followed.

I caught up with them. "Please take Happy back to the hotel with you," I pleaded. "I'm staying the night here with Hal. I don't think he should be here on his own."

Following his ultimatum to Fran, Hal had passed out on a Louis XV sofa, and was snoring loudly.

Happy had curled up in a boudoir chair, and not accustomed to heavy drinking, was also asleep. I woke her, and urged her to go in the limo with Fran, Sir Arthur and Lola. Drowsy, but in her usual complacent way, Happy toddled out to the limo in time to settle herself there and go back to sleep.

Mafalda, who for all her Fundamentalist leanings had consumed more alcohol than I had, now used her cell phone to call for a taxi. She'd noticed there was no telephone in the house: another dire warning of how dangerous the place was.

With Mafalda gone, and damp air swirling into the open-plan room, I covered Hal with a Spanish shawl that I borrowed from the piano.

I wanted desperately to go to sleep. Lucky, I didn't.

At two a.m., like clockwork as if on schedule, a motorboat drew up to the deep water dock beyond our beach. Arab whispers followed. I felt my skin crawl as if cockroaches were gliding over me. What to do? I ran to lamp after lamp, flooded all the rooms with glaring light, and added the noise of the TV at full blast.

Searching the closets for something to defend us with, I found a snorkeler's spear gun. I loaded its ammunition, aimed the spear gun into the open loggia and fired round after round.

Soon I heard the chug-chug of the motorboat's engine diminishing as it sailed away.

Hal slept through it all.

The following morning Hal seemed quite restored to his usual commanding self. He unpacked his lap top and checked his e-mails.

"There's something from my head office about that Harry Bloom fellow I asked them to investigate. Yes, the McDonald's people would much appreciate a donation to the Ronald McDonald Children's Charity. No, McDonald's had never employed a Harry Bloom in any capacity."

He let me read the e-mail. "Interesting," I commented. "Let's get back to the hotel. BUT AS THERE'S NO TELEPHONE HERE, I THINK YOU'D BEST E-MAIL HAPPY. You know her email address. Tell her to send us a taxi."

We had a long wait. Hal, newly a bachelor, had thought to order in plenty of alcohol, but no food. There wasn't even coffee. My stomach was rumbling, and I had to make do with a jar of cocktail peanuts.

Hal's good humor had vanished by the time we returned to our hotel. He'd lost his suite by checking out the day before. With Dubai's racing in full swing, he had no choice but to take a paltry single room where he most definitely would not wish to continue to entertain Mafalda.

She showed up for lunch.

I suggested we continue last night's interrupted party at the race course in its top restaurant. Hal agreed. Which was lucky, because he was going to have to pick up a hefty bill which I couldn't afford.

There was some rivalry among the women competing for who was wearing the most outrageous hat.

"Mine!" Fran announced in her deepest contralto. "I paid five hundred pounds for this fucking topper."

"No, it's mine: I paid only thirty pounds at Peter Jones, but it's got this crazy feather," Mafalda crowed.

Happy said nothing. She'd tried to disguise her huge belly in a new maternity dress which was of Arab design fitting for a Fundamentalist, but she wore last year's best Royal Ascot hat, which she'd chosen because it was *not outrageous*.

Suddenly, Lola blubbered: "MY GOD, look over there. Behind that woman in the pink cartwheel hat. Just behind her: there's my husband. There's Sven."

I looked quickly, but all I could see was the cartwheel hat, which was covering the head of the man behind her. I could make out his body, and the awful checked suit he wore, but no face.

Lola tore out of our restaurant, running like a meteor in search of the man.

Minutes later she returned, her face as deflated as a kid's balloon the day after a party. "I couldn't find him," she groaned.

"You must have been mistaken," I said kindly: "If he was in Dubai, I'm sure he wouldn't be so foolish as to come to such a public place."

"No mistake. His face was—uh—changed. Not so—uh—handsome. His golden hair was covered with a black trilby. He'd let his eyebrows grow thick, and he had a droopy mustache. But I know his walk, and that special way that he favors his right shoulder. My Sven *is* here, in Dubai. I'm going to find him."

Lola gathered up her handbag and car keys.

"I can't go with you, not before our race is run. But I advise you, Lola, not to pursue this. If you did see Sven, I believe he's here for some purpose. I'm certain he doesn't want to be tracked by anyone. You might even lead the police to him. Something none of us want. I've been in a Dubai jail, I know how he'll be treated."

Happy placed a restraining hand on Lola's arm. "Please wait. He may come to you at our hotel, if he's really here."

Lola shook off Happy's curled fingers. She rushed out of the racecourse.

This wasn't my day. Our horse came in Second, a placing I always hate because it meant my boy could have won but for some mistake on the part of the jockey, or the unexpected change in the going.

Fortunately that horse belonged to Hal Murphy, who'd proved over and over again what a sportsmanlike owner he was. Lucky that Fran's filly was scheduled for the next day, when I'd have time to personally test the going and give more detailed counsel to her jockey.

When Happy and I were alone in our bedroom, with Timmy asleep in his cot, she snuggled up close to me, and whispered: "It *were* Sven. I'd a good look. I reckon he's had more plastic surgery, but not to make him more attractive. That be impossible. No, he'd come to the races for a reason, just like y'all said. A changed man. Ah hopes not to be a *dead* man soon."

"Damn fool, to appear in such a public place."

"Must have had a good reason. That, or the threat of a bullet to his head."

"Why, do you—" I was interrupted by the intercom telephone. I hoped its jangling wouldn't waken Timmy.

Happy answered the call. "It's Sven!" she sang out to me. "He wants to know what room Lola's in!" Returning to the mouthpiece, she added: "Sven, she's in the Sir Arthur Snodgrass suite, with him and Fran. Oh, Sven! Do Be Careful."

I said: "I don't think we should join them. Sven must want some time alone with his wife."

"Yeah man! And Ah wants a good time with *my husband.*"

We got under the covers, and we DID have a good time.

Fran's filly won her race the next day. I didn't lose Fran as an owner. In fact, she finally ordered me to go to Ireland to bid on a new yearling. Her improved mood wasn't due to Sven's reappearance. He'd only stayed the one night with Lola, and then went on the run again.

I love Dublin. When I'd just left my regiment following the finalizing of the Vance Owen Treaty that ended the Bosnia War, I checked into the Kildare Street and University Club, which I was able to use through its reciprocity with my London Club, the Cavalry and Guards.

Dublin's men's clubs, with their woodwork heavy with peat smoke and their faded chintz furnishings, appealed greatly after tank warfare. I cultivated a taste for Guinness, and even learned to stomach their grey slimy lamb stews.

But I wasn't to remain long at that comfortsble old-fashioned club, because most unexpectedly my darling wife arrived after I'd been alone for merely two days. Was she worried I might meet another Irina or Lois, and get involved in yet another extra-marital affair?

I wasn't to know. Happy arrived with her usual mountain of Timmy's luggage, plus baby clothes for Irish and Dorothy. The entire family! But there was no Amah to help with feeding, bathing and playing with the "chillun." It became imperative I find a hotel that took small children, and hire a capable baby sitter.

"Ah's decided Ah should see the Book of Kells, or at least a copy. Ah wants to kiss the Blarney Stone, Ah wants t'learn me about the Lindisfarne Gospels, and such like."

Ouch. When I'd reveled in my renewed bachelor status during the past two nights, I'd forgotten Happy's fascination with antiquities. And Ireland had her fair share!

Happy was her usual brainy self when we attended the sales. She picked out a fine yearling that was going for a fair price. "Got t'inspect his legs. These Irish, they be mighty clever unloadin' a hoss what looks sound, but ain't."

After a vet pronounced the yearling as having no palate and therefore prone to swallowing his tongue, Happy found a filly that was down on condition but had alert intelligent eyes. I bought the filly for Fran.

With that job behind me, Happy started on her "tourin'."

Timmy had kissed the Blarney Stone, and Happy had just attempted to squeeze her enormous belly into position to accomplish the same, when her water broke.

Again, as in Dubai two years ago, we had to make for the nearest local hospital.

It was ultra-clean, and although the facilities appeared to be out of Dickins' era, no complications ensued.

Within three hours, almost painlessly, Happy was delivered of a large son.

"What-all shall we name this chile?" Happy asked, when she regained her voice.

We were in a semi-private room that Happy was sharing with an expectant mother who was practicing heavy breathing in preparation for the birth of her own child.

In answer, I said: "We could call him Erin, since he was born here. But my darling, you need to rest, and not to worry your precious head over anything."

"Nope. Not Erin, we done already got little Irish. I say let's us call him Richard, for you."

I kissed my wife, gently but for a long time.

Meanwhile, a bona fide miracle was taking place in Richard's bassinet. Timmy had come into the room to stare at our newborn. Timmy had extended a finger toward the bassinet—and, then came the miracle—just like Dorothy had done with me in Dubai, this newborn curled his tiny hand around Timmy's finger like a shrimp around a shell.

Timmy's face took on a look of ecstasy.

Sliding into Happy's Kentucky accent, Timmy yodeled: "Ah's got me a brother! This be *my* brother. Mine, all mine, because we be boys together. Richard, y'all hear? We's a team! The Timmy and Richard team!"

I had to interrupt this scene, much as I didn't want to, because Timmy started to press one of his precious M & M candies into Richard's uncurling hand. Next, Timmy will be wanting to feed Richard on a McDonald's hamburger!

"Easy there, son. Here's a bottle of special water. Try to place the nipple in Richard's mouth. And see if he'll drink."

Richard did. He sucked at the water as if was mother's milk. Which it wasn't. After her experience in Kentucky with that crazy serial killer, Happy had sworn off nursing her "chillun."

Timmy's face returned to its look of ecstasy. He'd offered to give nourishment to Richard, and his teammate had responded.

This miracle was complete.

We couldn't leave Ireland in a hurry. Happy spent five days in that hospital. She'd had stitches that didn't heal properly.

When she read the local newspapers and saw that races were coming up at The Curragh, she wasn't anxious to leave the country. After leaving the hospital, and declaring herself fit for everything, we left all four children with a willing nurse and headed for the racecourse.

It would be Happy's first experience of racing in Ireland, and she gloried in it like a kid at a birthday party. The deceptive simplicity of the Irish ladies' clothes, made by expensive couturiers to look unshowy, delighted her and filled her with a desire to emulate them. But her stomach was still too swollen to merit serious shopping, and she went to her first day's racing in a maternity dress. No hat. And when she suddenly felt faint, I had to rely on the St. Lazarus Ambulance ladies to seat her in a wheelchair.

"Lookee there! Ah seen Sven," she whispered, as soon as she'd settled herself in the wheelchair. "There, just past the Finish Line. Wearin' a trilby, just like Lola said he had."

This time I saw Sven clearly, his head as well as his body in his hideous checked suit. No doubt about this fellow: he was Sven, although not as beautiful as I remembered. He wouldn't be a candidate to work as a male model now.

Happy grabbed my arm. "Give me your cell phone. Ah'm goin' to telephone Lois and tell her to come over here to Ireland on the next plane."

She did. I drove to the airport to collect Lola and brought her to our hotel, where Happy had corralled Sven to stay for dinner.

The Jensens, or whatever their name would be legally, had a tender reunion. Lola had news: "I'm pregnant. A gift from our one night together in Dubai."

Happy hugged her, and we tactfully disappeared promptly after dinner. Sven made reservations for the bridal suite at an upmarket bed and breakfast not far from the Curragh, and they drove off together through the Irish mists.

They didn't surface for two halcyon days, during which—according to Lola during a lengthy conversation with Happy—they made love nonstop.

"She'll be lucky, Ah reckon, not to lose the baby at thet rate," Happy laughed.

Fran and Sir Arthur Snodgrass flew to Ireland and checked into our seedy hotel. Fran could well have afforded the Shelbourne, Dublin's traditional best for racing folk, but she still had her pennypinching ways.

"Lola, pregnant!" Fran became furious at that news. "She has her wedding before I do, and now she's having a baby before I'm even married!" Her famous contralto voice cracked. "And for all we know, her Sven's a murderer."

"No, ma'am. Ah's mighty sho he ain't no killer. Maybe next to *be murdered.* Thet ain't the same."

Nobody contradicts Happy on the subject of murderers, not even Fran. She shut up on that score, but took out her anger on me, criticizing the filly I'd bought.

"Looks like she has a fucking case of tuberculosis. Never saw anything so skinny. Bloody awful animal. Rick you said she was a bargain: cheap enough maybe, but a bad buy."

To escape Fran's wrath, Happy and I checked into that same bed and breakfast that had given the Jensens so much joy.

It was an eerie place. It may have started out as an overgrown farmhouse, but it had attained some grandeur at one point. There were valuable pieces of furniture, too worn to sell, torn velvet drapes, and walls clothed in faded silk with rectangular and oblong give-aways that once paintings had hung where the silk wasn't faded.

A fey little crippled man, not five feet tall, looking like an elf, welcomed us into the grander rooms. "A Rembrandt hung on that unfaded rectangular, and a Vermeer where it's oblong."

"Fit for a museum," I suggested, playing along.

In all seriousness, the elf nodded his oversized head. "After World War II a famous Nazi General lived here with his elegant wife. They owned the pictures and brought in these antiques. His name was Scorzini. And famous he was. Do yez remember when a Nazi Geneeral flew in a glider plane to rescue Mussolini? That was Scorzini."

"I do recall something like that."

"And when Hitler needed to name a replacement Chancellor after the under-the-table bomb incident, he gave Scorzini that job, sir. Aye, and Scorzini told the staff here that Hitler's arm was injured in the blast, and he may have lost it." The elf put a finger to his left eye, as if that would clarify the story.

"Y'all got any ghosts in this here ho-tel?" Happy asked, to break the tension.

"There are visitors who claim to have seen a lady in a long brown dress, style of a century ago. But she means no harm. Ye'll have ye a good night's sleep."

It wasn't slsep I wanted. Now that Happy was restored to her usual libido, I wanted good sex.

We had plenty.

Two days later Happy insisted we relieve the babysitter. She felt worried about Richard, and Timmy.

No cause for that. Timmy had completely taken over the surveillance, feeding, and general caregiving for Richard. He scolded the babysitter if Richard wouldn't eat. He watched with the scrutiny of a surgeon when Richard was bathed. He sang his own favorite lullabyes to make Richard go to slumberland.

Happy and I watched this phenomenon with immense satisfaction. Timmy's all-embracing smother-love wasn't doing Richard any harm. He was blossoming like a well-watered posey.

It was Fran that caused a legitimate worry. She was threatening to leave my stables and take all her horseflesh with her. She'd rattled that threat at me before, but this time she could back it up because she'd met a trainer in Ireland who was trying to get her away from me.

Called Oscar Lent, he might well have succeeded if Fran's interest hadn't been totally diverted by really serious news.

Fran burst into our bedroom the morning after we'd returned to Dublin. Happy was wearing nothing but the hotel toweling robe, and I wasn't even wearing that. I was in my underpants, with my chin covered in shaving cream.

"Arthur's been de-selected," she screamed. "He's no longer an MP, and we've been told he may have his knighthood taken away." Sobbing, she went into Happy's opening arms, and got wet from the damp robe. "I'll never be Lady Snodgrass now."

I poured a cup of coffee for Fran from the hotel's breakfast supply. Fran couldn't hold the cup straight and splashed coffee on her blouse, burning herself. Murphy's Law: if anything else could go wrong, it would.

Arthur followed Fran into the room. Snarling, he roughly pulled her arm. "You coming to London now, or no?"

"I haven't decided." Fran whined, she couldn't look Arthur in the eye.

"Now, or never."

"I haven't packed."

Arthur gave Fran a withering glance, and stalked out of our room. No goodbye for either of us. No kiss for Fran.

I cleaned the shaving soap off my face. Happy grabbed her old sweater to wrap it around Fran's shoulders.

Fran seemed to be going into shock.

Happy helped her into our open bed, and pulled up the covers. In an instant, Fran fell asleep.

"I'd say she'd had a line or two of cocaine this morning," I said sadly. "This may be the beginning of a skid into oblivion for Fran."

"What's 'de-select' mean?"

"The heavy hitters of his constituency must have implemented rules causing him to be kicked out."

Lola came silently into our room. She was very pale, and had an acute attack of morning sickness that sent her to our toilet to vomit. When she emerged, using a finger to work some of our toothpaste around the inside of her mouth, she said through the suds: "Arthur's been stripped of his knighthood. The Department of Defense claimed he sold military secrets to the Saudis."

"To our *Ben?*"

"No. He's just a playboy prince. This is deadly serious. People involved have died."

Happy nodded. "First Stinky, then Ali, and Harry Bloom."

Incredulous, I stared at my darling wife. "You'd guessed some of this?"

"Weren't no guess. My Pa smoked out a gun-runner in our Kentucky hills. Same *sort of man as them guys.*"

I said: "Happy, it's time you tell us what you know."

"Sho 'nuf. But it ain't written in stone, like them arche-o-logical treasures what Harry Bloom was meant to visit."

"Would you mind elaborating?"

"Ah looked up on your computer t'learn me about each of them countries he traveled to. Each one of them had revolutionaries who'd buy guns. East Timor? The president got shot. Pakistan? Benazir Bhutto assassinated. Chad? The so-called freedom fighters took over the capital. Sri Lanka? Them Tamil Tigers been busy for years."

"So when Sven went to Colombia, it wasn't to buy polo ponies only: he'd made contact with the FARC."

"Sho 'nuf. And Ali was a middleman. When Ah saw his house in Cairo, Ah knows he couldn't afford to pay no $1,250,000 on his own. Trace the check, and Ah's ready to bet it traces back to Arthur."

Lola drank the cold coffee I'd earlier poured for Fran. She said weakly: "I can't believe Arthur had anything to do with the murders of those three men."

"Would you rather we suspected Sven?" I asked.

Lola said nothing more.

Happy continued, gently because she hated to upset Lola further: "Didn't y'all think it was mighty strange thet Arthur was off to Dalmatia selling beachfront lots? And lately he was sayin' he'd go to Egypt to a new Red Sea resort to sell lots there. Lola! Ah thinks y'all got t'warn Sven to watch his back."

Lola interrupted: "Happy, *you* don't suspect Sven*!*"

"Thet's right. Ah doesn't. Never would have introduced you two if'n Ah thought Sven's a murderer. Had him to my home. Invited him last night for dinner. No way!Sven reminded me of a revenue agent my Pa liked: agent what worked for the gover-n-ment"

I stared at my darling wife: astonished!

I asked her: "Then who killed Stinky, in Miami?"

"Ah reckons Sven had gone down in the safe ele-va-tor. Then some of Arthur's hoods pushed Stinky down the opened shaft."

"Ali?"

"He'd got too greedy. Tryin' to sell thet filly what didn't really belong to him. Another of Arthur's hoods throttled his windpipe, then planted that chunk o' pork. Crazy."

"And Harry Bloom?"

"He must have got too greedy, al-so. Wanted a bigger cut off the prices of them guns they sold."

Again Lola interrupted. "I've got to stop Sven from taking the plane to London. He'd be on the same one as Arthur. He'd never land alive at Heathrow. Rick, can I borrow the keys of your rental car?"

"Ah's comin' with y'all," Happy grabbed my keys and led Lola to the hotel's car park. Happy, so recently out of the hospital after that infection from suppurating stitches, and pregnant Lola, were hardly the best driver and navigator for the ride. But speeding far beyond the limit, they soon caught up with Arthur's rental job.

A near fatal car chase followed, with Arthur now showing his unscrupulous character. He cut in front, went parallel, hammered the side of Happy's car and finally drove it off the road.

Steam billowed out of its engine. The two women left the car in case it caught fire and exploded.

A speed cop brought his vehicle alongside. He had a strong Dublin accent. "I clocked you going eighty kilometers an hour." He brought out an official-looking pad and wrote down my rental car's license plate, Happy's name, and handed her a citation.

Lola offered him fifty punts to forget about the incident.

"You trying to bribe me, lady?" he grunted. "That's worse than a felony. That could land you years in prison."

Happy tried Kentucky charm. "Officer, Ah's not familiar with the speed limits y'all have here in Ireland. Ah's a visitor from Amer-i-ca."

"I've got a cousin in Memphis, Tennessee. You ever been to Memphis? You sound like she does." His tone, gruff, was not too unpleasant.

"Memphis be a long ways from my Kentucky hills. But Ah's met folks from there who was real nice."

More cordially, the speed cop tore up the summons. "There's a petrol station about a mile East. You could phone for a taxi there."

He saluted, and drove off. Lola and Happy trudged silently to the petrol station. But, before asking for a taxi, Lola tried to have Sven paged at the airport. No luck.

By the time they arrived at the airport in a very tardy taxi, the plane for London had left. We returned to London the following day.

None of us heard from Sven for another month. "No news was good news," Lola whispered when she joined us in our Epsom cottage. "No one could have been killed on that plane. Maybe Sven had managed to get on an earlier flight."

There had been a minimal write-up about Arthur's de-selection on page 23 of our London newspaper.

Lola was infuriated by a subsequent article that compared Arthur's losing his knighthood to Lester Piggott having suffered the same. **"Poor old Lester, all he did was let his accountant make a mistake over his taxes,"** she growled. **"Arthur's been having people killed."**

Without Snodgrass, Fran had become a changed woman. She needed sex or cocaine. She couldn't do without both. Her figure sagged. Her skin took on a ghastly grey tone. Her hair went flat. I had good reason to fear she'd give up on horseracing and sell her bloodstock.

Thank God for Happy! We were back in our own bedroom in Epsom one unseasonably warm morning, when Happy looked up from changing Richard's diaper, and said: "Fran needs a good man in her life. And not any old one will do. Remember how keen she was on that future Earl, Jeremy Grace? Ah seen him in the supermarket while you was on early mornin' gallops. Jeremy hasn't got a girl; Ah done asked him."

Dour, I grunted: "No, it won't work. He dumped Fran before because of her cocaine habit."

"Ah says if 'n she gets the right man, Fran will go off the coke."

"Tell that to all those drying out places like The Priory."

"Ah could. Maybe Ah should. Could make a pile o' money. But it's true."

"My darling wife, you should stick to riding horses. Fran's been a heavy user for a very long time. No way will she give it up."

"Ah's done invited Jeremy fo' dinner. Fran's comin' too."

No arguing with Happy!

I wasn't looking forward to dinner. But to be on the safe side with such an important owner invited, I hired caterers to come in with platters of ready-prepared food. No Kentucky Fried Chicken and grits for our Fran.

She took one look at her dinner partner and her disgruntled face softened like jelly on a summer's day. "Jeremy!" She almost panted, she was so excited by the prospect of spending prime time with him. Her skin took on a glow, her hair was flung from side to side airing it, and she freshened the crimson on her lips.

Jeremy was equally dazzled. He wasn't seeing the frustrated, quarrelsome spinster that Fran had become. For Jeremy, she was still the opera star who crooned her way into his heart singing Christmas carols for him on the Christmas Eve when they met here three years ago.

Happy's plan proved a total success.

Later that night, when we were celebrating in each other's arms in bed, Happy sang out: "The joy from bein' loved cures everythin'."

Chapter 15

The next morning, Happy wore her most serious expression. "Rick, Ah thinks it's im-por-tant we talks to Jeremy about Arthur Snodgrass. Forget what Fran may tell him: she never guessed the truth. But Jeremy was in the M-I5 and could maybe help us get more of a low-down on Arthur. His game, and his whereabouts."

"Jeremy left that arm of the government. He had great respect for such as Mr. Dearlove when he was head of it, but he couldn't quite get on with some of the new people there."

"Ask him. First chance y'all gets."

I did. Jeremy, who like me, had once unjustly been a suspect when working to clear up a crime, came up trumps.

We met on the gallops when I was exercising ELIZABETH THE GREAT. He had a new hunter, to replace the one so brutally killed three years ago. I said: "Jeremy, could you put a trace on Arthur Snodgrass?"

Too much of a gentleman to make a smart-ass remark about the man who had preceded him in Fran's bed, he said with profound seriousness: "Not I, but I'll ask a friend who still has access to certain files."

Chapter 16

The week of another Royal Ascot was approaching and I had more than enough work to do down at the stables. Two of my two-year-old colts were coughing. Normal, this time of year, like nursery kids they seem to get sick most often in the mild spring weather.

Happy decided to go to London to look for Ascot hats. Anyway, that was her excuse when her real purpose was to go call on Fran.

With unhappy memories of two people who'd been murdered in that apartment, it was not a place that Happy would have usually chosen for her few spare hours in London.

"Ah just don't und-er-stand why y'all stays in this gloomy buildin'," she said to Fran, after being ushered into the drawing room. Fran had managed to clean up the poop that had been such an ugly part of being nearly strangled. But she had not rid the kitchen of a large bowl of cocaine.

Happy noticed there were recent finger marks in the cocaine powder. "Y'all been usin?" she asked. She looked around for a cocaine pipe, then remembered that Fran preferred to roll up a new ten pound note from which to snort.

"Hap, I thought you were coming to see my new décor," Fran said. "No lecture, please."

"Ah sho 'nuf loves the décor-a-tion. Kept thet old rug, though, Ah sees."

"Fuck all, why not? There's only one spot, and it was new, only two years ago. Not left over from when my mother lived here. Hap, want some tea?"

"Sho 'nuf. Got used to tea." Happy settled in for a long chat. "When would y'all like to talk about Jeremy?"

Fran brought in two cracked cups and a seedy teapot missing its lid. Her miserly habits had extended to non-replacement of her household bits and pieces. She poured the tea, nibbled at a biscuit from an opened packet, and said, "Not today. I've had bad news again from Las Vegas. The casino won't pay me anything like what Celine Dion got last year."

"Sorry to hear thet." Happy tried to smother a grin, because she well knew the enormous amount Fran had been offered by that casino. She said, speaking carefully, "Let's y'all and me be plannin' to go see Stonehenge. We can talk more on the drive there."

"Stonehenge?" Fran looked at Happy as if she was crazy. "Nothing but a circle of huge stones. Why would you want to go *there?*"

"Ah favors old stones. But also Ah wants to see Stonehenge befo'e another vandal hits them stones with a hammer!"

"A hammer?"

"Yep, vandal hit one with a hammer. But Ah still cares to go. When Ah was in Egypt, Ah went to see a King's tomb where the sun hits the altar once a year, just like Ah'm told the sun hits the right spot at Stonehenge for the Summer Solstice."

"Oh, I suppose that's interesting for some people," she said, echoing Lola, Fran poured another cup of tea for herself, but neglected to offer seconds to Happy. "We'll talk about this trip another time. Last time you brought it up, I thought what you really wanted was to go there in comfort in my limo. Meanwhile, your husband better win for me at the Ascot races in May."

He did. Fran ended up receiving her trophy in last year's hat, too stingy to go buy one for the May races. She didn't consider them up to the standard of June's Royal Ascot extravaganza. I do. I love the May races at Ascot.

Too bad that dear Hal had missed out on receiving *his* trophy for HAL'S COMET'S win. But I received an ecstatic e-mail from him congratulating both of us.

Hal had more to be ecstatic about; he'd fixed up with Mafalda to have a date during Royal Ascot week. Oh, Oh. We weren't going to get rid of Mafalda from our circle easily.

Fran had not been pleased with the running of her colt that won. We were not offered flutes of champagne. I got grumbles, and sneers about the jockey who had won by a large margin. Fran pouted, "Stupid jockey. He's revealed to the frigging bookies just how fucking brilliant my horse is."

She toned down her use of four letter words when Jeremy joined us. Like a scene from My Fair Lady, Fran had screamed a torrent of vulgarity when her horse approached the winning post, but caught herself in time to adopt a more distinguished pose during tea with Jeremy afterwards.

Fran really wanted to ensnare Jeremy. She was prepared to make a few sacrifices.

Chapter 17

Early June had races that gave me a tonic. I won races for Fran and Hal again, and for Ben. ANCHOR, of course, performed on schedule.

Hal must have sorely wished he'd kept ANCHOR, in spite of Ben having "made an offer he couldn't refuse." This year, Hal's Ascot week was all about showing off to Mafalda. She'd appeared in outfits that were in surprisingly good taste: suits from Belleville Sassoon, hats from Herbert Johnson. Nothing extravagant. Not even her shoes gave away her middle-Eastern preferences. No Jimmy Choo five inch heels, she kept strictly to the sedate buckled heel-and-toe covered pumps favored by the Queen. Mafalda was reeling in Hal like a champion deepsea fisher trawls a marlin.

"Ah expects y'all will soon see a big diamond on Mafalda's third finger left hand," Happy chortled.

Happy was on top of her form. With May's races over, like a racehorse chomping at its bit to lunge down a course, Happy prepared for her trip to Stonehenge. She'd convinced Fran to accompany her. The limo had been duly provided and they set off for the monument for the Summer Solstice.

When Happy was standing in a prime position to view that awesome event, she whispered: "This be the time of year when the sun's the farthest from the equ-a-tor."

She enjoyed the antics put on for tourists by the so-called Druids, costumed in flowing white garments.

Fran sneered. "I was in an opera once where there were Druids. 'Norma!' Much better costumes, I fucking assure you."

Happy had no comments on the subject of operas. She knew when to shut up because a subject was beyond her grasp.

The two women had rented audio tapes that explained the history of Stonehenge. Fran had turned off hers, but Happy listened avidly.

"Stonehenge dates back over 4,500 years. Not much is known about the people who built it, but recent finds have clarified much that has hitherto relied on guesswork. Due to a find of a nearby village that could support one thousand souls, it is believed that a religious theme brought visitors to the henge from all over Britain. This larger henge of stones could be the cult of the dead: ancestor worship. The wooden henge near the village could be the cult of life and fertility."

"Fertility!"

"Sho 'nuf?" Happy exclaimed, and shut off the audio. "Ah doesn't want no more babies. We'd best get out of here."

Happy had chosen to be alone with Fran for this outing on a dual purpose. Yes, she wanted to go to Stonehenge in a limo, but she also wanted to set Fran straight on what she must do to become Jeremy's wife.

When they were settled back in the limo and driving away from Stonehenge, Fran got the lecture she'd previously avoided.

"Fran, y'all needs to make a break from usin' cocaine, and from them fo'r letter words. Jeremy Grace, as the next Earl in his family, has limits to what he can accept in a wife. Ah knows he loves y'all. Really and true-like. Ah knows he'd have wedded y'all three years ago if it hadn't been for the coke. And in them days, y'all took great care not to use bawdy language."

"I'd tell you to get fucking lost if we weren't in the middle of nowhere. Long walk back to Epsom."

"Fran, please! If y'all was wedded and Jeremy's givin' a party in the House of Lords, would y'all tell the guests to fuck off if they said somethin' not right? Or when he takes y'all to a garden party at Buckingham Palace, and Her Majesty passes by where it was hard to see, call out:'shit'?"

"So I'll rein in on the language. But not the coke."

"Then there won't be a weddin'; Jeremy told me three years ago he wanted healthy chillun. He thinks that usin' will stop you from givin' him healthy ones. That 's why he stood you up at The Dorchester then, thet last time you'd made a date."

Silence from Fran. She sat thinking as the limo sped past the great lake that hovers near the Stonehenge district. Their car circled ancient Salisbury, and Happy peered at its cathedral's great spire. "Ah'd love to stop and visit thet there church. Ah never seen such a tall steeple."

Fran adopting a supercilious manner, grunted: "We're not stopping anywhere. I've seen enough old stones for one day."

Her driver had the temerity to interrupt: "Madam, that cathedral has some of the most prestigious, interesting stone carvings, propped up in its central patio, that you could find anywhere in the world. And the most wonderful, enormous clock, said to be the first ever to chime the hours. As for Stonehenge, it is a megalithic monument. You would have to go to Africa to find the likes of its several concentric stone circles."

"Spare me the remainder of your spiel!" Fran ordered sharply. "I'm not paying you to act like a tour guide."

In a school marm voice, Happy warmed to the subject: "Ah's heard like those rocks what make up Stonehenge, they was shipped on log rafts from where they was quarried."

"Oh, shut up!" Fran spat. "When *are you going to shut up?"*

"When Ah's finished." Happy smoothed her voice as she smoothed the creases in her skirt. "One mo'e thing. Ah believes y'all could make Jeremy so happy if y'all would give up on them rap songs and go back to opera."

"Now you are talking rot. Give up making twenty million pounds sterling a year in exchange for a measly five million I'd earn in opera?"

"Ain't five million sterlin' same as ten million dollars! How could y'all ever spend ten million dollars?" Happy wheezed.

"I'm aiming for one hundred million sterling in five years. It would take me TWENTY years at only five million!"

"Jeremy's worth it."

Silence came down like a snowstorm.

The car passed village after village, all of them with Gothic churches Happy would love to visit. The silence form Fran lingered on. Happy, like a clever lawyer, left her last words hang sedately. Fran pretended to be asleep, but her breathing came in gasping spurts.

When she deposited Happy at our Epsom door, Fran instructed her driver to take her back to London. No carrots or apples for Fran's horses that day. Not that she remembered very frequently to bring them treats.

Chapter 18

Fran remembered very soon to cut out the four letter vocabulary and eliminate her lines of coke. It took longer to ease out of her rap contracts. But she did.

One fine morning, after Whitsun, when robins pecked at the velvety grass in our garden Fran and Jeremy appeared at our front door. "*I've been made a Dame in the Queen's birthday honors,*" Fran announced gleefully.

Jeremy crowed, "Now we'll find out if she was marrying me for the future title. Tell me, Fran, my angel: are we still engaged?"

"You know we are!" Fran kissed him so hard I was afraid she might have broken his front teeth.

Jeremy responded by giving her an antique family ring, an heirloom of rosecut diamonds he'd hidden in his waistcoat pocket.

Their wedding plans – as set out to us that morning – did not include the three ballrooms at Claridge's. Fran wanted nothing that would remind her of Lola's wedding. She'd given to charity the wedding dress ordered from Mrs. Emmanuel for the non-wedding to Arthur Snodgrass. Oxfam was richer for it. Fran had bought a simple white satin gown off the peg that had shoulders embroidered with seed pearls, but nothing more elaborate than that. Of course, she borrowed the Grace family tiara, another of Jeremy's heirlooms.

Parsimonious Fran not only saved the cost of hiring ballrooms, she was spared contracting a singer for the ceremony. When Jeremy's uncle offered the family castle as the venue for their reception, Filipa Grant, who'd been dumped as Fran's soprano duo partner for their now-canceled rap recording had still come forward and offered to warble Ave Maria. As Filipa explained: "I was sitting on a dinny when I heard we weren't going to be doing rap. I didn't waste time to get a contract to sing Adina's role in L'ELISIR d' AMORE. No hard feelings. Glad to sing for free here for Fran."

Jeremy didn't want a London wedding. Always favoring the countryside, he opted for a chapel-sized church in the near vicinity of the castle. Fran invited my three eldest children to be her only attendants. Timmy was to be ring bearer. Our little girls were bridesmaids.

Their day opened with rain, but by three in the afternoon, the clouds had given way to sunshine and wind. Fran's elaborate veil swirled and billowed. Her tiara went askew. Two of our little children, in 18th century style costumes as for a portrait by Sir Joshua Reynolds, would have preferred to play in the puddles, but they were marshaled down the aisle by a suddenly stern Happy. Timmy dropped the ring and it went cartwheeling down the aisle. But he caught it. Our tiny girls scattered rose petals from baskets, then thought that must be naughty, so they halted the wedding procession while they recovered every last rose petal from the uneven stone floor.

Crowded shoulder to shoulder in the tiny chapel was the most unlikely assortment of people. On Fran's side were her oddly got-up rap singer colleagues, their agents and producers. In addition she had a scattering of the more outlandish members of opera's firmament. Fran's only conservative friend, Ellie, had to be on her cousin Jeremy's side of the aisle, and she had opted to wear a retro dress from the 1930s found in one of her favorite second-hand shops.

Jeremy looked elegant in a turn-of-the-century frock coat dug out of a trunk in the castle's attic. It suited his Knight of the Round Table face. His guests were the cream of British society, many of whom were his relations. Among the grandest was a royal: HRH Prince Michael of Kent, a fellow Eleventh Hussar, known to be supportive of members of his regiment.

Ladies on his side of the aisle varied from wearing dresses bought off the peg from a village shop, and couture gowns worth thousands ordered made to measure from Paris. One elderly Duchess was noted for arriving in a housedress spotted with kitchen grease, although her shoes had been made to order from Lobb. The younger relations eschewed extravagant hats, preferring the newer look of a twist of dyed horsehair topped with feathers and silk flowers.

This motley crew might have been expected to snub one another: the stars from the music world looking down on mere society luminaries. Not so: the Duchess set the tone by asking for an autograph from Filipa.

Happy adored the party, but had to cut short her enjoyment of it when Timmy insisted we go home to tend to his beloved Richard.

I'm told Fran was driven away in one of Jeremy's family coaches drawn by a single white horse. As I wasn't present I can't swear to this, but I'd bet that was one horse she didn't study too critically.

Fran cut short her honeymoon only for the ceremony during which she would be invested as a Dame of the British Empire by Her Majesty at Buckingham Palace.

She invited both of us to come too. Fran entered the hall with others about to be knighted or elevated to become a Dame, while we were separated to go into a vast elegant room with other guests of those being honored.

We'd been wishing there was air-conditioning during a rather long wait before the Queen quietly entered along with a few courtiers. One courtier would whisper to whomever was next in line to be decorated, that person would either curtsey or give a brief neck-curved bow, and then the Queen would put the medal on to a previously fitted attachment. When a man knelt, one knee rested on a conveniently placed stool. For some of those honored, the Queen had a word. For others, she merely did her duty and got on to the next line. She was simply gowned in a knee length light wool dress. No hat. No tiara. No crown.

"Ah sho' admires her," Happy whispered, "standin' up all this time and doin' the same things over and over."

When it became Fran's turn, we both held our breaths that she wouldn't disgrace herself by using one of her foul four letter words. In fact, she said nothing at all, dumfounded, a trouper who for the first time experienced a form of stage fright.

Surprise! The Queen did have a word for Fran. Her Majesty said, in her clear, almost girlish voice, "I much enjoyed hearing you sing as Liu in TURANDOT." That was Fran's finest hour. No doubt about it.

Outside the palace, the press surged around her, like seaweed after a storm. There were famous footballers, academics, an orchestra conductor, and various film stars but it was to Fran the press moved.

If these vultures were expecting Fran to make one of her famous mistakes by coming out with a four letter word, they were disappointed. She smiled sweetly for the cameras, showing her medal.

Then she invited us to the Goring Hotel, which was within walking distance of the palace, saving penny pinching Fran the price of a limo to drive us away.

We were to see The Queen again, the day before Royal Ascot began. Jeremy's uncle, the old Earl, was a Knight of the Garter, and feeling too ill to attend the garter ceremony, he'd delegated Jeremy to attend. Lucky us, we were included.

We saw Her Majesty in full regalia for the garter service.

The Queen came walking form Windsor Castle swathed in a magnificent velvet cape embroidered with the garter emblem, with its famous motto HONI SOIT QUI MAL Y PENSE. Her Majesty's shoulders were festooned with flat white satin ribbons. On her head, she wore a soft velvet beret with ostrich feathers attached. The Duke of Edinburgh and the Prince of Wales accompanied her, similarly attired. Prince William joined them in his debut appearance as a Member of the Order of the Garter. His velvet beret was *huge.*

We got a close look at Camilla, too. *She'd been relegated to being an onlooker, just like us. But HRH The Duchess of Cornwall did merit a front seat in the chapel.*

Happy and I sat well back under the banners and stained glass windows bearing the coats of arms of earlier knights.

What a wealth of pageantry we'd experienced on those two days. But I still looked forward to those magical five days of Royal Ascot as my favorites on the calendar. There we not only get to see the Queen, but with any luck, after all our hard work, we might have a horse that wins and that could mean the Queen presents us with a trophy.

I had one reservation: Mafalda's presence there. Would Happy's prediction come true and Mafalda would end up with an engagement ring from Hal?

Chapter 19

June's Ascot races had long been a target for Hal's new filly, ELIZABETH THE GREAT. With weddings and ceremonies behind me, it was time to put my nose to the grindstone. ELIZABETH THE GREAT had won a race earlier, so she was no longer a maiden racehorse. I'd been preparing her for the turns and gradients of the Ascot race course and felt confident she could win.

Happy decided to make a fashion statement this year. She'd bought an unusual Jamaican cartwheel at Harvey "Nicks" and it suited her well. Her figure had slimmed down from the tub she'd carried during her pregnancy, and the fitted silk suit she chose enhanced her natural curves.

ELIZABETH THE GREAT won her race. But Hal had foregone attending Ascot on that day in order to escort Mafalda to a lunch at the EGYPTIAN EMBASSY, so Happy and I got to stand on the dais with Her Majesty presenting the trophy for the race.

Once again, my gracious lady monarch thrilled Happy by inquiring about our new baby. "I hear you have just had a son, and he is well," the Queen said in her cut-crystal accent.

"That's right," Happy spluttered, then remembered her manners, and added, "Ma'am."

Again, as Her Majesty had done two years earlier, HM turned to our jockey to congratulate him on his winning ride. Happy's moment was over. The Queen returned to the royal box.

We'd been told: "Horses away." It was time to leave the winner's circle. A few minutes would lapse before the next race.

Our head lad, Tom, led away ELIZABETH THE GREAT. Happy and I decided to go to an open-air restaurant to meet my Yorkshire owners Bea and Bill for drinks. Before we reached the restaurant, I suddenly saw that odd brown bowler above the heads of other patrons in the restaurant. Sven!

Lola wasn't with us. She'd stayed in her apartment with their baby. I stared at Sven and hurried over to him to say hello with or without Lola being there. He stared in return then turned his back.

Snubbed! The brown bowler wasn't tipped nor was a welcome word uttered.

I thought: what's the matter with this guy? Has he forgotten how to speak English?

Happy rescued me, and led the way away from more drinks with Bill and Bea, back to the unsaddling enclosure for a private word. "That man ain't Sven."

"He certainly looks like him."

"Ain't Sven. Ah's known fo' some time Sven has a twin brother."

"I thought the change was due to a theatre's make-up expert. But, I say! A twin, that explains a lot. I've been wondering, every time I saw that unfashionable brown derby: why on earth Sven would use that as a helpful disguise if he didn't want to draw attention to himself."

Happy shrugged, "This man *did want to call attention*. He makes his contact at races, where there's sho' to be a crowd. Didn't y'all catch him talkin' to Arthur Snodgrass once?"

"You know I did. God in heaven! Good old Sven has a twin who isn't a good guy at all! They must incarnate the Yan and the Yin. Good and evil. I'm going to face this guy down and ask him if he knows of Arthur's whereabouts."

"Careful, my sweet. Ah believes this man plays dirty."

I didn't listen. I threaded my way through the crowds, doubly nervous because HAL'S COMET'S race was coming up and I needed to be saddling him.

But with the Sven problem dominating my mind, I left that job to Tom, our trustworthy Head Groom. I nailed Sven's twin standing at the rail alone, while the general public had gone to place bets.

I said: "I'm a friend of Sven's."

He looked at me as if I was crazy. Then I realized he probably didn't speak English. And he wouldn't know his twin as Sven. There had to be another name for Sven in Chechnya.

While I stood beside him, Sven's double was accosted by an odd-looking man, heavyset with a pronounced slouch, also sporting a large mustache and a brown bowler.

Although the sound of a loudspeaker announcing the next race partially blotted out what he whispered, I recognized a name, "SNODGRASS".

"IL EST MORT," Sven's twin said in French. Lousy French. But I understood that Arthur was dead. He continued: "MORT! Cesium chloride." The last two words were understood internationally. I knew that our government had been trying for years to have cesium chloride replaced for medical and research radiation because terrorists could use it in a 'dirty' bomb. This told me that Arthur had graduated from smuggling guns to dealing in nuclear substances: a switch that would be considered treason by Chechens, as he must have been negotiating with formerly Russian break-away countries to buy enriched uranium.

God in heaven!

Sven's twin hurtled away to join the bettors swarming near the Tote's windows. The man wearing the matching brown derby went with him.

I rushed to join Happy in the paddock to judge HAL'S COMET's action. I watched his jockey lift himself into his saddle with ease and confidence, take his reins, settle himself, and test the stirrups. All was well with HAL'S COMET. He made two turns of the paddock and then we watched Hal's colors on his jockey as he gentled him down the field to the starting gate.

Cesium chloride! Cesium chloride! Those words seared into my brain as I watched HAL'S COMET handle the opposition, wearing it down while he thundered ahead. At the line, he was pipped by a more experienced colt but hadn't disgraced himself by coming in Second.

Standing at the Second pole, commiserating with the jockey for not winning and listening to his insider description of what went on during the race, I turned a polite ear to him but all I could think of was CESIUM CHLORIDE.

After we boxed HAL'S COMET and I sat in our car to dial Hal at the Egyptian Embassy and give him a full account of his colt's race plus encouraging him to believe he would win next time out, I asked him to have his company's experts do a research job on cesium chloride.

Chapter 20

Jeremy and Fran had returned from their honeymoon. They were living in the revamped gatekeeper's cottage they had done up as their home while experiencing that British aristocrat's thing of waiting for the day Jeremy would inherit title and castle. I went to see them. I needed time alone with Jeremy to discuss the late Arthur Snodgrass.

I tried to shoo Happy to go home to the "chillun."

She'd have none of that. So it was both of us who cornered Jeremy in his study, where I spilled the info about Sven having a twin.

A twin whose searing words were cesium chloride.

We'd both known ever since Happy's abduction in Dubai that Jeremy had connections with MI5, although he'd long assumed the style of a country gentleman whose sole interest was riding to hounds.

But Jeremy was very quick to twig to the significance of cesium chloride.

"So that bugger Snodgrass had turned to trading in nuclear." Jeremy bit the bullet to clarify the conversation.

"It would seem so."

Happy intervened. "Ah's worried about what could happen at the next top race meetin' like in Paris, at the Arc, the first Sunday in October."

In a pedantic tone, Jeremy said: "Oh, I doubt there will be a dirty bomb placed in the Longchamp stands. What would be the point? It won't reverberate around the world if a few couturier's models showing the new Fall Fashions get burned to crisps in the stands at the Paris racecourse."

"Ah wasn't thinkin' of no DIRTY BOMB. Ah's thinkin' mo'e like what a terrorist could do usin' a suicide bomber. Like kill President Nicholas Sarkozy."

Silence. Jeremy and I digested her idea. It left a sour taste in *my* mouth.

Jeremy spoke up first. "The President of France! Yes, *that would reverberate around the world."*

I said very quietly. "How? Who could do that? Sven's twin is too conspicuous. We'd never let him get near enough to the President."

Jeremy added: "The Longchamp grandstand was updated to protect dignitaries from just that type of threat. There's a bullet-proof shield in the paddock."

"Ah's been thinkin' about thet. How? And when? Where exactly. Ah's figured out them problems. Listen up: won't be no bullet. Be a suicide bomber with one of them bomber vests. Hidden under a woman's clothes. A furrin' woman, in one of them nation'l costumes. She'd run at The President when he gits out of his fancy limousine before President Sarkozy can safely enter his private box in the stands."

"It's possible," Jeremy mused.

More silence. Even heavier. Finally, Jeremy broke the impact of the moment. "Yes, it could be done. Happy, you've been to the Arc de Triomphe Race in Paris. Studied the form. Yes, foreign ladies do wear their national costumes. I saw the Mongolian Ambassador's wife in a spectacular hat with a four inch spike and an embroidered coat to her ankles. It was a very tight coat, no lady could hide a bomber vest under such a coat. But the custom of some Muslim women to wear burkas could enable them to hide a suicide vest on one occasion when the President of France comes to the Arc de Triomphe Race Day. On one occasion I was present when he was followed by a marvelous display of Hussars in semi armor and wearing helmets with plumes. No. It's when he stands stationary, usually as the MARSEILLAISE national anthem is being played, that the Hussars provided a gorgeous show. But not an effective deterrent to a suicide bomber. There's always that dangerous moment when the President steps out of his limo. The ideal moment would come for a suicide bomber to attack. Heaven's above, *Happy! You may have guessed the Chechens' plan."*

Chapter 21

The first Sunday in October is the traditional date for the Arc de Triomphe Race to be run at Longchamp Racecourse,

This year we were all four present at Longchamp Racecourse that first Sunday in October because Fran's filly was entered in the first race. There we were joined by Ben, who was in his jolliest Muslim-playboy mood. Although still a practicing Muslim, I suspected he'd had several martinis before coming to the races because his breath certainly suggested that fact. While some other Arab owners wore contemporary-styled business suits, Ben had opted for his national costume. He looked very imposing with his head topped by a flowing headdress with its black circlet, his single button shirt peeping out from a long white tunic, with its accompanying white cape over white trousers.

On the grandstand's fourth floor, we had all lunched at the expensive Panoramique Restaurant as guests of Jeremy. The tables had been garlanded with fresh yellow chrysanthemums, while cascades of red geraniums flowed down from its balcony. We savored lobster, and quail with the finest wines and a hot chocolate souffle'. Wonderful!

All the ladies in the restaurant displayed extravagant hats and the best couturier outfits Paris could muster. Hal and Mafalda were at an another table, Mafalda's ring outshone the rings of all the other women present.

But the conversation over lunch was not frivolous. My darling Happy set the tone revealing one of her incredible insights.

"Ah's read me an ar-ti-cle in the noospaper written by them folks wut works fo' the Asso-cia-ted Press. Ah believes in them thar folks. It told how in Baghdad, the I-raq Police caught up with a fifty-year-old I-raqi woman who admitted she'd done re-cruited more than eighty girls to blow themselves up as su-i-cide bombers. This here woman, called Samira Ahmed Jassim, but also known as The Mother Of Believers, said as how she was part of a plot to have girls raped. Turn them into suicide bombers."

"This article claimed they were raped on purpose?"

"Sho' thing. Then when them girls felt they wus ruined to be future wives or mothers, havin' been raped, which be mo'e than shameful in a Muslim country, them girls, sent to this woman fo' motherly advice, were then convinced that to escape from shame and to reclaim their honor, they should let themselves be wired to be blown up. This ogre woman claimed she had personally masterminded twenty-eight bombings."

I said, "I guess that the Muslim prohibition against men touching women who are not their wives, daughters, or sisters meant that male security forces couldn't search these girls."

"Yeah. Po'r girls. Some o' them barely in their teens."

Jeremy Grace ventured a thought. "Have you heard about the Quantum Entanglement theory? I have, and I've been profoundly influenced by it. There's a group of top scientists involved in this, and also the former US astronaut Ed Mitchell. He spoke to me about how a precursor of Darwin had already worked out the origins of the species. He reminded me of Plato's description of how a man chained to a wall with his back to the room would see light throwing shadows on the wall and it is that we see what's out there, just the shadows. Mitchell reckons that in another sixty years, we'll be on the threshold of knowing more, but we're nowhere near yet. Ed Mitchell uses identical twins' extra perception skills as related to intuitively *knowing* a sibling's needs as an example of Quantum Entanglement. Maybe Sven is trapped in just such an entanglement. His twin's evil, and has caused a good man like Sven to cross the lines of decency."

Fran hooted. "I'm a twin. But Carrie and I certainly had no entanglement."

Jeremy commented, "I heard that you weren't an identical twin. You and Carrie didn't come from the same egg. Mitchell meant *identical* twins."

Jeremy's conversational skills reminded me of a smooth pebble thrown out over water, skipping down and up. But I felt intrigued by his bringing up the Quantum Entanglement and agreed that it could add light to solving this case.

"Let's go watch the President arrive in his limousine," Jeremy suggested finally. I knew how he meant it, NOT offering a fun experience, but in dread of what might happen.

Foolish me, I didn't stop Happy from coming along. *I should have finessed that idea by suggesting she go to the trainer's carpark where she could telephone home to check her cell phone for news of our children.*

I left the Panoramique lunch hall to join the surge of guests who had abandoned their parties to join the throngs of rubberneckers viewing the dignified progress of the President's cavalcade, with his limo heading the accompanying group of government officials. I had a good view of that parade as their limousines wended through the auburn autumn-tinged trees of the Bois de Boulogne.

In the leading limousine I glimpsed a vignette of President Sarkosy's ex-model gorgeous wife Carla. She was chatting animatedly, her famous lips dancing.

Our crowd of onlookers mobbed closer, ever more tightly. The women among us craned to see what color Carla Sarkozy had chosen to wear for her Longchamp outfit. Bets had been wagered on that color. Big bets.

We men stood stock-still, pretending to admire the perfect condition of the limos. In truth, we were all ogling for another glimpse of Carla.

I wondered if President Sarkozy was secretly fondling his gorgeous wife's thighs, out of view below the limo's windows. Hadn't I read somewhere that President Sarkozy had a condition whereby his penis was in a constant state of erection? Were his trousers tailored to hide that?

Carla Sarkozy broke tradition by not wearing a hat. Not good for the milliners' trade! Her loose hair hung unfettered by any kind of pins as her hair swung like a surfboard in a heavy sea.

Her dress was almost transparent, revealing she wore little or nothing underneath.

That didn't seem to bother President Sarkozy. Wasn't he famous for not minding her nude photographs that had appeared lately from the days when Carla was a noted model? I believe he said he didn't mind because he was proud for people to see how beautiful his wife's body was.

I'd arrived at the spot where the President's limo would dislodge him and the gorgeous Carla. The others of Jeremy's lunch party had loitered behind while he'd paid the restaurant's huge bill. But Ben and Happy were catching up.

Happy strode beside Ben. He walked briskly, until they approached the outer perimeter of where the crowd anticipated the President's arrival and descent from his limousine to go into his box.

Suddenly, Ben stopped. With a bejeweled finger, he pointed out a Muslim woman costumed in heavy robes.

In a highly disgusted tone, Ben growled, "How dare that woman mix my national costume so incorrectly with rubbish? Look at her shoes, totally inappropriate. She's a fake."

Then he pointed to Sven's twin, who was tackily outfitted in a brown morning coat to match his awful bowler hat. It was the same type of hat that King George V admonished the twentieth Prince of Wales for wearing, saying, "That's a rat catcher's hat."

Sven's twin had been escorting the oddly costumed Muslim woman.

Now he started to rush away from her. Near where the President's limousine would stop, he threw himself to the ground and began to writhe on the cement with foaming bubbles erupting from his mouth. He seemed to be having an epileptic fit.

The crowd parted like the Red Sea for Moses, providing a channel for the fake Saudi woman to reach the President.

Happy, who had visited Egypt and Jordan last year and accompanied me three times to Dubai, knew correct Muslim attire. She recognized that this woman *was* a fake Saudi, and that Sven's twin had invented a fake epileptic fit for a diversionary tactic.

"Thet woman's here to kill President Sarkozy," Happy breathed.

In a nanosecond my Happy had got through the crowd, fast as a racehorse pounding toward a Finish Line. She nabbed the woman, grabbing her thick waist, restraining her as if she was handling an unbroken colt. Happy must have felt a suicide bomber-vest under the woman's robes. In another nanosecond, just as The President's limousine slowed to a stop where the woman had taken up a position, Happy shoved the fake Muslim toward the nearest Women's Toilets. There, I could not hope to follow!

With Happy's steel-like muscles working their wonders, the teenage woman offered no contest. From underneath her veil came desperate sobs. Because she'd failed? Or because there would be no place for her to go, to live, or to have a future.

Apparently, as I was to learn later, my Happy evacuated the toilet area by barking out the imminent danger from the woman's suicide bomb.

Alerted, the Security forces came into play. A uniformed member of the Security Corps rushed to recruit more Security. Bomb disposal experts arrived at the toilets, where Happy had imprisoned the bomber inside a cubicle.

Happy reverted to Kentucky-hill speak. "Come on in y'all. We got us a suicide bomber." She opened the cubicle door to reveal a weeping teenage Chechen girl, squatting on the floor, her tears wetting the veil that still hid her face. "Don't y'all be a-feared of this here girl now. She done missed her chance to kill the President and his wife. She ain't goin' to blow herself up for no toilets."

Steadfastly, Happy stood by while the bomb experts defused and removed the woman's lethal vest. Happy waited until the woman was arrested under the Anti-terrorism Act and taken away "to help with inquiries" for the maximum time allowed by French law. In France, there's probably another way of arresting people. I'm not familiar with the Napoleonic Code.

Sven's brother was arrested simultaneously, outside, near the racecourse's nearest exit. His brown bowler hat had gone skidding away. Without it, he looked a lot less like Sven, because he was almost bald.

Sven and Lola emerged from the General Admittance stands to join us in the paddock. Sven had missed the scene where his twin had played an epileptic to distract Security from protecting the President.

Without briefing him about his twin, Happy placed her arms around Sven, and said, "Ah sho' understands how much y'all loved yourn brother." But she didn't give him the usual cheek brushed kiss.

Sven thought it was the worst that would happen that day. He went off smiling with Lola to the car park to go home to their baby. He'd learn from the next morning's newspaper how his twin had been arrested under the Anti-terrorism Act.

Happy had gone into the paddock. With consummate expertise, she helped our jockey ease into the saddle, checked his stirrups, and gave a loving pat to Fran's filly.

My incredible wife had possibly saved the life of France's President Sarkozy today, but Happy's first concern now was for the filly to have a good run.

The filly won her race. No trophy for us in Paris, but I received a very welcome call from the USA. Fran's best colt, now a three year old, I'd entered into the Arkansas Derby, and he won too. I'd accomplished Fran's major demand on my services. I'D WON A DERBY FOR FRAN!

From that high, I returned home to learn that Tim had wet his bed. Again! Nothing for it but to do the Father thing: change Timmy's sheets and dress him in clean pajamas. He fell asleep, thank God, in a trice.

Chapter 22

When we were in our kingsize bed, I wanted to make love. But, for once, Happy preferred talk.

"Ah'd watched on tel-e-vision when the Chechens, fightin' Russia, took hostages in thet Moscow the-a-ter and all of them – hostages, and innocent the-a-ter goers – was gassed to death. Again, couple years later, two women suicide bombers killed 40 folks in Moscow subways. Also, Ah'd watched thet long doc-u-mentary showin' all them thousand hostages chillun, with their mothers and teachers held by Chechen terrorists on thet first day of school in Beslan. How many died? Shot, after three days drinkin' urine because the terrorists had no water for them! Until Ah seen them pictures, Ah sho felt Chechenya deserved Independence. When ah re-a-lized thet Sven's twin brother were involved in fundin' it, by tradin' in munitions supplyin' terrorists to kill and invalid people, mostly women folk and chillun, Ah couldn't chance he was aimin' today fo' what Jeremy called 'to do something that would re-ver-ber-ate around the world.' Ah's sorry fo' Sven, tryin' them other times t' cover fo' his twin. But today when Ah seen thet twin o' Sven's fall into a fake ep-i-lepsy fit, Ah didn't stop to worry if'n Ah'd be leavin' mah babies mother-less. Ah just had to stop thet bomber."

"So Sven was a terrorist?"

"Nah. Sven weren't never no terrorist. He'd left Chechnya as a teenager. Got himself a scholarship in England. Hung around them polo fields. Learned him thet there be good business in buyin' 'n sellin' polo ponies."

"And that's all? He never did anything else?"

"Yeah man. Nothin' else, but buyin' 'n sellin' polo ponies. Went to Colombia fo' ponies fo' the Americans. Took American ponies to England. Sold English ponies to them Russian trillionaire Oli-ga-chs and them Dubai po-tent-ates."

"But we saw Sven with Stinky, Ali, Harry, Bloom and Snodgrass."

"Sho'. He been trackin' them. Worried they be lethal compe-ti-tors fo' his brother in thet there mun-i-tions business. He were right. Them guys would have murdered his twin if'n he hadn't got to them first."

"Sven's twin killed all four?"

"Don't know as how he killed them personally. But, sho' thing, thet twin brother had them killed. They'd been tradin' guns with him earlier. Gunrunners, all. When them guys wanted out to trade fo' nuclear from the break-away former Russian nations wut were ready to sell nuclear, the twin had them murdered. Not Sven."

"How did Ali get $1,250,000 for the filly?"

"Nevuh done had one million two hundred 'n fifty thousand. Ali were tied to gunrunners who wanted to launder thet dirty money buyin' fillies who were winners."

When she'd got that longish declaration off her chest, I played with her lovely nipples. My Happy responded as I'd hoped she would. It was glorious.

The End

Models Murdered in Milan

Characters Models Murdered in Milan

Rick Harrow, narrator, an English trainer of racehorses
Happy Harrow, his jockey wife who moonlights as a sleuth, very motherly to their four children
Fran Purcell Cabrach, opera and rap singer, makes millions but is a pennypincher
Lord Cabrach, her brilliant but longsuffering husband
Maheen, step-daughter of Rick's most generous owner
Hal Murphy, Canadian millionaire racehorse owner
Mafalda Murphy, Hal's outrageous wife, a former courtesan
Flavia, Fiona, and Nina, Maheen's successive roommates
Miss Parizzi, difficult and mysterious owner of a school for aspiring models
Draga, called by the students The Dragon Lady, a Romanian refugee
Brian Murphy, oversexed spoiled son of overly-generous Hal.
Bruno, a Romanian tenor who loves Nina

Chapter 1

Why was I mixed up in the mess caused by a teenage girl's headless torso found floating in Milan's Navigli Grande Canal? God only knows. Milan's out of my line of country. I train racehorses in England, and had never been to Italy. But that was soon to be changed by one telephone call.

The telephone rang in the tack room I'd converted into my office at our stables in England's Epsom. Only my wife, Happy, a retired jockey, and my richest owners had this private number. What was this call going to be about? Good, or awful!

I hurried to answer. The caller was my opera star owner, Fran Purcell now the Hon. Mrs. Grace, who was dallying with singing rap for more money.

She warbled, "I've been offered a contract by Milan's La Scala Opera House to sing there this season. I've checked out the horse races at the Milan racetrack, and there are three that would suit my best fillies. What do you say? Will you take them to Milan to run there while I honor the singing contract?"

Fran had adopted a more distinguished act since I'd last seen her, no doubt to please Jeremy, her husband of three months. She wore less stage makeup, which previously had been embarrassingly gross here in the home counties. Her couture clothes were appropriate for the bride of a future earl: no more sequins and bosom-revealing décolletage. Now it was tweeds, low heels and a twin set for our future countess. Fran's upper teeth had been straightened years ago when she entered the singing business, but recently she'd had her lower ones capped. Important for when she needed to open her mouth wide for those high notes. Most importantly, she seemed to have eradicated the ghastly four letter language that had sullied her vocabulary.

She exuded top drawer culture, no doubt preferred by her husband, Jeremy.

I said carefully, "Your word is my command, Mrs. Grace. As a matter of fact, I'd been looking for races for those fillies of yours, and Milan's could be just the ticket. But I'll just mention that the Milan Execs are very slow at paying up, if your fillies *do* win."

"Huh! No slimy Ities will ever defraud *me*, Rick. They'd have to get up very early in the morning to hope to do me down." She hung up without saving goodbye, leaving an ugly vacuum in my tack room.

The next morning our daily lady resigned from looking after our chillun. She pleaded sick. Good God. Happy was stretching herself beyond endurance. I decided to send an SOS to our dear AMAH, to ask her to come to Milan to help with the kids. I'd pay for her return ticket, cost what it may.

I almost knocked down my tiny darling wife as I rushed to leave the stables. Happy had heard my final words. In her cheerful way, she laughed out loud when meeting me on our manure-strewn path, '*IF* your fillies win' ain't no joke. Them fillies be jumpin' out o' their skins, wantin' to race. Where's thet song bird wantin' to take them?"

Happy's Kentucky hill country accent became more marked when she laughed out a comment.

"Milan."

"And where-all be thet?"

"Northern Italy. You'll love it. You can do your relaxation thing by searching out ancient architecture. And you can take all four kids. ITALIANS LOVE KIDS, AND WILL WELCOME THEM."

"Sho 'nuf? But wut about Fran? She don't like kids."

Happy's laughter became infectious. I grinned, chortled and hugged her. "Doesn't matter. We won't be taking them to the opera house." With our arms entwined around each other, we went up the hill to our thatched cottage. There, Happy left me to begin packing for Milan. Not good. She always traveled with mountains of unnecessary items for our kids. But listening to her humming "Comin' Round The Mountain" I got on with my own chores without a care.

Fran tolerated Happy, but just! Although she should have felt enduring gratitude to my darling Happy for putting closure to her twin sister's murder.

My darling wife, who after the joy of riding the winner of a race in Tokyo had decided to rest on the laurels of her career as a jockey in order to teach dressage, now was of less interest to Fran. Happy's talent for unmasking murderers had served its purpose, as far as Fran was concerned. Or so Fran thought.

Pennypinching Fran had liked it when as a licensed jockey Happy had often exercised her fillies for free. She had taken notice of Happy's win on HAPPY'S ESCAPE in Tokyo and planned to use her in a race with one of her own stars.

My opera singer wanted jockeys who could push horses to beat others past the winning post. Fran wasn't interested in people teaching obedience to horses with the aim of instructing them to do the classic steps of Lippizaners.

Happy's new interest hadn't prevented her from solving four murders since Fran's sister had been strangled. With Fran, Happy's successes with those cases didn't count. Fran, so self-absorbed, boxed herself in to the worlds of music, horseracing, and sex.

Marriage to the Hon. Jeremy Grace hadn't slaked Fran's thirst for sex. No doubt Jeremy provided the necessary. But could I easily forget her past lovers: that saxophonist Goofy, Santa Anita's Nelson, the dangerous Sir Arthur Snodgrass, and probably that asshole of a swindler Shelley who tried to sell her a lame horse?

Had Fran recently fallen for a Milan gigolo, and that's the real reason why I'll be shipping her fillies to race there? I was guessing that the gigolo came on scene earlier and THEN the contract at La Scala!

Chapter 2

Next day, unfazed by Fran's snub, my darling wife had perched her delicious behind on my desk, and speedily queried, "Do y'all think Hal Murphy might send his fillies to Milan? And pay MY fare and Timmy's? Ourn three littler ones c'n go fo' free. Ain't Hal our most gen-er-ous Owner? Ah's read thet there be great hist-o-ric ruins in I-taly. Ah'd sho love to visit them places."

Oh? I'm well aware that Happy has a thing for archeological wonders. Hadn't she visited them in Egypt at Karnak, Memphis and Giza? In Ireland kissed the Blarney Stone? Seen sunrise at Stonehenge? And threatened to drive to Alice Springs when we were in Australia, to view its gigantic nature-made rock?

But Milan's a commercial city, known for fashion and textiles. If Happy accompanies me, with our four "chillun," will she be touring the surrounding region all of the time? And whom do we know in Milan who'd be a babysitter? I dote on my children, but to win in Milan I knew I'd got to give my all to our fillies.

Happy, smiling widely, was busily dialing Hal's telephone in Canada. "Hello, is Mr. Murphy there?" she asked, when a female voice responded. "I'd like to—"

Mafalda, the Egyptian courtesan who'd ably managed to get Hal to place a ring on the wedding finger of that very much used left hand, now sent her large voice across the Atlantic to fill my redesigned tack room with her heavily-accented fractured English "Hallo! Happy-girl! I recognize your Kentucky accent. You don't seem to improve on your English." She pronounced that last word "Ang-lish."

My darling wife *did* forego pointing out that Mafalda's use of the English language left much to be desired. Sweetly, as if she was sucking on cotton candy at a Kentucky Fair, she crooned, "Mafalda, darlin', Ah wants a word with Hal. Please!"

"Anyting you wishes to say to my husband, you can say to myself."

Oh, Oh! I didn't like the sound of that. Always in future would we both need to go through Mafalda for a word with Hal? Not good. I knew for certain that Mafalda thought she understood about racehorses ever since she showed up at the horse sales in St. Petersburg when we bought the Russian filly. She didn't know a damn thing, except the prices of good horseflesh! Would Mafalda, only a recent bride, become one of those wives who answer the family telephone and become a human barrier to reach the head of the household? I hoped not.

Happy had grown fond of Mafalda in St. Petersburg when Mafalda was the underdog to Ali's wife. Now, that fondness might fade faster than a glacier hit by a hot sun in summer. Happy hadn't approved of Selina, the first courtesan she'd met, kept by a fellow Trainer, Selim. But Mafalda had successfully caused my Baptist wife to put aside her reservations, as a virgin does a lover. Until today, Happy had made an exception for Mafalda and *her lack of morals.*

Happy hadn't anticipated unacceptable commands from her erstwhile friend.

I took the telephone receiver from Happy's willing hand. Perhaps a man's voice would control Mafalda? "This is Rick Harrow, Mrs. Murphy. I need to speak to Hal."

"Anyting you want to say to Hal, you ought to say to me."

"Mrs. Murphy, MAFALDA, put Hal on the wire."

Using her courtesan name did the trick. There was a rustling of silks, and then the firm tones of Hal Murphy gladdened my ear. "Rick! Life's good, eh? I'm still on honeymoon, and believe me, thet's aboot as good as life gets. But what can I do for you? My horses all right?"

"All in great form, sir. Hal." I corrected myself. My rough diamond Canadian owner didn't like me to use SIR, he preferred his nickname. "I'm studying the form for races that will take place in Milan, and I see at least two that would suit your fillies. Not much for them here or in France. How about I ship them to Milan?"

I genuinely meant that Milan's races could offer Hal's fillies a chance to do their stuff when there were no suitable races for them at the same time in England.

"Great idea. Mafalda has a little daughter in school there. Give my precious bride a chance to see her baby. And Rick, be sure to bring Happy and your children along. I know my fillies always do their best for Happy. And she works her wonders best when she has your children on board."

Dear, generous Hal! We hadn't even had to ask for Happy and the "chillun" to come along.

Her forehead wrinkling, Happy took back the receiver and asked: "Mafalda has a little baby daughter, in Milan? Old enough for school? How wonderful. Ah'd love to meet her."

"Let me know the dates of those races and we will all get together in Milan. And yes, you should meet Mafalda's daughter. I KNOW you are a wonderful mother, but my Mafalda may suggest a few additional improvements to your mothering."

Hal rang off.

I did the necessary at my stables to prepare the other horses for upcoming races in England. But within weeks we were on a BA airplane for Milan.

Happy had never visited Italy. "Ah's thrilled to have a chance to see some of them Roman anti-qui-ties," she crooned over baby Richard's head as she fed him his bottle. Below us spawned the Italian Alps, aglitter with unseasonable sunshine. Happy strained to peer beyond the mountains in hopes of viewing a Roman monument. None came in view.

On the drive from Milan's airport we entered the city passing the Church of Santa Maria delle Guardia, that houses Leonardo da Vinci's famous painting The Last Supper.

I pointed out that round roofed beautiful building to Happy. She frowned, "Not int-er-ested in paintin's. Ah wants mon-u-ments."

When our taxi swerved past the incredible Fourteenth Century Duomo, that Gothic masterpiece with its adornment of 2,244 marble saints, Happy complained. "Not be old 'nuf to int-er-est me! Where be them Roman ruins Ah's seen on the Internet?"

"Roman ruins are mostly in Rome. The Forum, and also its coliseum. And—"

"We be goin' to Rome?"

"Not this trip, my darling. But maybe I can lure Fran to take a limo up to Verona. Not too far from Milan, farther north. Northwest, to be precise. There's a fine coliseum still in use there, I attended operas on its stage in season."

I was careful not to embroider that comment. I'd heard about those operas on its stage with my earlier great love, who over our many years together had been dying of leukemia. Janice, as she was called, was an opera fan. She passed away in my arms in a hotel in Verona, the night we'd managed to see part of LUCIA DI LAMMERMORE. After Janice's death I'd fallen into a terrible depression that might have lasted indefinitely had I not met and been comforted by Happy.

"Ah's lookin' forward to Verona, then."

Happy and I unloaded our four "chillun" and their mountain of luggage and settled in at the small pensione that had three rooms reserved for us in a modest quarter of old Milan. The pensione's belligerent owner had a sweet-tempered wife who proved only too pleased to earn more euros by babysitting our "chillun." But even so, Happy didn't get to roam the countryside for historic ruins.

The day after we'd unpacked, the Murphys arrived at Milan's grandest, most expensive hotel. We were summoned to their suite and told to come outfitted for a great gala party which would take place that evening. As clients of the hotel their names had been added to a list of donors for the charity, CONQUER AIDS.

The Murphys' suite was truly grandiose. The chairs and sofa were authentic Renaissance antiques. Their huge bed had a Ducal crown surmounting it. Draperies were embroidered with the same Duke's heraldry. Tough, I thought, for that duke to have had to sell his personal possessions: I hoped using them would not prove contagious and Hal would lose his Canadian dollars.

Mafalda was in a *noblesse oblige* mood. She swanned into the sitting room dressed in an Armani many-ruffled ballgown, more fitting for a teenage debutante. On her crinkly hair she wore a VERY recently acquired diamond tiara. Hal escorted her like a battleship defending against pirates. His dress sense was faulty, he'd worn white tie and tails to a black tie event. I worried he might be summoned as a waiter to bring a tray of drinks!

"Hallo, you two." Mafalda's tone had become very grand. She addressed us like a feudal princess giving orders to serfs. *"Tiens, tiens,"* she switched to French that was as fractured as her use of English, *"vous allez voir ma petite fille ce soir.* My little baby girl will be joining us at the ball. She's attend a most exclusive school, Miss Parizzi's. A school for most special talent girls. Maheen, my baby, play the piano. I've seen her little fingers fly over keyboards like hummingbirds over a vine."

We sauntered down to the lobby to look for the placement listing that would show us our seating. The placement poster was in a calligraphy mock gold lettering worthy of a medieval manuscript. The lobby should have pleased Happy's demand for antiquities, it held distinguished thrones purloined from Ducal palaces.

The ballroom was decorated in a far earlier style. It had examples of early Grecian friezes cast in plaster. There were concrete statues imitating Greek gods. But the main centerpiece was a reproduction of The Three Graces. And, to accentuate the theme, each table for ten had a plastic copy of The Three Graces surrounded by autumn leaves of red and orange. The plastic copies imitated the famous sculpture created by Antonio Canova for the Sixth Duke of Bedford; the table ornaments were not grand enough to create a nostalgia for the Classic Ancient Greek interpretations of the Karitas, daughters of Zeus. But Happy longed to own one of those plastic copies of Canova's. Would it be tasteless for her to take home our centerpiece?

The evening's décor was supposed to evoke thoughts of ancient Rome, but Canova's neo-classical imitation took pride of place although many centuries out of line.

As we entered the ballroom there was a flurry of activity from a threesome of adolescent girls who were completely NAKED except for a dusting of gold-colored powder.

A small circular floor had been raised above the parquet. The three girls took their assigned places there in the circular positions made famous by Carnova's The Three Graces. One prop had been added because the three girls were not of equal height, the eldest being short and squat. She needed a square shaped stool to help her create the illusion of three girls of similar heights, as in the Three Graces. Not only were their heights different: their breasts varied in size. The eldest, squat girl had enormous breasts that hung like melons without the help of greenhouse nets. A bra would have helped, but the order for this night was that she should be nude. She had almond-shaped eyes that denoted an eastern heritage. Thanks to the gold dust it wasn't possible to determine the color of her skin. She wore a gold tinted wig, identical to those of the other two girls, otherwise it would have been easy to guess her race. Her companions were both tall, skinny and Caucasion. Both had small underdeveloped breasts, with the tallest of the two girls drooping hers due to a round-shouldered stoop.

I guessed their ages to veer between sixteen and seventeen.

The three girls held their joint pose for several minutes, like children *playing* at "statues." Eventually two of the girls exited behind shrubbery while a pair of huge wings were produced and affixed on either side of the tallest girl's collarbone. With the wings in place, she emerged again to take a new stance on the elevated floor. Winged Victory? She held that pose for less than a minute, until her place on the stool was taken by the next tallest girl who sat on the stoop and cupped her hands under her chin, copying Maillol's Le Penseur, The Thinker? Last came the short, squat girl whose lower arms had been painted with a grey cream that made them seem to disappear: Venus De Milo?

"Sacre Dieu!" I heard a screech from Mafalda. "Cannot be. Cannot. Can NOT. MY Maheen? Nude! Naked, in front of all these people?" Mafalda swept on to the circular floor, her tiara dipping crazily to her chin. She yanked at the small girl's wig. It came off in Mafalda's hand. Mafalda gave a yelp of certain recognition, and would have lunged to slap the girl but the girl was too quick and darted away behind the foliage. Evidently, she knew only too well how forceful Mafalda's slap could be.

Chapter 3

Mafalda made a fist and groaned an oath. Biting her lips, she retreated to our table, where she grabbed the plastic copy of the Three Graces and hurled it to the marble floor. It broke in two. Happy scooped up the two pieces. "Ah c'n fix this'n with superglue. Ah can put it in mah babies' bedroom."

Hal Murphy, startled by a facet of Mafalda's personality hitherto hidden from him, coughed apologetically and said in Happy's direction, "Sure, you can have that damned piece of junk. Mafalda wouldn't have wanted it, she only accepts what's authentic. That girl coated in gold dust? Pretty cute, I thought. Nice pair of tits. Big ones. She's no six year old, like I was led to believe. Is she!"

Mafalda shook her curly head, then quickly reverted to the role she'd been playing of adoring wife. She pronged a fork into the shrimp cocktail on his plate and thrust it between Hal's open lips. Hal never lost his smile.

Happy and I waded through the seven course dinner that followed. It tasted marginally better than charity dinners in England, but neither of us could enjoy the food because Mafalda blasted on about the disgrace her daughter had brought upon the Murphy family.

Hal listened stoically, eating everything from each plate as it arrived, and downing the accompanying wines. He seemed determined not to bark at Mafalda. Now and then he'd pat her fluttering hands as if they were pigeons that had escaped from their dovecote.

We were trapped between dessert and coffee to listen to the ball's chairman saying Thank You to sponsors, all named, and then give a final over-long speech on the necessity of fighting AIDS. "Thirty-two million cases worldwide. This plague must be stopped. We must cure those who suffer from the disease in order to spare others from being infected."

Damn! I was having to pay a babysitter to listen to that old broken record. All I could think of was that the thirty two million people with AIDS could have controlled their sexual impulses or used clean needles. Then the money raised to attack this plague could have been used to fight cancers, malaria, or heart disease, diseases that kill non-users and heterosexual folks.

We couldn't leave the ballroom. Hal Murphy's name was to be mentioned as the charity's main donor. I knew we had to applaud him and maybe start the applause because these Milan folk wouldn't recognize the name Murphy as a great philanthropist.

I peeked behind the wall of shrubbery and saw that the three girls from the statues event were only being served *their* dinner at the tail end of the self-congratulatory speeches.

They finished their dinners just as we were released from our table after applauding Hal.

Happy led the way to the hotel's front entrance, where we found ourselves in a long queue waiting for taxis. How I wished we could have escaped that queue and the speeches!

Now fully clothed in fashionable long dresses and capes, first one and then the other of the two tall girls from the statues' event were collected by fawning parents. One fond Mama bundled her adolescent prize into their auto, proclaiming, "Aren't I lucky to have such a talented daughter!" *She hadn't seen her adored child starkers at the ball.*

The second tall girl was also met by English-speaking parents. In her case it was Papa who crooned over his kid, telling everyone within hearing distance, "My daughter will be a top model. She has everything going for her!"

I thought, "Not wonderful breasts. But then she might yet straighten her posture and save them from drooping."

The plump, short girl waited forlornly. No one had come to collect *her. I knew that her mother and step-father were still receiving plaudits in the ballroom.* No way, in her present mood, would livid Mafalda offer to see her daughter back to Miss Parizzi's, "exclusive" school.

Happy solved her problem. She jumped the queue to reach the girl. "Y'all be Maheen? Howdy. Ah's Happy Harrow, mah husband and Ah works fo' Hal Murphy. We's plannin' to take a taxi. C'd we run y'all back to school?"

Maheen stared sadly at Happy. In mid-Atlantic English, with overtones of a British boarding school's accent, she said, "I'd thought my mother would at least order a car to take me back. I don't see one coming. I think she may have cancelled it, because she's furious with me for being in the Statues sequence. Did you see us? Were we so terrible?"

"Mighty purty, if y'all asks me. Real cul-tured like. Turned the place into a mu-se-um. Ah *likes* museums. In museums Ah gets to see them ant-ti-qui-ties wut Ah loves."

The girl's face brightened like a sky where clouds have parted. "Antiquities? Th*ey are my main interest too.* My mother wants me to be a model. But, I'm short, and sort of fat. *I want to be an archeologist."*

"No kiddin'?" Happy gave the girl a hug. She looked at the girl as if they had just been joined at the hip. Archeological treasures were Happy's most enduring interest! Outside of sex with me, that is, I HOPED as I heard the end of that comment. "Where are y'all headed? Cost a lot to take y'all there?"

"Not if we take the subway. There's a station right near my school."

I spoke up, having joined them as they left the queue. "Our pensione is near a station, too. Do you know the Darsen Quarter, beside the Navigli Grande Canal? We're not far from the station that serves it."

"Know it? I adore going to the Navigli Canals. To both. The Grande and the Pevese. My favorite places, outside of archeological digs! I love the old romantic buildings, and their specialty shops. They used to be the heart of a network of canals. Gorgeous. I go there a lot. Easy stop from the station near our school. The girls from my school give the Navigli canals a nine out of ten.".

The three of us headed for the subway station. Happy's new organza gown got mud on its hem from water that splashed up from the wind-whipped Grande Canal. Maheen's suitcase, containing an alternative costume, bumped alongside her plump knees. Maheen pointed with ribald humor, "We three girls had to bring a suitcase with costumes in case the hotel management complained about our nudity."

Happy giggled along with Maheen. The two could have been the same age. But with her next comment Maheen slipped back from her patina of sophistication into childhood. "I get scared coming alone to the canals. Real scared."

There was no explanation. Happy jollied Maheen until they reached her austere school building with its grim prison-like barred door. We parted there, with Maheen slipping past a battered looking old concierge, whose face was as traced with lines as a spider's web.

Maheen waved briefly, and disappeared into the school's murky interior.

The next morning, with the arrival of our English language newspaper at breakfast we saw a picture of the Navigli Canal, with a brief description of the dismembered headless body of a teenage girl who'd been found floating in its turgid waters.

Happy was reading the accompanying story when our bedroom telephone rang. The sobbing voice of a desperately upset teenager flooded our space. It was Maheen calling, "Did you see the newspaper? The girl in the canal, she was my roommate until yesterday."

Chapter 4

Why was Maheen placing this burden of care on Happy? It had been evident to me that the two had bonded and Happy had proffered real friendship. But the two were markedly opposite. My blond aquamarine-eyed wife, although also tiny, was slim and was blessed with a strength that came from having a loving husband, a welcoming old time Kentucky father, four healthy children and careers that had blossomed. Maheen, fat and Nubian skinned with her fuzzy hair, huge boobs, a face scarred by loneliness and an obviously-fragile emotional state could not be called a similar type. With no visible Upper Egypt father, and a tyrannical mother who had tried to pass her off as a six-year-old to hide her own age, little Maheen had reasons to be a complainer. But many other more underprivileged girls had risen to great heights, for instance Byzantium's Empress Theodora, imitated by Maheen's mother, also a courtesan from an Egyptian brothel who married BIG.

Happy said what she imagined Maheen wanted to hear, "Yes. We'all read the news account. Sorry y'all lost yourn room-mate. Can we'all do anythin' to help?

"Meet me at the Navigli Grande Canal. I've got to see the horror scene. Personally. You can go by subway. Meet me in the boutique where they sell Starbucks Coffee."

"Sho 'nuf. Mah husband needs to go down to the stables, Ah'll come soon's he leaves."

That didn't suit *me*. I needed Happy's expertise down at the stables. She had a marvelous knack controlling Fran's Soviet filly. But, I shrugged off my disappointment. I broke Trainer rule number four, don't push a horse too much without proper assistance. And God knows Happy's talent went far beyond "proper assistance." I kissed her. We went our separate ways. I took the subway. She walked.

Soon Happy left our more comfortable neighborhood, where apartments had washer dryers for family laundry and wide balconies for leisure time.

She entered a poor quarter where laundry was stretched on lines operated by pulleys overhead from building to building, and the elderly sat on stools beside cracked pavements to get a breath of fresh air.

Leaving that area of weary housewives shod in plastic flipflops, Happy emerged into a lush square of restored houses where exquisite model-type girls preened in their Jimmy Choo five-inch heels. What a contrast! These girls were either practicing to model on catwalks, or they were already famous. The square's few men steered among gorgeous youngsters who were teenage models of both sexes. Among the older men were sophisticated gigolos. A few of the older men were predators trolling for paid company, they showed off their Rolex watches and Armani suits as they strolled the sidewalks. There were fewer older women. These had deserted the streets knowing they could not compete with their younger rivals for any admiring compliments or a whore's pay. The scarce older women scuttled like lizards into the boutiques to buy clothes that would hopefully transform them and bring them hoped-for renewed youth.

Happy described this to me later. On her arrival next to the Navigli Grande Canal she sought out the boutique that blazoned it sold Starbucks coffee. It was sandwiched between two five story shuttered houses with their pavement looking as if gigantic popcorn had fallen there thanks to a multitude of umbrellas topping sidewalk tables.

Under the sign that advertised Starbucks she'd grabbed a recently vacated table. She was astonished at the size of the euro tip still waiting for collection by a harried waitress. It gave her a clue as to how much cash was spent in the Navigli area.

Suddenly a rush of schoolgirls filed along the canal. The newcomers came chattering, and trying to imitate the seasoned models' stilted walk and hip-pushing posture. Happy guessed these girls had emerged from the nearby subway station. She craned to see if Maheen was among them.

She was. But Maheen, her short body curved into the letter "C" from depression, scuttled almost like a cockroach to the empty chair at Happy's table. Maheen, weeping, came blowing her nose to be able to breathe, Maheen pointed to the Grande Canal's far end. She struggled to speak. "There, it was there that the polizia found the trunk and limbs of poor Sofia's body."

"Sofia, your roommate?"

No words. Only a nod from Maheen.

Happy persisted. "Had Sofia been at Miss Parizzi's School very long? And how long y'all been there?"

A grunt, and then a cough. Finally two words, "Three years."

"Ah's been told by Mafalda as y'all was in England to school."

Another nod, accompanied by a few squeaked-out words, "My mother doesn't actually count how long I'm anywhere. Three years ago I was in a British school."

"So y'all were thirteen then."

Two nods. "My mother thought I'd grow tall after puberty. She wanted me to be a model. She chose Mizz Parizzi's because it was cheap, and the old bitch gets jobs for her girls as models. Miss Parizzi's famous for her mantra: Heads high, butts tucked, Venus Mount high, shoulders down. Not much use to a girl who's short and has heavy breasts." A long silence, then gulps. "Sofia *did* grow tall, got an agent, got a modeling contract."

"Did Ah see Sofia at the AIDS ball? Were she in the statues' act?"

Shake of the head. "Sofia didn't need to go naked to get noticed. Not after she'd already made it as a model. She was at an audition that night. Early evening." Three gulps. "Her agent had shuffled a video around the fashion houses showing her on a catwalk. Producers wanted to see her in person. Poor Sofia. She had permission from school to take the subway. Went alone. She never, oh it's too horrible, never got back to school."

While Maheen was racked with a fresh attack of tears, another rush of schoolgirls flooded the square. Happy guessed a subway train had pulled in to disgorge them at the nearby station. Two of the girls brought over chairs to Happy's table.

More brightly, Maheen chirped, "Happy, meet Flavia and Fiona. The two other statues in our Three Graces act."

Happy had to scan their faces thoroughly to recognize these two without their sprinkling of gold powder and gold wigs. The two had much in common, both six feet tall and slim. Both wearing high fashion, very short skirts and extremely tall heels. But the similarities stopped there. Fiona spoke English with a Scottish burr, was red-headed and porcelain skinned. Flavia had a heavy Italian accent, and showed bloodlines from an Othello-type North African with her smoldering chocolate retinas and bulbous lips. Both proffered instant friendship to Happy.

Fiona asked, "Did you see our act at the AIDS ball?" She seemed ultra proud of her participation.

"Yeah, sho did. It gave a great start to the evenin'."

"I was Cleta. That's the name Spartans gave the original," Flavia boasted, her eyes alight. "Sexy, huh? Now I've got the attention of an agent, maybe I'll get to do a video for prospective employers."

Cautiously, Happy asked, "What did your parents think of y'all bein' in the Three Graces act?" Happy instantly recalled an Italian Papa collecting this girl from the hotel's front entrance.

"Papa? He didn't know about me being naked. Desnuda! He felt proud I'd been invited to such a fine hotel to do a show, and that might speed up my chances of becoming a model. Signorina Parizzi's fees are too expensive for us. Caro. Carissimo."

"And does your Pa knows y'all were naked?" she queried Fiona.

"Good Lord, no! Father's a strict Presbyterian. He and the Mater collected me at the hotel because they were in Milan at a conference for textile manufacturers. Our family make tartans, and some ghillies' tweeds. You know, tweeds for private estates. Some Lairds and gamekeepers keep to that old custom of having an estate tweed."

Happy *didn't* know. She turned to Maheen to bring her back into the conversation. "Maheen, them Three Graces seem to have weathered the cent-u-ries."

"Yes. Isn't it fascinating to think that the Spartans spoke of them? And more than a thousand years later Raphael made a painting of them." She sighed, but it came out a light rush of air, nothing dramatic. "I wish I could get to a dig and find artifacts from the days of the Spartans. Just last week I read that a group of archeologists in Bulgaria dug up four perfectly intact wheels decorated with metal work showing a high degree of culture."

Happy listened attentively. Not only was the subject of archeology close to her heart—she called it 'learnin' about them old stones"—but she'd become intrigued listening to these two girls and Maheen. There was such a difference in the way the taller girls had reacted to Sofia's gruesome murder. The taller two had known the murdered teenage model, yet neither of them mentioned Sofia, nor did they seem too perturbed at what had happened to her. Only Maheen, when she'd first arrived, had shown compassion.

Really crude, Flavia said, "Thanks to that dumb bitch Sofia's murder, we've got a halfday off from school."

Fiona concurred, "Cool. And, Maheen, now that you haven't anyone rooming with you, how about having me move in? You've got the biggest, sunniest room in the building."

"If you want to," Maheen hung her head. Her posture had gone bad again and she was resting her large breasts on the table's formica top. "Someone's got to clear out her closet and drawers. I don't know if her parents will want her old clothes, and bits. I don't."

Flavia said, "I'd like that DVD player she'd just bought."

Fiona added. "The fashion house that had contracted her sent over a brilliant pair of shorts and top. She was to do a summer shoot. Could I have them?"

"Don't know. Don't have any idea of how her parents will react. They haven't arrived from Perugia. They know the polizia aren't going to release what's left of her body for burial."

Happy asked quietly, "Any news as to if the po-lice have found her head?"

More weeping from Maheen. No nods.

Flavia trumpeted, "Exciting, isn't it? A headless body, just like in a penny-dreadful. Much good it did the killer to behead Sofia, her body was identified within hours. Oh, let's forget all this grim stuff. Come on, girls. Let's go to that French goods boutique across the way. There's a sign in the window says SOLDES, that means sales. Come on."

Flavia rose from her chair, leaving untouched her caffe latte, no doubt wanting to preserve her model type figure. Maheen remained planted at Happy's table. She grunted, and shook her head. No words, just the grunt.

Laughing, her two schoolmates wandered out and crossed the street to disappear into the boutique that offered *soldes*.

Happy indulged Maheen's need for silence, but after she paid the bill for their coffees and left a fair tip, she remained at the table to ask, "Maheen, tell me about them two girls. How come y'all's so friendly? Don't seem like no kind of company fo' y'all."

Maheen eased, lightened up. "Those two are all right. Self-centered, I guess. But aren't most girls who want to be models? Got to be prettier, taller, more svelte, and have better dress sense than most. Cool. But the truth is that we three are all lonely, looking for love maybe. Flavia's over-sexed. Talks about going to bed with guys. I doubt she has, wouldn't she have got pregnant? But that's all she wants to talk about, yak, yak, yak. Intercourse, except she calls it 'fucking.' She has a boyfriend of sorts. Not very romantic. He lives somewhere far away. In Italy, but hours from here. So mostly Flavia makes up stories of having intercourse, when we know she hasn't even seen him. We girls are permitted cell phones, but Flavia never even gets a call from him. Fiona? She's an *emo*."

"Don't know as Ah's heard thet word befo'e. Wut's an emo?"

"Someone who's too emotional. Boy, or girl. Fiona's a dreamer, gets all excited just talking about a man she's met. Excited in, well you know what way I mean. Sexually excited. Acts like she's having an orgasm just talking about him."

Happy pondered the fact that Maheen was familiar with the term *orgasm*.

Reconsidering, and remembering that Maheen's mother had been a paid courtesan for many years, she shrugged and carried on with her questions.

"Do y'all *like* Fiona?"

"Sure. She's really cool. I've been thinking of inviting her to be my new roommate."

At that moment they both saw an hysterical Fiona waving desperately at them from in front of the boutique she'd gone to visit. She used her arms like the starter at a car race. Screaming from across the road, she yelled, "Don't leave me! Help! Come here!"

Happy quickly led Maheen across the asphalt. "Wut's happened? Fiona, y'all must calm down."

"Hell, no! Help! Help! Flavia's disappeared. VANISHED."

Gravely, Happy asked, "Vanished? Wut y'all mean?"

"Disappeared. We'd both found dresses we wanted. I went into one changing room. Flavia went into the other. When I went to buy the dress, I couldn't get any answer from Flavia's changing room. No Flavia. Help! Help! We got permission from Miss Parizzi to come here together. 'Stick together,' she ordered us. I'll get HELL from her if I go back to school without Flavia. Miss Parizzi will ground me for a month."

Happy, who'd had dire thoughts of a murdered headless Flavia floating in the canal, was shaken by Fiona's crass comment, how she was primarily worried that she might get a grounding from Miss Parizzi.'

Maheen commented, "We'd better call the polizia."

"No! No!" Fiona grabbed at Maheen's free arm and shook it hard. "This whole thing could get into the newspapers. My parents could read about it. They'll be furious I was let out of school to go to the Naviglia Canal boutiques. I told Miz Parizzi that I'd left dresses to be altered, and that after I collected them I wanted to have dinner at Paper Moon."

"Maheen, y'all have any other idea wut we could do?"

"Yes, I do. I KNOW Flavia. I'll bet she's gone off to look for that boyfriend she wants to fuck. I can find her, if that's all this is. Come on, Fiona. I'll take you back to school, then I'll collect my credit card and—if Mrs. Harrow will go with me—we'll hunt for Flavia."

Totally willing, Happy agreed to go on a girl-safari with Maheen. Her gut instinct felt this was an acceptable plan. At best it could lead to the Navagli Canal murderer in time to save Flavia. And if this was nothing more than a naughty teenager's escapade in search of sex, so be it.

Chapter 5

Maheen managed to evade the school's caretaker by getting Fiona to put on an hysterical scene. Fiona pretended to froth at the mouth. When the caretaker said, "I seen three girls leave here this evening. Now there be only two returning."

Fiona screamed, "Three. We are three," and she pointed to my Happy, as if my wife was a student.

Half-blind, the old man stared through dirty bi-focals. At last, nodding, he opened the school's austere heavy-nailed door. Her curiosity rising, Happy followed the two teenagers and had a good look around the hallway. It led to a floor above. Maheen led the way upstairs, a finger to her lips signaling they should be quiet.

Maheen's room was certainly large and airy. She went speedily to a desk, removed her credit card, and waved goodbye to Fiona. Leading the way down a gloomy hall, she stopped at a tired square opening in the wall. She pushed a button, there followed a creaking noise, and a square door slid open. Happy looked into a shaft and recognized the tired works of a dumbwaiter. She watched as Maheen slid on to an oversized tray, and gestured that Happy should squeeze beside her. Maheen closed the square door and pulled on the cables that sent the dumbwaiter down into a fetid cellar. There, Maheen pushed Happy out a coal shaft into the building's back perimeter. Maheen began to run. Happy kept up. When they had reached a quiet street well beyond the school's sparse garden, Maheen said, "Don't worry. I've used this system before when I want to get out of the damned school. Come on. Let's get to the subway and find the train station."

Without explanation, Maheen chose to go to the station that provided trains running in the general direction of the southern coast leading from Italy to France. When Maheen finally told Happy where they were headed, she smirked, "Flavia's boyfriend lives in Ventimiglia. That used to be an important border town on the Riviera. But when the European Union ended borders between member states, poor old Ventimiglia went into decline. Tonight there's going to be a party there. The whole town's going festive. I'm betting Flavia wants to party with her boyfriend."

Happy had furrowed her brow. "Ventimiglia? Ah recalls thet were the town in THE JACKAL where the murderer gets stopped and examined if he done had a rifle with him. He did, but he'd brought it to the border unassembled and faked like it were part of his car's muffler." My Happy hadn't lost her longheld fascination for movies.

"No cars tonight. We'll have to foot it from the train station to the seafront. There should be an enormous crowd. Cool. Maybe we'll get to see fireworks."

And there *were* fireworks. They lit up the looming mountain that peered down at the seacoast town while a far older village nestled in its skirts. The village church was silhouetted by the fireworks, and suddenly Maheen yelled, "Up there! That's Flavia, up there. Next to the village church."

Maheen strained to see. But the fireworks had lessened, fading to sparklers, and all she could make out were hundreds of upturned faces now in shadow.

Following Maheen she crossed a long bridge and climbed a vertical lane that led to the church.

"Flavia, Flavia," Maheen yelled again, louder. Now a new surge of fireworks imitated chrysanthemums and in their yellow glow Happy recognized Flavia. She was weeping, her tear stained face a mess of streaked mascara and running blusher.

When they reached Flavia she fell into Maheen's welcoming arms. "He hates me," she moaned. "He told me to get away, I was ruining his fun. And he got a girl with him, his right hand inside her blouse. While I watched he put his left hand up her skirt, and told me I was no good at making love but this Marta knew what to do."

"Don't cry. He isn't worth it." Maheen hugged Flavia, but Flavia flew into a spitting rage. Her saliva coated Maheen's eyelids.

"Fat stupid bitch. Maheen, you can't appreciate a real man. Because no man will ever want you. Andrea's all man. It's me who isn't good enough for him," Fiona stopped spitting and started to stalk away.

Happy passed her like a champion racehorse reaching the Finish Line. "Y'all ain't goin' anywheres without usn." She grabbed Flavia by her long hair, as if it was a horse's mane. Pulling her without relaxing the tight grip, Happy reached the train station. There, most tourists were straining to go home now that the fireworks had ended. No one bothered to raise an eyebrow at Happy's tough-love handling of a subdued Flavia.

Once their train pulled out into the star encrusted night, Happy released Flavia. Fiona went to the late-nite restaurant car to bring three cups of coffee.

By the time the train reached Milan, the three sleepy girls rushed to the subway station to wait for the last car headed for the Parizzi School's station.

At Miss Parizzi's there was no caretaker to answer the bell. The two boarders sneaked back into the building using the coal chute. Happy waved goodbye, and started her long walk to the pensione.

Chapter 6

Happy didn't hear from Maheen for two days.

That was just as well, because now *we* had a grievous worry of our own. While we were making love last night, I'd felt a lump in Happy's right breast. Happy gave a dire squeek, but did not follow that up by ceasing to caress me. When we had finished and were on our "Cloud Nine" which is invariably exquisite, I tried to bring up the subject of the lump I'd felt. Happy had placed two fingers on my lips.

"Not now. We's too happy fo' miseries. Talk about it in the mo'nin'."

I didn't sleep. I couldn't. Not with a threat of cancer of the breast looming for my darling wife. Cancer! How I hate the word, in all its various forms. My longtime live-in sweetheart had died of leukemia shortly before I'd met Happy. Without Happy at my side I might have contemplated suicide.

She'd saved me from that. How can I save her now? Oh God, when I recall the blood transfusions, the searches for the matching bone marrow, and recalled the agony of fellow patients in the hospital who had the dreaded radiation, strapped down while enclosed in a cage of plaster of paris! Then there were the others with chemotherapy, losing their hair and being constantly nauseated.

And will surgeons remove my darling Happy's precious breasts?

Had I brought on this breast cancer by being too rough when playing with her nipples or squeezing them? Oh God, how guilty I felt when I thought of how many times I held them tight all through the night while we slept!

That morning, when dawn broke, I hurriedly dressed for morning stables and then hurried back to the pensione to escort Happy to a cancer clinic for a biopsy.

We were informed that the results of that test would take several days. Damn, damn, damn! How will I ever get through those days, worrying for my wonderful-Happy's well being? I chewed my fingernails to the flesh, and

I'm afraid I was rather hard on our fillies having insisted they do double gallops because it calmed me to watch them.

Those two days were two of the worst of my life. I acted tenderly toward Happy, but she brushed off my concerns as if they were moths. "We's goin' to be just fine. If thet doctor takes off my breast, Ah'll just buy me one of them bra-ssier-es what has a fake spongy filler. Ah's done with nursin' kids, so's don't make me no mind."

Darling Happy had not fallen into depression, but I certainly did. I wondered how God could visit such misery on a good woman, an excellent mother, a loving wife, a dedicated worker at her job, and a champion for the rights of female jockeys. How?

An odd happenstance at this time was that instead of wanting to hear stories of racing lore from me my Happy decided to tell me horror stories.

"Ah's been thinkin' about what sort of monster we's dealin' with in this here Milan. Y'all knows how Ah con-cen-trates on wut Ah reads in them noospapers. Monsters, plenty wrote about them in the noospapers. Remember the father in Austria wut kept his elder daughter em-prisoned in a basement to breed babies off her until she done got an in-fec-tion with the last one and had to go to a hospital where the truth come out? Ah's wonderin' wut they did with their garbage, wut they did to wash 'n dry clothes, diapers too.!How come the girl's mother never suspected wut was goin' on in her basement? Then there was thet man in the USA wut killed his wife and mother-in-law, and when put in jail he plucked out one eye then later tore out the other 'n ate it! Yeah man, and wut about thet girl livin' with her folks near Orlando, where we was last year? Thet woman, called Casey Anthony, had a three-year-old girl called Caylee. Casey, twenty-two years old at the time, used chlor-o-form to keep the chil' quiet when she went out dancin' with a boyfriend. Casey Anthony used thet chlor-o-form trick one time too many seems like, 'n little Caylee died. Casey put her tiny body in the trunk of her car until it smelled so bad she buried it in the woods some hundred yards from her parents' house. Monsters! Plenty diff-er-ent types out there."

As the day wore on, Happy deflected her fears by plunging into Maheen's problems.

In my black misery, I was in no mood to commiserate with the dejected daughter of my favorite owner's Egyptian wife. Happy, however, thrust herself into Maheen's problem as if she had nothing on her mind.

When finally the telephone rang in her bedroom and she recognized Maheen's cut-crystal British accent, she responded feelingly at her news.

Maheen's opening words were: "Mizz Harrow, Fiona has left Mizz Parizzi's."

"Sho 'nuf? Them parents got sc-a-red thet their baby could be murdered!"

"Nope. Fiona's parents dragged her back to Scotland, fed up paying the school fees without her getting any modeling contracts. They'd never really had been able to afford the fees. Made huge sacrifices for Fiona. She's furious. No chance to find the knight on a white horse she could fall in love with. Not in her part of Scotland. She calls Scotland 'jail.'"

"So, who be yo'r cand-i-date for a new roommate now?"

"Nina Rospovitch. Gets the biggest allowance of any of us. Can afford to treat me to taxis to the Navigli complex."

"Y'all *still* wants to go to thet place?"

"Of course. No other place as cool in all of Milan."

"Is Nina boy-crazy"

"Nope. Likes older men."

Chapter 7

Happy hardly had time to digest this news when Fran hurtled into her bedroom. "I've met the most divine tenor. His name's Bruno. He's a Romanian. Was a big star in the Bucharest Opera. Hopes to make it big here. He's got the title role in Pagliacci. Gorgeous voice, but he's not one of those homo tenors. Very sexy. And he's crazy about me. Can't wait to bed me."

No comment from Happy that Fran had been less than four days without her Jeremy. She knew that Jeremy suffered from rich-wife syndrome. He'd remained in London because there he'd had a chance for a highly paid job.

Personally, when I met this Bruno, I didn't care for his obnoxious arrogant manners and foul breath. But Fran blossomed when she was in his unattractive presence. "I sing better after listening to him practice his arias," she declared effusively. "I'm in better voice now, aren't I, darling Bruno?"

It was obvious to me that Bruno had pushed to enter Fran's circle because she was already a big star, and he hoped that some of her stardust would settle on him.

Vulgar, vain and verbose this Bruno rubbed me the wrong way as if I was a cat being brushed the wrong way with wire.

"You like-a the sex?" he asked in a low, overly familiar tone as we washed hands in the men's room of the bar in our pensione. "I like-a the sex. Ever since I boy, I masturbate until I could get a woman. I was only ten when I fuck waitress. She taught me tricks I still use."

In a growl, I spat out, "That's your affair, not mine."

"Ah, *affair*. Most be-au-ti-ful word in English language. In Romania, under the dictator Ceauscau, we singers were limited as to how much sex we got We were not to tire ourselves. Not that way. But I live in six floor walk-up. Me, I tire climbing stairs. Sex easy. When I boy, I thought of nothing but sex. Not food, sex. Not sleep, sex. Not—"

I cut short his reminiscences. Turning my back, I hurried to the patio where I could see Happy was tearing open an envelope with her clinic's name emblazoned.

"Have you?" I couldn't complete a sentence. I stared at the paper in her hand. It contained a very long diagnosis *in Italian. Happy had to hand it to the pensione's owner to read it out to her.*

"No cancer," he proclaimed, as sententiously as Mussolini addressing his fascists. "Was a benign cyst."

My shoulders heaved with relief. I took Happy in my arms, and I felt tears burning my lids. I was still holding her in utter joy when, within minutes of our receiving this news, Maheen brought Nina to see us in the pensione's patio, while Bruno was still there plying Fran with champagne.

He spilled champagne on the table, as he stared at Nina. A transformation came over him as overwhelming as when a full moon erupts from behind veiling clouds.

Bruno promptly dumped Fran for this troublesome teenager. Nina *was* trouble. She not only failed to show any respect for Fran's position in the opera world, she proceeded to tell me how to train racehorses. "My mother has racehorses," she proclaimed. "She was in a syndicate that won the Irish Derby last year. Cozy with the Magniers. Now *they* have the world's greatest trainer. You, Mr. Harrow, should take lessons from him. And you, Mrs. Grace, should consider changing stables and begging the Magniers to let you be in their syndicate."

Ouch. God knows I need to keep Fran as an owner, whether to love her or not even *like* her.

I needn't have worried that our Fran would follow any recommendations from naughty Nina. Because within two more days Nina had escaped from her school to go to live with Bruno. Thanks to the school's assistant head mistress, Draga Copescu. She was a tall model-like woman whom the boarders had christened The Dragon Lady. This Draga Copescu had helped Nina to join Bruno.

Chapter 8

When she'd first met her, Happy had made a huge effort to understand Nina's personality. Nina seemed permanently on a make-believe catwalk, never studying, never demonstrating affection for anybody. The catwalk was all. Her ambitions, her physical desires, her deportment, everything in her life seemed aimed at being accepted as a model and making her way to the top on the fashion scene. When Nina ran away from her school to live with Bruno, Happy decided that Nina's character was like a kaleidoscope, one twist and all change.

Happy met Maheen at a pizzeria the following Saturday afternoon. Maheen complained about her erstwhile roommate. "Nina was no fun to be around. Not like any other roommate I've ever had. I'm guessing, but I'll bet that during her early years in Russia the discipline demanded from anybody who wanted to get to the summit of any art form, well, it must have broken plenty of other girls so they didn't make it. With Nina's mother having married money and brought her to the West, Nina wasn't going to fail to get what she wanted."

"Did she borrow yourn clothes? Did she ask y'all to lend her your moher's hand-me-down Chanel purse?"

"You know she did! There's hardly anything in my closet she hasn't tried on. But I'm so short and she's so tall, that it's only tops and the purse she'd use."

"When do y'all expects to see her again?"

"Maybe tomorrow. She moved out of school, and why not? Bruno offered to have Nina live with him in his apartment, and she loves it there. He has mirrors all over the place, on the ceilings too. She can twirl and practice her catwalk prancing all she wants. No nasty Dragon Draga to tell Nina she's got to stop pirouetting and start studying."

"Tell me about Draga. She be from Russia too?"

"No. Romania. Same kind of place. Discipline, discipline. She's older, so she lived under the Ceausescu rule. Must have been horrible. Not much food. Did you know that when the orphanages ran out of food they gave the kids blood? Some international agency shipped Romania plenty of blood, so that it was more plentiful than milk. And in some cases the blood was contaminated with HIV, and the orphans got AIDS."

"Sho did read about thet in a noos-pa-per."

"The Dragon Lady came from one of those very orphanages. Didn't catch anything there. Worse luck for us. Only caught a bad temper."

"So when did Draga get out of Romania?"

"Couple months ago. She must have worked like hell to make it here. She was sent to a prison to be a warden, but got out of that by applying to help out in a fish market where she helped prepare the daily catch for the stalls. She said it stank something awful. Managed to go to some college's night classes where they taught foreign languages, learned French, Italian and English."

"Does she make good money at this-here school?"

"I wouldn't think so. But she can have lots of food, because most of the girls won't touch it and there's plenty left over. But, just like us girls, she wants to keep her figure. Wants to be a model."

"She be ugly!"

"Draga doesn't think she's ugly. *She* thinks she's gorgeous. Thinks she's much better looking than any of us girls in school."

"She told y'all somethin' like that?"

"No. No way. She doesn't chat with us girls. But there's a Sister Agnes who comes to our school to check on our health. Draga monopolizes her. Sister Agnes says that if Draga doesn't ever get to be a model, she wants to study medicine."

"Sho 'nuf? But don't it take lots of money to study med-i-cine?"

"Who knows? I never looked into it. A doctor! That's the last thing I'd want to be."

"Wut *do* y'all want to be?"

"An archeologist. I'd love to work on digs, find something nobody in our century ever saw before. I think Nina might have joined with me on that, if she hadn't had her head so filled with being a model. I'm sure her mother wouldn't care what Nina does."

"Why not?"

"Because Nina's mother, Elisabeta, is like so many of the Russians we see here. She wants to buy, buy, buy, and couldn't care less what happens to her kid. She's bought an apartment in Paris, a house in Miami, a penthouse in Monte Carlo, yes, penthouse because the real estate agents assured her if she was high up enough there the other Russians' buildings couldn't spoil her views. When she first got married she went crazy buying clothes, and paintings. Then she needed more and more homes to house the clothes and walls for the paintings."

"Does Nina's mother know thet Nina's livin' with Bruno?"

"The school's not going to tell. Won't want to lose its fees."

"Sho 'nuf. Ah re-calls thet when Flavia went missin' not a word was said. But, Bruno? He ain't the easiest man in Milan. Ah never could understand how Fran took up with him. She got a real nice husband back in England."

Maheen laughed. "*Back* in England. There's your answer. That prima donna wants a man by her side here. And in her bed, here. Or so my own mother would say."

Happy eased off on that topic, remembering Mafalda's career had included that spot of courtesan work.

"Wut could them two have in common, Bruno and Nina?"

"They both remember being hungry as children. Bruno told Nina he has mirrors on the ceiling because although he was starring at the Bucharest Opera House his salary was so low the best he had to live in was a loft where the roof leaked. He gets a feeling of security with overhead mirrors stopping any possible leaks."

Happy kept to herself her own opinion of Bruno's reasons for wanting mirrors on the ceiling of his bedroom.

She learned more about Bruno's bedroom when Maheen left the pizzeria to go back to her school. Her empty seat was hurriedly filled by the unexpected arrival of a trapped-seeming Nina, who bared her teeth like a snarling wildcat.

This was a very altered Nina. Her clothes hadn't been borrowed, they'd been *bought* at the most expensive boutiques in this fashion conscious city. Her makeup had been applied by a professional makeup artist. Her hair was streaked with golden highlights and cut into a bizarre angular shape.

"I want to talk to you, Mrs. Harrow. Yes, talk. Or, really ask you questions. Questions. You have so many babies, so close together. You want babies, every year?"

"Ah loves mah chillun. Don't matter they come close together."

"Da. **But I *don't* want any children. And I'm scared I'm going to get pregnant. I'm living with Bruno now, we share a bed. If you follow what I mean.**"

"Better y'all asks yo'r Ma about thet side o' babymakin'."

"Not possible. As we say in Russia, not convenient. My mother will never discuss sex with me. Sex is why I've been brought out of Russia. She didn't really want me around her new husband, I'm so tall and she'd like to have passed me off as a pre-teen. But her brother, my Uncle Igor, he was fucking me. My mother said I could have a monster baby because Uncle Igor and I are close relatives."

"If y'all had stayed at school, y'all might have learned what to do. Ah cain't help. Ah cain't meddle in this."

"Mrs. Harrow, you being a married woman, couldn't you do me a favor and go into a chemist's shop and buy some birth control pills for me? I've tried the Black Market, but these Italians are funny about selling them to underage girls. Underage? And I feel so old, now. THERE'S ANOTHER THING. Another thing! When Uncle Igor did *it*, it didn't hurt. He was small, down there. But Bruno, although he's shorter than me, he's got a big thing and it hurts me."

Happy mulled over that bit of information until, like an expert skydiver who has tested the parachute of a novice, she took the plunge. "Rick, he bought me some K-Y when Ah's felt raw after birthin' mah babies." Lifting the pizzaria's menu in a signal she wanted her bill, Happy prepared to end this conversation. Suddenly she was learning more about Nina's character than she was prepared to digest.

She didn't have to end it, because Nina's mother arrived and took over. "I'm Elisabeta, will you order a glass of champagne for me?" She took two chairs, one for her gym-slimmed backside and the other for her oversized Gucci purse.

Elisabeta had also made use of Milan's top couturiers and make-up artists. But she'd paid them to look younger while Nina was trying to appear older. Elisabeta's miniskirt barely covered her venus mount, her brassiere hauled up what had been sagging. Six inches shorter than her daughter, she wore shoes with six inch heels.

Before a waiter could produce a flute of champagne, Nina lunged from her seat and bundled into her mother's lap. All of her six feet tall body managed to crowd on to Elisabeta's honed frame. Neither mother nor daughter seemed at all perturbed by the pastiche they were creating, nor how much they damaged their expensive Corso Venezia clothes.

Elisabeta ran a bony hand through Nina's angular cut, "What happened to your beautiful long hair? And does your school permit you to wear so much makeup?"

A long, weighty silence followed. Would Nina lie? Pretend she was still in the school? And was Elisabeta about to do a Vesuvius? Become a human volcano spurting vocal lava?

Happy studied the bill the waiter had brought. A fat hand covered hers as she pulled out a credit card for payment. Bruno's hand. Stealthily he'd arrived in the café.

With his other hand he tossed a twenty euro note on the table. "Mrs. Harrow, allow me to treat. Ah, and is champagne for Elisabeta? Good. Stay, dear Mrs. Harrow, as we will now have long friendly talk."

The hovering waiter had placed a flute of champagne in front of Nina's vacated place. Adroitly Bruno pushed the flute of champagne to be in front of Elisabeta. No proper Russian matriarch, like a chorus girl on a date she poked her index finger into the champagne and then sucked the finger to test the wine's quality. "Better champagne at the Bice," she pronounced, as if she'd been invited to a wine-tasting.

Happy stayed. She felt a tremor as if a curtain was about to rise on a controversial performance, as she had when in Sydney she'd seen MADAME BUTTERFLY.

Bruno, the professional tenor, set this stage for a grand aria. He took Nina's vacant chair, leaned forward like Scarpetta in TOSCA, and said, "Elisabeta, I most happy to see you. I much want your permission to marry Nina."

Vesuvius stopped rumbling. No more threat of verbal lava.

Nina's face had mixed expressions vying for place, like seaweed and foam on a wave. Joy, surprise, anxiety. But Elisabeta's face was one-faceted. "Oh! But I just pay her school fees for new term. Will the school refund my money?"

Although the scene had been skillfully stage-managed, this was one aspect Bruno had not foreseen. "I will repay you, if not."

"Meanwhile, where will Nina live? Not with me and my husband! Not if there is to be long wait while you plan big wedding."

"I have beautiful apartment in New York waiting for me for my Metropolitan Opera season. Plenty money. I send Nina to modeling school there. Big wedding? No! If you sign papers give permission, we can be married at the end of this week."

Finally, Nina who like a lamb sent to market had been left out of their dealings, forced out a word, "Please."

Happy swooped on that word. "Miz Elisabeta, cain't y'all see thet Nina—"

Bruno's voice dropped from tenor to baritone, exploding over Happy's initiative. "Nina will be pleased. All good, for her. In New York. I get contract for recordings. Like I say before, Big Money. But cannot leave Milan before I sing Pagliacci. Is tomorrow night. Gala performance at La Scala. I invite you as my guest."

Elisabeta wasn't ready to give up her battle line. But, like the doomed Maginot Line, her armament only aimed in one direction. "You pay for wedding dress? Or, you pay for wedding supper? You pay for honeymoon!"

Bruno nodded acceptance to all of Elisabeta's demands. Sotto voce, he whispered in Happy's ear, "Nina has tight cunt. I like. Not size of swimming pool such as Fran has. Too many men in Fran's life. I will be only man for Nina."

On that note Happy left the pizzaria and hailed a taxi. She noticed that for all his boasting about Big Money, Bruno had come in the cheapest rental car available in Milan, which he had illegally parked on a yellow line.

At the pensione, after cuddles for the "chillun" and an early dinner, we hurried to our welcoming bed. But Happy wasn't ready for sex. She wanted to talk, to pour out to me all she had heard and seen that day.

She did.

Later, she added, "Ah's been invited to PAGLIACCI. By Bruno. Will y'all take time to go to thet?"

"And why not? It's a beautiful, and very short opera. Usually shares the bill with CAVALLERIA RUSTICANA. Our horses will be asleep. We'll go!"

"Wut's this PAGLIACCI?

"It's a sad story put to music by Leoncavallo. Has a great history. The first ever record to sell one million copies was of Caruso singing in the role of Canio, *Vesti La Giubba*. Toscanini conducted for its premier. The story's core is simple, jealousy. The action takes place around a group of smalltime actors who go from town to town. Canio's wife, Nedda, is cheating on him with Silvio, who asks Nedda to elope with him. But there's another character, Tonio, who wanted to sleep with Nedda and was told by her to get lost. Coincidentally the play they put on for Assumption tells a similar story. Canio, who plays Pagliacci, gets the info from Tonio that Nedda's put horns on him. He stabs Nedda and, still on stage, knifes Silvio. Briefly then, that's the PAGLIACCI libretto."

"Them tickets got prices on them like y'all wouldn't believe! And just to see such a sad opera? Do y'all thinks we got to buy expensive wedding presents for Bruno and Nina since he give usn such expensive tickets?"

"Sorry, but no. We're way over budget as it is. And we still have to stay on at the pensione to see our horses run here."

With merry eyes, Happy whispered, "Ah's thinkin' just a tube of K-Y."

Chapter 9

La Scala! I've read about it, seen videos of it, but had never before been present for a performance in this delectable opera house. Newly refurbished, and re-opened after much needed renovations, the glittering result was soul warming. Its six tiers glistened from its superb lighting.

Budget or no budget I'd treated Happy to a new dress for the occasion of Bruno's gala performance. She'd lost all the weight put on during her latest pregnancy, and pirouetted appropriately for me in front of the meager mirror in our bedroom. With shoes to match by Dolce & Gabbana, the effect was stunning. She boasted she'd found her twinkling studded evening bag for a fiver in the flea market at Porta Ticinese in Milan's medieval section. For my Cinderella wife to arrive in style, I'd chartered a mini-limo to swish us past the Sforza Castle down the Dante Boulevard to enter the great plaza leading to La Scala Opera House.

I felt a male pride in my gorgeous young wife as we entered La Scala's magnificent lobby to jostle with Milan's finest. When the third warning bell rang to summon latecomers to their seats, we found that ours were particularly good.

After the heart-tearing overture there came the famous whoosh of the rising curtain. When Bruno, outfitted like an itinerant small town's actor in the 1865 era, and, looking taller, took his stance on the stage, there was a warm feeling of comradeship that overwhelmed me. I hadn't been fond of Bruno, because I've never warmed to Fran's successive lovers, but watching him now I did have a feeling of real friendship for him, a man who had come to the West as a refugee from a brutal dictatorship to reach this evening's heights.

That taller look added glamour. His trousers hid the backs of his shoes, maybe he was wearing "elevators." He had the exhilarated glow of a bridegroom-to-be, and was in fine voice. At the end of his first aria there was a worrying pause, perhaps caused by surprise at the quality of his performance, but then the highly critical Milanese audience gave him stupendous applause. Bruno's *Qual Fiamma Avea Nel Guardo* had made musical history He had entered La Scala's record books alongside the likes of Maria Callas.

In spite of his bulky frame Bruno did a good job of the knife scene when he first threatened Nedda. Just before the curtain came down for the first interval, Bruno gave his rendition of that great aria Vesti La Giubba. For this aria Bruno received a standing ovation.

Invited backstage for the intermission, we left the glamorous Milanese opera snobs to simmer over the finer notes from the songs they had just heard. A flunky showed us how to find Bruno, who for this night had the main star dressing room.

The corridor was eerily quiet. We stepped into the room, after discreetly—THANK GOD—knocking, to find Bruno devastated. His stage make-up had run from weeping. His wig had been removed and he still wore a band of netting to keep his own hair in place, but this wasn't doing its job because Bruno's hair was a mess. Grabbing Happy, he LET OUT A DEMONIC YELP.

"Police been here. Told me. Nina dead. Her body found floating in Alzaia Naviglio Paves. Fingers, all fingers cut off."

Bruno broke down. He couldn't speak any more. Thrusting his way around the room like a caged animal, he wiped flowing tears with the sleeves from the clown's costume he'd put on for PAGLIACCI's second act.

Happy, not wanting to rub vinegar in the wound, still had to ask, "Not the Alzaia Navigli Canal—"

Bruno cut her off. "You are thinking this copy-cat crime? No. Not same canal. Not torso cut from arms and legs. Fingers only. I will learn more details after Second Act."

I asked, "You're going on stage? You're going to finish the opera?" Astounded, I patted his shoulders as if we were 'old boys' who'd played rugger together at Eton. "Beg off. I'll explain to the management. There must be an understudy for such an important role."

"No. I sing. I give best performance of my career. My mother always told 'Bruno you must suffer to reach heights of greatness.' I *am* suffering."

There followed a delay beyond the scheduled intermission of twenty minutes. But no one in the audience complained. Strutting in the bars, a second flute of champagne calmed the glitterati. Only those burghers who had come by train or bus and feared losing the last coach had long faces. The news of yet another dead girl's body having been found floating in a Milan canal was not to interrupt a gala performance of PAGLIACCI.

Bruno got six curtain calls for this performance. After his final very professional bow, he disappeared behind the lowering curtain.

Milan's A-list opera buffs stayed on for CAVALLERIA RUSTICANA.

Happy insisted we return to Bruno's dressing room to give him what comfort we could offer. We found him on his knees, back turned to an hysterical Elisabeta who was flailing him with sharp blows. When he saw us, he moaned pitifully, "I hard man, but not strike woman."

I pushed myself between Bruno and Elisabeta, receiving the last of her interrupted blows. How to handle this inept Bruno? Here was a shredded man, pulped by his own misery and Elisabeta's towering hatred. Only a few minutes earlier he had taken his bows as a rising star who had delivered a brilliant performance in one of the world's most famous opera houses. Now he was a sniveling wreck. What to do?

I helped him to his feet. "Bruno, when we were ushered inside, the flunky told me there's a pack of howling paparazzi beyond the corridor. They—"

"No. Reporters, I cannot see." Bruno sopped up his tears. Ignoring Elisabeta, whose fury was Olympic, he said, "Yes, I escape. There is back door. Back door behind room. We take. Happy go first, they not expect young woman. I leave for New York in morning. Go apartment. Pack. We listen radio, more news."

We waited while Bruno changed out of his clown costume into a bridegroom-to-be outfit. Elisabeta, her face contorted with rage, skulked out of the room into the corridor. We could hear the baying of the paparazzi.

Happy, on cue, led the way out to a dimly lit back door and into an alley. This alley had decidedly not been renovated. It was filthy, the walls peeling, and I thought I saw a rat scuttle from behind a garbage can.

Milan's opera buffs had remained in the brightly lit Opera House, savoring their third or fourth flutes of champagne, waiting, never to miss a note of CAVALLERIA RUSTICANA. Outside, while we waited for our limo, we saw one long-haired intellectual type desperately examining his wrist watch in hopes he might still make a bus.

When the limo failed to appear, I summoned a taxi from across the wide venue that leads to La Scala. A slow moving one had come from the direction of the Duomo, Milan's grandiose city heart.

Bruno gave his address. We three took the back seat together. The taxi left the La Scala's carefully manicured site, ending in a less opulent neighborhood. After climbing to a top floor in a grimy building, we found Bruno's apartment was much as Happy had heard it described. Heavily mirrored.

Barely able to talk, Bruno mumbled, "Apartment belong to movie actor. Vain. But mirrors good. Help me improve posture when I practice arias."

He went into the bedroom, and began to toss clothes into a suitcase that was brought down from yet another mirrored space. While he went searching for his passport, Happy took a good looksee into the bedroom closet and noticed that Nina had collected very expensive clothes during the few days of her time with Bruno.

Her forehead wrinkling, Happy asked, "Bruno, Ah hates to mention this, but could Ah bring these fashion items to Maheen? She be too short to wear them dresses, or slacks, but she sho' could use them blouses. She could give to them other girls in the school what she cain't wear."

Bruno didn't dignify her query with anything more than a brief nod. Happy proceeded to stuff the clothes into two pillowcases from the prominent double bed. She averted her eyes as best she could from that bed, it had too many ifs.

Listening to the radio's horrific details about Nina's mutilated hands, I went into the kitchenette and made coffee from a can of instant Nescafe. There were only two mugs for it, but Happy shook her head, she didn't want any. Bruno and I quaffed the coffee, and without any more talk we gave hugs, and left. In the corridor we could hear Bruno's radio blaring more news of Nina's murder.

In the taxi we passed newspaper sellers who had already stacked the early editions. I asked the taxi driver to pull up to one and bought a paper even though neither of us could read Italian. "Morta," one headline screamed, and that much both of us understood only too well. Beside the long, leading article there were photos of the girl whose body had been found previously in the Navigli Grande canal. Much was made of the fact that the first girl's body had been mutilated far more than had Nina's.

What did the loss of Nina's fingers mean?

I think we got an inkling from an unsolicited source in the cozy patio of our pensione. The place was run like a private party, with strangers off the street treated like special guests and welcome to sit at any table, including those that were occupied.

Later that evening, with the 'chillun' asleep, Happy had joined me for a tête-à-tête supper, when a total stranger sat down uninvited to strike up a conversation at our table.

"How do you do? I'm Dr. Jason Speelman, from Oxford University. I heard you speaking in Etonian tones, and thought you wouldn't mind if I shared your table."

I'd risen from my chair as I would have for any person attaching himself to our table. I grinned, shoved out my right hand and gave his a squeeze. Happy didn't look so pleased: she preferred to have our private time together PRIVATE.

Dr. Jason Speelman must have been living in a hotel room, felt lonely, and needed a chance to talk. He couldn't be made to shut up, and neither of us got a word in edgewise.

"My field is psychology. Criminal psychology, in case you are familiar with the science."

Happy didn't volunteer that she'd worked as a sleuth to unmask four murderers.

"Criminal psychology, yes. It becomes more fascinating by the year. Freud never scratched the surface. The human mind takes so many twists. Abnormal, antisocial behavior—"

Happy suddenly yawned. I knew she didn't care much for clinical wordage.

Unmindful that he'd lost one member of his audience, Dr. Speelman pursued his theme. Like many men, he discounted the female listener, directing himself only to the male member of the team, believing that only males were worth giving information to.

"Serial killers, for instance. Take what makes *them tick.*" Now *regretting that he'd lost half of his audience, he carefully chose to speak in layman's terms.* "It's my belief that a serial killer is often motivated by his own anxieties. I'll spell out already," *he added condescending to reach what he considered would be Happy's level of comprehension,* "Often as not, the serial killer strikes again and again in order to allay his demons."

"Ah's goin' to bed, now." Happy rose from the table. "Rick, you be up soon?"

I nodded.

Dr. Speelman looked like a penguin hit by an unusually hot breeze. "Sir, I hope you can stay a while longer. My field is so interesting. By the way, what is it you do?"

He still didn't know my name. Nor had he asked for it. My profession? As a goodbye, I said, "I help my sleuth wife uncover serial killers. Goodnight."

Dr. Speelman had neglected to rise from his seat when Happy left the table, and had again when I left.

Upstairs, cuddling my delicious wife, I said, "Sorry you had to tolerate that bore."

Happy kissing me on that favorite place of mine, whispered, "Don't matter none. Not now, when y'all come up so quick."

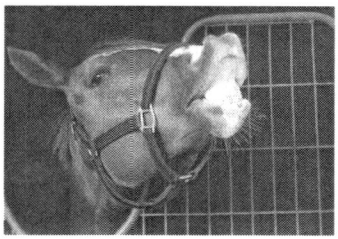

Chapter 10

"Maheen! Ah's got to go see her soon as can be," Happy groaned, as I paid the babysitter and had yet another bad encounter with the disgruntled owner of our pensione, who'd made it very clear that he didn't appreciate being awakened at all hours.

We looked in, very quietly, on our sleeping infants, and finally got into our own welcoming bed.

Happy, very alert, was still intent on the subject of Maheen. "She ain't got no lovin'—mother to help her. And Ah's not much good at helpin' anybody, seein' as how thet Nina done asked me fo' help and Ah let her down."

"Darling, please don't suffer from any guilt over this. There's some monster out there who's doing these things, and from the way I see it you couldn't have prevented Nina's murder."

"Ah could. Ah could have offered to send her to our house in Epsom, and she could've gone to London from there to look fo' a models' school."

"I doubt you'd have been able to get to the pitch with that Elisabeta in the wings."

"Yeah man! Ah knows thet sort of mother. In ourn Kentucky village there be a mother like Elisabeta who goes whorin' to Louisville. Not too different from Mafalda, either. Mafalda ain't been no mother to Maheen until she married Hal Murphy, and put on her good-mother act."

It took some doing to get Happy off the subject of mothering, but with caresses and kisses and rubbing the back of her neck in the way that sends her into orbit, I finally got good sex.

Chapter 11

Mothers! They come in all different kinds. Hadn't Happy and I been exposed to an amazing variety at the Caring For Tots kindergarten, and the Honeyville Gym? Kentucky had spawned some of the best and the worst. Joanne had dumped her three months old daughter on the rejected husband she didn't love in order to dally with a slick lover. Hal's first wife, crippled Clara, had been an excellent mother for years while she struggled with arthritis. But then one day she went—elbows in crutches—to a gigolo who only wanted the fat alimony Hal was forced to pay.

Now there was Mafalda. Was she as nasty a piece of work as I suspected? Or had she some hidden qualities which might show up under duress?

Chapter 12

Good mother or not, Mafalda arrived back in Milan the following morning. Hal had taken her to Rome for the final gala dinner for the Aids charity. There, they had unexpectedly been greeted by Hal's teenage son, who had flown in from Canada unannounced.

Byron Murphy, eighteen, had taken it on himself to leave school in Canada for a gap year at the American College in Florence. As both of his parents had remarried and were not overly anxious to check on his whereabouts, and a married sister who hadn't seen him for two years, Byron did much as he pleased.

Shorter and less bullish-looking than his father, Byron had grace and polish. His blond hair had been tended by a barber usually visited by famous actors. His preppy clothes were strictly Brooks Brothers. He wore no tie. Or socks, preferring quality leather shoes on his skin.

Unlike his father Byron had no noticeable Canadian accent, eschewing the aboot or oot of his father's generation. He had one affectation, he used snuff and made a great business of bringing out an antique Georgian-era snuff box to pinch a few grains. Snuff, not cocaine.

Happy and I met the Murphy prodigal son at lunch in the Hotel de Milan. Happy warmed to him, I was carefully non-commital because as an Englishman I never like to act too friendly with boys unless the wrong idea crosses a father's suspicious mind.

Lunch, Murphy style, was superlative. We began with melon and prosciutto ham, continued with veal piccatta garnished with local white truffle mushrooms, and ended with a cassata that featured pistachio ice cream, sandwiched between chocolate and coffee mousses. Instead of a chef's bon bouche at the beginning of the meal we were sent an assortment of homemade candies to finish. There was a rose for the first course, a Santa Beatrice red for the veal, and champagne with the pud.

Maheen's name was never mentioned. Not one single time. Instead, Mafalda was all over Byron, playing the loving new step-mother. I hadn't seen her working so over-the-top since she had been zeroing in on the late very unattractive Ali in Moscow during her courtesan period.

It took a diplomatic suggestion from Happy to get Mafalda to listen up about Maheen. "Ah's sho' Byron would like to meet some of them bee-u-tiful girls at Maheen's school. So many of them girls wants to be models. Pretty 'nuf to make it big, Ah'd say. Ah's got Nina's clothes for them wut wants some. Wut say we drive to the school?"

Byron, who in spite of his overly careful choice of barber and tailor, was no homosexual, brightened. All during lunch he'd looked very uncomfortable, shoving off Mafalda's overly caring manner. I saw him pull away his hand when for the tenth time she tried to stroke it. "Yes. Girls' school. Models? I'm for it."

Hal, ever ready to provide what people wanted, went to Reception and ordered a limo. Mafalda had turned quiet. Had she heard that Maheen's most recent roommate had been murdered? Her perfect body thrown into a canal, her fingers cut off?

We weren't given a chance to find out. From the hotel's main doorway a prima donna was making a noticeable entrance, Fran! In true star form she demanded to be shown the best table in the restaurant. Without a hello to us, she went to Hal. "I know *you*, you're the big owner from Canada. You'd know which is the best restaurant in this hotel. I won't be fucked off into some coffee shop." Pennypinching Fran for once seemed determined to spend generously on the best food in the finest hotel. Unlike when she went with us to Saratoga and stayed at an American version of a Bed & Breakfast.

In fact, she'd arrived too late to be served in the main restaurant. Hal realized that fact, strode back to the maitre d's podium and handed him a large tip. "For the latecomers to get a table."

Fran hadn't arrived alone. No. She came accompanied by an older Scot. Not wearing a kilt this far south of Glasgow, but with his oversized chin and gruff speech, I could guess he was from the Highlands. I found it surprising that a Scot would be a gigolo. The Scots were a race of fighters, ready to go to any country's little war to shoot at any enemy. Like Sir David Stirling, founder of the famed SAS, they rarely stayed in their Highlands. But to act the gigolo, for a prima donna such as Fran?

She didn't miss out taking a long look at handsome Byron, but from the subsequent mouth downturn judged him too young.

Fran would have marched onwards to the table being prepared for her, but Happy caught her arm.

"Hello, Fran. Ah guess as how y'all didn't see usn." Her soft tone changed. Amazingly, for Happy, she wheedled, "Fran please send a message to Bruno. He's feelin' awful down. This should have been his weddin' day, but his bride done been murdered. He's leavin' fo' New York in an hour."

"That son of a bitch? I should send him a fucking message? No way!" Fran shrugged off Happy's arm and swept on into the dining room.

I couldn't help but notice that my fellow Britisher had winced at Fran's bad language. I judged he hadn't known Fran long. Not been exposed earlier to her personal choice of gutter speak. Shoving out a hand, I said to him, "Rick Harrow. Racehorse trainer. You are?"

"Ian Stokes. Real estate." His accent was Winchester, not Scots. He'd been to a British school and gained a British accent. He gave a brief bow to both Happy and Mafalda, a nod of thanks to Hal, snubbed Byron, and prepared to follow Fran to their table like a trained Pekinese. But first, he answered my further query.

"London, or local?"

"Ex-London. Now, local. Involved in creating a new residential area near the St. Ambrose Church."

"Heart of the city."

"Guarantees buyers." Obviously not a great conversationalist, Ian's brief retorts were cut short in any event by a commanding gesture from Fran. Seated at the table she'd been studying the wine menu. Pennypinching, wondering if a mediocre red would do, or if she should get cheap champagne? He left us, responding promptly to Fran's gesture.

"Good lookin' ain't he?" Happy grinned. "Wut y'all want to bet he's sellin' some real es-tate to Fran?"

"Not taking that bet," I laughed. "I'd say she's leading him on, having him *think* she'll buy a villa, but of course she never will. Too many recording dates in too many other cities."

"Limo's here," Hal called out.

No waiting around allowed. We joined Mafalda, Hal, and Byron, seated on a curving U-shaped back seat that could have held seven more passengers. There was a bar included under the air-conditioning outlet. Hal served Mafalda a drink, offered me one, and Happy, had one himself, but noticeably didn't include Byron.

Happy asked the limo driver, "Do y'all speak English?" After a decisive nod from the driver, she continued, "Are we goin' past the St. Ambrose Church? Can y'all tell us a little about the area?"

"I learned my English on Thoid Avenue and Thoidy Thoid Street in Manhattan. If you like geneology, I'll tell you Mayor Giuliani is related to me. St. Ambrose? A very special saint. **He** taught St. Augustine. Yeah, father of the church, who came from North Africa to Milan to sit at the feet of the great Ambrose. There's a carnivale in the area thanks to St. A. It lasts longer than Ash Wednesday, continues on through Thursday Friday and Saturday.

Sabado Grosso. The Carnivale Ambrosiano. St. A. invented a new rite for the church, a rite still used in Milan today. People like this area. Until the bodies of those mutilated girls appeared in the canal, this was a very happy place."

"Tell him to shut up, I hate drivers who play tour operators," Byron interrupted curtly. With no stylish manner to ease his churlishness.

The driver shut up.

In an uncomfortable silence we drove toward the school. It was an idyllic day with the perfect blue of the Lombardy sky to lighten our mood. We passed a Roman column that Happy would surely have loved to know about, what with her passion for "old stones" but she cut out attempting any more questions. Were we all to be told what we could do by this smooth adolescent?

I recalled seeing a French magazine being sold at our local newsstand. It ran a headline announcing an article in its interior titled something like: "Are our children overly dominant?"

Byron was developing into quite a surprise. Could he be an example of the Second Generation syndrome? Where the children of the newly rich think it's cool to pretend to be aristocrats? Plutocrats?

He leaped out ahead of Mafalda or Happy, not bothering to hold the door for them or help them down the limo's step. He banged on the school's copper studded front door. The Dragon opened it, she stared in amazement at this arrogant youngster. She looked startled, like a trout fisherman who has reeled in a barracuda.

I doubt that the Dragon would have addressed Byron if she hadn't recognized Mafalda in the party. A fee paying mother. "You have come to see Maheen." She voiced a statement, not a query.

Byron spoke out fearlessly, "The girls who want to be models, that's who."

Now Draga handled Byron like a fisherman who throws back a minnow. She'd taken a second look at Byron, and decided he was no barracuda and could be given the toss. "We have serious students here. Do come in Madame Mafalda. I apologize, do come in." She turned her long back on Byron. Happy and I were admitted along with Hal, as afterthoughts.

Who was in the school's narrow lobby? Ian Stokes! How did he get here before we did? What happened to lunch with Fran? Why was he here?

In the curt phrases to which he'd accustomed us, he snapped, "You here too? Came on my motorcycle. After Fran offered a drink, not lunch. Not bothered to wait for that. I'm sure she won't buy a villa."

He'd answered all my silent questions, except WHY?

The WHY ran into the lobby. "Hi, Dad!" A pre-teener hugged Ian. "It's so cool of you to come today. I expected, uh, I think I expected you tomorrow."

Draga scolded, "Tricia, you aren't properly dressed for a visit from your father."

Behind Tricia sidled Maheen. No hug for Mafalda. No hug *from* Mafalda.

Maheen perked up at seeing Happy. What is it that teenage girls find so welcoming about Happy? Because she's barely five years out of her teens?

"Sho' good to see y'all." Happy hugged *her.* "Lookee here, yo' new Step-Daddy done brought usn all a surprise. He be a son, Byron, straight from Canada."

"Florence," Byron corrected rudely. "I've been at the American School there for a WEEK now. Say, I thought there were girls here who want to be models!" He gave a really tasteless stare at Maheen's short stature. No way would short, plump Maheen ever qualify to be a model on a Milan runway. Or on a runway anywhere else.

Maheen handled that churlishness. "We don't all want to be models. I want to be an archeologist. Here, I'll introduce you to Flavia. She's about to be offered a contract by Chloe. She has pretty hands, gets to be photographed with those five hundred euro bags. Have you seen the Ferragamo ad, with just a hand and a gigantic purse?"

Flavia, six feet two inches in her loafers, had arrived quietly. She peered down at Byron as if she was on the top of the Eiffel Tower. He was staring at her hands. But Byron, after a minute realizing that his height wasn't going to make a favorable impression on Flavia, to compensate for his five feet six inch figure, he leaped on to the lobby's one chair. Now *he looked down on Flavia as the Empire State Building does on the Chrysler.*

"Get down from chair," barked Draga. But she restrained from yanking the boy from his position. Hal did that.

Ian cut into this nasty scene by crooning to his daughter, "Tricia, How about taking the back seat on my motorcycle? Got a new 'des res' for sale near the clinic at Lecco. Come along."

They left the lobby. Ian ushered his daughter through the imposing doorway, and soon the noise of a motorcycle roared into the silence. It diminished after a few minutes and finally slithered away.

Happy lightened the residual gloom. "Maheen, Ah's brought some clothes Ah thought y'all could use. They be Nina's things. But Bruno said as how Ah could take them to y'all. Don't fit? Give it to them other girls here."

Maheen off-loaded Bruno's two pillowcases that Happy had lugged to lunch and brought along to the school in Hal's chartered limo. Slowly, reluctantly almost like a superstitious African primitive, Maheen handled them as if these clothes contained some bad kharma.

Flavia had no such qualms. She made a grab for the dresses that had spilled out of the first pillowcase, and, like a modern Cinderella, was soon trying on the shoes from the second pillowcase.

Picking around them as if they were cactus, Maheen selected a Celine T-shirt and a diamante studded evening bag. "I guess I'll keep these."

Happy asked her, "What happened to Nina's Chanel bag? I couldn't find it in Bruno's apartment."

"Oh that was nabbed the first minute we heard Nina had been killed. Girl from Finland grabbed it from our bedroom closet. She's a real nerd."

Byron swept between Flavia and Maheen. "Got a great idea, Flavia. You and me, we take the limo. Dad can send for another. I want to show you some sights."

He took Flavia's free arm, divested her of the dresses and shoes, and led her out though the big doorway. Hal said nothing. He shrugged, and lifted his eyebrows for Mafalda to read that he was powerless to stop his son from going off. Like an astute army officer, he'd decided to save his ammunition for a more demanding occasion.

Outside, the limo's motor flared, and then a crunching of gravel followed as Hal's limo left the driveway.

Hal said to Draga, "I'd like to use the school's phone to call for another limo." He drew out the limo companies' card and squinted at a number printed there.

With little enthusiasm, Draga handed him the telephone.

From central Milan we heard an Italian basso voice saying, "Pronto?"

Hal gave the school's address in faltering Italian. I was at a loss for words to help out in the situation. Again, Happy defused another unpleasant moment by asking, "Maheen, will you take me up to your room? Ah'd like to take a look. Maybe Nina left behind some—'

"Oh, Nina left behind her iPod. I'll give it to you to take to her mother."

Happy followed Maheen up a winding staircase. Maheen's room was at the far end of an ugly bile-green corridor painted the harsh color popular with old hospitals. From that forbidding corridor they entered her large room that was diffused with sunlight. "Like it? I grabbed this room, first day of the new term. More windows, see?"

"Nice. Real nice." Happy noted that Maheen felt no evil karma here.

"Mrs. Harlow, we're in what used to be a convent. Belongs to the Diocese of St. Ambrosio. When vocations to be nuns dried up, the diocese decided to rent it out for a school. The first headmistress insisted on building out a new studyroom full of windows. And to even that out for the façade, she had this room made. Seven windows!" Maheen busied herself wrapping heavy paper around the T-shirt and evening bag. "I really don't want these things of Nina's. Won't you take them to someone else? Flavia got enough."

Happy didn't hesitate. "Sho 'nuf. Since Nina's fingers gone missin' Ah thinks the po-lice could be glad to have them for DNA." Happy took the package and waited for the iPod.

"Hold on, Mrs. Harrow. Now I can't find the thing. Nina's iPod. I can't imagine who'd want it. It's just full of the music she pranced to, practicing being on the catwalk. Music that's got the funk."

"But ain't they be many girls in this school practicin' to be models?"

Maheen nodded. "But Nina liked Russian jazz. The old kind that helped bring down the Iron Curtain. Nobody else in this school goes for that. No, and anyway only the Finnish girl has asked me for Nina's iPod. Probably meant to wipe Nina's music. You know, the Finns and the Russians have a huge hate going. Seems I recall that the Finns lost a war to the Russians. Anyway, she won't be able to get the iPod. If I find it, I'll give it to you."

"Ah thanks y'all kindly. Ah has another idea for usn. Why don't Ah get per-miss-ion to take y'all out for a day lookin' at some ar-cheo-ology? Ah's goin' to ask the Dragon Lady."

Draga stood in the doorway of Maheen's room. She came accompanied by an older woman who had a faint mustache on her upper lip and had shaved hair from the two sides of her face.

Glowering, the two women were trapped in a contrived silence.

"Oh, Miss Parizzi, sorry. I'm sure Mrs. Harrow didn't mean anything by what she called Miss Draga. Let me introduce you. Miss Parizzi, this is Mrs. Harrow, whose husband works for my step-father. Mrs. Harrow, meet Miss Parizzi, our Headmistress."

"Pleased, Ah'm sho glad to meet y'all."

Miss Parizzi still said nothing. Maheen had scrambled into an upright shoulders-squared stance like a new recruit. Obviously in awe of Miss Parizzi, she urged her inside the room. Draga held back, seething from hearing her unpleasant nickname.

Neither woman entered the room. Why? Happy, always ready to delve back into her memories of Kentucky lore, thought how that mustache might denote that Mizz Parizzi liked young girls more than she should. The two women turned away and marched single file down the corridor.

"Limo's here," Hal sang out again. Happy hurried downstairs, gave a hug to Maheen, and we four crowded into a smaller car. No limo. The car company must have run out of them. There were no hugs given between Mafalda and Maheen before we left the lobby. But Hal, always dependant on earning brownie points by being open-handed with his money, peeled off five twenty euro notes and handed them to Maheen before playing captain of this ship in the car.

Maheen had her own ideas on how to spend part of the money. She called out, "Tomorrow let's go to Dolce & Gabbana. Lopez's stylist, a woman called Andrea Liberman, featured that gorgeous J. Lo in a white silk dress that showed off her bust. As my tits are about the best I've got to show off, I want to see what the dress cost. Maybe I could have it copied at the Navigli

Canal shop I know about that takes your own measurements and makes sure the dress of your choice really fits. Cheap, too."

"Shucks, Maheen. Y'all *really* wants to go back to thet Navigli Canal place?"

"I'm telling you, it's cheaper. What the Parisians call a 'copyiste.' But I'm not planning to go there at night. I've got other shops to visit there. I like the silk shirts with zippers up the front that are featured at doSena. Also, now that my mother's married to a millionaire, maybe she can afford the jewelry an American woman, Louise Lanzi, who lives in Milan makes. Different designs, lots of color. The prices are staggering, from $1000 to $10,000. I want to check out this lady's stuff for my Mom. But not yet. And certainly not tonight."

Later that evening, when Happy and I were close under the covers of our bed relishing the cooler autumn night, Happy came out with a startling idea. "Ah thinks thet school Mafalda found be run by a lesbian. Took thet job runnin' thet school to prey on avail-a-ble girls. Most of them be pretty, graceful, foreign. Honey fo' a bee. Makes me wonder."

"About a tie-in with the murders of those would-be models?"

"Maybe. Got mo'e thinkin' to do befo'e Ah sums this one up."

I ruminated on that. When I was at Eton there had been a House Master who was homosexual. We "new boys" laughed at his feminine gestures. Nicknamed him "Walks on eggs." But by our Third Year we'd been clued in to his ugly practice of using his position of authority to "adopt THAT position." By the time I'd left Eton and become a parent of a young son I never thought back to "Walks on eggs" without shuddering. To this day I can't understand how any parent could be so uncaring as not to vet a housemaster's proclivities before sending a child to live under that person's care. Had Mafalda taken the trouble to vet Miss Parizzi? No!

Chapter 13

Fran Purcell monopolized most of our time during the next few days. Not only were two of her fillies about to run at Milan's race course, but she was contracted to sing in two operas at La Scala. Not in starring roles, but as the contralto half of the star's duets.

"What crap! Why do I bother going to so much bloody bother to sing in opera? I make so much more money with rap!" Fran complained to Happy, sitting in the tiny crowded patio of our pensione. Happy knew that pennypinching Fran wouldn't pay the bill, so she'd restricted herself to ordering coffees. Fran continued, "I've developed a public persona, I realize that now. I've covered up my honest shyness with swearing and using four letter words. But I've been lying to myself, cheating myself, thinking I was growing into a finer artist when I was really only escaping into a role I created for myself."

Happy, who hadn't quite followed all of Fran's verbal meanderings, nodded politely. Fran continued, "My heart isn't into opera. Having to be so careful of my vocal chords, never going anywhere there's smokers, staying out of wind, avoiding iced drinks. What the hell, no fun! I've plagiarized Maria Callas's style. I've stolen ideas from other singers. I've become nothing but a ruddy thief, where opera's concerned."

"Ah likes the way y'all sings. It's real pretty."

Fran treated this last comment as if a man-eating tiger had ripped off one of her arms. Her voice rising to nearly a soprano's, she squeaked, "Pretty? That's all? I'm beginning to hate my job. If all the public thinks is that I've a 'pretty' voice. Bullshit. Believe me, I'm beginning to think I'll retire soon. The music industry's so tough. Fickle, and mean."

I said, "Fran, don't belittle your talent. You have awesome breath control, a great range, flexible phrasing, and I like your technique even if it IS borrowed."

"Don't give with the shitty flattery, thank you very much. When I want to hear from you, it's only concerning the welfare of my horses Are the fillies fit to run?"

"Bursting out of their skins."

"Okay then, let's go into lunch. I take it this lousy little pensione won't have air-conditioning. Can't have any fucking air-conditioning playing havoc with my voice."

I had no smart-ass response to that. Instead, concentrating on my memories of her finest performances, I recalled the shimmering tones she could produce. I concentrated on how her body had quivered with the intensity of her attempt to reach for the best her voice could offer. I thought again of how impressed I'd been with the delicacy and clarity with which Fran illuminated demanding passages. Oh, Fran was a true professional, who could elevate the senses of her most critical audiences. It wasn't up to me to be a smart-ass.

We entered the pensione's cheerful, clean dining room and sat down at one of the smaller tables. Most of the pensione's clients had large families and the majority of tables were set up for ten diners or more. The owner's wife gave out menus, then whipped away the used cloth left by the last diners and placed a detergent-clean cloth on the formica top.

Fran announced in her loud voice that could carry to the highest gallery of an opera house, "No dairy foods for me. Not good for my voice."

"Spaghetti, madame?"

"With no cheese, yes. Absolutely no cheese, don't go sprinkling that parmesan over the spaghetti. No parmesan!"

Timmy emerged from the pensione's inside hall. He climbed into my lap, sprawling like a friendly Labrador dog. Timmy knew he wasn't supposed to join the grown-ups. Was I going to have a rebellious son like Hal's Byron?

Using Happy's Kentucky accent, he drawled, "Richard done gone to sleep. Them sisters of mine are nappin'. Amah's ironin' clothes. Ah wants spaghetti too."

Spaghetti! Not a quick trip to the nearest McDonald's? Spaghetti forTim, then.

Fran ignored Tim. As she had ignored our need for cash when he'd been kidnapped two years previously. She continued to talk about herself, "I need to treat my vocal chords with some bloody respect. They earn my crappy living. By the way, what did you both think of Ian? Handsome. But maybe not too much in the top storey."

I supplied a short comment. "He seems an able enough real estate man. Same age as I am, forty-three, I'd guess. Loves his pre-teen daughter. Tricia's her name, I think I've got that right."

"Not interested in buying any fucking real estate in Italy. Whatever for? I'm out of here once the fillies have had their runs and I've sung in my two operas. I think I'll give Ian a miss, in future."

Happy and I exchanged knowing glances. We were both fully aware that Ian had no plans for including Fran in *his* future. He'd guessed she wouldn't be a client for the real estate he flogs, and also he must have judged how stingy she is when he saw what a cheap wine she'd ordered for them in the restaurant earlier.

"No fucking news on the murderer of those mutilated girls?" Fran changed the subject. One that Happy and I had carefully avoided.

Happy volunteered a reply, "Ah's been givin' these here crimes some thought. Need more knowin' about them folks what 's in-volved. But, tell me, Fran. Did y'all happen to mention to Bruno thet Ah's done some sleuthin', befo'e?"

Coldly, Fran snapped, "Why do you ask?"

"Bruno, he done told me he thought thet Nina's murder could be done by some what-he-called copycat. Why would he bring up somethin' like thet to me? Y'all done said like Ah'd solved murders?"

"Fuck it, suppose I did? What harm was in that? Yes, I did tell him you'd solved the murder of my sister, Carla, and those other three musicians: Sybil, Goofie and Munchie. I told him you'd helped catch a serial murderer of nursing mothers. That you'd figured out how a double suicide was really a murder and a suicide. That a terrorist was the final link in a chain of another set of related murders. He was fascinated. Kept him out of the clutches of that girl, Nina, for one night at least."

Fran had shut up my Happy. It took a tantrum from Tim to alter the mood. "McDonald's, I want to go to McDonald's. I hate this spaghetti. That's all we ever get here, spaghetti."

Tim was being Tim again. He'd climbed down from my lap when he saw the plates of spaghetti arrive. Now he was stamping a foot. I suspected he'd climbed into my lap only to avoid having to pull over a chair for himself.

But that day Happy had endured enough bad manners from undisciplined sons. "Y'all's goin' to bed without dinner," she said authoritatively. "Down home in Kentucky we' all don't never talk to grown folk like thet."

She marched Tim out of the dining room and I could hear the two sets of shoes slapping on the pensione's stone staircase. I knew that she knew that Amah would no doubt sneak a plate of food to Tim, later.

Fran leaned her head close to mine, and whispered, "*WAS* Nina's murder a copycat crime? Her body wasn't chopped up. Just lost her fingers."

I didn't like the burning in her eyes. Since when had Fran become bloodthirsty? This new characteristic made her ugly. In response I simply shrugged, and concentrated on my spaghetti. Fran's eyes had reminded me of the eyes of a claw-beaked seagull I'd seen picking at the corpse of a drowned beached dog.

Chapter 14

In our bed that night, Happy remarked, "Seems like Fran done changed a lot from the Fran we used to know. Could she have been thet jealous of Nina?"

"Jealous of what? Six years difference in their ages? Fran's a famous singer. Rich! Jealous of a poor little Russian immigrant because Bruno took her to live with him? That wouldn't have happened if Fran hadn't thrown him out."

"Yeah man, thet be true. But it weren't only Fran wanted to get rid of Bruno. He told me that the sex with Fran didn't suit him. Wrong size. Said somethin' like he bein' in a swimmin' pool when he be inside of her."

I had to laugh. Thank God, I thought, that I'm not like some trainers who feel they have to sleep with their lady owners to give them value for money. Fran? No thanks!

The bedside telephone rang. It was Hal Murphy to tell me he'd put a trace on his son, Byron. The first limo driver had returned to base with a story that he'd left the two kids at the Torre Palazzone in a Tuscan corner near Sienna.

I thought, that's a long way from Milan. A limo ride there would have cost Hal a packet. I said, "Do you want me to go with you to fetch them, Sir?"

"No. Not you. This is going to take some doing. I checked up on the place. Respectable. It's a fortified castle converted into a hotel. Located in its own hamlet. Your wife would love the main building, dates from 1000 A.D. There's an ancient stone tower, a 15th Century farmhouse, a Renaissance chapel that's been converted into a bedroom. Definitely, a job for Happy. Job for a woman."

Happy had been listening in on the Italian-style extra headphone. She was nodding enthusiastically.

Hal continued, "It may be too late to save the girl's virginity, but still Happy's the one to go collect her. Look worse if a man goes. Will you ask

Happy? I'll send a limo around to you in ten minutes. Time's of the essence. Don't want the police arresting Byron. The girl's under age. Big trouble!"

Job for a woman! Then why doesn't he send his wife, Mafalda? Why mine?

The limo arrived in precisely ten minutes. Happy, dressed in jeans and a thick sweater against the sudden autumn night chill, was relieved to recognize the driver. Same man. No doubt he'd been bought off, tipped handsomely by Hal to keep his info to himself. Not give it to the police. Nor to the paparazzi.

I saw her to the limo in my toweling robe. I felt the chill, but I was more concerned whether Happy would be harmed by a furious Byron. A man enjoying coitus does not lightly tolerate being interrupted.

Waved off, Happy settled in the limo for a sleep. When the driver woke her it was still night, but the city's lights had been replaced by flickering candles illuminating a few of the dawn resisting leaded windows of a great castle. Striding in their light, aided by the waning moon, Happy reached the imposing doorway. Its doors were closed against the night. No vigilant porter welcomed her or asked what she wanted. There was a bell. Happy rang it. She didn't hear its peal, but after a long wait she was given the up-and-down by a formidable older woman, who'd emerged into the hall. Dressed in a negligee fit for a bride, but a bride of several generations ago because it was made of hand worked lace trimmed with fur, this woman matched the aging castle's style. With her fierce gaze and worn cheeks that had seen splendid parties and a not-so-splendid decline, her cracked voice was full of reproach.

For the guardian of such a grand place, her question was too ordinary. "What do you want at this hour?" She added reproachfully, "We have only eleven bedrooms here, and they're all taken. You haven't inquired for a reservation!"

"Ah's come fo' young Mr. Murphy, and his friend. Ah works fo' his father. Hi, my name's Happy Harrow. What's your'n?"

"I'm Madame von Rapp. The receptionist and porters have gone to their beds long ago. You cannot barge in here and demand to take away two of our guests."

"They be minors. And Ah's got a letter of au-thor-i-ty from Hal Murphy, the father. Show me their room. They be ordered to come with me."

"You must think I am very stupid, or weak. I will certainly not take you anywhere. How do I know you are not a brothel-keeper come to spirit away that girl."

"Don't know nothin' about no brothels. Ah's a jockey. My husband trains race hosses and we both works fo' THE Hal Murphy." Happy dialed Hal's cell phone number. Hal's large growl echoed through the hall. Happy handed her cell phone to Madame von Rupp.

Hal's growl turned into a spate of very hard orders. Mrs. Von Rupp's creased face began to look like a pillowcase that had been slept on.

Seemingly defeated, Madame von Rupp shrugged, and led Happy upstairs. She knocked on a closed door. When there was no response Madame von Rupp rattled a large bunch of keys, found one that fit the lock, and pushed open the door.

Byron was asleep, fully clothed, on the double bed. Flavia was crunched into a chair, stripped to the waist, also asleep. Her miniskirt was slightly torn, and its hem around her waist.

"Wake up, y'all," Happy barked, suddenly a jockey who knew how to control rebellious horses. She strode across the bedroom, gave Byron a stern shake, and went to cover Flavia's breasts with the blouse that was strewn on the floor.

"What the hell," Byron sputtered. But he jumped out of the bed, embarrassed.

Flavia shook herself awake. Without any excuses, she put on her blouse and pulled down her skirt.

"Y'all's gettin' into Hal's limo, *now!*" She collected Byron's wallet and passport from the night table, pulled Flavia from her chair and marched them both to the hall. Madame von Rupp followed down the stairs, frowning. In a grande dame manner she took a stance beside the hotel's main door. Like a Lady of the Manor, she shook hands with Byron. Cooler as regarded Flavia, she waved her to the limo as a chatelaine might have ordered a dog to its kennel.

Madame von Rupp called to Byron, "Goodbye Percival. I've spoken to your father. He's given me his credit card number to pay your bill. One thing, promise me this story will not be in the newspapers."

"You better believe it," Byron called back.

Inside the limo, as it sped through the hotel's grounds past its ancient stone tower and into the scarlet-streaked dawn, Happy grilled him, "So wut's with the Percival? Y'all give thet woman a false name?"

"Duh! Look in my passport. Percival's my real first name. Was I going through school being called Percy-boy? No. I've always used my middle name. Why should I use a fancy boy's name just because my Dad's got delusions of grandeur. Wants me to get into High Society. Even Byron doesn't suit me. I'd never become a poet. Any objections?"

"Sho not. Not about a name. Ob-ject-tions to wut happened last night with Flavia."

"Nothing happened." Byron took a snide look at Flavia, who was asleep stretched out fully on the limo's far side. "We couldn't do IT. Flavia's got a wall down there it would take a concrete-breaker to crash through. I'm no sex machine. She'll have to get a doctor to use a scalpel on her hymen before she can have her wedding night."

Byron followed Flavia's example, stretched out on to the limo's other couch, and promptly went to sleep.

Happy, shrugging, found a comfortable position as if she was riding a long distance horse, and devoted herself to staring out at the unfolding Tuscan scenery. Every so often the limo would speed past a castle with myriads of turrets and towers, or a domed church. Equally fascinating for Happy were the small abandoned homes where once children had played and lovers had caressed each other in marital beds. She felt touched by the thoughts that were engendered, and too entranced by old stones to sleep.

Chapter 15

With Flavia returned to her school, after hard words from Miss Parizzi, and Byron returned forcibly into Hal's suite, Happy finally made it back into our own bed. But there was no time for sex.

Happy had missed going out with the first lot of my string for morning exercise. I'd delayed, taking more time than usual over the horses' high protein early morning feed, hoping she'd make it back to Milan in time to join me at work. Not for sex, too late for that. Work. But no, Happy had given up sleep and sex to bring back Flavia and Byron.

But she did show up at the stables we'd been allocated for trainers with horses entered into Milan's current races.

She busied herself with rags to block out draughts to protect our lot from catching colds during the autumn's longer, colder nights. I found her pale, and needing a shower when I returned with our string.

"Darling, how did it go at that Torre Palazonne place? Very elegant décor? Gorgeous antiques?" I asked, hurrying her to a rental car to return to our hotel.

"Didn't see no such elegant fixin's. Yeah man, Ah doesn't doubt thet the ho-tel had 'em, but Ah seen nothin' but a lobby and Byron's bedroom."

"Will Byron be up for rape? Rape of a minor?"

"Nah. Couldn't do it. Couldn't get inside her. All Hal's had to pay out was fo' the room. And the limo rides."

When we'd returned to our hotel, before Happy could get a shower or a kip, Fran arrived and was barking orders at me from the pensione's empty patio. "Get the best vet in this fucking town. I've heard from the lad that Aida's got heat in a foreleg."

"True. The vet's been already and assured me that with care she'll be able to run her race."

Fran bleated, "Why don't you ever tell me these things? Why do I have to get shitty news relayed by a stable lad?"

Rule Number Six for trainers, Never answer a question for which there's no easy reply. I ordered an expensive bottle of wine, although it was still mid-morning. When it arrived I lifted the bottle high to expose its label. "On me," I grunted, so that miserly Fran wouldn't think she'd have to pay for the wine.

After downing two quick goblets of Pouilly Fuisé, Fran relaxed and resumed yesterday's topic, talking about her favorite subject: herself, and her music career.

On the arrival of the bottle I'd ordered, Happy had left us to get some sleep. She knew that the wine was for Fran, and that Fran would most certainly drink up most of it, while doing all the talking.

Fran started straight away complaining about the first opera in which she was to appear. "Tomorrow night's arias are going to stink. Might as well put a male skunk in the audience."

"Has that ever been done?"

"Shit, don't you know anything about opera lore? Of course it's been done. And when I was a kid I remember reading how rats were loosed in London's Colisseum by an Orthodox Jewish group protesting some nazi conductor's appearance there."

I laughed, thinking that must have emptied out the hall faster than Fran singing with laryngitis.

A limo drew up outside the pensione. Uninvited, the Murphy couple had arrived. Hal and Mafalda entered the patio and joined us, but that didn't cramp Fran's verbal flow. She hardly welcomed them, and seemed resentful when two more goblets were brought out for them to share her bottle. After a very short "hello" she marched on with info about herself and her opera appearances.

"Tomorrow night's opera is ARIODANTE, and for once I get to play the lead role. There are so few of them for a contralto, or even for a deep mezzo soprano, which is what I really am. Usually, almost always I have the secondary role, as a maid or a priestess's acolyte, or whatever. I didn't mind when my twin Carla had the starring soprano role. I really loved the way our voices melded in our duets. But next Saturday, it's Wagner's PARSIFAL. Hate the damn thing, although I get to be Kundry. Damned opera takes five hours. Half the audience is asleep, and the standees have paralyzed legs."

Hal boomed, "PARSIFAL's wonderful. I've recorded The Pilgrims' Song from lots of different opera groups. You'll be great as Kundry. For once we opera buffs will get a woman in her thirties who doesn't weigh two hundred pounds."

Fran acted deaf to that comment. It didn't contain a big enough compliment to attract her attention. She spoke on, like a locomotive hauling endless cars with no caboose in sight. "If I could, I'd restrict myself to lyric operas. Or operettas, with happy endings. I hate sending my fans home with dour expressions because the star with the leading role has to die. Andrew Lloyd Webber's got it right. Keep the audience in a jolly mood."

Again I restrained myself. I didn't correct Fran with "What was the happy ending in EVITA, when she died of leukemia in her twenties? Where was the jolly mood in THE WHITE LADY? When she reappears as a ghost?" But there was no way I was going to take on Fran. I was spared the trouble by Mafalda.

"Fran, you wouldn't be so self-centered if you had a child. You and Jeremy should start a family."

"What!" Fran's exclamation could be heard on the pensione's top floor.

A Spanish-speaking hotel guest shouted down, *"Callase, no se da cuenta que estamos dormiendo?"*

To make sure that Fran understood she was to shut up, the Spaniard tossed a banana skin from his window. It narrowly missed Fran's head and landed flat in front of her place setting. On her plate it looked like a spent condom.

Acidly, Fran glared up at the third storey window and waved with the banana peel. No stopping our Fran! Then she rounded on Mafalda, "And be a perfect mother, like you?"

I'd never expected to see a courtesan blush, but Mafalda reddened.

Mafalda caught Fran's implied criticism of her mothering skills like a bullet between the eyes. But, she tilted against Fran, a female Don Quixote. "I knew you had a bad side," she spat out, "but you'd best aim your poison at somebody else. I can do poison too."

Hal pulled up a chair to sit between them. "Eh? What's going on here? Two beautiful ladies acting like cats with their claws out? We must be drinking the wrong wine. Waiter, bring us a magnum of Moet Chandon champagne."

Hal had never warmed to Fran. When their fillies ran against each other he would put on an act that he'd gone to Eton and believed in fair play. Adopted a MayThe Best Horse Win attitude. But under his hairy pelt there was a furnace burning with red coals.

Chapter 16

When my owners left, I rushed up the pensione's steps to our bedroom, Feeling horny, I was longing to have sex, but when I saw Happy sleeping peacefully I restrained myself in time not to wake her.

Instead, I sat down to the sparsely fitted desk to study the state of our finances. The pile of bills was daunting. I was deep into ways of paying them, when the bedside telephone jangled.

I heard Maheen on the blower.

"MR. HARROW, MAY I SPEAK TO MRS. HARROW, PLEASE?"

Happy's arm came waving from the bedclothes. I handed over the telephone.

Happy's face emerged, she clasped the telephone to one ear. "Wut can Ah do fo' y'all?"

"Mrs. Harrow, Flavia's back and now the whole school's been given a free day. Could you and I go see some of Milan's antiquities? I've just learned that the city's much older than I thought. Founded by Gauls, around 400 B.C. **Much before the Romans arrived. Could you pick me up?"**

Happy groaned. She looked at me with some desperation. I could read from her raised eyebrows that she felt she'd done enough for other people's children. She'd like a day with her own.

She was about to invent an excuse, but Amah knocked and entered our room with all four children neatly turned out for a nearby park. Happy had been finessed. Resigned, she tried to infuse her voice with some show of caring, and said: "Maheen, give me a couple of hours. Ah'll come fo' y'all after lunch."

"Oh, but Mrs. Harrow, there's so much to see. And who knows when the school will give us another away-day. Most of the other girls are going to a fashion show. There were tickets left for it in Nina's room, and the girls figured they'd plead misery and all get in."

"So y'all go to the fashion show too."

"No thanks. Antiquities! I've just read that a discovery was made in Pella, where Alexander The Great was born, with archeologists unearthing armor, jewelry, and pottery. Oh, if only someday I could be in on something like that! But, please, PLEASE, let's go see what we can today. You be here in an hour? I'm ready now."

When Happy reached the school she found Maheen reading the account of the archeological find in northern Greece. "Oh, Mrs. Harrow, the helmets were so beautifully worked, they were made of gold foil, and have pictures of lions and deer etched. Wonderful! Do look."

Happy didn't share her enthusiasm. Happy's interest was in old stones. But she read the article as a concession, and then bundled Maheen into the hired car that she had taken—with driver—for three hours.

Who was sitting in front with the driver? Byron Murphy!

"Uh, hello," Maheen said without much of a welcome. "You'd better keep out of sight at this school. You're persona non grata around here."

"Are those Latin words an invitation for us to hook up?" Byron gave out a huge laugh. "The headmistress and someone called Miss Draga have already seen me. They were all piling into a minivan to go to a fashion show. I'd come here to take another look at the girls in this school. All too tall, I felt like a hut among skyscrapers."

"Forget any hooking up. My, but you've got a nerve! Mind you, if you want to share our car, we're going to explore archeological sites. I wouldn't think they'd be your cup of tea. But if you have nothing else to do, and you're already in the car, I suppose we'll have to take you along."

"Tea? What a disgusting drink. My mother used to serve it as a big deal. Silver tray, with fancy pots for sugar and cream. Cakes, sometimes sandwiches. Sure, I'm going with you. You're the only girl in this damned school who's my size."

Happy felt her hackles rising. Having lived through the Fran Purcell saga when the singer was engaged to a man who was having sex with his sister, Happy distrusted Byron's light bantering. He'd tried to seduce Flavia. Was his new half-sister to be next on his list?

Their driver had been given instructions earlier as to the route to the site they'd chosen for today's adventure. All the way across busy Milan, Byron kept his body half turned to face the back seat with a running commentary on current events. He made fun of Italy's tired politicians, Washington's newcomers, and settled on criticizing a group of Canadians that he knew about but whose names meant nothing to Happy nor to Maheen. Flavia's name, pointedly, was not mentioned.

When the good part of an hour had passed and they had not arrived at their destination, Happy began to worry if the three hours she'd paid for were going to be enough to see the monument and get back to the school.

When she was about to suggest they turn back, an incredibly beautiful pile of ancient stones loomed in front of the car. They climbed out, Happy feeling stiff as if she'd been too long in a saddle. Maheen dumped her to run past a guard and ask for the gallery that contained the Roman antiquities.

Left with Byron, Happy paid the three entrance fees—two student discounts, please—and entered the monument's hall. She didn't like its musty smell. She followed Maheen into a tunnel-like exhibition area, where unlike in most of northern Italy there was air-conditioning to protect its valuable objects. In the way of modern museums, this two thousand year old building had been thrust into the Twenty-First Century by an intestine-like winding gallery where the exhibits were shown on black velvet bases like jewels in a Cartier window. The intestine's walls were covered in black velvet, giving a somber feeling like entering a subway station's deepest tube.

Ecstatic, Maheen pushed past tourists who were ahead of her in the line, and she was oh-ing and ah-ing, when Happy's cell phone rang. Trapped in the velvet walled intestine, Happy took the call although there were signs in three languages at the monument's entrance prohibiting the use of cell phones.

It was an hysterical Mafalda whose Egyptian voice pierced the intestine's heavy velvet gloom. "Hal's had a heart attack! We were making love, and suddenly he was clutching his chest. Maheen should come to our hotel immediately. And if you know how to find that spoiled son of his, Byron, phone him to hurry here too. Hal may be dying."

The "spoiled son" heard the call, being shoulder to shoulder with Happy in the intestine. He sneered, "The old goat deserves what he got. He and that Egyptian woman have been at it like rabbits for weeks now."

It wasn't easy to locate Maheen. She'd skipped through the intestine and hurried to two halls beyond.

When Happy caught up, she said, "Sorry, honey. We'alls got to cut this short. Your Mama just phoned t'tell usn thet yo'r step-Daddy's had a heart at-tack. We's goin' straight to their hotel. I'll telephone from there and explain you'll be late gettin' back to school."

Great wife and partner that she is, my dear Happy phoned me next and suggested I go to the hotel too. She added, "Ah reckons thet Mafalda wants Maheen there so's she has a chance to in-her-it some o' Hal's money. Make use of a deathbed scene. But y'all could ask what he wants to do about his horses. Run them here, anyways. Even when he may have flown back to Canada?"

Chapter 17

When I arrived, there was no deathbed scene in Hal's suite. He was sitting at the suite's private bar dispensing drinks to Mafalda and Byron. Maheen had to wait to delve in the bar's fridge for a diet coke.

On a cocktail table nearby were the paraphernalia of a local heart doctor. I watched while the doctor busied himself taking Hal's blood pressure and then listened to Hal's breathing through an old-fashioned stethoscope. Grey-haired, overly thin, wearing black Rip Kirby framed eyeglasses, and a shiny navy blue suit, his style matched the vintage of his instruments.

In a thick Lombardy accent he said in Italian, *"No capisco. Niente."* In halting English he added, "You go hospital. Not drink alcohol." He removed Hal's drink from his shaking hand. But he poured a fresh one for himself. This doctor was Old School, the kind that stuck fingers down Caruso's throat which gave that greatest of tenors the infection that killed him.

"Hello, Sir," I forced a cheerful grin for Hal. I wanted to insist he go to whatever hospital the doctor decreed, but Rule Seven for trainers dealing with owners is Don't Boss Them Around. "Why don't we all proclaim a day off from whatever we've been doing, and—"

"Hell, no." Hal's usually large voice had shrunk. "Who would be looking after my horses? Eh? We are all continuing as we have been and that includes me."

Again, I grinned, this time sheepishly. I was wondering if he and Mafalda would "continue as" with non-stop sex.

I walked the doctor to the suite's door, and mumbled, "Please send on your bill. Soon. As Mr. Murphy may be going back to Canada."

I accepted a double whisky from Hal and brought one to Happy. She looked as if she needed it, with no sleep and too many worries. She took a few swallows, but concentrated on what Maheen was saying. "Nina was fun, when she arrived from Russia. So green. So amazed by all the modern comforts we had at school. Modern comforts, in that place? But what the school had was still amazing for Nina. She seemed to have a big heart, and shared with the other girls the awful candies her uncle had given her as a goodbye present. I don't know how much she really changed. Maybe what I saw was a veneer to make us think she'd grown sophisticated, and that she was totally obsessed with becoming a famous model."

"Did y'all think Nina would be murdered? Seein' as how she were sleepin' in the same bed and had the same clo-set as the first roommate who was murdered?"

"No! Never crossed my mind, or any one else's. The two girls came from different worlds."

"But they both wanted to be famous models."

"So? You think there's something in my room? Buried treasure, or a stash of drugs? There isn't. I looked!"

"Ah hasn't got mah thinkin' goin' yet. Still, Ah'd feel less concerned if y'all moved into this here ho-tel."

Byron came leering, with his emptied glass in hand. "A room, all to yourself, Maheen. You could have visitors any time you like."

Mafalda joined them. "I've been looking for another school for you, Maheen. There's a modeling school in Nice, not too far over the border in France. Three year course. Teach you how to apply makeup, walk gracefully. That kind of thing. You could go there tomorrow."

"But I don't want to be a model. Anyway, I'm too short, and too chubby. You know I love antiquities. My dream is to be at a dig when a tomb is opened and I get to hold a bracelet that no one has had on for two thousand years."

"All those great treasure troves have been found," Mafalda shrugged.

"No. Last week one tomb showed up in Egypt with wonderful things, and in Central America they found a woman's mummy and she was wearing an incredible mask for a ritual sacrifice, while in Greece—well, I've told you that already—an archeologist dug up a huge cache of Macedonian helmets finished with real gold."

Hal's quavering voice crossed the room. "Come here, Maheen. I'll give you 100 euros and you can go exploring next weekend. And you, too, Byron, I've got plans for your weekend." He unfurled a roll of bills and gave each 100 euros. "Now I'm tired and I've had enough visiting. Going to go to bed. Live a little longer, eh?"

Mafalda immediately crossed the room and helped Hal to rise from his chair. She didn't have another word for Maheen. I've read that whores have hearts of gold, but that doesn't seem to apply to courtesans because considering Mafalda's track record of neglecting her daughter, I can be a witness to the fact that courtesans are only out for themselves.

Happy cut through the icy atmosphere like a knife though cheese. "Come on y'all, Ah's got the car and driver downstairs. Ah c'n take Maheen back to her school."

I said to Hal, "Goodbye, Sir. If you want us to, we'll look around again tomorrow after morning stables."

"Bye," Happy echoed.

Not a word from Byron, who was glaring at the 100 euro bill as if it had bitten him. How much should he expect to get? No goodbye for us. No goodbye from us to him, either.

We left the three Murphys in their suite, found the car, and I prepared to give a bonus tip to the driver for his lost time.

Nearing the school, Happy said, "How come the girls only needed a minibus? If all the girls went?"

"Not the day students. The day school is what keeps the school afloat. That, and the kindergarden. Draga's good with the little kids. Smiles a lot at them and plays funny Romanian games. No, it was the boarders who went, because Miss Parizzi wanted it."

"Would one of them boarders have Nina's iPod?"

"Don't know. Could be! But then that one must be lieing, because I've asked all of them and not one will admit to taking it. And honestly, I don't think they'd want it with all that uncool Russian jazz in it."

"Ask. Ah'd like to know wut happened to it." The car drew up to the school. An elderly porter opened the door to an empty building. Happy gave Maheen a hug. I started to, then thought better of it, considering how any gesture from an older man towards a girl can now label the man as a pedophile.

Instead, I gallantly opened the car door for her and stood by silently as she greeted the porter. She waved goodbye to us, the school's door closed behind her. Our car drove off.

And, at last, except for the driver I was alone with my wife. I felt like doing a Henry V calling out "To France," only my call would be "To Bed."

Chapter 18

Happy did her learned-from-television striptease act, then we cuddled, and I began love making by caressing the back of her neck the way she likes it. Happy responded like a cat in heat. Wonderful! Our bed creaked and we moved to the overstuffed armchair to make less noise. But we couldn't tone down Happy's shrieks of pleasure, because that's the way she goes when having an orgasm.

The following morning, sex wasn't on my mind. I appeared promptly at the stables for morning gallops, not looking my best without having shaved.

Our traveling stable lad, Saul, said, "Mr. Harrow, you copying the Italian actors who let their five o'clock shadows show?" He grinned, because we were on good terms and he knew I could take a bit of ragging. When I'd grinned in return, his face grew as solemn as an undertaker's. "Bad news about that Soviet filly. She's coming into season."

Rubbing my unshaved chin, I looked in on SOVIET SMILE. Yes, she was coming into season, lifting her elegant tail in an arc in an equine invitation for sex. Good God! This was Fran's finest filly, and her greatest chance for winning a decent prize.

What to do?

I went in search of Happy to get her advice.

She looked in on SOVIET SMILE, rubbed her neck and whispered in her ear. Giving the filly a kindly pat, Happy told me, "She's comin' into season, all right. But not fo' a few days. Has she any entries like fo' t'morrow?"

"Well, uh, yes. On the off chance that something could interfere with her running in the big Milan prize, I DID pay the fee for a minor race tomorrow afternoon. Winning that won't satisfy Fran."

"But it could help make SOVIET SMILE breedable with a good stallion. Go fo' it!"

"How about you and I go back to our pensione for a bit of breed-ability,"

"Sho 'nuf. But Ah's done quite enough breedin' with the four chillun we got. Ah's up fo' a bit of fun mo'e like. Got to be quick, though. Ah's promised Flavia Ah'd take her to to the big shows of this-here Milan Fashion Week."

A rule for trainers, Never Turn Down An Opportunity. We went back to the pensione. Amah had taken all four kids to a park, and we had a very satisfying "bit of fun."

Happy collected Flavia and they took the Milan underground to the first show for which Miss Parizzi had supplied tickets. Flavia was in raptures. "Oh, Armani has changed its look. No more neat hairdos. None of those ugly skullcaps he's been featuring. His clothes have loosened up a bit, but still they're very elegant."

Flavia twisted her body as if she was modeling.

Happy, even in her five inch high heels, had to crane to see anything. The tickets were for standees. Movie stars and zillionaires sat in the front seats and first rows that fringed the catwalk.

"See all those pretty dresses? With jackets! And vests with evening gowns. I love them," Flavia tried to get closer but was stopped by a mustached woman who was as tough as a warder in a prison.

Happy murmured, "Lookee, one of them models is a honest-to-God movie star herself, Kate Blanchette. Ah loves them croc shoes in a turquoise color she's wearin'! Them shoes match plenty o' other dresses in the show. Plenty turquoise. And yeah man, Armani do have some trousers, but worn with even' gowns. Not fo' me. Ah likes mah ridin' pants fo' the hosses and evenin' gowns fo' parties."

The girls couldn't make any comments at the next show. They were given seats at Missoni's but Happy pointed to a sign that requested silence next to the No Smoking order. A hurricane of futuristic colors pervaded the Missoni show. Angela Missoni had altered her past performances and introduced a streamlined modernistic look that combined elegance with geometric prints.

The girls had managed to get tickets on the Sunday for the Moschino Cheap & Chic presentation, that appealed to Happy because it featured lots of the bows of a type she used to wear in her hair back in her Kentucky hills. Flavia commented on the long hair the models had shown off, with no heavy backcombing. "That's how I like to do my hair!" she squeaked, causing neatly coifed heads to turn from the front row.

At Dolce & Gabbana, the girls were thrilled to see the famous Kate Perry, who sang at the Monday night event.

What really turned on Flavia, was the news broadcast there that Milan's Politecnico University would shortly be offering a Masters Degree for fashion industry people who wanted to become specialists in on-line fashion sales.

Flavia breathed heavily, "I see it says here that Giorgio Armani will provide a scholarship for that, and also give the students work experience at Emporio Armani's on-line store. That's for me! As soon as I can leave Miss Parizzi's I'll take a quickee degree that lets me qualify!"

"How could y'all hope—"

"Everything can be bought today. I'll get a degree. Listen, Armani's business generates $3 billion a year in sales. Mr. Armani himself has said that he wants a big Internet presence because that way his brand can expand beyond clients who need a store near where they live or travel."

The two girls next stop was to visit the distinguished Milan Politecnico. Its gracious last century architecture imposed a serious note. This was no two-bit mail-order university. Flavia listened intently to the description of courses detailed by a woman wearing flat shoes with a highly stylized dress, and a hairdo fitting for an actress in Gone With The Wind:little curls over her ears. "We will offer the courses you need," she spoke clearly and distinctly although in fractured English. "Business planning, store management, accounting, communication, and logistics. There will be courses run by fashion industry professionals. Executives who have excelled in this world."

Flavia, her purse bursting with pamphlets supplied by the Politecnico, was deposited back at her own run-down school by an exhausted, bored Happy.

Maheen was waiting for the two girls in the front hall. She treated Happy as if they were of equal ages, "Mrs. Harrow, I've found something wonderful. I've just read about the most terrific woman who was as ahead of her time as an astronaut would have been four hundred years ago. She lived around 1100 anno domini, and ran her estates like a man. When her husband became a pest, she had him murdered. How about that?"

"Not sho Ah likes thet type o' woman."

"Oh, but she ran wars too, and led her troops astride a famous white horse. She fought for the Pope, but when she died he wouldn't make her a saint, because of that business of having murdered a husband."

"Ah sho hopes not! Ah counts saints as very special people."

"Her name? Mathilda of Canossa. In that first millennium, she became the most powerful woman in Europe, because she became a player in negotiations between the Roman Catholic Pope of that time and the Emperor of the Holy Roman Empire. The Pope, Gregory VII, was having a hard time consolidating the Church's outlying interests, and trying to keep the Holy Roman Emperor, Henry IV, from taking them over. Countess Mathilda had a vested interest in backing the Pope, because he'd helped her to inherit her title, estates, and money. Henry IV had wanted her out of the loop by insisting on something called the Salic Law, which prevented women from inheriting. But the smart Pope put that law aside."

"Honey, Ah's so tired Ah cain't hardly understand wut you're tellin' me."

"I'm talking about an incredible woman. She led her army against Henry IV several times, although he was a sort of cousin through her first marriage, to the horrible Godfry, who was a hunchback."

"Maheen, please. Mah eyes are closin'. Let me go home to my babies."

"Sure. But not yet. I'll get you interested in Mathilda, when I tell you she also got rid of her second husband, Welf of Bavaria. Seems he couldn't do IT, couldn't get her pregnant. So, goodbye Welfie-boy. Who, by the way was much younger than Mathilda. I don't know if Mathilda had him killed or not, he just disappeared from the radar."

"Honey, will you call a taxi fo' me? Ah's too whipped to take a bus or the subway."

"Okay. But let me finish about Mathilda. She never had a child, she left everything to the Vatican. So there's a great painting there of her by Farinati, I think I've pronounced his name correctly, and a statue by Bernini. That name I know I get right."

"Don't give me no art names just now. Please, the taxi."

Maheen pulled out her cell phone from a pocket of her dress. She dialed and ordered the cab. Turning to Happy, she added with marked interest, "I'm so anxious to go see what's left of the castle of Carnossa. Will you take me there?"

Happy had guessed that request was coming. She waited until she heard a radio taxi honking its horn outside. "Yeah man, Ah supposes so. But mebbe folks ain't permitted to go there."

"Yes. We are. The public's encouraged to visit her castles and the monasteries she built. When can we—"

"Bye, Maheen. Ah'll let y'all know when Ah can help on this. But first, Ah's got to do some mighty impo'tant work with Fran's fillies."

Feeling considerable relief Happy left the school's front step and, with a cheerful grunt, entered the waiting taxi.

Chapter 19

Fran's fillies were not about to give Happy any easing of the stresses which had been plaguing her for weeks. SOVIET SMILE had not officially entered into season and was running. So was SOVIET BALLOON, Fran's newest acquisition.

A major problem rose because Hal's STORMING MELODY was entered in the same race as SOVIET SMILE, because that little winner had been expected to run the following week. STORMING MELODY, also new to the stable, had only been purchased and prepared for his career in the past month.

Hal had left for the South of France. We'd had e-mails from Roquebrune Cap Martin. He informed me later, by telephone, that he wanted to listen in to the race and I was to position my cell phone near the course's main microphone so he could hear how the race was run. His excuse was that in the very selective up-market hotel they'd chosen, there was no television that could show the Milan races.

I met Fran early, a good hour before the opening race. The Milan course was beautiful, those Italians certainly knew how to use the season's flowers to best advantage. Wonderful smell, oleanders mixed with horse poop.

Fran was in a strange mood. She was playing the opera star more than the racehorse owner. She started right in as the diva, "I feel nauseous, I'm so fucking worried I'll goof at the La Scala. Shades of Maria Callas! I simply can't fuck up this appearance tomorrow night. Get me a winner today, Rick. I need a god-damn lift."

"We'll be trying our best." I didn't mention the Coming Into Season problem.

"I've been warming up with some arpeggios, the voice responds, but I feel the acting isn't good enough. Clear, pellucid, that's what I demand from my singing. But, the acting? I feel it's wooden. Buggered."

Happy and I treated Fran to lunch in the course's most expensive restaurant. In character, Fran never attempted to pick up the check.

We went down to the paddock with the other owners. I stared at the women, wondering why in this worldfamous center of fashion, they dressed in dowdy clothes.

Like in the Aviary World, the males looked smarter, although I've never liked Italian tailoring with its high peaked lapels and nipped in waists. Nobody wore a hat, although the sun was shining quite overpoweringly.

SOVIET SMILE looked magnificent. That sunshine caught glints of red in her coat and I could have sworn I noticed a flirty look in her huge eyes.

This was a mixed race, for colts and fillies. Believe me, those colts certainly HAD noticed her flirtatious glances. That included Hal's untried colt.

Standing in the Owners and Trainers stand, Happy and I kept Fran company. Her nerves were terribly on edge, She repeated, "I can't get less applause at La Scala than Bruno got. I just damned well can't."

She didn't notice that as the competitors galloped down to the starting gates, all the colts stayed back behind SOVIET SMILE. I certainly knew why: those colts had become aware that she was coming into season and they all wanted to be in the BEHIND position. Oh, oh. That wouldn't bode well for Hal's colt. Hal, no nouveau in the racing world, Hal could take his horses from my stable if he felt I'd done him wrong by putting his colt in a race with a filly coming into season.

The gates went up, the contenders bolted out. Of course, SOVIET SMILE was left alone in front, with the exception of a local Italian filly who was accustomed to getting her oats at this racecourse.

Down the course they raced. Oh God, STORMING MELODY had got a favored position on the rails. Rule 153 in England forbids a runner to make a manoeuvre in the interest of another from the same stable. And, YES, now STORMING MELODY eased away from the rails just as SOVIET SMILE had fallen back to get her second wind, and THEN ENDED UP IN THAT SAME POSITION ON THE RAILS. Oh my God, I hadn't warned the jockey not to do that, because I'd felt that STORMING MELODY was so green that he'd never get that position. I could be fined $5000 or more, and called up in front of the Jockey Club for not giving sufficient instructions before the race. I'd gone into detail with SOVIET SMILE's jockey, because I truly felt she'd have a good chance of winning. But there was an added reason why I hadn't counseled my other jockey: he was Italian and didn't speak English. And I still don't speak enough of that language to give meticulous instructions to a jockey.

I knew of important trainers who'd been called up before the BHA recently for using a pacemaker to take a good place on the rails, with orders to relinquish it to the stable's real contender.

There goes my reputation, and there goes my favorite owner!

Fran was still on her emotional landslide, worse than a rock falling precipitously during an avalanche.

But her filly won!

Now I was really for it. Trouble! With a capital T.

In all the excitement, I'd forgotten to dial Hal's number on my cell phone. Oh, but he'd be sure to read about what happened in THE RACING POST tomorrow.

While Fran received her small trophy, and I was presented by the racecourse execs with a watch, I noticed there was no gift for our winning jockey. All the execs acted as if he smelled as bad a five day old carcass.

Tomorrow was going to be a busy day, what with expecting an early morning call from Hal, and having to escort Fran to her performance at La Scala in the evening.

Chapter 20

But Happy wasn't in on any of that. Because the next morning the telephone rang very early. And the caller wasn't Hal.

It was an extremely flustered Flavia on the blower.

"Mrs. Harrow, please. Happy? Terrible news. Maheen never came back to school last night. Police are combing the canal for her body. Please come!"

Happy threw on her riding clothes and raced for the subway. She arrived at Flavia's school in time to find her young friend in the hall, waiting for a taxi.

"Oh, Mrs. Harrow. Thank goodness you've come. I've figured out where Maheen could be. Mantua, or in the near vicinity. I've asked Miss Parizzi's permission to go there. Got it. Tell me, do you have a credit card? The taxi could cost a small fortune."

"Credit card. Yeah man, but I ain't got no right to spend a lot of money. Not with four chillun needin' mountains of things."

"Won't Mr. Murphy pay you back, if you bring home his step-daughter?"

Happy thought over that possibility. A *yes* came up. "Ah says we goes."

Group singing interrupted her thoughts. "What's thet?"

"The kindergarten. The little kids have a singing lesson at this hour. They're singing a Romanian shepherd's tune that Draga taught them. She wrote words in Italian for them. 'I love life, I love music. I love fun.' Like that. And then the kids make up their own lines."

"No foolin'? Like wut?" Happy supposed she could teach our own "chillun" such a song.

"Like 'I love candy' or 'I love toys.'"

"Wut they singin' now?"

Flavia wrinkled her pert nose. "'I love TV.'"

"And is that Draga who's playin' the pi-ano fo' the chillun?"

"No. It's Miss Parizzi. She gave Draga the day off."

A taxi's horn tooted outside. "Wut we waitin' fo'?" Happy grabbed Flavia's right hand and pulled her to the front door.

In the taxi, Flavia made excuses. "Mrs. Harrow, I'm sorry to call you away from your husband. I watched the races yesterday and learned he's in trouble."

"Yeah man. Deep trouble. He's speakin' today to the execs of the Milan raceco'se."

"Awful for him. But he's got such a fine reputation, I'm sure they'll find him innocent of any conniving with the jockeys."

"Won't help none if we lose our two top owners. We'll be out of business.'

"That's not going to happen. Let's talk about something else. I want to fill you in on what motivated Maheen to rush off to the Mantua region."

"Go ahead. Ah's listenin'."

"Miss Parizzi gave us a lecture yesterday on the great women of the early days of the last millennium. Started with Queen Isabella, called the She-Wolf. She was married to the homosexual Edward II, who gave away her jewels and their wedding presents to his boy-friend Gaviston. She gave Edward II four children, but fell in love with a guy she met in The Tower, called Mortimer. They escaped together and raised an army in the Low Countries to invade England in September 1326, and capture Edward, whom they murdered. In fact, she was the last person to successfully invade England and kill its reigning monarch."

"Don't sound like no nice lady."

"Strong lady. There was also Eleanor of Aquitaine, who married first a French King, then an English King. Two of her sons became Kings of England, but she may have murdered her third son who wasn't very smart. According to Miss Parizzi the greatest of all the early ladies was Queen Elizabeth the First. But she ordered or permitted the murder of her cousin, Mary Queen of Scots. Not such a nice lady, either. We come to Countess Mathilda, who lived in a much earlier time, the Twelfth Century. She was another who was a murderer, and who led armies. She murdered her first husband, a hunchback, and maybe her second husband too. Maheen became determined to see Countess Mathilda's castle. Not that far from here, some miles outside of Mantua. Isabella, Eleanor, and Elizabeth had their castles in England, all too far away for her to go to just now."

"But Maheen liked early Roman ruins. Or the Gauls'. Why somethin' from the Twelfth Century?"

"Don't know. But I'll bet my allowance that she's gone to see Mathilda's castle."

Happy, exhausted, fell asleep for the remainder of their long journey. It was twilight when they arrived at Castle Canossa. It stood in approaching darkness, its eroded towers looming high against the sapphire sky, like Druids from a pagan ceremony who had turned to stone.

After giving orders to the taxi to fix a path with its headlights, Happy led Flavia carefully up a worn lane. Treading now with extreme caution, they approached the ruin's main tower. It had square openings where windows had once graced its façade. Suddenly the pin-point of a flashlight could be seen ahead. The gaping windows offered weird lighting. They heard footsteps running. The flashlight's beam arced, faded.

Someone screamed.

Happy shoved Flavia into a safe doorway and sped ahead. Her taxi's beam had less force as she went forward, but she managed to recognize two figures: Maheen's and Draga's. It was Draga who was screaming.

Maheen had positioned Draga to have no escape from being pushed down the castle's well.

Pummeling her hard, Maheen had the winning clout. Thrashing from side to side, attempting to avoid Maheen's blows, Draga's angled face had diminished from a wolf's to a drenched pussycat's. Gloom had taken control there. Her mouth was an elliptic O, like in the painting by Edvard Munch, The Scream. But no further noise came out of it.

With one great push, Happy ended the fracas. Separating Maheen from Draga, she would have posed a few questions, but Draga suddenly pulled a long knife from a sleeve. She attacked Happy, who slid away as if a competing horse had tried to take her daylight, and instead slashed at Draga with her jockey whip.

Happy's whip was never far from hand, because she kept it in her boot. Now she hit Draga aiming for the wrist wielding the knife. Many a dangerous colt had been bested by Happy's whip. Draga would prove no match for it. She dropped the knife, and ran.

She ran straight down the path lit by Happy's taxi, but swerved at the end to dash for the rental car that Maheen had leased for their trip here.

Revving the motor, Draga sped away in a zigzag course. Evidently, she had had little practice driving since getting her license.

Happy, Maheen, and Flavia crowded into the taxi. Happy gave the timeless order: "Follow thet car."

Not easy. Draga's erratic driving gave no indication of what she would do next. On the motorway, she opened up to 120 kilometers per hour.

The taxi driver objected to keeping up. "Me lose license," he complained. "You'd guessed Draga was the killers?"

"Sho 'nuf. Ah's know fo' some time thet someone in the school be thet monster. Once Maheen showed me thet el-e-vator she called 'a dumb waiter' Ah guessed thet the two girls' bodies went down to the basement in thet. Packed in garbage bags after the killer cut 'em. Each transferred to a suitcase. Then taken out through thet abandoned coal chute."

"Why to the Navigli Grande Canal?"

"So's the models there'd take no-tice. Thet's how Ah dis-re-garded any idée o' Miss Parizzi. She's a passive do-nothin' gay, and just enjoyed lookin' at beautiful girls who wanted to be models. Not see them daid. It *had* to be Draga, once Ah'd learned me thet she wanted to be a model. Givin' due warnin'. Thet's wut she was up to. Ah didn't know none about her knives. But Ah'd guessed it had to be someone higher-up than no student 'cause she'd need a pri-vate bathtub fo' cuttin' the bodies in. The students had to share."

The taxi would have lost Draga's rear lights if an alert motorway police officer from Lake Garda had not pushed to block Draga's onward rush. With a colleague, he rode ahead to a junction where Draga could be netted. She was.

Happy's taxi driver pulled up alongside the motorcycle policemen. Happy and Maheen confronted them.

Because Happy could not speak Italian, Maheen did the talking. She explained to the policemen that Draga was going to be indicted for the murder and dismembering of two of her school's students. Maheen displayed the long knife that Draga had used to threaten Happy.

Not buying Maheen's story outright, the policemen nevertheless manacled Draga and placed her in a newly arrived third policeman's car, which had stopped at the junction.

It was the taxi driver who convinced the Lake Garda policemen that Draga had pulled that knife on Happy.

She was allowed to speak to Miss Parizzi, using the first policeman's cell phone. Miss Parizzi confirmed that Flavia and Maheen were both students at her boarding school, and had permission to go to the Canossa Castle. Miss Parizzi did not offer a comment on Draga's character, adding only that she had given Draga permission to go to the Canossa Castle as a chaperone for Maheen.

Had Miss Parizzi had a secret lust for Draga. And couldn't bring herself to condemn a would-be lover?

The police officer took note of The Parizzi School's telephone number, inscribing it carefully in a worn Morocco leather notebook.

Relaxing back in the taxi, heading for Milan, Happy grilled Maheen. "Wut you be about, tryin' to shove Draga into thet well? Become like her, a murderer?"

"You forget Mrs. Harrow, that I'm an Egyptian. Egypt has a long history of strong women who believe in revenge. That damned, and I mean *damned to Hell* woman, Draga, had killed the two people closest to me in all my life. Really, the only people I've ever loved. My best roommates ever. But no, I wasn't going to kill her. Scare her! I knew that the well was dry and filled with rocks almost to the brim. She'd have fallen a few feet and maybe bruised herself. I wanted her to confess. LOOK! I'd brought a pocket tape recorder!"

"Thet be no good. Wouldn't be wut lawyers call 'ad-miss-able in court.'"

"Those policemen ended believing me. Want to learn a secret? One of the policemen, the short tubby one, the officer, he ran his hand up my skirt when I sat in the car with him."

"Ah sho hopes y'all give him a sharp slap."

"No. I liked it. Felt delicious."

"Sho 'nuf! Maybe it be time fo' y'all to enjoy a good man's lovemakin'."

"Not so lucky. Being groped in the back seat of a car isn't my idea of enjoying lovemaking. And you heard Fiona in Veintimiglia. How she told me I was too short and my boobs too big for any man to want me."

"Maheen, there be many stocky guys who prefer a tiny woman. Them towering gals make them feel like pygmies. Boobs too big? For modelin' clothes, maybe. But most real men like big boobs. Mah Rick says like he gets pleasured mo'e when Ah's pregnant and mah boobs swell to twice their normal size."

"Easy for you to talk. You've got your man. But my mother will keep me in schools where I won't meet a nice guy. She'd hate for me to get married, and have a baby making her a grandmother. No, my life won't change. Things will just go on being rotten."

"Ah believes in good changes happenin' like when Rick says *God's in his heaven and all's well with the world.*"

"All the changes I see are for the worse."

"Ah can tell y'all about a real good change. When Ah first went to Dubai, the A-rabs had camel races where three-year-old boys was used as jockeys. When a toddler fell off and broke his neck, he'd be replaced by another toddler. Reason bein' thet a toddler weighs less than a grown man, and them camels will race fo' water no matter who's in the saddle. Ah told lots of folks about this, and now the camels have mechanical jockeys on them. No mo'e kiddies diein' after a fall from them camels. These mechanical jockeys are fitted out with a cap and jacket in the racing colors of their owners and even have a mechanical whip thet twirls like the real thing. Now thet's a change fo' the better."

"You would try to explain away my doubts with a racing story! I tell you, I'm never going to find the man for me."

"Sho 'nuf, if'n y'all stays on yourn butt. Got to get out in the world. Make a move. Why not give the Lake Garda policeman a try? Ah's heard tell thet Lake Garda be a most ro-mantic place."

"I'll believe that when he puts a ring on my finger. But God won't let that happen."

"Why so? God's great."

"I hardly believe in one. What with my roommates being murdered, and my mother not giving a damn about me, how can I believe in a personal God! Someone wonderful I can pray to?"

"God exists. Ah knows it. Gives mah life meanin' and Ah also needs thet poss-i-bility thet Ah goes t' Heaven someday. Meet the Mama Ah never knew. Thanks to a God wut's fine, 'n lovin', 'n comfortin', 'n forgivin' which is why Ah takes me to church. Y'all would feel better about things if'n y'all went to church, too."

"Mosque. I'm a Muslim."

"So? Y'all thinks thet Buddhists, and Taoists, and the Jewish people, plus all them other faiths of Ah don't know them names . . . Thet the moniker makes a bit of difference when they pray? Their God's just as wonderful. Probably the *same* one, called somethin' else. You be Muslim? Well, thet's fine. Just as long as y'all *does pray.*"

"Happy, you guessed it, didn't you? That I was praying up there at the Canossa Castle? I didn't mean to. The prayer just popped out. I didn't want to die. Not just yet. And until you hit the Dragon Lady with your whip, I thought we'd both be carved up with her knife. So I called on Allah to save us."

Happy let out one of her huge laughs and gave Maheen a hug.

Flavia had been listening to all this talk, and had little to add. She just breathed out: "Wow."

When *they* arrived back at the school, Miss Parizzi stood looming like a gargoyle in the doorway. "Hurry, Maheen. You are wanted on the telephone by the La Garda polizia."

Trembling, whether from nerves or anticipation, Maheen strode quickly to the hall telephone and put the receiver to her ear. Instead of dire pleas, a waterfall of flirty come-ons poured from her bulbous lips following a brief bit of wordage from the La Garda police officer; obviously that same one who had made a play for her in the rear of his car.

When the call ended, Maheen crossed to where Happy had sat down on the one available chair. "Guess who!" she caroled, and hugged herself.

Miss Parizzi wasn't finished with Maheen. "Your mother has been screaming at me down the wire. She says you're to leave the school and go to Mrs. Harrow's pensione."

Her tone implied "good riddance."

Joyfully, Maheen stopped hugging herself to hug Happy. "Come on! Come on, let's leave this damn school. I don't want a single thing from my room. 'Uncle' Hal can buy me a new wardrobe. But I won't be getting it from the Navigli Canal shops. I'll go back to Lake Garda to buy everything there."

By the time Maheen and Happy reached the pensione, I'd already taken a room for his step-daughter on Hal's orders. But I made very sure the room was on another floor. I didn't want Maheen to hear us making love. Happy makes such a lot of noise when she has an orgasm. I wouldn't want Maheen to learn too soon what she could enjoy with her Lake Garda policeman.

And Maheen did find love with her short, tubby guy. It turned out that his grandmother was an Ethiopian, brought from Africa by his soldier grandfather when Italy abandoned its imperialist plans. An African-born girl with Upper Egypt connections was just that polizia's dream for the love of his life.

Maheen found plenty of 'old stones' to survey in the lake district.

With a five hundred euros allowance from Hal with which to refill her closet, Maheen had convinced Happy to travel to Lake Garda to raid its shops and search out antiquities. Up, up into the higher mountains they drove in a rental car, leaving dusty Milan far behind. The air became purer, the birds sang in larger groups, the late flowers sent out delicious scents.

"It's like having an early Christmas holiday, coming up here." Maheen seemed to grow taller as she sat up straight, corrected her posture, and grabbed one final dollop from Miss Parizzi's teachings: "bust up, bottom tucked, shoulders down, neck long."

Her police officer was wearing civvies when they arrived at the Cielo Bellissimo shop he'd advised them to visit. He didn't look as dashing without his uniform. His brown-as-old-wood hair was receding. A fact that had been hidden by his uniform's cap. His suit was poorly cut, and his tie was too big and garish.

London educated Maheen never flinched. "I love your name, Luca Palacio," she said dreamily.

"How you find my name?" The officer chortled. He would have been delighted with Maheen's opening words if she'd said she liked pigs.

"I telephoned ahead to the Captain at your station. My name's Maheen. I was born in Egypt, but my father was probably Ethiopian. My mother won't discuss anything about him. So far as she's concerned, he never existed."

"An Immaculate Conception?" Luca pushed ahead into the shop. "Your mother must be like an amoeba."

"No. Like something else." Maheen cut short any further comments.

When Luca demonstrated a certain controlling attitude by proceeding to choose Maheen's clothes for her, Happy kept her distance and let the two get at being romantic in their own ways.

Strolling from the shop, Happy peered out at the lake with a pivoting glance that swung like the beam of a lighthouse. The jagged mountains had become swathed in advancing mists. The puttering tourists' boats melded into its horizon like so many lost birds. She'd heard that Mary Shelley had been inspired to write about Frankenstein's monster while staying at a nearby lake, and did not doubt that the eerie atmosphere would have launched that story. She shivered.

Returning toward the town, she shrugged at the Moorish window treatments of some of the houses. "They ain't be old 'nuf to in-ter-est me!"

Back in the shop. Luca was telling Maheen about his beloved Ethiopian grandmother. Maheen was blooming, and had been transfigured into a pretty girl.

Happy, glad to see what a becoming change had come over her short fat friend, teased her, "Maheen, y'all has become a flirt."

Luca invited the two girls to a pizza parlor. It was crowded with large Italian families that included grandmothers, mothers and mothers-in-law, fathers, fathers-in law and a multitude of gorging children. The place was surprisingly quiet, because every last guest was too busily eating, for conversation.

Not so Maheen and Luca. Leaving Happy out of it, they proceeded to further their probings about each other's earlier lives, their hopes, and preferences.

"I like coffee ice cream," Maheen said.

"I like coffee ice cream too." Luca echoed.

"I want to go to see those ancient columns at Axum, from Ethiopia's earliest history. Maybe from the time of the Queen of Sheba."

"My lovely grandmother told me she'd been to Axum. Seen them. She was one of the people who signed the demand that Italy return the monument from Axum that Mussolini stole. And was so pleased that it is now back in place in Axum."

"Oh Luca, would you be a sport and go south to the Italian border with France, where there's a huge column I want to see at a place called La Turbie?"

"Bella, of course I go. We go together!"

The following day Luca drove Maheen and Happy to La Turbie to see the Roman monument there. Not enough! Not for the two amateur archeologists. Maheen and Happy convinced Luca to extend their trip to Rome, to see its Colisseum, Flavion's amphitheater, the Arch of Constantine, and the Forum.

Thanks to Maheen and Luca, Happy saw plenty of 'old stones' before we left Italy.

But eventually I had to claim her and refocus that incredible energy back to horseracing. No argument. Happy, satiated with "old stones," launched herself into reprising her newest interest: championing the rights of women jockeys to get an equal chance at the best races.

After all, ten per cent of $1 million was $100,000 while ten percent of an off-day's small race tag of $4000 was a mere $400. Hardly worth risking your neck for.

With the passing of the weeks we'd been in Italy, our fillies had easily adapted to the local hay and water. They weren't as comfortable with the going at the track, but when the harsh summer drought eased into autumn's gentle rains, they took more readily to their gallops. Morning stables, evening stables, they worked well. I clocked their speeds, which increased daily.

"Ah spoke to Soviet Lil this mornin' 'n she told me as how the miseries in her hooves done faded away."

Happy managed to help our other best filly by eradicating the heat in her foreleg. Happy had written to her Pa for a tried-and-true Kentucky balm which had done the trick. Believe it or not, made of roosters' combs.

The afternoon of Soviet Lil's race threatened us with too much rain. The Milan sky glowered and raged like an unkind mother-in-law. There was thunder and its bride, lightning. But the short squalls that hit the racecourse were over by the time our filly ran. She loved the ground. In the top fillies' race she ate it up, her cured hooves flying out of the mud while the other fillies struggled to pull theirs out of the mire. Happy had made her point about giving good rides to girl jockeys and Fran had agreed for this filly to have a woman in the saddle. Experienced and brilliant, this woman helped her mount to ease past all the other contenders and breeze up toward the Finish Line. SHE WON.

So it was that on this particular rain-threatened afternoon a girl jockey was to get her ten per cent from a worthwhile purse.

Happy's campaign was working. Very often previously, girl jockeys earned ten per cent of miserable purses that barely paid the rent in a pensione.

I heard a familiarly strident voice coming over the rails from the Visitors' stands. Pointing to a smaller race with a purse in liras amounting to less than $2000, "Hardly worth risking your neck for!" commented Maheen to Luca, the two having arrived for our race to cheer the filly to the Finish Line.

Personally, I was content with the watch I'd won thanks to the filly's success at the race course. And, of course, I felt relieved that my stable would get *its* ten percent of the prize money. God knows, our home near Epsom was prone to a leaking roof and the stables needed constant damp eradication. Our ten percent would disappear fast enough when we returned to Epsom.

Fran wasn't so content with *her* winnings, because she didn't manage to squeeze them quickly out of those "Ities." On the race card a sizeable prize was listed. But she was made to wait for her money, a wait which I knew could mean a period of several years. And Fran loves money so much!

A surprise bit of news meant that Fran could put some of her promptly-paid earnings from singing at La Scala to good use. Her news? Fran was pregnant! She admitted to Happy that when Jeremy came to Milan to hear her sing in AIDA he got her pregnant. They'd celebrated later in bed, downing champagne while they exulted she'd ended her La Scala season with a triumph. Great! Happy and I could look forward to judging her talent as a mother.

Lucky Jeremy. Maybe he would have an heir for his title.

I was truly glad for Jeremy. I wasn't about to be a snitch and tell him about her sex detour with Bruno.

Jeremy kept repeating non-stop what bliss he'd enjoyed between the sheets with Fran. Ha! No way would that compete with the rapture I get in bed with my Happy!

THE END

Madrid's Mocking Murders

CHARACTERS Madrid's Mocking Murders

Rick Harrow, a British trainer of racehorses
Hillary aka Happy Harrow, Rick's Kentucky hills wife, an apprentice jockey who moonlights as a sleuth
Hal Murphy, Rick's most generous owner
Mafalda Murphy, Hal's ex-courtesan wife
Maheen, Mafalda's seventeen-year old daughter
Luca Palacio, Italian police officer in love with Maheen
Fran Purcell, Lady Cabrach, Rick's opera star owner
Earl of Cabrach, Fran's ex-M15 husband
Brian Murphy, Hal's rebellious difficult son
Rick's Dad, who visits the younger Harrows
Nashville Mary, who becomes Dad's girlfriend
Lord Hogan, a mysterious Blairite peer
M. Talleyrand, a flirt
Monsieur Germain Galé, rich textile industrialist
Madame Eva Galé, his reserved but elegant wife
Giselle Pont, warm-hearted mother uncaring wife
Dr. Pont, distant father and husband
Ghislaine Pont, fourteen-year old, loves to collect recipes
Norman Steele, a hustler portrait painter
Sadie Hogan, lives as Lord Hogan's daughter, she has a secret
Madrid doctor
Hotel manager and wife
The Harrow children, Timothy, Dorothy, Irish, Richard

Cove Creek and son

Chapter 1

It was just before midnight, with a gale blowing. I had my long legs scissored while I sat by the telephone in my tack room waiting to hear whether Fran's best mare had yet foaled.

Fran Purcell, one of England's most famous opera stars, had recently added to her professional name of Purcell the title of Countess of Cabrach. Fran's husband's uncle had just died, which meant he was no longer in waiting as the Hon. He had inherited and become an Earl. Fran's title had increased her demanding ways to volcano pitch. Like flaming lava flowing down towards a helpless village, her telephone calls burned into my tack room.

"Fuck you," the new Countess exploded with her customary rough language. "If you lose this mare's foal, I'll take away every ounce of my horseflesh training in your stable."

The telephone rang again as soon as I'd replaced the receiver. With the calm tone of a much experienced vet, Dr. Morse said, "It's time. But it looks like a breech birth. You'd better come to her stall, Mr. Harrow."

Very bad news. I knew he didn't want the responsibility of proceeding with a caesarian. Astute Dr. Morse wanted me to carry the burden.

I rushed to Soviet Gal's stall. She lay on clean straw, her huge brown head in my wife's lap.

Baptized Hillary, my wife goes by the nickname Happy, because generally she has an extremely joyful manner. Tonight, she was weeping. Fat tears trickled down to the end of her pert nose. She wiped them Kentucky style, with the back of her free hand. With her right hand she stroked Soviet Gal's tangled mane while attempting to whisper in her ear.

Happy alleges she talks to our string. After a sloppy kiss on the mare's cheek, Happy moaned to me: "This here po'r mare done got the same problem as 'most killed me with our Dorothy in Dubai. Tell Dr. Morse he c'n cut her. Please! She's sufferin' somethin' awful."

Compassionately, I listened. But the loss of Fran's bloodstock would ruin our stable. I knew I had to be highly professional in this case. I turned to Dr. Morse, who already had Soviet Gal's blood on his birthing apron. I groaned: "What's your final say?"

"With your go-ahead, I'll do the caesarian. No chance otherwise. Too much blood lost. Both the mare and the foal will die, if I don't operate."

I nodded. With my right thumb I made an upright sign, meaning "Go for it!"

Dr. Morse produced an enormous needle. I knew what it contained. Anesthetic. He plunged the needle home. Soon Soviet Gal's bulging eyes closed. Not in death. She kept breathing throughout Dr. Morse's messy procedure. Many minutes after watching the vet pull at four tiny hooves, she foaled.

I took the goo-covered foal in my arms and sucked into its mouth. A male, he expelled a jaw full of goo AND BREATHED! Now both mare and foal were breathing normally, and I could relax. But Happy didn't relax. Still crouched beside Soviet Gal, she wiped at the goo and blood that had spilled on to her jeans, but maintained her vigil.

We both knew that the foal should try to stand and begin to nurse from between one to six hours from now. Happy could be very stiff in her joints by morning.

But the miracle of birth hadn't ended. Soon Soviet Gal slowly opened her enormous eyes to gaze at her foal. I'd placed him in the straw near her nose. She could enjoy the scent of him! She nuzzled her foal and then tried to rise. Her operation had been well sewn up and bandaged, but it must have been extremely painful for Soviet Gal to get erect. Finally, she managed that and began to lick off the goo that was still all over the foal. When that was completed, the foal tried to get up. He first took a stance on his knobbly knees. With eyes wide open and ears cocked slightly backwards, he wove and ducked until, ANOTHER MIRACLE, he stood. Now he was high enough to search for Soviet Gal's sweet little udder. It had several nipples, but fortunately we hadn't had in that birth what is so dreaded by trainers: twins. Only one nipple was needed. This little foal cocked his head and began to suck. Crises over!

Reeling, needing to clutch at a hay rack, Happy drew herself to a position where she could caress the mare. Not the foal. No. Happy had more sense than to intrude on Soviet Gal's mothering.

Together we thanked Dr. Morse, who had steadfastly remained nearby swilling cups of our awful coffee. Then we trailed back up the manure-strewn path to our cottage.

Too early to telephone Fran with the good news! So we went to our own bed. Not to make love. To sleep.

Chapter 2

Fran Purcell, the very grand Countess of Cabrach, had no qualms about waking *us* up. With a shrill voice she berated me for not giving her the news that Soviet Gal had given birth to a colt and that both had weathered the night.

"Can't you ever do anything right?" Fran ended her tirade. Yes. I'd won seven races for her on three continents, surely *that* should be counted as RIGHT.

Calmly, almost reverently as I judged was expected by the new Countess, I smoothly said: "Now you've got a foal. With any luck he should be running in two years and then at three maybe he'll make good at classic distances."

"Up your ass! I want to know if Soviet Gal will be racing again soon."

"Happy says that Soviet Gal told her she's in the brooding mood now. Wants a stallion, not a Finishing Post."

"Shit! Well I'll let that go for the moment. I have other plans on the griddle. Plans that concern me."

In a surprisingly diplomatic tone, Happy proceeded to speak to Fran, having grasped the telephone receiver. "Hi, y'all. Wonderful thet yourn Soviet Gal got through thet caesarian. Ah knows how tough thet can be. Ah's had one of them too. Wut news y'all goin' to tell usn?"

Speaking in a high ground accent learned from her cradle, which was not a cockney one, Fran scolded grandly: "You wouldn't know what a ZARZUELA is, dear Happy. In your Kentucky hills the people won't know about Zarzuelas. But I'll explain it to you: it is a form of country folk music from old Spanish times adapted to fit a play. The form is old and stale. Audiences dwindled to nobody in the largest Zarzuela theatre in Madrid, so it's been converted to an opera house. And I've been offered the star roles in two new opera productions there."

I guessed what was coming next. Spot on. Fran now told us that we were to pack our bags to take two of her best fillies to Madrid to race in upcoming classics there. And, as she had so often before, she'd added we were not to bring our four children. She wouldn't be paying for lodgings big enough for six and their Amah.

"Right you are, Countess," I said, to oil things using her much-belated title, "but we'll pay for our own rooms, and Happy will insist we take along our 'chillun'."

I well knew the dates for those Madrid classics.

With Happy's help I slaved to bring Fran's fillies up to condition to race them in time. Not easy. Her fillies had been given too much work this year and were tiring of the game. Like Soviet Gal, at least one of them was getting broody and longed to be covered by a stallion. Fran, penny pinching as ever, wouldn't pay the going prices for the great stallions and for now I preferred to go on racing these two, rather than having one or both sent to inferior bloodlines.

Only days away from our flight to Madrid, I received an entirely different set of orders from Fran. "Fuck it, I've decided to give those two fillies another chance before they go to Madrid. I want you to pack them off to Germany."

"Baden Baden."

"Exactly. That shitty Iffezheim race course."

"Countess, it's too late for me to enter them in any decent races there."

"You managed to get Hal Murphy's slogger into the Kentucky Derby last year."

"Hal Murphy was prepared to pay an enormous late fee charge."

"If these races are small ones, my fillies will win them! Worth it. Pay!"

"Countess, your two fillies will be worn out by the time the Madrid races get going."

"The hell you say! I'll be the judge of how much racing they can bear. Pay! Ship them out tomorrow. And you be there in Germany to receive them." She hung up.

I dialed her cell phone. "Countess," I poured on with the title, "I can't make it tomorrow. I've got a runner at Doncaster."

"Send the stable lad to represent you. MY fillies go to Iffezheim tomorrow. I HAD intended to go watch my fillies there myself, but Prime Minister Gorden Brown is permitting my Jeremy to make his maiden speech in the House of Lords tomorrow. Unusual, to say the least. But then, Jeremy had served his country well when he was in MI5."

I noticed that Fran didn't leave off Gordon Brown's title. All titles meant a lot to Fran now. She'd adore being in SPAIN WITH ITS VIBRANT MONARCHY, WHERE HER TITLE WILL RESOUND SPLENDIDLY. Or so I'm sure she supposed.

Happy had turned on the speaker phone and listened attentively. Once the call from Fran had finished, she asked me, "Ain't Fran very pregnant to be startin' a new contract singin' in thet there Madrid?"

I nodded. "Jeremy may want to slow her down; he's really excited about having an heir."

"Maybe a girl," Happy laughed playfully. "Grow up to be a jockey, not a countess."

I dutifully sent off Tom, my head lad, to represent me at Doncaster. And our horse lost. Fortunately that horse belonged to Hal Murphy, the least demanding owner in our stable.

All for nothing. The Iffezheim executives wouldn't relax their rules for a hefty payment, and Fran's fillies were denied a chance to run in this week's races. Thank God. I hated the prospect of ruining two fine future mares their chances in Madrid where winning would guarantee they would be accepted as brides for the best stallions.

Chapter 3

Before we left for Madrid, I followed Fran's lead and attended Jeremy's big day at the House of Lords. Feeling loyal to Jeremy after he'd acted so selflessly to help my Happy when she was abducted in Dubai, I couldn't let his installation be missed.

It's always a treat to go to the Upper House. I admire its great classic architecture, even if it isn't that ancient, having been rebuilt when most of the older building burned down. I strolled through its really ancient mead hall with the high rafters overhead still containing tennis balls from the Sixteenth Century when the future King Henry the Eighth played here.

I dutifully climbed the seemingly never-ending steps to the visitors' gallery, keeping well out of sight of Fran, who'd copped a front seat.

There was a tightening of my gut when Jeremy appeared in the traditional white-ermine-trimmed scarlet robes, accompanied by his two sponsors, other 'hereditaries' who'd somehow managed to remain in the House, now crammed with Brown's adherents. I knew one of them, Lord Rotherwick, who's remained in favor due to his all abiding interest in saving forests.

Jeremy had the good sense to keep his maiden speech short. What's the old saying? "Be bright, be right, be brief, be gone." Jeremy followed that advice, spoke a very few words extolling the MI5 and MI6, ended by declaring, "I'm proud to be British." He and his sponsors promptly headed for the Cholmondeley Room in the lower parts of the House.

To reach Jeremy's drinks party I passed those magnificent renaissance tapestries and the oil portraits which were among the earliest known to man.

I gave Jeremy a solemn bear hug, had one whisky, and went looking for the House of Lords' Gift Shop. Whom did I find there? Happy!

She looked as flustered as a cat that had just given birth to kittens. She fluttered those long, long eyelashes over her pool blue eyes. "Ah's too late fo' Jeremy's par-ty. A-shamed t'barge in about now. But, as Ah's spent the five pounds t'come by taxi, Ah's decided to get some use of thet trip. Came in t'the shop. Bought me a present fo' Hal Murphy, t'make a-mends fo' leavin' his hosses t'Tom, and plannin' to go with y'all t'thet there Madrid."

The shop assistant stared at Happy. I doubt he'd ever heard a Kentucky Hills' accent in this place before. I said, "Darling Happy! Always thoughtful, always clever. Yes, Hal may well resent that we're going off to Madrid to run Fran's fillies." Turning to the shop assistant, I added, "I'll take a bottle of that House of Lords port that has the special label. Wrap it for shipping, please. And the whisky bottle too. It's to go to Canada."

Happy put out a restraining hand, palm up. "Naw, just as Ah was leavin' Epsom, an e-mail come in from Hal. He's goin' to Madrid. Flyin' in t'night, to join us. Wants to run Admirals Barge at the Zarzuela racetrack."

Marveling that Happy already knew the name of Madrid's racecourse, I stared at the many rows of whisky bottles containing the wide variety of brands overwhelming other items in this shop. I didn't want Happy to think I doubted her ability to be a quick learner as regarded foreign racecourses. I wiped my face as clean of expression as a plate that had just emerged from a dishwasher.

Paying for the two bottles, I suggested, "Come on, Happy. You've never been to the Houses of Parliament. I'm going to take you next door to the Commons, since you've missed the best of the Lords."

Thanks to the stickers on our lapels that had been provided by Jeremy's good offices, we passed through the complicated security processes to enter that Lower House. I led Happy up the long flights of steps that went to the Visitors' Gallery. What a shock to see so much new security: the very new bullet-proof glass and grenade avoidance methods that had been added since my last visit here. I'd been to the Lower House during the IRA attacks in London, and hadn't noticed THIS much security then.

We listened to an interminable monologue about the dangers to shipping in the Gulf of Aden, and to Somalia from pirates. Then I gave up our seats to two tourists and guided Happy into my favorite rooms. I shouldn't describe them as rooms, rather as huge galleries. Using my free arm, the other around Happy's delicious waist, I made an arc toward the tall portrait of Queen Alexandra to accentuate the beauty caught there by its painter. Going on to another enormous gallery, I showed Happy the work of an artist who had captured royals of a far earlier era: Holbein.

Feeling satiated with superior art, I was helping Happy into a taxi outside the Lower House when I saw the car park where MP Airey Neave's car had been blown apart by a detonating bomb. Airey Neave! The then Prime Minster Margaret Thatcher's great friend! And I was starkly reminded of that phrase uttered by Michael Corleone in GODFATHER TWO, where Corleone says: "If history teaches anything it tells us you can kill anyone."

Would we be safe in Madrid?

Chapter 4

Of course we traveled to Madrid with our four children but not the nanny. I needed Happy, and she needed the chillun, but Amah's old bones refused the trip. I bought a sturdy steel walker for her to help Amah move around our house and left without her.

I'd forgotten that airports used to smell of cigarette smoke, having been in so very many where nicotine was out of fashion. But the Madrid Airport proved to be an exception. Fran, who'd flown in our same airplane, in tourist like us, gave with an unusually severe torrent of four letter words. I tried to avoid that, but it was like trying to get out of the way of a cracking glacier. No luck.

"Fuck this filthy place," she shouted. "I'll have my vocal chords buggered for weeks from this cigarette smoke."

Penny pinching Fran hadn't ordered a limo in advance, and she joined us in the long line of exiting passengers waiting for taxis.

Unfortunately for my darling Happy, she tried to improve the atmosphere by saying, "Dear Fran, Ah's learned me thet the racetrack's name be the same as them Zar-zu-ellas wut used to be played at yourn Opery House."

Huffily, Fran turned her elegant back on Happy. She didn't deign to comment. Earlier Fran had tried to pull a bit of one-upmanship on Happy by downplaying Happy's general knowledge and was now caught by the short and curlies.

Oh, oh. Not a great idea on Happy's part. She should have kept her use of Google to herself.

Two taxis were necessary to transport all of my tribe's belongings because darling Happy had fallen once again into the trap of bringing too much baby paraphernalia.

Fran, of course, had grabbed the first taxi that had become available and we'd been left on the crowded curb to wait for two more.

It turned out that the Zarzuela Racecourse was located quite close to the airport. Great. I'd be able to contract my favorite jockeys who could ride here in Spain early in the afternoon and make it back to Britain for evening races.

We drove northwest of Madrid through the town called Aravac, and then I had my first glimpse of the two sprawling acres that contained Zarzuela's newly renovated stands that were protected under a scalloped concrete awning.

I'd booked rooms at the Hotel Eurostar. With ninety-one available, I'd picked two on a corner in consideration of other guests who could conceivably be bothered by my babies' intermittent crying spells. There was a swimming pool, paddle courts and large gardens. Just what the "doctor" ordered. Best of all, I got a discount for our party of six.

Its style was "airport modern" and lacked any of the Spanish graces that would no doubt be features at the more costly but still inexpensive hotel that Fran had chosen in the center of the capital. I'd seen its picture on Google, and there were plenty of Moorish turrets from which to warn "Moros En La Costa." I knew she'd ordered a piano to be installed in her room: no trepidations for Fran that SHE might disturb other guests.

While we unpacked in our small cubbyhole, that had few amenities but had lots of promise thanks to its king-sized bed, Happy surprised me by ruminating about Fran's upcoming opera role. "Ain't she in thet there opery called THAIS wut features an Egypt-i-an courtesan? I know it do; I looked it up on Google. Real naughty lady wut lu-res a monk to fall from grace."

Google again. What would Happy do without it? As I'm a Google addict too, I can't complain.

"Yes. THAIS. I hope that Hal Murphy and his Egyptian bride won't be here in Madrid when Fran sings in that role. You, my precious wife, are most perceptive: to guess that Mafalda wouldn't be too pleased to have to sit through Massenet's masterpiece. Yes, yes. I haven't forgotten either that Mafalda caught Hal while she was still living the life of a courtesan."

"High paid call-girl," Happy trumpeted like a whale ejecting its spray. Happy had lost any fondness she had originally felt for Mafalda, when she'd seen the latter treat her daughter Maheen so poorly. Maheen, who was in a new school in Milan, was programmed to arrive in Madrid for her half-term holiday. God willing that wouldn't coincide with Fran singing in THAIS, with Mafalda and Maheen in the front row seats Hal would buy.

Happy giggled. "Fran told me she's goin' to be in two shows here. Ah heard Fran practicin' some song from t'other opery called LA RONDINE. By thet there favo'rite comp-o-ser of hers, Puccini. Yeah man. 'Nother call girl, called Magda has a maid, Lisette. Fran don't get to play the kept woman

THIS time. Just her maid. Them two have a great song, a du-et, *O MIO BABBINO CARO*. Ah'll have to keep me a straight face fo' thet."

We shared a laugh. My, my. But Happy's getting very erudite. I knew she'd picked up some kitchen Italian when we had our long sojourn in Milan. Wonderful, though, that she could actually pronounce the words of an aria so easily. With no Kentucky hills accent apparent.

I wanted to get her in to our waiting king-size bed. No such luck. The hotel manager's wife appeared at our door with a stricken look on her caramel-colored face. She was weeping. "Richard *enfermo*," she wailed.

Happy dashed out of our bedroom down the corridor to where the two boys shared a small room. She found Timothy peering hysterically into Richard's crib. Happy could hear the baby struggling for breath.

"Timothy, go to yourn father," she ordered peremptorily. Like a captain at his wheel in a storm, Happy's face had taken on a determined expression. HER baby wasn't going to die, not if she was in charge.

I dialed Reception. I met with a language barrier. The one employee who spoke English was having his dinner. "Doctor!" I repeated several times, and when that word brought no help I tried "Medico," which I'd learned in the army.

Minutes later the hotel doctor appeared.

He was elderly, kind-looking but terribly inefficient. When I took him to Richard's room, his one piece of medical advice was, "Open the windows." Maybe that was the extent of his English vocabulary.

Happy wasn't about to accept inefficiency. She pulled out her cell phone and dialed the emergency number of the American Consulate. She demanded the address in Madrid of a first rate hospital with a pediatrics unit, then instructed that a room should be prepared there for Richard. Within minutes she'd wrapped Richard in layers of baby blankets, clothed Timothy in a winter weight jacket against the approaching night air, kissed our two girls settled with the manager's wife in an adjoining room, and had hailed a taxi to take the four of us to the Madrid hospital.

No touring for us this time. Happy didn't stop her cooing to Richard even when we passed an archeological dig, although archaeology is her favorite subject. By the time we'd entered the vast outskirts of Madrid, Happy was as hoarse as a wedding singer after three marriages in one day.

Our taxi driver spoke no English, but he found the hospital like a homing pigeon. Happy had scrawled its address on a bit of paper. Her instructions had been followed to the letter. At Admittance we were given an English-speaking nurse who hurried us to Richard's private room.

The hospital was extremely clean, far more sanitary than most of our British hospitals. I'd seen dust on window panes, and even spots of blood on a wall in a hospital near Banbury. Before we adults and Timmy could proceed down the inner corridors we were obliged to don ankle-length smocks, and had shower caps placed on our heads and over our shoes.

No giggles from Happy in regard to how we looked. She and Timothy remained equally grim. Tim, who had been kidnapped two years ago in Kentucky with a resulting psychological problem that meant he could not love anyone, had been cured when Richard was born. Richard was his all. Tim wouldn't eat or sleep until Richard was fed and then crooned to slumberland. There had been no question in our minds this night that we must take Tim with us to the hospital.

All three of us were unsteady on our legs. The stress had kicked in with a vengeance.

There were three plastic chairs in the room, more suitable for a patio set under a beach umbrella.

We sat down heavily, gasping like lost travelers in a desert. Unusually for him, Tim stretched out one hand to place it in Happy's palm. "Will Richard die?" he asked.

"Not if Ah c'n help it!" Happy groaned through clenched teeth.

A young doctor entered the room. Very polite, he had the manners of a Grandee. He kissed Happy's hand, welcomed me to Spain, and drew a small toy from a trouser pocket to give to Tim. The toy was similar to what Tim craves from McDonald's. Tim's eyes grew less blank. He accepted the toy and put it in his own trouser pocket.

The doctor spoke with an Oxford accent, "Your son Richard will undergo a series of tests. We must know what we're going to fight. Put a name to the enemy. I suggest you go back to your hotel and return tomorrow morning. There's nothing you can do here."

Happy moaned, "Ah wants to stay near mah son's crib."

"He's going into an oxygen tent for the moment. He won't be able to see you. Then, when I feel he is strong enough, I'll order the tests to begin. Go home."

My cell phone rang. I went out into the corridor to take the call. Completed, I relayed its info to Happy where she still stood next to Richard's hospital crib.

"We've been summoned," I dropped my shoulders.

"Fran?"

"Yes, it was Fran. No compassion. Not a word of sympathy for either of us, although I'd told her straight off about Richard."

"Where-all we be summoned?"

"To her hotel room. Believe it, she's already picked up some guy. A portrait painter, and she's modeling for him." I stared at the ceiling as if I could see there the faces of men Fran had picked up in Los Angeles, London and Milan.

The fact that she was pregnant with Jeremy's much-wanted heir had not deterred Fran from her usual pursuits.

"Ah's goin' back to ourn girl chillun. They needs me too. As for Tim, he don't need no lessons in whoorin' from Fran at his age."

"Please, Happy. I've a feeling in my gut that you should come with me."

Happy, even when wanting to do her mothering for our little daughters, now relented and collected Tim from Richard's crib-side. Happy has never been one to argue with me or question my requests.

We had a long wait for a taxi.

Madrid's night air was hardly wholesome. With all the traffic expelling carbon monoxide and houses equalizing the sudden drop in temperature with coal fires that spewed additional gases, Tim was soon acting out that he was choking.

"Shape up!" Happy had her moments when she disciplined Tim as she would a renegade horse. Tim grew quiet, and I feared he might fall back into that sullen mode he'd adopted for so long in the year before Richard's birth.

Fran's hotel was very different from ours. It had pretensions of grandeur. Designed to appear as if it had been built in the Grande Époque, there were velvet hangings at doors as well as at windows and heavy tapestry-covered furniture. The carpets were cheap imitations of the patterns of well-known oriental rugs. The chandeliers had plastic drops, not crystal.

A creaking elevator lifted us to Fran's high floor. We found her room easily. It had a reek of turpentine from the variety of artist's supplies that had taken over Fran's room.

"Meet Sir Norman Steele," Fran's voice was exultant. "We met downstairs in the hotel bar." She was seated in a fake Louis XV mahogany chair, with a factory made tapestry behind her. On Norman's easel there was a sketch in charcoal that had caught Fran's individualism. The sketch was in a prominent place, where a tasseled lamp shade gave it a glow. A tall thin thirty-year-old was attempting to improve the sketch's nose in the portrait by wiping at it with a coin-sized ball of bread.

"Hello," he muttered, not taking his eyes from staring at his sketch.

"Howdy," Happy bit out the minimum. She said nothing to Fran. It was obvious that Happy didn't feel that Fran deserved a word when Fran had neglected to inquire about Richard.

Tim said, "I need to go potty."

Happy acted on Tim's need by immediately finding the toilet. It was in a room of its own, apart from another room for basin and bathtub, European style. Happy would have remained in there indefinitely if Fran hadn't commanded, "Come with us to dinner."

At that late hour? Yes. I'd forgotten that in Spain the hours for eating out were usually near midnight.

Chapter 5

There was a delay. Sir Norman Steele needed to wash his brushes, although he hadn't used anything other than charcoal. We waited. When he emerged from the bathroom he flashed his large teeth at me. "Old Etonian? I didn't make it there from my prep school. I recognize the posture. Were you a wet boy? I rowed for my private school."

Apparently he wanted to be friends, two men together in opposition to the two girls.

Norman was well-dressed. Although they were paint spattered and very used, his Pinks shirt, Anderson and Shepherd cord trousers and Lobb suede shoes belonged to a gent's wardrobe. Trumper's, the London clubmen's barber, had done a good cut but his hair had grown too long and needed a repeat visit. I couldn't quite place his accent. Unlike Professor Higgins in MY FAIR LADY, I was unable to locate his birthplace from his vowels and consonants. But I doubted that his title was legitimate. I hadn't traveled with my Debrett's, it was too heavy. Without it I couldn't rely on its stud book listings to check if he'd been knighted or was a Baronet. My gut told me he was neither, and Fran had added "Sir" to impress us.

His charcoal sketch was a good likeness. It exaggerated the beauty which had blossomed since her pregnancy. Her sharpish features had taken on a layer of fat. Even her flat chest had improved, there was a hint of two future swellings that presaged breastfeeding.

Fran had chosen to be portrayed in her Lisette costume from LA RONDINE. It suited her, and she had fond memories of great successes in that role.

In an unusually exuberant mood, Fran led us down to the ground floor, having suggestively pushed against Norman in the elevator. She had no qualms about appearing in her Lisette costume in a restaurant. "Where shall we go to eat? What's your favorite restaurant?" she asked Norman.

Tightlipped, he quickly responded, "Let's stay here in your hotel. Such a charming place."

Not that CHARMING. Its restaurant smelled of cabbage. The fake antique motif was carried throughout with more awful plastic chandeliers and threadbare tapestry-covered chairs. I guessed that the dinners could be automatically charged to Fran's hotel bill, and that was why Norman found this place CHARMING.

We'd scarcely been seated and had ordered from the three-course-menu when a stout woman came rushing to our table, her eyes bulging as she stared at Fran. "You're the world's greatest contralto," she gushed. She spoke with an Eastern Seaboard American accent, "I heard you as Lisette in LA RONDINE. I'd heard Oropesa in that same role at the Met too, and you were so much better. No comparison."

Fran sat up straighter. She thrust out her chest. How she exulted in that praise. She reminded me of the time I saw former Prime Minister Margaret Thatcher, also in a restaurant, at a time when she'd been shoved out of office and when she got applauded as she'd entered the restaurant. Lady Thatcher's face had glowed. From a stance as a businesswoman intent on getting on with her memoirs, she'd returned to her glory days as the woman who'd fought and won a war eight thousand miles from her base. Now Fran's face wore a similar expression.

It didn't last long. As soon as the American woman scuttled away her Knight on a White Charger began to diminish in stature. Norman left the table repeatedly to make calls on his cell phone. I suspected he'd contacted a friend to call him back when the desserts were on the table. Norman had no intention of paying the bill or being in its vicinity. On cue, his phone rang, and he excused himself. "Sorry, got to go. Have a late sitting with the Hernandez Aza family." He disappeared.

"Oh, the Hernandez Azas! Did you hear? Fuck it, they're among the richest in Spain. Own miles of beachfront near Marbella." Fran wiped the remains of chocolate icing from an open mouth. "They can certainly afford his fee of $30,000."

I protested, "You can't mean you're going to pay that man $30,000 to paint your portrait! Fran, think of the wonderful filly you could buy with that money."

Penny pinching Fran had never balked at spending for the best horseflesh. But, a portrait?

She bit out, "I want that portrait. I'm only paying $30,000. It will be around for hundreds of years. How long does the career last for a filly? Three years? Four at most. Even the great Dahlia faded after the age of five."

Fran knew her equine facts. No doubting that. What did she know about portrait painters? Hadn't I seen portraits hanging on the gates of Hyde Park, where "the starving artists" exhibit on Sundays, selling oil originals for a tenner?

Dinner over, Happy stood up. She announced, "Ah's goin' back t'the hos-pi-tal, Ah's takin' Timmy. Y'all c'n stay with Fran, Rick."

I stood up too. Fran was out of luck. She'd have to go back to her room and be lonely. I was in no mood to talk horseflesh with her this night.

Chapter 6

Tim was placed on my shoulders and wrapped in my jacket while we waited for a taxi outside in the now-cold night air. Somewhere close by in a night club's show a guitar was being plucked, troubadour style. We heard the tapping of heels as gypsy girls danced the flamenco. When a taxi arrived the driver was speedily given Happy's bit of paper with the hospital's address. He, too, knew the hospital's location. Did Madrileños use taxis instead of ambulances? Maybe cheaper.

To our astonishment, the same young doctor was still on duty and hovering over Tim's oxygen tent.

He explained, "I was going to be relieved, but something caught my eye on his x-ray. I don't think your son's ill."

"Not somethin' picked up on the plane flyin' here?" Happy's voice quavered, but there was a note of hope.

"Señora, I think he swallowed a wheel off a toy and it's lodged in his thorax. Serious, because the object could move into his lung. We might have to operate and remove the lung. But this is not a disease."

Remove my little boy's lung? He'd never be on a par with his generation of schoolboys to play their games and compete on their level. One lung left!

A screech from Tim interrupted my horrible fears. Not a shocked screech. A guilty one.

As he often does when scolded, Tim relapsed into his mother's Kentucky-hills accent. "Ah knows as how Ah's not supposed to feed him none. Weren't feedin' him. But Ah's let him play with mah toy truck. He done swallowed the wheel."

Three pairs of adults' eyes stared at Tim. He hung his head. If I didn't know how much he loved Richard, I'd have cuffed him. But I knew he couldn't have meant for Richard to come to any harm. He should have spoken up sooner. Right! He hadn't, but he'd come clean in time.

The doctor moved into fast mode. Demanding two interns, he had them help place Richard on a gurney and shunt him down the long empty corridor. Would I see Richard alive again?

Night in a hospital is pitiful. We saw a cadaver shuttled to the hospital's morgue. We heard plaintive cries and moans. Mostly, there was dreadful silence.

Tim had fallen asleep against Happy's left arm. I'd dozed. Happy never stirred, not sleeping. When finally I recognized the young doctor's hearty step, I rose and grabbed his shoulders with both hands.

"Richard all right?"

The young doctor looked exhausted. He'd been on duty for fourteen hours before he'd spotted the wheel in Richard's thorax.

"Procedures over. It was a success. You can see your son in the recovery room in a few minutes."

Poor little Richard. When we recognized his lined face, it seemed to have shrunk like a plum that became a prune.

"C'n we take him with us?"

"Señora, that's not to be recommended." The young doctor wiped his hand over the beads of sweat on his forehead. "Tomorrow. Come back and we'll see how he'd got on and if you can take him to your hotel tomorrow."

We were all three very solemn on our return trip.

Tim slept most of the way, and I had to carry him in my arms to the room he'd shared with poor little Richard. I tucked him under the sheets and he never stirred.

Back in our room, next to that still-waiting king-size bed a red light was blinking on the telephone. I lifted the receiver and pressed the light's button. Hal's Canadian accent filled the room, "We're at The Ritz. Seen Fran. She was at the bar with some fellow who does portraits. Fran's having one made of herself. I'd like to have one of my darling Mafalda. Maybe with her little girl, our Maheen. She's due here next week for her half-term holiday. Call me." I replaced the receiver, but the red light was still blinking.

Again I pressed the button, expecting Hal to give me orders for Admiral's Barge. It seemed that Hal had to duplicate everything Fran did. Her fillies run at Zarzuela? His Admiral's Barge had to run there too. A portrait of Fran would demand a portrait of Mafalda and maybe of Maheen. Was Hal in a race to show off he was as good as or better than Fran at anything? Oh God, I hoped not.

The red light blinking was not to herald orders from Hal. The voice was my father's from his home in distant Warwickshire, distant by miles but even more so by his life-style and Edwardian Era manners. "Dear boy," I heard, "I've always wanted to go to Spain. Seems like this may be my opportunity. How would you feel about my coming to Madrid? I've always wanted to see the castles in Spain, ever since I was posted to Gibraltar and forbidden to cross the frontier."

The red light stopped blinking, having cut off the end of his message. How did I feel? Like the farmer in the children's ditty The Farmer In The Dell. I'd brought my wife, she'd brought our children, my opera singer owner had appeared, my Canadian owner had followed with his bride and warning us her daughter might arrive soon. Next to be in Madrid will be my father. Our group was expanding at a furious rate.

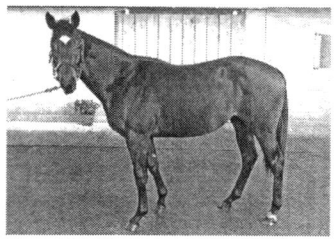

Chapter 7

After checking out Hal's horse at the Zarzuela racecourse's stalls for visiting competitors, Happy and I headed again by taxi for Madrid.

This sojourn in Spain was proving expensive.

We went straight to the Ritz, were guided to Suite 206 and entered it to find Mafalda posing for a portrait with Norman Steele already nearing completion of her charcoal sketch.

Hal gave us matching bear hugs, but kept a finger to his lips signaling we shouldn't interrupt Norman Steele at his work. Mafalda nodded briefly only to return to stretching her neck to make it appear slimmer and longer.

Mafalda's portrait was not a good likeness. Mafalda had put on weight since we first met her in Russia with a Manolo five inch heel caught in the copper rail of a bar while she downed a double whisky.

The love handles I'd noticed when we were in Milan now had turned into a heavy tire around her burgeoning waist. Her ankles had thickened, and on her hands there were blue veins stretching like the ends of a spider's web. Norman Steele's sketch, with Mafalda using one hand cupped under her double chin to hide more welts of fat, showed a younger thinner woman.

Acting on the show of friendship Norman Steele had offered in Fran's room, I gave him a salute, army-style. He responded by putting down his charcoal, and suggesting Mafalda take a break.

"Hello," he said to me. "I met your friends downstairs at the bar, and when they told me they'd come to Madrid to race a horse trained by you, I introduced myself as a portrait artist commissioned by another of your owners to do a neck and shoulders."

I smiled politely, but when Norman took up his charcoal and began to thin Mafalda's nostrils, I suggested to Hal we go into his bedroom for a chat.

"How much you paying this Norman?" I asked straight out.

"Ten thousand for Mafalda's head, another ten if Maheen's is added to the finished portrait."

"Amazing. He's getting thirty thousand from Fran."

"Sure thing. He told me about that. But she wanted the top of her Lisette costume to show. The bertha, featuring her shoulders. I guess she's vain about those shoulders."

I nodded. "Fran's vain about a lot." While speaking, I wondered again, what it was with Hal and Fran. Did he have to compete with her about everything? The horses, the trips, and now the portrait artist?

Muttering, almost under my breath, I said, "Fran mentioned a sum of three hundred thousand dollars for one portrait he's done."

"True. And I know about the story. It seems that in the Hernandez Aza family there were originally four children, only one daughter went missing. The father wanted the missing girl to be included. He wanted a portrait like the famous one by Fransico Goya of Ferdinand VII, his queen wife and princely children. Norman agreed on fifty thousand per head."

While I chatted up Hal, my Happy had taken on Mafalda, who was trapped to sit immobile. Happy grilled her about Maheen, knowing full well that there was no motherly love there in spite of Mafalda's new fatty maternal-look.

"When's Maheen comin' here?"

"Not soon, I hope." Mafalda bit out without turning her head.

"Will her nice Luca come too? He sure 'nuf loves her. Won't want no way to have her take a va-ca-tion without him."

"Don't speak to me about that dreadful policeman. I want better for my daughter. And she's still only seventeen. Too young for a boyfriend."

Happy bit her tongue. She'd been poised to remind Mafalda of the many lovers she'd surely had by seventeen. But Happy knows where our bread is buttered, and that we can't afford to lose Hal as an owner. Hal would dump us if commanded to do so by Mafalda.

Norman called another halt.

"Let's go back down to the bar. I need a drink," he called to Hal.

We trailed downstairs into the Ritz's magnificent, truly luxurious lobby. Here the tapestries were authentic and the chairs Regency or earlier.

While the group ordered drinks, I went to Reception to inquire for the cheapest room. I knew it would be expensive, but felt that Dad would rather have the smallest available in a first-class hotel than a spacious suite in a crummy place.

But expensive was too expensive. I didn't make a reservation.

We found Fran at the Ritz bar. She didn't seem too pleased that Mafalda had commissioned and sat for her portrait.

"Norman!" She exclaimed, "You're a dirty disloyal scoundrel. You're giving Mafalda the time you should be devoting to my portrait."

Norman had no chance to reply. Again an opera buff approached Fran. Our star turned on her microphone persona expecting a similar accolade to the one she'd received in her own hotel.

But this woman, skinny as a rail and with a face as ugly as barbed wire, spat out, "You're the awful bitch who stole Angela Gheorghiu's thunder in LA RONDINE. But you haven't got a great voice, more like a frog croaking."

Fran blushed. That must have been a first for her. She turned away from the woman without a riposte. Standing tall, swaying her rail-like shoulders, the woman swept away.

Cowed, our group remained mute for a moment. But Happy, always the diplomat, broke the bad spell with a call for their drinks, "Here's to hog wash," she joked, "Ah c'n bet we'ns will git worse than mah Pa's moonshine."

I downed a double scotch, while our Muslim Mafalda downed hers just as fast. I noticed she didn't ask what the theme of that opera was. No doubt she was well versed that LA RONDINE's story concerned a kept woman who gambled on true love. Not at all what she wanted underlined near Hal.

Chapter 8

After having Richard discharged from the hospital, we'd dressed him warmly and took him with us to look for accommodation for Dad. We found a reasonable semi-suite for Dad at the back end of Fran's hotel. No view, no easy access. He might wet his pants before reaching his bathroom from the hotel's very distant lobby.

Dad arrived by taxi, with very little luggage. He hadn't changed in appearance. He still sported the same short back and sides haircut he'd adopted while with his regiment in World War II. His hair was thinner, but there was enough to cover any approaching bald spots. He had the same mustache, clipped except for a flirtatious curve down from each nostril; not a Salvador Dali mustachio, nor a Hitler brush, but very much his own style. He wore the identical blue striped suit he'd appeared in whenever going up to town. His shoes were black, he kept the brown suede tie-ups for the country. A glowing light brightened his tiring eyes. His smile was timid, but hopeful.

We were on hand to greet him, accompanied by all four children. As he hadn't ever seen Richard, that was the first Harrow he kissed. Then he worked his way up through Irish, Dorothy, Timmy, and Happy, until giving me a restrained hug very unlike the one I'd received from effusive Hal. When he met Fran in the hall, he bowed like a courtier at a Garden Party when the ranks part like the Red Sea for an approaching member of the Royal Family.

We went downstairs to the hotel's unprepossessing bar.

Having just ordered drinks, I felt startled to watch another elderly thin woman approaching our table. I squirmed, worrying that again Fran might be insulted. Instead this lady ignored Fran, and directed herself to my Dad.

"Hello there," she said in a soft Tennessee accent, prompting my Happy to look up with pleasure as she recognized it. "Ah's met you-all in Lon-don. Re-mem-ber? Last week. At thet Shakes-peare plots festival!"

Now it was Dad's turn to blush. Honestly, like a teenager. "I rarely go up to London," he said apologetically. Of course he rose immediately from his chair, with his courtly manners he'd never had done otherwise when a lady first appeared. Slowly I rose from mine too. Dad continued in a lighter tone. "Yes, madam, I do recall we had a few words about Shakespeare."

"About there bein' only forty-four plots, and Shakespeare used most of 'em, as Ah recalls."

I bowed as if she was the Queen of England, that short neck-curve bow.

Dad said politely, "I'm Timothy Harrow, and this is my son Rick with his family, and Lady Cabrach." Dad would never use anything but her title, never stooping to employ her professional name: Frances Purcell.

"Mah name's Mary North. But Ah'm from the South," the newcomer giggled lightly, it was obvious she'd made that remark very many times in her life. She nodded at the rest of my family, and hardly took any notice of Fran. This Mary North was no opera buff. "Ah's a writer. Folks in Nashville know mah work. Few outsiders heard of me, though. Thet's why Ah's still studyin'. You-all know what Ah means. To git better at thet there writin'."

Happy chimed in. "Ah's from Ken-tucky. Y'all knows thet's the home o' the best hossflesh. Mah husband's a trainer. Y'all knows wut thet means, a hoss trainer. Ah's a jockey," she shoved out a hand and grasped Mary's tightly "C'm on, sit y'self down. Have a drink on usn."

Mary North was thin. She had a curvaceous bust, very attractive whether or not it had help from a brassiere. Chocolate brown eyes suggested Spanish blood, but she dispelled that notion immediately by proclaiming: "Ah's de-scended from folks wut come over on the Mayflower. Joined thet there Mayflower So-ci-ety, Ah done has. Lot o' work, tracin' all the bornin' and dyin' o' so many an-cestors but Ah's managed and now Ah's a full-fledged member. When Ah was in England Ah visited thet there Plymouth rock, Ah 'sho did." Pausing for breath, she turned carefully to Dad, and added. "Ah knows thet some gentlemen don't like women wut talks too much. Sorry, if Ah's bored you-all."

Dad didn't blush now. He certainly recognized that Mary North was making a play for him, but he liked it and his face took on a glow like a firefly at dusk. "Dear lady, please speak on."

The rest of my party could have left. Dad and Mary had eyes only for each other.

My God, but these two elderly pensioners were certainly bonding fast. Is it because they had little time left on earth?

I noticed that Fran was anything but pleased that no attention had come her way. She was bristling and I could sense the earthquake that was about to tear apart this dining room.

Quickly, I suggested, "Let's the eight of us go out on to the terrace." Not a great idea, considering that approaching night air was beginning to cool the tiles. But I followed through and led our group outside, leaving the two pensioners to get to know each other better. I could hear Dad's voice, "Dear lady, do tell me more about your home in Nashville."

Mary's lilting reply to that invitation resounded through the terrace's open French doors. "Well, if you-all insists. It's the world-center of Country music. It—."

I couldn't hear the rest. But Dad must have eaten up every word because he'd made no move to join us on the terrace.

Fran brought up a subject that she was sure would grab our attention. "I think the Hernandez Aza girl was murdered. The fourth Hernandez Aza child, the one that Norman had to add into his portrait even though she'd gone missing."

Happy's antenna responded in precisely the way Fran had foreseen. "Ah's had a thought in thet there di-rection mahself," she said, nodding with that sage look she gets when murder is mentioned. My darling Happy had fingered six serial killers. One of them had murdered Fran's twin sister.

Fran hadn't forgotten that.

"Have you seen the Hernandez Aza family portrait?" I asked.

"Shit, of course not. It's hanging in the Hernandez Azas' palace and I haven't been invited there. But I've seen a print of it. Very outstanding piece of art. Beautiful, but there's a pathos. Like in the greatest operas."

"Mostly when a chile goes missin' and there be no findin' it in under five days, usually it's been killed." Happy ruminated.

I queried further, "How old was this child?"

"Crap. Stupid question. Wasn't exactly a child. Eleven. Maybe twelve. I noticed there was a budding of breasts. Pretty kid. Maybe rebellious. Like I was, around that age. Strong face. Observant eyes. I wouldn't want to share a stage with a kid like her, because nobody would look at me."

Happy, who so often compared people to characters from the movies, said, "Like Dorothy in The Wizard of Oz?"

Fran raised her shoulders and her eyebrows. "Hell, I guess you could say so. Listen, I'm freezing out here. Let's go back into the dining room and tell the old man to hurry up and go fuck that woman so we can warm up."

"We're heading home." I bundled my babies into a taxi without a further word to Dad. Happy did her diplomatic ploy, apologized to Fran and piled in next to me. All of my party fell asleep long before we reached Aravac and the Eurostar Hotel.

I left it to the drowsy manager's wife to settle our sprigs between sheets. I wanted to get Happy between ours. And finally, yes, I lured Happy to respond to lovemaking.

Sublime.

Chapter 9

Fran woke me with specific queries about her fillies. I should have been long gone for early morning stables, but the wonderful delicious superb lovemaking with Happy had kept me awake until dawn and I'd barely fallen asleep when the telephone call came in from Fran.

"Bugger you, Rick," Fran's voice hit like an iceberg. "Do I have to get another trainer to look after my horseflesh?"

"Your fillies are in great condition," I said, faltering.

Happy woke up. She took the receiver. "Fran, y'all knows thet mah Rick has a magic way with fillies. We's both goin' down t'see them just about now. Y'all ain't got no call t'be askeered. Nothin's wrong with them there fillies. Ah guarantees it."

She said a careful goodbye, dressed and made two cups of coffee from the packets provided by the hotel. We didn't wait for the electric kettle to give us boiling water. Happy used what there was from the tap. She arranged with the hotel for a babysitter to care for our kids, and once they were settled with a pleasant girl, we headed for the stables.

Zarzuela Park's stables for visiting horses was located a mile from the Eurostar. We walked. The dawn air was still cold although sunlight peeked through nearby trees. I shivered.

Happy smiled. "Like a mornin' in mah Ken-tucky hills," she said. A frown washed away her smile like a curtain of rain hitting flowers. "Ah thinks as Fran's gettin' mo'e biggity than ever. Ah doesn't want t'be beholden to her. Any chance thet our Hal will help out with the cost o' ourn ho-tel?"

"Darling, you know he will. We have but to ask. The trouble is we're always asking."

"Could yourn Dad help?"

"We've managed without going to him. Oh, I know the bills are piling up. What I need to do is win some races here and earn our ten percent."

* * *

Thank God all three of our contenders looked to be in prime condition. When we had them unboxed and Happy took them one by one on the gallops, I thought everything was going like clockwork. We could win with them, and pay our bills.

Happy had a very different opinion. Breathing in bursts from exercising three horses, she panted. "Admiral's Barge told me he don't like the goin' here. Ah's got a plain old hojous feelin' he ain't goin' to try. Be ourn least hoss."

Not good! Happy talked to our string and came out with the salient facts. What could be wrong with the Zarzuela Course? We'd brought his bottled water and Epsom hay. It had rained within the week and softened what had been challenging going. I needed to win with Admirals Barge in particular because Hal was my most generous owner. And if I was going to have to ask for a loan, it wouldn't do for this horse to lose.

Worse, when I was settling Admirals Barge in his box, who should appear there but Hal's son!

Byron Murphy wasn't a favorite with us. He'd given Happy a difficult time in Milan when he eloped with a student from Maheen's school and Happy had been recruited to cross most of northern Italy to find the lovers before the girl lost her virginity.

Happy had succeeded in locating the two rebels, and the girl's virginity had remained intact thanks to Byron being unable to break her hymen. It was too tough.

He'd never been fond of us since that time. So the feeling of dislike was mutual.

Fortunately for us Hal didn't favor Byron. The teenager had caused too much serious trouble at home in Canada and later in Italy.

Nevertheless Happy gave him a big hello. "Byron, Ah knows y'all ain't got a lick o' sense, but Ah's glad to see y'all still likes hosses."

"My Pater sent me to you," Byron said grumpily. His highlighted hair had grown to his collar, giving him a supposed matinee idol style. His small eyes sent swiveled glances around the stable. "This place stinks. Don't these Spaniards believe in mucking out the damned manure?"

Happy ignored his whining complaint. She asked, "Wut all do Hal want?"

"Mrs. Harrow that's for me not to tell and for you to find out. I've got a taxi outside ticking up a horrendous fare. You two had best get going, and leave these horses to their grooms."

Happy followed in Byron's wake. She must have been remembering the cost of the limo Hal had hired in Italy to send her to find the lovers. At the time she'd told me it cost more than a round trip fare to the United States.

I gave instructions to the groom and then caught Byron's taxi before it sped toward Madrid. Happy and I were outfitted for exercising horses, not for the Ritz Hotel. We probably were tainted with that manure smell Byron had complained about.

Well, I'm a horse trainer and my Happy's a jockey. Manure smells belong in our lives!

We did get a tepid stare from the uniformed doorman at the Ritz's entrance. Never mind. A luscious blonde girl arrived at the same time who was identically outfitted, having obviously exercised a horse. She didn't smell, but her long blonde hair was in a mess, and a telltale green stain on her collar indicated to me that she'd kissed a recently-fed horse.

Happy stopped the girl. "Y'all work at the Zarzuela track?" she asked, extending one of her grubby hands.

"I've been exercising my horse at a livery stables' gallops," the girl said in an unpretentious way. "I'm Sadie Hogan. What's your name?"

"Sadie? Like Sadie Hawkins in the Lil Abner play? Shucks, Ah ain't got nothin' special fo' a name. Mine's awful. Hillary! Just call me lil ole' Happy. Everybody does."

Byron elbowed Happy away from the girl. He extended his manicured paw. "And I'm Byron Murphy. Come in to the bar with me and have a drink."

I guessed that Byron must often use his father's accounts to give drinks to girls. I said, "We're going up to your father's suite."

Pleasantly, Sadie queried, "Byron, isn't your father Hal Murphy? Gosh, that's the same man I'm supposed to go see. My Daddy wants me to take a peek at a portrait he's commissioned by Norman Steele."

Byron shrugged. He took a detour away from the bar. "Follow me to the elevators."

Happy chimed in, "Ah's goin' there too. We'all works fo' Mr. Murphy. He sent Byron to go bring us to his suite this mo'nin' and Ah's can act as cha-per-one."

Sadie twinkled her way into the nearest lift. She didn't appear to be the kind of girl who needed a chaperone. Almost rugged, her mindset was surely on horses, not sex.

We had a great surprise on entering Hal's suite. His step-daughter, Maheen, had arrived from her school in Italy.

Maheen was very changed. When we'd last seen her during the Milan models murders, she'd still retained the aura of a schoolgirl. This Maheen was a mature woman.

It was obvious that Maheen's virginity had gone. She had the bloom of a woman who'd found her man. Luca Palacio, the police officer who'd been instrumental in saving Maheen and Happy from the serial murderer who'd dispatched other young women, had done a good job of helping Maheen to achieve orgasm. No question.

After hugs, I said, "Hello, Maheen. Welcome to Madrid," then added, "Is Luca about to follow? Will he arrive here soon?"

Maheen's face garlanded with rising smiles. "Yes, yes. His superiors are sending him to investigate what the Spanish police are doing to protect tourists, after that terrible train slaughter. Lake Garda wants to give its tourists plenty of confidence that they can feel safe coming by train."

"Will Luca be staying in the center of Madrid? Happy and I elected to be near the Zarzuela racecourse. Near a town called Aravac."

"Is it cheaper to stay out of the capital? We're saving to get married."

A bellow tore across the room like the winds of a hurricane. "Married! You're only seventeen!" Mafalda swept out of her bedroom and slapped Maheen across her left cheek. "How dare you talk of marriage? You want to make me a grandmother!"

Maheen put some saliva on three fingers and rubbed her sore cheek. "You're going to be a grandmother whether I get married or not."

Happy hugged Maheen. "Mah darlin' friend. Is y'all pregnant?"

"I hope so."

Sadie had been staring nonplused at this scene. Happy, laughing lightly, careful not to offend her owner's wife, brought Sadie into the conversation, "Maheen, this be Sadie Hogan. She just met all of usn. But she do have a spe-ci-fic reason fo' bein' here. Her Daddy wants her to see the Norman Price po'trait Hal done ordered." Happy took a deep breath before pouring on a compliment that could cool Mafalda's fury. "It be very be-au-ti-ful, just like yourn Ma."

The eye of the storm deflated, Mafalda walked across the room and pulled a linen sheet away from the oil portrait that now replaced the charcoal sketch.

Hal roared into the salon. He bear hugged Maheen. "Great to have you here, kid. Isn't the portrait gorgeous? Just like your fabulous mother. Don't you agree, Rick?"

Caught in the crosshairs, I mumbled, "Lovely. Norman Price knows his business."

True, busy as he must have been this week working on Fran's portrait, he'd managed to create a masterpiece of subtlety, evading a mirror-like resemblance yet producing an attractive Mafalda.

Handing me a tumbler of whisky, Hal boomed, "Wonderful picture. Aboot perfect, but it needs one addition. You, Maheen! I want a Madonna and child portrait."

Maheen swallowed hard. "I'm preggers, Hal. I'll soon have a bump showing. You want three generations?"

"Pregnant! Great, I've always wanted to be a grandfather. Let's open a bottle of champagne on that." He noticed Sadie, who was moving her head as if she was watching a ping pong match, studying Mafalda's face one minute and then staring at Norman's portrait. Hal was intrigued. "And who are you, young lady?" He offered a flute of champagne to her.

"She be Sadie Hogan, Hal," Happy answered for the girl. "She loves hosses just like usn. And she be the same age as Maheen. Them two can be real good friends."

Sadie grinned. She went for that idea. She'd warmed to Maheen the moment we'd entered the suite. Accepting the champagne, she swallowed and then said, "I don't usually drink. But my Daddy says I've got to have a debut party and so I've got to learn to like this stuff."

"Wut's a day-boo party?" Happy queried.

"I'll be eighteen soon. If we still lived in England, Daddy would be giving me a ball. But we're tax exiles. Stuck in Spain because Daddy saves a pile in taxes. He's told me I can choose my own kind of party."

"Why not a Sadie Hawkins party?" Maheen laughed hard. "I've already caught my man, but if you're still looking that could be a great way to get you a guy. You've got the right name for it."

Amazed, a strangled look of astonishment washed over Sadie's sun-freckled face. "Oh! I've hated the idea of a debut party. But a Sadie Hawkins Day do? Love it!"

Mafalda, bored that no one had given any further compliments on her beauty as captured in the oil painting, now growled, "I'm hungry. Let's go down for dinner. This Sadie can come too, if she can handle Maheen."

Dinner! A great idea. Happy and I had had no breakfast. Looking at how much weight Mafalda had put on during the past month, I knew we'd be encouraged to work our way through an entire menu.

We had seven courses, with all the accompanying wines.

Chapter 10

It was just my luck that Fran entered the dining hall while we were still on a cheese course following dessert. I didn't want to have to admit to Fran that we'd left the stables earlier without checking on her fillies.

Fran was not alone. Norman Steele was with her. He strode away from Fran to come to our table to greet Mafalda, and be introduced to Maheen.

Dumped by Norman, left publicly to find a table on her own, Fran was fuming. I hoped that Happy and I could escape her wrath by inventing an excuse to leave Hal's dinner party. No such Luck.

Norman zeroed in on Sadie, delaying us.

He asked Sadie, "How is Lord Hogan? He's called me several times. Wanting to have me start your portrait. By Jove, I'll be only too happy to get started. I've seen how charming you are."

Plunk, another future client, after another compliment. But Sadie wasn't an easy target. She shook her head. "I'm not going to be one of those simpering girls who'd love to look like I was on the cover of VOGUE. No thanks."

"Lady Sadie, I assure you that I visualize a canvas where you are sharing the space with a horse's head." Norman was quick to catch Sadie's frown at the supposed compliment, upping her to the grade of Lady when Sadie only rated the Hon. He added, "Your favorite horse. And you, you will be wearing a velvet safety helmet and the clothes you use to compete in horseshows."

Sadie had no quick retort to that offer. I wedged in a suggestion. "Happy and I are going to go looking for my Dad. Maheen, would you like to come too? And Sadie?"

I left my unfinished demi tasse and bowed to thank Mafalda for dinner, then added, "Hal, come see Admirals Barge tomorrow. You could familiarize yourself with the racecourse at the same time."

Happy gave me a sharp kick in the shins. I'd forgotten she'd told me that Admiral's Barge wasn't pleased with the going at Zarzuela. Damn! I'm in Spain to run horses, not to sit around gabbing about oil paintings.

But our wonderful, dear friend Hal let me off the hook. He said in his boom box voice: "Rick, you go along and find your Father. Take Byron with you. I'd like to have him get to know this lovely Sadie."

We five of us went to Dad's hotel. He'd left. We scoured the vicinity and came to a huge restaurant called La Dorada. I could see Dad through its window. He had Mary with him, and the two were chatting. They were also holding hands, leaving their fish dinners to go cold in curdled sauce.

Mary and Dad were touching foreheads, so close that they were consuming each other's breaths. The Scene touched me more deeply than I would have thought possible.

Quietly, I turned to my group and said, "Let's find another restaurant."

Byron pulled a guidebook from his pocket and began to reel off the names of moderate eateries.

To my amazement, Sadie swarmed like a bee from a hive towards Byron and spat, "We'll go to El Botin. My father's favorite place. Very expensive! And you, Byron Murphy can pick up the bill."

El Botin featured rows of roasted piglets looking at you as you entered. Not appetizing for everyone, those dead piglets' faces! Sadie grabbed Maheen and Happy, leading them to the ladies rest room.

Secluded there, Sadie proceeded to tell the other two girls that Byron had goosed her in the elevator. "Dirty, nasty, dork. Put his fingers in between my legs and tried . . . well, you can imagine! I'm determined he'll get stuck with a huge bill."

But Byron lucked out. Instead, once we were seated at a table, Sadie suddenly sang out, "Daddy! Over here! We'll make space for you at this table."

Lord Hogan crossed past the leering dead piglets and joined us. Portly, dressed as if going to his bank, he had a dark grey Saville Row suit, patent shoes, and the club tie of a club whose emblem I didn't recognize. Immediately, he kissed his daughter, and said, "I'll not only join you, I'll make this my party."

Sadie didn't kiss him in return. She introduced all of us by our correct names. Sadie was good at memorizing, apparently. She ordered the plat du jour as a competent hostess well-versed in playing that role for her father.

"Have you seen the portrait of that Mrs. Murphy?" Lord Hogan asked immediately. "I'm really keen to have Norman get started on Sadie's. Norman did a great job on my picture. Did it in London when I'd just been named to the Lords. In my ermine."

I guessed that this particular peer was a Blairite, elevated to the peerage for some monetary favor done for former Prime Minister Blair. Never one of my favorites, I'd been disgusted when Blair had squeezed most of the hereditary peers out of the Upper House. Lord Hogan was evidently a self-made man. Maybe he'd started his career as a barrow boy.

Spot on. Lord Hogan, holding the stage, continued, "I began my upward thrust as a barrow boy, you know. I'm only a Life Peer. So it doesn't matter that I don't have a son. Sadie's my jewel. And someday she'll give me grandsons to spoil."

Sadie glowered at that remark. Obviously she'd heard him make it before and hated it every time. She said mischievously, "Why don't we take this party home with us after dinner and you can show them your portrait from when Blair made you a peer?"

Spot on! Again I'd guessed right at Lord Hogan's incongruous past. After a dinner that didn't feature roasted piglets, we took three taxis to a distant nouveau-riche neighborhood.

All its houses were palatial, although none of them had appropriate gardens.

Crowded on small lots, these monoliths were not authentic in any way. Too new, too garish, too over-the-top as regarded architecture. Inside, the hall was too big and featured a cement fireplace large enough to roast a deer. The drawing room was ostentatious, and above its too-new marble mantelpiece there was a built-in frame for a towering portrait. Lord Hogan's picture was almost ridiculous. His robes didn't fit, his shoes showed under them, and his baron's coronet had been too featured on a table beside him with one hand outstretched to it. Not a gent's portrait.

I quietly glimpsed Sadie's face. She was controlling a sneer.

"Magnificent, isn't it?" Lord Hogan beamed. "I love this picture. And I want a head and shoulders of my Sadie for over there, above the Chinese cabinet."

All of us stared at the cabinet. It was no antique. Its gold gleamed as brightly as a rising sun. But yes, on this room's crammed walls it offered the only open space for a good-sized portrait. Not a $100,000 one like Lord Hogan's. This picture would cost no more than $30,000 even if it included a horse's head.

An embarrassing question came next. Sadie asked Maheen, "What did your mother do before she married Mr. Murphy? I noticed that in her portrait there was no hint of her background."

Maheen's natural tan went to a blush. Murmuring, almost stuttering, she blurted, "My mother's Egyptian. In her day there weren't many jobs for women. None really for her class. Jobs were for servants, yes. Or weavers of rugs, that sort of thing, yes. But, she liked to travel. Uh, yes, went to Paris, Moscow, like that."

None of us pursued the subject. A pall had come over us.

Sadie said, "Come on. Let's go into the billiard room, and I'll challenge anyone of you to a game."

Unfortunately, only Byron accepted that challenge. We all wandered into the room. Lord Hogan must have thought any self-made peer must own a billiard room, but Lord Hogan had never learned to aim a cue. It was Byron, who licking his outwardly mobile lower lip, picked out a very new cue and skillfully sent a ball into the table's far diagonal pocket. It didn't take a rocket scientist to figure that Byron had spent his years in college playing billiards.

Sadie equaled his every play. I wondered if she could be as adept at riding horses. I'd be very happy to invite her to help Happy exercise our string.

I wasn't to know. Happy said, "We got usn four young chillun wut need us back at ourn ho-tel. Thanks fo' dinner and takin' usn to yourn home. But we's got to get away."

A uniformed butler was ordered to call for a taxi. I offered to give a lift to Maheen to the Ritz. But as soon as we'd delivered her safely, I told the taxi driver to take us to the nearest train station. We took a train home to save money.

What sweet bliss to be back home and between two sheets with my Happy. I wanted to initiate lovemaking, but Happy had been bitten by an urge to talk about our evening.

She repeated to me what Sadie had told her about being goosed by Byron. "And Ah thinks Byron's on drugs."

"Not our problem," I tried to soothe her, and tried to forget this news.

Happy went on to another tack. "Ah's been thinkin' what ails Admiral's Barge. Could be he needs shoein' by a local ferr-ier. Remember wut Hal told us when Dubber be sick in Hong Kong? 'When sick in China, get a Chinese doctor.' Well, Ah's convinced we'all needs git a local ferr-ier."

On that, Happy turned to me, opened her mouth and received my tongue. We had a glorious night of lovemaking.

Chapter 11

Happy was right. Admiral's Barge needed different shoes for a racecourse in a different country.

We also had Fran's fillies fitted with the different shoes. Magic! Their gallops improved, and our future promised successes at the Zarzuela track.

With Admiral's Barge back to his normal speed, I felt we could return to Madrid and see my Dad. No way did HE want to see US!

We found Dad at his hotel. He'd changed his hair style, allowing it to grow long at the neck. Not as long as Byron's style, but noteworthy. He'd exchanged his bottle bottom eyeglasses for an Armani pair of tinted sunglasses containing his prescription. His trousers had wide flares!

Mary North wore the same dress we'd seen on her at every meeting. It had a huge skirt and a low décolletage. She could have been Dolly Parton on stage. But she sang Tammy Wynette's signature tune as we entered the room, "Stand By Your Man."

I guessed that Mary was sharing the room in order to save on one for herself plus hard-to-find taxis in the dead of night. Before, she'd slipped out, alone, probably to take a bus.

"Where to?" I asked my darling wife.

"Let's usn call Sadie and see if she invites usn to judge her hosses."

Great idea! Sadie thought so too, and said she'd meet us in the railway station on our way to her livery stables with an intervening stop at her home.

To get my bearings, we went to the huge signs in Spanish and English announcing SALIDAS DEPARTURES. From there I hurried to the parking lot. On the way, as Sadie waved to us, we heard a stranger say to her something in Spanish that made her blush.

"Want me to sock that guy?"

Sadie said, "Thanks, Rick. But there's no need. That man was simply complying with an old Spanish custom called a *piropo*, giving me a left-handed compliment. He said, "I want to sleep with you."

As Sadie repeated his phrase in English, another man stepped up and said: "He'd be crazy to waste time SLEEPING with you. I could offer something much better."

That guy I made to kick in the shins, but was stopped by my darling wife.

"Ricky Honey, don't y'all fret. Thet's a com-pli-ment in this here country."

Sadie's car was a Mercedes convertible. I got stuck in the cramped rear seat while the two girls laughed their way back to that pretentious mansion.

Inside the hall, Sadie whispered archly, "Norman is here to add a decoration to his portrait that Daddy has just received for his charitable contributions." She stifled a giggle. "You've got to see Norman! He wears a terrible, old Panama straw hat when he's working on something he'd already finished."

We entered the so-called Study, where the portrait had been placed on an easel. Lord Hogan was posing like a show pigeon with its chest thrust forward. Norman held a florid decoration in one hand while sketching its design to paint it as an addition to the portrait, prominently featured on the pictured baron's chest.

Lord Hogan's face seemed to flush with pleasure at seeing his daughter. He hadn't expected her to arrive. "Darling child, you didn't go to the stables yet?"

"Nope. Thought I'd come to have a look at how Norman's progressing." The giggle broke out. "I notice he's got on his Panama hat."

Norman growled from under its brim. "Always, always wear my hat when I'm finishing up. So you're off to the stables?"

"In a minute."

Norman surprised us with his input. "I'd like to see those stables. Take a look at your horses. To select the one that will be with you in your portrait."

"No way, Norman. I'm trying out a horse that's been lame. I want Mr. Harrow to take his measure. He knows horses. You don't."

Norman said nothing.

Breaking the polar moment, Lord Hogan offered jauntily: "Rick, You must come with me on the shoot I've organized for tomorrow. We expect enormous bags. As many as three thousand birds. As many as General Franco ever shot in a day."

"Thanks," I countered, "but no thanks. I haven't raised a gun in anger for years. I prefer to see birds mating, or whatever, not being shot at."

"I won't take 'no' for an answer. This shooting party's costing me a fortune. You'll enjoy the lunch, if nothing else."

We left after I'd agreed to join his party. Couldn't be rude to Happy's new friends.

But I could hear the whispers of the two girls up in the front seat of the Mercedes convertible. Sadie asked, "How could you have married a man so much older than yourself? I couldn't. Never in a million years."

"Ah fell in love with him. Ah's still in love with him. He be so special with me."

When we drove up the gravel driveway to the stables I felt relieved not to have to hear the tail end of that conversation. Instead, I heard a chorus of "hellos" from other debutante types who stabled their horses at this livery. Obviously, from the waves and smiles they gave her, Sadie was very popular with these girls. Maybe she was only First Generation posh, but they accepted her as she had the right cut glass accent and wore the in-thing understated clothes.

"Meet Hannah and Rachel," Sadie presented two flirtatious types, one a super blonde and the other a stunning brunette. Both Hannah and Rachel wore impeccably cut hacking outfits topped by the regulation velvet helmet.

The two gave Sadie the Spanish double shoulder pats and gave us the once-over. Hannah warmed up to Happy, even after she'd heard the Kentucky-hills accent. Rachel was stand-offish. Both scuttled away at the approach of two middle aged women, one of whom was also kitted out by Saville Row while the fatter of the women had probably bought her tired blue jeans and cowboy jacket from a charity shop.

"Meet the owners of this Livery Stable," gushed Sadie. "They've saved my horseflesh from all kinds of dramas."

Happy and I shook hands with them.

The fat lady said in a Bayswater accent, "Please call me Phyllis. We use only first names here. Protects the girls who come from lesser families, you know." She had a shy twinkle in her eyes. They were partially hidden behind square framed glasses that did nothing to add to her appearance.

Her companion, taller and thin, with the beaked nose often seen in portraits of Norman-descent aristocrats, shot cautious looks at both of us. Astute, her expression showed she'd guessed at our careers. Was it that obvious I'm a trainer and Happy's a jockey? Maybe our worn boots gave away the information. Or perhaps our legs are outwardly curved like those of a retired colonel from a cavalry regiment. The smell of horses could linger from gallops earlier, which was another give-away.

"I'm Camilla," growled tall-and-thin. Her voice was extremely low. She could have sung in a males-only choir. Were these two women like a married pair?

Camilla and Phyllis had done a good job with their livery business. The hay nets were full. As we watched, grooms came to fill water buckets, scour the flooring and spread sweet-smelling straw. All the horses were bouncing with health, their coats gleaming from constant brushing and their manes well combed. I looked into the eyes of several and had strong equine glances come my way.

Happy said, "My name's Hillary, but just call me Ole' Happy. Ever'body does." From her dancing lips I could see she'd summed up how this livery worked, and approved.

Sadie had left us to go for her horse. She led out her lame favorite for our inspection. Magnificent animal, but strictly for hacking, not racing.

My earliest memories included tales of how Sergeant Murphy, bought for the heir to a US carpet fortune Laddie Sanford, had gone from being a mere hunter in the field to winning Liverpool's Grand National. Exceptions prove the rule. But this animal I knew would never place in a horserace. I nodded appreciatively for Sadie's benefit, but left the diagnostics to Happy.

"Sho be lame," she let out a huge sigh. Happy ran her hands down the bad leg. She nodded balefully. "Y'all needs to ease the swelling and repair thet there wound on his right hindquarter. If'n there be a Hyperbolic Healing Center in Madrid, y'all should take him fo' the vet to see. Listen up to mah Rick, he'll explain."

I echoed, "Hyperbolic Healing Center." I doubted that Sadie and the two older ladies would understand Happy's Kentucky-hills accent. "The treatment works by the use of high pressure chambers similar to those used to treat scuba divers. The chamber is filled with 100 percent oxygen, and the pressure inside is increased to the equivalent of being 66 feet underwater. This increased pressure creates a higher concentration of oxygen in the blood."

Camilla pursed her lips. She understood, all right, but was a doubter. Phyllis grinned eagerly, but I'm sure she'd understood nothing.

I continued, "The effect of this treatment in these chambers is reduced swelling because it has helped the white blood cells which fight infection. Not an inexpensive procedure. In addition to a 10-foot wide hyperbolic chamber you need the control console and a skilled technician to operate it, plus knowledgeable grooms. "Could we hope to get this for Sadie's pet?"

A serious head shake from Camilla. "No. Not yet. Not here. But there are very skilled vets available and we have one who is overseeing this animal's condition. Your darling is better, isn't he dear Sadie?"

I left it at that. No hyperbolic chamber. Not my fault. I changed the subject. "Sadie, how about bringing out another horse. I'd like to see you in the saddle."

So would Camilla! I noticed that her eyes gleamed when Sadie opened her legs to swing up into the saddle to take the reins of a sound young colt.

Sadie proved to be an expert. She had a fine seat, and total control. When Sadie dismounted to offer the reins to Happy, I heard a most unladylike oath. "Shit, it's that damned Norman. He's followed us here."

With Happy cantering away to the exercise trails, I turned to observe Norman's approach. He had a large sketch pad under one arm, and replaced the soiled Panama hat with a spanking-new yachtsman's cap. Norman was certainly into hats!

"Hello, Rick," he was slightly breathless from hurrying toward us, fearful we'd leave without waiting for him to join our party.

Sadie glared at him. "What are you doing here? Didn't Daddy want you to finish adding his new decoration?"

"Done that. Your father was very pleased to send me here. Now just show me your horses and I'll pick the one to share space in your portrait."

With no rejoiner ready, Sadie shrugged and led Norman inside the barn. She pointed to the ugliest horse there, a speckled roan with a long blaze from lips to forehead and freckles on the pink around his nostrils. "His name's Fagan," she sneered, "and you'll be a Grand Maitre if you can make him look attractive."

Ignoring Sadie's insulting tone, Norman produced his charcoal and proceeded to sketch Fagan's head. Slowly a minor miracle occurred. Fagan became a very special horse, with an expression that broadcast he was loved.

A change came over Sadie. She softened. "You've captured the fact that I love him. You are a Grand Maitre."

Sadie ran to where Norman was rubbing away a stain on the picture, and kissed him!

Happy, returned, now dismounted and handed her mount's rein to a waiting groom. She poked me in the ribs and whispered, "What about thet? Didn't y'all hear her say she couldn't ever go for an older man? Looks like she done got other thoughts now."

Returning to the railroad station, Sadie had Norman up front with her while Happy and I shared the narrow rear seat. But I enjoyed the ride, because Happy's hair was caught by the wind in this convertible, and she'd never looked lovelier.

I couldn't wait to arrive back at our hotel and carry her to our king-size bed.

Chapter 12

Our lovemaking was blissful and I was still at it by dawn when the bedside telephone screeched in on my concentration. I kissed Happy lightly, signaling a stop, and answered the call.

Fran, again. But she wasn't demanding this time. She sounded distraught. "I've caught a fucking cold. And Dress Rehearsal is tomorrow night. This is terrible; my voice is going. I sound like a fog horn in mid-winter. But I'm going on stage. I'm a real trooper, right? 'The show must go on' and all that crap. Anyway, I've put aside tickets for you and Happy to come to it. Have you any suggestions to get me through this thing? Your kids are always getting colds. You must be an expert at-"

"I'm not. And Fran, I wouldn't dare to prescribe anything for you. Your vocal chords are your fortune. You must get a good doctor."

"A good one! Like that Italian one who put his filthy fingers down the throat of the great Enrico Caruso, giving him the infection from which he died! Thank you, but no!"

Happy took the phone. "Mah Pa always said to take plenty of moonshine with hot water and lemon." She hung up laughing.

"We'll lose Fran to another trainer," I muttered gloomily.

"Y'all hear what-all she done offered us fo' the oper-y? Dress Rehearsal tickets. But ah recalls as how thet po'r Romanian tenor Bruno, wut we-all done helped when his fi-ancé got killed, he got us ex-pen-sive seats, bestest ones at La Scala, fo' openin' night. I sho wish Fran weren't so tight-fisted."

"She buys the best bloodstock available. And I get to train her best buys. That's good enough for me."

"I wonder if'n she in-vited Hal and Mafalda to come to the Dress Rehearsal. Ain't this the oper-y about a cour-te-san?"

"It is. You like a good laugh, my darling. Keep your eyes on Mafalda, and see how long it takes for her to work out what this opera is about."

Happy did just that. We dressed up for the Dress Rehearsal. I wore a tie and business suit. Happy chose her 'bestest' silk dress, a confection of layers of undulating silk that turned me on so much I could hardly watch the "oper-y."

Dress Rehearsal was a big deal that night. It was to be the first time ever that this old theater would be used for grand opera. The stage was quite large, as it had been used for the zarzuelas of Spanish folk lore with large casts. The acoustics had been improved with special small cloud-like forms hanging from the high ceiling. The seats were new and comfortable. The lighting was fantastic.

Two unfortunate happenings marred the evening. First, it became evident from the moment the star appeared on stage that she couldn't sing. She coughed repeatedly into a soon-dampened handkerchief, not a huge one of the type that Luciano Pavorotti had favored, but a meager poor excuse of a linen square hardly more practical than a Kleenex. Fran spoke her lines rather than trill them, and even speaking those poor lines caused paroxysms of more coughing. Her nose dripped liquid snot. Occasionally one drop would linger on the tip. Her eyes were bloodshot.

Fran soldiered on, living to the utmost her 'the show must go on' mantra. In the audience there were quizzical looks exchanged, and restless feet tapped under the seats.

And then, with the First Act still in its beginning, Mafalda finally worked out that this opera concerned a woman of her former profession. She heaved like a whale whose blow hole was hampered by seaweed. Struggling to rise from what was a cramped space for someone as heavy as she'd become, Mafalda uttered complaints loud enough to drown out Fran's attempts to stick to her role.

With Hal and Maheen in tow, like two tugboats fighting a tempestuous tide, Mafalda hurled out of the theater. Their limo had been ordered for two hours later, when the performance was scheduled to end. With no taxis in sight. Mafalda's language descended to curses that would shock the inmates of a Cairo brothel.

I know. I'd heard those curses in Cairo, exchanged by taxi drivers caught in jammed traffic. I'd exited from the theater with Happy in Hal's wake. I didn't want to chance losing my most generous owner. Lucky! Because although it was the cheapest rental car available in Madrid, I did have transport and could offer to drive the Murphy group to their hotel. And did. Moreover, I had a tidbit of bait with which to calm Hal.

While weaving in and out of the cars of late night revelers, I said, "Hal, old friend, I've been invited to a shoot tomorrow. I know how you love to get quail in Canada. How about you joining the party? I hear there will be upwards of three thousand birds released. Quail, pigeons, pheasants? Whatever, I'm going."

Seated next to me in the front, leaving the three ladies in the back, Hal stopped frowning. He turned to me, his eyes alight, "Delighted, Rick old chap. Nothing except being in bed with Mafalda could make me happier."

I kept the rental car to get us back home to check on our children.

Early the next morning I still had the car and could avoid yet another train ride into Madrid. I felt a little less embarrassed driving up to Lord Hogan's mansion in this car, and Happy's face glowed as she offered Sadie the box filled with local delicacies she'd had made at our hotel. Lord Hogan's guests were all correctly attired. Holland & Holland had supplied not only their guns and cartridges but their elegantly cut shooting jackets, caps, and plus-fours. One, who was a duke, wore red socks. I'd heard that dukes favor red socks. I had nothing better than my old, tired leather jacket, and probably could have passed for a beater if I hadn't been loaned two guns worth about forty thousand pounds.

Six Land Rovers ushered us in a safari-like procession to the estate where the shoot was scheduled. Standing in the mist rising from its grounds, we were each issued a 'Secretario' for a loader. I asked and was given the lowest butt in the line, where I was expected to see the fewest birds. I hadn't been on a shoot since I was thirteen, and had experienced the 'entry into manhood' rite that for our county people was equivalent to a Jewish boy's Bar Mitzvah. Truthfully, I hate this sport, shooting birds. I hate to see anything die.

Lord Hogan in *sotto voce* said, "In Spain we permit these 'Secretarios' to bet on the bags of our guests. The best-bag boy gets a lot of money. Watch out that your 'Secretario' doesn't poach another guest's bird, or lie as to your total."

He added nothing. I was on my own, except for the dicey 'Secretarios.' Mine was called Pedro, and he turned out to be a sweetie-pie who behaved impeccably and overlooked my absolutely dreadful performance before and after lunch.

Hot soup and sherry were offered between the morning drives. I accepted both. Lunch was superb, served by butlers in a clean but deliberately primitive hut.

I had watched Hal with amazement: he'd been brilliant in the field. Two cartridges, two birds. He never poached a neighbor's bird, nor did he swing around to shoot behind. Unlike the former U.S. Vice-President Dick Cheney, he never shot at man-level, aiming always to the sky. Dear Hal had obviously taken part in many top drawer shoots in Canada, learned the etiquette, and practiced the sport to bring his participation to a high level. As my Australian counterparts had caroled in Melbourne, "Good on ye, Hal."

Lord Hogan had welcomed Hal as another self-made tycoon. He'd recognized Hal's rough diamond ways as similar to his own. He'd developed a camaraderie, and was winding his right arm around Hal at every opportunity.

Hal had an additional chance next day to prove his sportsmanship. We ran Admirals Barge in the three p.m. race and he came in Second. I'd imported a British jockey who'd ridden him before. The weather was dry, and the competition below par. Yet our runner misfired. Hal didn't complain.

"Admirals Barge will do better next time. I'm aboot ready to return to Canada, but I'd like to see him have another run here before leaving. Maybe his bad hoof hadn't quite healed."

Fran was far less of a forgiving owner. When our British jockey missed his flight from Gatwick to Madrid, I'd asked Happy to ride Soviet Girl because that skittish filly wouldn't accept just any rider. Our British fellow had ridden her at Goodwood, and she'd seemed to like him. But she adored Happy, and proved that every morning and evening at her gallops.

Happy didn't have a good ride. Soviet Girl acted sluggish coming out of the stalls, trailing the field. Happy gave her a friendly but no-nonsense kick in the ribs dictating more speed. Soviet Girl responded well, chasing the two leaders, ending Second in her race. That position paid well, but Fran whined and then berated Happy in her adopted gutter language. Ouch.

Later, when we were back at the hotel consoling each other in our king-size bed, Happy explained that she had no bad feelings towards Fran. "She be born into a fancy home on thet there Ebury Street, in London, Ah remembers well t'were a duplex a-part-ment. She went to a ritzy school, where proper lang-u-age were used. But Ah's figured Fran likes to shock folks with them fo'r letter words. Folks wut comes up to congra-tu-late the greatest contralto they ever hear, n' Ah's watched them chins drop in horr-or. Yeah man. Ah's done become used to thet. Ah reckons thet our Fran's got a hang-up. Maybe never felt as pretty or as clever as her twin sister, and has to shock folks or turn a nasty side."

I could have added a word about Fran's miserliness. But didn't.

Chapter 13

Our next day was filled with a less acceptable experience following yet another command from Fran. We were summoned by Fran to attend a bullfight.

"Shit, I don't have to start rehearsing for Ariadne, and my other filly isn't booked for her race until next Saturday. I've bought three tickets. Rick, you can drive me to the building."

Penny pinching Fran would buy tickets for something she really wanted to see, but she wasn't hiring a limo or taking a taxi. Of course I offered to drive her, and hired another car to take the three of us to the Las Ventas bullring.

It was very imposing. The arena's architecture was bastard-Moorish, but its windows had the graceful pointed arches, and its great doors were high as a Mosque's. The color pink had been a mistake, considering that blood would soon be flowing. Blood from the picadors' horses, and blood from the bulls. In the arena, where a fabled procession of matadors and picadors was now unfolding, I found in it a triumphant mix of ancient and modern that worked. It excited the crowds of onlookers. It would push the matadors to do their utmost. All this colossal input created magic. These matadors accumulated huge wealth, as I suppose they should as they put their lives in the mix.

Music was much a part of the magic. The first blast of trumpets accompanied the procession of matadors. The flashy music matched the costumes. The matadors were clothed in vibrant 'suits of lights, *trajes de luces*,' embroidered with sequins that twinkled as bright as diamonds in the mid-day sun. On the matadors' heads were odd flat black horizontal caps in a style of centuries ago. Some hats had a pigtail sewn to them, while others among the matadors had grown their own plaits. These men had enormous grace, and walked like ballet dancers.

Behind the matadors came the picadors, dressed in more somber colors, wearing leather chaps to protect them from the sharp horns of the muira bulls soon to be fought.

The picadors had the first go. Their job was to weaken the bull by drawing blood. The picadors were mounted on very old, expendable horses.

Out rushed a bull. It didn't charge in a straight line, but dismayed by the shouts of the crowd and the unfamiliar setting the bull swayed like a drunken sailor. Approaching the bull with his lance aimed at the bulge behind that horned head, the picador forcefully thrust home. But this bull threw back his body and then charged. His horns connected with the elderly horse's stomach and out poured its intestines.

"No!" Screamed my darling wife. "Stop thet!"

The Picador was too far out of range to hear. Fran had bought cheap seats.

Urged on by the bloodthirsty crowd, another picador took up his stance and again thrust home his lance's spearhead, and his horse too was gutted.

Happy left her seat, clutching at her open mouth.

"Sientese, majadera!" Complained a couple whose view she was interrupting.

Swaying as if she was about to faint, my usually-strong wife hurried up through the stand and looked for the Ladies toilets to vomit.

"I'll come back to drive you to your hotel later," I gasped to Fran, then hurried after my Happy. She'd found the toilets, and I stood outside them waiting like the husband of a pregnant wife who'd needed to retch.

When Happy finally emerged she had wept so much that the rims of her eyes were blistering red. I placed both of my arms around her to comfort her, and together like the babes in the woods we managed to leave Las Ventas.

I took Happy to Dad's hotel, and was in luck because both lovebirds were in his tiny suite. The Nashville Shakespeare buff was holding both of Dad's hands and reciting poetry to him. She didn't let go of those hands as we wandered through his open door.

"Well Ah nevuh, what you-all bin doin?" Nashville Mary asked my shattered wife.

"Ah seen a hoss had its in-tes-tines ripped out," Happy wailed.

I left her to give an account of our damned afternoon while I recouped the rental car and rushed back to Las Ventas in hopes that I could find Fran and avoid a scolding that now always included a threat to leave my stable.

The very grand arena looked very different in the late afternoon sun, with no crowds shoving to get inside. Now the grounds were empty. The fifty thousand paying bullfighting enthusiasts could be heard braying for blood on the other side of its walls.

The arena's pink colored walls took on a rosy glow from the late afternoon autumn sun. I strode quickly to where Fran was still glued to her seat.

She gushed like the mother of a child ballet dancer who has just witnessed her darling's first pirouettes. "Isn't this the most fucking glorious sight you've ever seen? Those huge bulls with their huge balls dangling. Sexy, that's what this is. No wonder the Spaniards love watching bullfights. It gets you primed for an orgasm. I must find Norman, back in Madrid, quickly. I hate to waste good foreplay and watching these bulls is better than foreplay."

It suited me to leave promptly. We avoided the crowds, I was able to locate my rental car in the huge car park, and was delighted to deposit Fran at her hotel and go to find Happy in Dad's room. No derby winner had ever tried harder for speed.

Chapter 14

I found Happy relaxed, chatting with Nashville-Mary. The women were holding hands. Nashville-Mary had released my Dad's.

I grabbed them. Lucky that I did grab Dad's, because I noticed they were feverish. They were also very frail, bony and shaky.

"Dad, I think we should call a doctor for you."

"Certainly not, Rick. Never felt better in my life. Take your little woman back to your own hotel, and leave me to my Mary. I'll be fine."

Trained to be obedient to my father, my regiment, and my owners I left Dad into Nashville-Mary's care.

After returning the rental car, Happy and I took our usual cut-rate train back to our village and spent a cozy evening with our 'chillun'.

God was in his heaven and all seemed right in our world.

But as so often happens in my life, just when everything seems so rosy, a disaster wrecks it.

Early the next morning, while we were breakfasting after gallops, a telephone call came in from Maheen. She was weeping.

"Sadie's gone missing. She left home early yesterday to try to canter a horse that's been lame. She hasn't been seen since. Never arrived at her stable. Never came home last night."

"Damn!" I grunted. "That will be Byron again."

Happy took the telephone. She'd listened to the news. "Naw," Happy was adamant. She wore that sleuth expression that warns of dire troubles. "Not Byron. Worse. There be too much show o' money around Sadie's house we seen. Money thet could be what's causin' this trouble, or sick sex. Ah's got a gut feelin' somethin's mighty wrong with someone close to Sadie. A lesb at the livery stable? Them two deb-u-tantes: Rachel or Hannah. Someone. Ah's got some thinkin' to do."

I took back the receiver. "Maheen, we'll come up to Madrid."

Good thing I offered that, because before we could leave our hotel another disaster call hit us for six. It came from Nashville-Mary, "Your Dad's very sick. Yo'all best cum up soonest 'n git him a doctor."

"Get him to a hospital," I barked. "Telephone me at the Ritz. I'll be in Maheen Murphy's room. Give me the name of the hospital. We're on our way to Madrid, fastest."

We weren't. We'd missed the express. There was a half hour delay before a snail-slow local appeared.

"Damn, damn, damn," I complained when we'd boarded the train, and stopped at every milk collection venue. "Damn all these brat kids who impose themselves on our lives. My Dad must come first."

Happy kept her opinion of these complaints to herself. When we arrived at the Ritz, we found ourselves in the same elevator as my Dad.

"My God, Dad. I thought you'd gone to a hospital."

"No. Not ready to die, yet. Hospitals are for dieing. I feel fine. Had a word with a doctor who assured me I hadn't had a stroke, nor even a heart seizure. Just too much lovemaking with Mary. That's what caused my breathlessness."

"Dad!"

"Mary made too much out of my breathlessness. I adore her. I adore making love to her. But this doctor told me not more than once a day."

The elevator was arriving at Maheen's floor. "Dad, how? Why? I don't understand. So how many times a day were you at it?"

"Three. Sometimes more if you count after midnight as another day. Wonderful. And all thanks to Viagra. It works for me, works a charm."

Speechless, I let Happy and Dad leave the elevator before me. When I caught up with Dad, I asked, "Where's Mary now?"

"I've run out of Viagra. She's gone to a pharmacy to buy more."

I stared at my father. His springy step, his straight back were not what I remembered from my last visit to him in Warwickshire. There, he'd been using a cane, and his shoulders had been rounded. His back had curved like an oldster's with advanced osteoporosis. Before today I could bet my life that Dad had foresworn sex after my mother had died giving birth to me. Or had he? Were those two hour long weekly visits into Banbury for sex? No wonder I'm always so horny! Like father, like son.

Maheen's door was open. We glimpsed her at a side table, grasping a telephone. Her brown cheeks were streaked with tears. Holding her free hand was the father of her unborn baby, Luca. He was wearing his Italian police officer's uniform, not civvies.

Luca took the receiver from Maheen. "I'll speak to the police for you."

To my surprise, Luca rattled off his questions in Spanish.

When he replaced the receiver and Happy had given him a hug, I asked, "And where did you pick up this lingo? None of us can speak a word of Spanish. Happy uses her kitchen-Italian here."

Luca's grin was infectious. Maheen stopped crying, smiled bleakly, and listened. He said, "My Ethiopian grandmother couldn't stand the winters on Lake Garda. Too cold and damp. We went to Seville from October to May, and you know how quickly kids pick up a language. But I haven't had any helpful information from my Madrid counterparts. No news of Sadie. She must be dead."

Happy wasn't smiling. In an aside to me, she whispered, "Maybe Sadie not be dead. Strong girl. Strong 'nuf to control difficult hosses. Thet girl she fight off any pre-da-tor. She fight not t'be kid-napped, raped, or Ah doesn't know what."

Maheen turned on the TV. A bulletin was interrupting a sitcom. We watched it as Luca translated. He read the latest from an announcement. He explained, "It says a girl's mutilated body has been found in the parking lot of the Las Ventas Stadium. Closed to the public today. The bullfighting season ended yesterday, and the arena isn't readied enough yet for political rallies, or concerts."

I cut Luca short. "What girl? How, mutilated?"

"The girl's not Sadie Hogan," he burst out with that news. "This body has been identified from dental records as the Hernandez Aza girl. Remember Norman told you that a daughter of the Hernandez Aza family had disappeared and he'd been contracted to add her face and shoulders into the family group portrait?"

Norman entered Maheen's room. He had his large sketch pad with him. He listened to the news bulletin, and shook his head. "Terrible news. The Hernandez Aza parents are going to be devastated. We should all leave flowers in front of their mansion, like Londoners did for Diana, Princess of Wales. I feel real pain even though I never saw that child. I painted her into the portrait from a photograph."

Luca continued to translate, "*Bene,* this girl was mutilated with a screwdriver. Eyes dug out. The screwdriver was found still in place piercing her jugular vein. Now viewers are being advised to use discretion in permitting children to see the picture released by forensic."

"Forensic," Happy echoed. She choked on the word, and seemed about to vomit again. What did her vomiting spells mean? At the bullfight, and now here?

I began to wonder if Happy was pregnant.

We didn't have time to debate whether to go to buy flowers for this girl we hadn't known. Nice suggestion, but not for us. The telephone rang and Maheen answered. Her face, already damp from the earlier tears, now took on a frenzied look.

"Happy, you must leave at once. The manager of your hotel is on the telephone with terrible news. Your babysitter died an hour ago from meningitis, and your little Irish is running a very high fever."

We bolted.

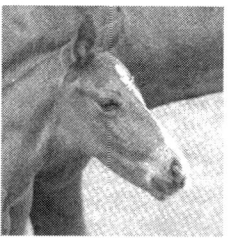

Chapter 15

We couldn't bear to wait for a train. I haggled in English with a taxi driver and brought him down to a price I could afford. He was well worth his fare. He darted through back streets to reach the autobahn and flew over the speed limit to reach our hotel.

The manager's wife was in tears. She had Tim and Dorothy hanging on to her skirt, while she carried baby Richard. "We have a doctor with your daughter now. But I thought it best to keep these other three of your children away from their sister."

Good sense. I shook her available hand and rushed upstairs to our rooms. From the smell of disinfectant I could trace the visiting doctor.

Happy hurtled behind me, gasping, "How bad be this men-in-gi-tis?"

"It's a terrible disease, an inflammation of the membrane that encloses the brain and the spinal cord." I didn't add that it often killed within twenty-four hours.

In Irish's room the doctor was wearing a surgical mask as protection against contagion. He was leaning over Irish, shaking his head. "No use taking her to this village hospital. No facilities for children. No isolation wing. Our hospital is mainly for injured jockeys. Sprains, hematology problems, usually occurring after a jockey takes a bad fall. Even for those, we usually send the worst cases to Madrid." He spoke English correctly, but with an American accent that indicated he'd studied medicine in the United States.

"What do you suggest as the best procedure?"

"Time. If the fever breaks . . . Well, there might be some hope."

Happy spoke up. "In Kentucky we'd wrap the baby in cold wet cloths."

"No. Please don't do that," the doctor handed surgical masks to me and to Happy. I put mine on. Happy didn't.

That worried me. I recall from my history lessons that Queen Victoria's daughter, the Princess of Hesse, had died from diphtheria, having caught it caring for her sick child.

But Happy wanted Irish to recognize her and be comforted by looking at her mother's unhampered face. Happy removed her coat and drew a chair up as close as was possible to Irish's crib. She placed a hand on Irish's forehead. With her other hand she stroked her feverish cheek.

I drew the doctor into the corridor. "What about an oxygen tent?"

"No. I wouldn't recommend that now." He went into our room and crossed to the bathroom to wash and dry his hands. He had a packet of disinfectants and rubbed each hand with the contents. He offered a packet to me. I shook my head. What for? I hadn't touched Irish, much as I would have liked to. She hadn't touched the handle of the door that I'd touched, she was too tiny to have reached it and there was nothing else in her room that could have contaminated me.

Oh, Irish, my youngest daughter, to whom I'd given so little of my time. What I had given was always reduced to being shared with her brothers and sister. Dorothy, my favorite. Tim, after his kidnapping had been Happy's concern. Richard, Tim's idol. Poor little Irish, she hadn't received her fair share of caring. And now this!

The doctor presented his bill, was paid, and he left. The hours dragged by. Happy never left the crib side. I looked in sporadically, noting that Irish's little face seemed to have shrunk more each time I saw it.

After midnight, I heard Happy rising from behind the crib. She came into the corridor, her eyes streaming. "Irish be dead," she groaned. "And there ain't no Baptist Minister in this here town to say prayers."

I led Happy to the crib side and together we said the Our Father. The hotel manager appeared as if waiting for Irish's death. He didn't speak English as well as his wife did. "I call Undertaker. Same as for babysitter. Not all will take diseased."

Dawn brought the Undertaker's van. Darling Irish was placed in a plastic body bag the size of what we used for garbage in England. I was shown a catalogue of caskets. Not much choice for infants. I bought the best.

"When be the funeral?" Happy choked out.

The Undertaker's under-under-assistant shrugged. He understood the word funeral. Not too different from *funerales* in Spanish.

We went to bed. No lovemaking *this* morning, but like terrified children we hung on to each other our bodies entwined.

I woke up first. Pink slivers of sunlight crossed the carpet of our room announcing the impending sunset. I touched Happy's forehead to test for fever. Thank God, none.

The hotel manager's wife had thoughtfully ordered that no calls be passed to our room. But, after I'd had a brief word with Hal to explain the circumstances, and received his truly sincere condolences with an offer to help financially with these medical and funeral expenses, a jangling call came in from Fran.

No condolences. She barked, "Tomorrow night's my debut in Ariadne. I haven't time to listen to your shitty gripes. But I want to know the latest news on the condition of my Soviet Heiress. Is she going to be fit enough to run?"

I was tempted to hang up on Fran. But I bit back my anger. "She'll be fit by Saturday. We are arranging a funeral for our Irish. It will be tomorrow, I believe. We won't be able to go to hear you in Ariadne." Fran hadn't invited us, but that was unimportant. I repeated, "We have the funeral tomorrow. When that's over, by Saturday, we'll accompany you to the races. See you in the Owners and Trainers Stand."

No. Fran didn't demand that I collect her in Madrid, and drive her to the races. No! Thank God for that, because at a time of severe crises small things can loom so large and drive you crazy.

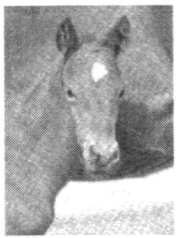

Chapter 16

Fran surprised us by turning up for the funeral at the town's crematorium. More, she sang a solo of ABIDE WITH ME, Happy's favorite hymn. Fran is certainly a kaleidoscope character. She didn't hug either of us after the ceremony. Too afraid of catching a germ. But she'd hired a limo to bring her to the funeral and for later, to get her on time for her opening night.

Oh, that funeral! I couldn't bear to look at Irish's tiny casket until it was placed on the moving trundle that was headed toward metal curtains to the flames of this crematorium. We'd been told that due to her highly contagious meningitis she could not be given a funeral in a chapel, and she had to be cremated. I lunged to the casket and threw myself on it to hug it like President John Kennedy had done when his infant son Patrick died within hours of birth.

I'd never suffered before like I did at that moment. My darling wife, amazingly controlled, drew me away from the casket and it moved along past the curtains to be burned with its precious cargo.

"No wake," Happy declared softly. "We be needin' quiet time."

We returned alone to our hotel room, slept, and then devoted ourselves to our surviving three children. Irish's crib had been removed, and Dorothy wanted to know why.

"She be gone t'Heaven," Happy said, kissing Dorothy. "We been real blessed t'have had her these two years. But God loves her so much he wanted this angel back in Heaven."

Tim pouted. He wanted more attention so he slid again into imitating Happy's Kentucky-Hills accent. "Y'all bin gone fo' hours. Ah's real tired of waitin' around to see y'all. Ah's tired of this here hotel. Ah wants to git me some fun."

"We'll go see the horses at Zarzuela."

"Nah, Ah's tired of hosses. Ah wants to go to McDonald's and git me some real food."

Nothing for it but to discover where we could find a McDonald's.

"Madrid," the hotel manager informed us. "You want taxi?"

No. Dorothy and Richard would travel for free on the train, and Tim was half fare. It was still cheaper to go by train.

Arriving in Madrid we needed a taxi to take us to McDonald's and afterwards to the Ritz. Happy wanted to go to Maheen for the latest news on Sadie, or Byron.

McDonald's did the trick for the two older kids. Dorothy had caught Tim's enthusiasm for McDonald's food and take-home toys. They ate their burgers down to the bun's last crumb, while I tried not to weep thinking of how Irish should have been here eating with us too.

At the Ritz, Maheen welcomed us warmly albeit with tears for Irish. She cradled Richard in her arms, practicing for when she'd have her own now-about-to-be-born baby. Luca was in her room, and I guessed he'd like a picture of Maheen with the baby far more than the Norman one where she was a minor addition. "No news about Sadie. News of Byron? You'd best ask Hal about him."

We crossed the corridor to Hal's suite. We found him in front of Mafalda's portrait, studying it intently. Mafalda, nervous, shifted from side to side. Not good, because her love handles became very obvious as they jiggled under her close-fitting dress.

After condolences, Hal pointed to the painting. "For so much money, it sure doesn't look like my Mafalda. He got Maheen aboot right, although I'm not sure I like the way he gussied her up to look like some tarty model."

I went to peer at their portrait. Yes, there was no resemblance to the Mafalda we knew. She'd been glamorized beyond recognition. Her neck was as long as any painted by Modigliani. Her mouth had the Leonardo de Vinci mysterious smile of his famous lady the Mona Lisa. Her hair streamed in an imaginary wind like that of Botacelli's Venus emerging from the sea. The portrait was a caricature.

In Norman's version of Maheen you could see a likeness. Norman had slimmed her lips, narrowed her nose and lightened the brown of her eyes. But like the professional models who once having left a studio released the pins in their hair, opted to wear T-shirt and jeans, and removed makeup to be transformed into the really ordinary girls they were, Norman presented Maheen as Maheen.

Mafalda didn't know whether to be pleased or furious.

Norman entered their suite as the Murphys were debating. He'd brought his Panama hat. "I'm ready to sign this work if you're pleased with it." He aimed his statement at the Murphys, ignoring Maheen.

In reply, Hal went to the desk and wrote a check. Norman put on his Panama hat to accept it. "Well, that's that," he grumbled, as if not content with the sum paid. He added, "With portrait painters it's drought or downpour. I've been paid by you, by the Hernandez Azas, and Lord Hogan, but where's the next commission coming from? Mr. Murphy, how about a nice head and shoulders of yourself for your Board Room in Canada."

"No thanks." Hal crossed to the suite's bar. "Champagne, or whisky?"

Norman wasn't finished with his pitch. "How about one of your son, Byron?"

Hal's eyes flashed fire. "A portrait of Byron? No! No thanks. I don't want him to be portrayed as some pansy. When he went off to his boys' boarding school I made sure he had boxing lessons so he could ward off any pansy advances there."

Happy intervened, "Boxin' lessons?" She opened the bar's refrigerator and served a coca cola to Tim and took one for herself. "Ah's read in this mornin's English lan-gu-age noospaper thet a boxin' match be proposed fo' the Las Ventas bullring. Mebbe Byron done got involved in thet."

"My dear Happy, I don't give Byron enough money to play the entrepreneur. He couldn't back a boxing match. I want him to get a proper job now that he's refused to return to his university. I give him very small handouts. That's all. He has no other money except for a Trust I set up. A tough Trust to break. It can only be opened up for charity donations."

Happy continued, "But thet there boxin' match be fo' a charity."

"Which charity?"

"To fight cancer."

Hal went to the telephone and asked the Ritz operator to connect him with the leading cancer charity. We heard him, *sounding incredulous,* repeat, "Byron Murphy! Byron Murphy? You are certain he's backing a boxing match?" Hal grabbed a pencil and wrote on a ready pad. "Thank you, yes. I'd appreciate his address and telephone number."

Within seconds we recognized Byron's voice coming from the telephone. "Yes, Dad. I was able to use Trust money. Yes, next week's the big match. You'll be proud of me. And don't think I'm not going to make a packet out of this. I sure am!"

Hal slumped into a nearby chair. Hanging up without a goodbye, he said to all of us, "My son! My son, a leech who'll use a charity to leech money."

His complaint was cut short when the telephone rang from across the hall from Maheen's open room. She rushed to answer the call. "Yes, Lord Hogan. We'll be right over."

We'd followed Maheen into her room and I asked, "Does Lord Hogan have any news of Sadie?"

"Not exactly. But I think we should go over there. Luca, my dearest, will you please come too? We might have need of a connection to the Madrid police."

I recall how useful Maheen's intuition had been when Happy was solving the Milan serial killer mystery. Maheen was hot on this case now.

We shared a taxi, crowded with my three children in tow. Arriving, we immediately sensed there was a dreadful pall in the Hogan mansion.

No butler. Lord Hogan opened the enormous front door. We were hit by bad odors.

In the great hall a huge vase was still dominating, but its flowers were wilted and a stench came from putrid water that needed changing like a fish tank untended for too many days.

There were more wilted flowers in every room through which we passed. A fireplace smelled bad from a forgotten blaze where now there was nothing but charcoal and ashes.

Lord Hogan stopped in front of Sadie's unfinished portrait. There was a sad empty section in the top left corner which had been scheduled to feature the head of her favorite horse.

"Thank you for coming," Lord Hogan spoke formally. He had a large, very damp handkerchief and blotted his eyes with it continually. "I was surfing the Internet, tried Google and keyed in the name Hillary Harrow. Happy! It said that you, Happy, are a famous sleuth who has fingered five serial murderers. Help me, Happy. I fear we'll never see my Sadie again. I was once a barrow boy who worked shoulder to shoulder with some of the worst scum in England. I managed to elude their projected crimes. But now I need you, Happy. I can't handle this crime. I'm too close to it."

He honked into the handkerchief, and wiped his nose.

Happy gave him a long look. She forgave that she hadn't received condolences from him after Irish's death. Because she certainly knew the pain of losing a daughter, and could understand why he could think of nobody other than his Sadie.

Cadgilly, Lord Hogan spoke as if he'd just awoken from a sleepwalking jaunt. Happy stared at him, reserving her opinion of his behavior. "Can you help?" He repeated his query to Happy, but after catching a glimpse of Luca, he turned to him and examined Luca's police uniform as if he'd never seen one before. He added, speaking directly now to Luca, "Can you help?"

Luca nodded. "I would hope I could help."

"Have you a connection with the British police? Uh, what is that uniform you're wearing?"

"Italian police. I'm attached to the Lake Garda force, visiting Madrid to study what their police have done since terrorists bombed the train that killed so many tourists. We don't want that to happen at Lake Garda's train station."

"The Madrid police? They haven't been helpful at all. They said lots of girls Sadie's age run away from home. From parents who place too many constraints on their children, old-fashioned restrictions on their daughters. Too many restrictions aren't for this modern age. They think my daughter ran off with a boyfriend."

"Could be right. We have that problem in Italy with old-fashioned parents who can't comprehend modern era ways."

"Do you have any other connections?"

"The British police. Yes, I can access Scotland Yard."

"Anyone else?"

"Interpol."

"I'd like to hire you. What do you charge?"

"Nothing, except to the Lake Garda polizia for my regular salary. I'll do what I can to advance your case to please my Maheen. She cares a lot about what may have happened to Sadie."

Maheen put in her opinion, "I'm very afraid there will be a sad outcome. No way did Sadie just run off with a boy."

Happy added, "Ah's read about some pro-fe-ssor at the Uni-ver-sity of Ari-zona who's called Professor Brilliant. Honest to Betsy. Thet's his real name. He's discovered a new way to get criminals. Somethin' to do with their hair! Works better than usin' DNA."

Lord Hogan listened avidly. He pocketed his wet handkerchief. "I want help from everyone I can get. I want every person on this case to use whatever means are available. Newest technology? Yes!"

I sighed. Lord Hogan seemed to be getting up his hopes, but I had a gut feeling that Maheen had the answer: Sadie was dead.

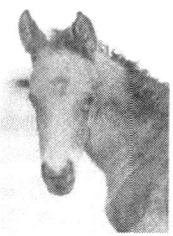

Chapter 17

Two days later we met again at the deteriorating mansion. The smell was worse. Now the flowers had dried out, but the putrid water remained.

Lord Hogan met our group at the door, and ushered us inside the hall. No drinks were offered.

The group included Hal, Mafalda, Maheen, Luca, Happy, and I.

Luca was in civvies. "I'm leaving for Lake Garda," he excused himself from taking further part in the case. "Sorry, Lord Hogan, but none of my contacts could offer any leads. They gave the usual comment, 'working on the case.' Not good enough. But, I'll lose my own job if I don't report back to my superiors what I learned about terrorism on trains."

Lord Hogan was working with two wet handkerchiefs. The tip of his nose and both nostrils were scaling from over use of handkerchiefs. He said, "I've summoned you here because I'm sure you saw on TV that a girl's body has been found with similar injuries as the Hernandez Aza girl had suffered. Eyes gouged out. A screw driver in her jugular. Is this new body Sadie's?"

Luca shrugged. "It will be at forensic now. There will be a situation room with bright minds going over possibilities. I don't like the fact that there are the same injuries. Makes this *look* like a serial killer's at work. But that isn't necessarily true, we could be dealing with a copy-cat murderer or not! Mrs. Harrow, you've traced serial killers, what do you think?"

Happy shook her head like a child who's been to Disneyworld and couldn't believe she'd seen Mickey Mouse. "Ah's not made up mah mind on this here case." Happy had seen the TV news, translated by Luca.

Hal surprised us by forwarding a theory. "Maybe these girls weren't as innocent as we like to think. Maybe they acted like Nabokov's Lolita, and preyed on a man until he snapped."

The roar from Lord Hogan shook the rafters of his mansion. "My daughter was a totally innocent girl. You will learn that is the truth if you just telephone the Madrid police. Dial them now!"

I bypassed his roar and said, "The Hernandez Aza girl was only eleven."

Hal insisted with his grand idea, "There have been Bad Seeds younger than eleven."

Lord Hogan ignored that comment. "Come see her painting. I've had it photographed by a professional and sent a copy to the police. Norman had caught the fresh-air life she chose. No make-up, no teased hair or fancy riding habit. Painted Sadie in a T-shirt."

Norman appeared, joining us to admire his portrait. He'd found the front door open and followed the familiar route to the study.

"I think the police have released my picture of the Hernandez Aza girl to the main TV channels. It's a far, far better thing than to show the awful photos taken where she was found murdered." Norman paraphrased Charles Dickins' book Tale Of Two Cities.

Happy asked, "And where-all was thet? We ain't been told yet where-all she were found."

"Yes. It was on the noonday news. But then you don't speak Spanish. I do, and I know that the place was the grounds of the Las Ventas bullring."

"Horrible place. So many bulls and horses killed there. Now a human being. Could be she were a lovely girl!" Happy shuddered. She pulled out her handkerchief and wiped away tears.

"The Madrid police were so stupid. They haven't done a thing right," Norman pointed out. "You wouldn't believe how careless they were about not messing up the murder scene. Didn't take fingerprints of the people allowed on the grounds. Didn't preserve valuable DNA from the body and from clothes found nearby."

Lord Hogan groaned, "Don't."

"My friend," Norman went to the very dusty bar, polished a glass with a dish cloth and poured out a double whisky for himself. "You mustn't dwell on this bad scene. Remember Sadie as she was in her picture, all youth and charm."

Hal intruded again. "I read somewhere that garroting was the method for capital punishment convictions in Spain, yes, as late as in the 1960's. Perhaps the killer has a fixation about garroting and that's the reason for the screwdriver in the victims' throat. Eh? I think the body the police found was that of a pre-teen prostitute."

"Oh, please don't," Lord Hogan began to sob. He didn't have a ready handkerchief, and used the bar's dishcloth to blot his tears.

Mafalda, who had kept silent, came out with a thought that veered away from the TV news. "I've been given a flyer at our hotel for a concert at Las Ventas with José Carreras and Monserrat Cabal. The bull ring officials will have a lot to do to jolly up the place after such a gruesome murder."

Maheen added, "And then Byron will be running his boxing match for charity, there."

Lord Hogan shook his head as if it was a machine filled with popcorn. He took Luca's arm. "Call the police for me. I need to know if the girl that's been found is Sadie."

Chapter 18

Luca didn't need to call. His cell phone was pulsating. He retrieved it from a buttoned pocket, listened, and then turned directly to Lord Hogan. "Madrid police on the line. Forensic doesn't think the girl murdered at Las Ventas is Sadie. Can you go down to the morgue and help in identification?"

Like a sunrise after a downpour the room filled with Lord Hogan's yell. "Yes. Straight away. Get a taxi. Get three taxis. We must all go."

Three taxis weren't readily available. We managed to find two.

Maheen, Luca, Happy, and Lord Hogan went in one, with Norman and I following accompanied by the senior Murphys.

Our taxi took a roundabout route to jack up the fare. Our driver must have taken one look at Hal and correctly judged him to be an easy touch.

Reaching the police station, we relied on Norman to speak enough Spanish for us to gain access to the morgue.

We found Lord Hogan perched beside a heroic-sized metal tray containing the mutilated body of a teenage girl. He was staring at her. Great distress changed his features. Sunrise had given way to rainclouds. "Not my Sadie, but she's someone's daughter."

Our group split up on the sidewalk outside the police station. I planned to go see Dad, with Happy in tow. An officer hailed two taxis for us. They stopped very promptly for the police! Maheen and Luca left us to collect his suitcase and continue on to the airport. Maheen was trying not to cry, saving her tearful goodbye for the airport.

Norman shrugged at the non-event, "Stupid Madrid police, dragging Lord Hogan down here when they have the photograph of my portrait of her and could damn well see this girl wasn't Sadie."

He told us he needed fresh air and strode off, walking briskly.

Generous Hal, although he well knew that my Dad's hotel was on the opposite side of Madrid from the Ritz, insisted he'd have his taxi drop us off.

We were very quiet in our taxi. Hal must have been thinking of the daughter he'd had with his ex-wife Clara, whom he seldom saw when in Canada.

Happy and I were still absorbed with pangs of longing for Irish.

Chapter 19

Dad wasn't at his hotel. But Fran was. We glimpsed her with one foot straddling the bar's lower brass rail. She was wearing Manolo Blahnik shoes with five inch heels, and looked as if too much alcohol had made her unsteady.

Damn! She saw us. We couldn't get away. We were trapped at the concierge's desk, made to listen politely while the old codger raved on about my father's affair with Nashville-Mary and how wonderful it was to see a man in his eighties so much in love. Envy, no doubt.

Fran stood next to the concierge, winking, and gossiping. The concierge managed a smirk. "The chambermaids never can get in to make up his bed. He's making love in the morning and in the afternoon. And when the chambermaids want to turn down the bed sheets, come evening your father is still making love."

Fran listened to this with her nostrils quivering. For a pregnant woman, she was certainly still in heat. "I've met a divine man," she crowed, leading us to a table near the bar. "I'll have him come over to meet you in a minute. But fuck all, he's a bit of a snob. Rick, you with your Etonian manners, you'll pass. But it's Happy, with her hog-calling language I'm doubtful will make the grade."

Happy grinned as if this nasty comment was as sweet as caramel candy. She didn't miss a thing, my Happy. However, she didn't carry grudges, and often overlooked an unkindness when she figured the perpetrator was having a hard time.

"Wut y'all goin' on about? Fran, Ah wants t'hear how thet per-for-mance at the opery went."

"Superbly, of course. I got six curtain calls for my Zerbinetta. Stole the show from the girl who had Ariadne's role. But then I always give credit where bloody credit is due. And Richard Strauss can produce some heavy music. Ariadne's arias were difficult to follow. While my sublime long aria

254

was light and cheerful, appropriate for the star of a commedia troupe. In Zerbinetta, good old Richard Strauss gave audiences what they really enjoy, a spritely character."

She'd spoken in a loud voice that carried across the room. Almost on cue, a bleached-blonde middle aged man approached our table. He stopped in front of Fran and kissed her hand.

Fran gushed, "Oh darling, these are the Harrows. He's my trainer and she sometimes rides out on my horses for me. Harrows, this is the Marquis de Talleyrand."

I did the little neck arched bow I usually reserve for royalty. Although I knew from my school books that the great Eighteenth Century Marquis de Talleyrand had left no heir. Not one who could use the clever Marquis de Talleyrand's title. That masterful man, a politicians' politician, had died in the early nineteenth century without legitimate issue. What surprised me was that Fran, now a proper countess listed in DEBRETT would be fooled by a bottle of peroxide and a kiss on the hand.

"Darling Francoise, how well you look. My friend Dr. Pont has certainly cleared up that little rheum that had troubled you." His use of English was impeccable.

"Yes, darling. Totally. I was in great voice last night, as you'd know if you'd read the critics' comments. All thanks to your wonderful Dr. Pont."

Oh, oh. That did not bode well for her marriage to Jeremy. Not good, that Jeremy had missed both her opera performances in Madrid. And had not taken any part in finding a doctor to cure Fran's cold. Jeremy should have hired the best nose and throat man in Britain and flown him out here. Perhaps it was undiplomatic of me, but I asked, "And how's Jeremy?"

Fran frowned. Not for long. Fran knew well that frowns cause wrinkles. She tossed her head, gently, so as not to mess her expensive hairdo. "Jeremy? Always so busy in the Lords, trying to find the way out of Afghanistan for our troops."

"Oh?" Talleyrand seemed inordinately interested.

"Yes. And he's come up with an excellent plan. Jeremy has suggested that the Afghanistan government permit small farmers to grow their poppies, but with smaller harvests. That way the farmers wouldn't lose all their traditional income, only have a smaller one."

I was surprised at Fran's careful English. No four letter words in front of Talleyrand. Oh, no. And poppies? She must know quite a lot about the harvesting of poppies considering her years of heroin use.

Next it was Talleyrand's turn to surprise. And not in a way that pleased me. Talleyrand swerved his admiring glance from Fran to concentrate it on my Happy. He kissed her hand. My unsophisticated Baptist jerked her hand away, but was flattered nevertheless. God, this must not be the start of another of those flirtations that so rocked my marriage when those two Australians tried to seduce my wife last year.

Will I ever forget Rus, driving us to Sydney all those hours singing Dancing Matilda with Happy until I thought I'd scream! Any threat from Rus had ended when the careless man took his sick baby out in the rain in order to buy wine for himself. That, followed by horrible Rex in Saratoga, who was shown the door quickly when Happy burned his probing hand with a borrowed cigarette.

But they were not as skillful as Talleyrand. I recalled in Gone With The Wind when Rhett Butler said to Scarlett something along the lines of 'you've had one husband who was too young, another too old, now you'll find out what a real man is like' and that quote bothered me. I could guess that Talleyrand was a master at sex.

Fran guessed that too. She bristled like a porcupine whose quills were vibrating. Speaking as if she were ejecting darts, Fran snapped, "Call over to our friends the Ponts, tell them to leave their table and join ours. And you, YOU come sit beside me." Fran squeezed an extra chair between Happy and herself, then jumped into the seat next to Happy, leaving the extra one for Talleyrand. He was not to sit with my wife. Not if Fran could help it.

She gestured to two waiters, then directed them to unclip four half-moon leaves that transformed this square table into a round one, seating eight.

Dr. Pont and his wife joined us promptly. No doubt they liked the look of the magnum of champagne that Fran had ordered. I could see that the glasses they'd abandoned were empty.

"I'm Rick Harrow, Lady Cabrach's horse trainer," I introduced myself when Talleyrand made no effort to do so.

Happy joined in, "And Ah be his wife. Name of Hillary, but most folks call me just plain Happy. Y'all got any chillun?"

"Chillun?" Talleyrand's fine knowledge of the English language didn't include Kentucky-Hills talk.

I translated, "Children."

Madame Pont chimed in, "I'm Giselle. Yes, we have a child, a daughter. Our girl's called Ghislaine. With the same initials, she can someday inherit all my engraved silver."

Mafalda approved of that. "I'm Mafalda Murphy, and I too have a daughter with the same initial. She's called Maheen."

We all nodded politely. Giselle added, "Interesting names."

Mafalda enlightened her. "I'm Egyptian. So is my daughter."

In a deep, rumbling tone Dr. Pont intervened. "Ah! Egypt! I'm proud that France has had such a fine historical record there. Napoleon's forces discovered how to translate Egypt's hieroglyphics thanks to the Rosetta Stone."

No comment from Mafalda. She looked displeased. Hal explained why, "My wife doesn't look with favor on any army that invaded Egypt, from the ancient Babylonians' to General Rommel's."

Changing the subject, Dr. Pont peered at the label on the magnum of champagne. "Ah! Pommery! A longtime winner, made by the de Polignac family. A great family which intermarried with the original makers."

Talleyrand queried, "Good friend, did you know Prince Henri-Melchior de Polignac? The one who was killed when the small airplane he was piloting crashed against telephone wires when he swooped down near ground level to inspect the family's vines?"

"Yes, I knew him. And his father, Prince Guy de Polignac. Prince Guy initiated a Nobel Prize-like award for each year's best vintage, in memory of his son."

Fran bit out, "Well, drink up. I suggest that we four go upstairs to see my portrait. I'd like your advice as to if it needs anything added. Not you, Harrows. You two are always in such a hurry to go home. So, go home. And, you Murphys? I don't believe you need to see my portrait again. After all, you have your own Norman portrait."

Dismissed, we left the hotel like two students who'd been chastened by their headmaster, and sent home, but felt that was no punishment. Home! Yes, we were delighted to be on our way there.

The Murphys stayed at the enlarged table to drink up what remained in that magnum of champagne. They looked abandoned, only two at a table for eight.

Chapter 20

We next met as an eightsome on the night of Byron's charity boxing match. But the eightsome grew to ten.

During the past two weeks Fran's best filly had developed a sore on her right front heel, and I'd had to postpone her run until that was cured. The result was that we'd been kept in Spain until she could run.

Our three limos were in line in the parking lot. The two Murphys had invited Happy and me to share theirs. Fran and Talleyrand were in the second. Fran had broken her Penny pinching rules to impress Talleyrand. No scrounging a ride when Talleyrand was present. The third contained Dr. Pont, his wife Giselle, their daughter Ghislaine and two newcomers, Germain and Eva Galé. The Galés had obviously paid for that limo. The Galés reeked of old money, and lots of it.

"Where-all's Maheen?" Happy asked as soon as she saw that the Murphys were alone.

Hal replied, somewhat sheepishly. "We haven't heard a word since she went to the airport with Luca. We imagine she's staying at Lake Garda to be near him."

As a group I counted that twelve of us walked toward the grand entrance of the Las Ventas bullfighting ring. Along the way we passed an open tent. I noted that waiters in red jackets were carrying in large platters of food covered with foil wrap.

Not twelve, I counted again and realized we were thirteen people. That didn't bode well. I'm not a superstitious man, but thirteen? I've never liked that number. When there were thirteen horses in a race, or we'd draw the thirteenth stall, every time I lost with that number.

Happy had warmed to Giselle. "Ah sho like wut y'all's wearin'. Right pretty," she said sincerely.

In fact, Giselle's gown was awful. It had a tiny waist covered in silver sequins over red satin and below there was an enormous skirt in the same red satin embroidered by white feathers. If I'd been Dr. Pont I'd have felt very embarrassed. But the paparazzi adored her over-the-top look. Good for selling newspapers. Next to Giselle came her daughter, Ghislaine, who'd arrived in a nondescript half-length more suitable for graduation from a convent school than an A-list charity event. No photos were taken of her outfit.

Their backers, the Galés, were discreet in their choices. Germain Galé wore a tired black tie smoking jacket that had seen many parties. His wife, Eva, was in a simple white silk column of a gown that was deceptive in its simplicity, because a close examination revealed it had been designed and cut by a master of the craft.

We'd been introduced very briefly, as if we didn't count for much. Talleyrand was all over the Galés. He recognized quality, all right. And big money.

Talleyrand whispered, "Germain Galé owns one of the greatest silk factories in France. Been in his family over two hundred years. Located in Lyons. Ever hear of Napoleon's great love, Desirée, whom he lost to his General Bernadotte, who became Queen of Sweden? Desirée's father was a silk merchant. A Galé provided him with silk!"

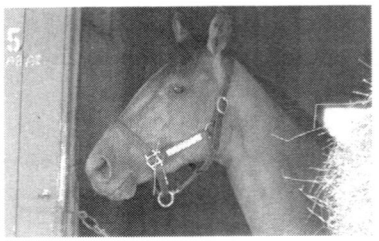

Chapter 21

The boxing match turned out to be a disaster.

We had prime front row seats, thanks to Hal's generosity. The Galés and Ponts were not far behind, in the third row. At least we weren't seated in a line totaling thirteen.

Everything went wrong from the start. I'd never seen Byron's wonder boy, the boxer who was being promoted along with the charity event. When I caught sight of him entering the ring, I felt a tremor go through me. He had bad eyes.

I recalled how Joseph Hume Dudgeon, one of the world's greatest judges of sportsmanship, always said, "You can tell a good one by the eyes."

This man in the silver and scarlet trunks was not a good one.

His name, Cannonball Jones. That cannonball tag forewarned how he would fight.

And it would not be by the Marques of Queensberry's rules. He came out with his head down to ram his opponent before the poor man could get up his gloves. Ram, ram, ram. He aimed at the head, neck, and stomach. Then he rammed lower down, and his opponent began to howl like a wounded animal being peppered by gunshot instead of a clean rifle shot.

Five minutes into the first round, the fight was stopped. The referee had been alerted that the local authorities would not put up with so much brutality.

An announcement came over the loud speaker saying that all tickets to the boxing match would be refunded, but that those present who had paid for the dinner dance in the tent should proceed there immediately.

Lights began to go out inside the bullring.

A very deflated, and totally anxious Byron joined his father. "I'm ruined," he said. "And what can we possibly do to entertain five hundred guests from eight p.m. to ten, when the dinner will be served? Food's here, but the drinks haven't arrived yet. I can't even offer a glass of wine."

We left the darkened bullring, and crossed the half lit parking lot going toward the tent. I couldn't help but wonder in that eerie light just exactly where the body of the teenage prostitute had been found whom the Madrid police had mistakenly tagged as Sadie Hogan.

Hal said, "There should be better lights here. Someone could fall, and then—Byron—you'll be sued."

Byron countered, "I took out insurance against anyone being injured inside or outside this damned bullring. Much good that will do me, now that all tickets have to be reimbursed."

Hal insisted with his theme, "You could have insured against the fight being cancelled."

"I did. But only if caused by heavy rain. My worst problem is that it won't be granted charity status if it's classified as a non-event. And for the Americans here, that's very serious because they won't be able to charge the tickets against their income tax."

An ever-surprising side to Fran's complex personality now cheered us. Fran came charging across the car park's asphalted surface, calling to Byron. "Fuck you, what a mess, but I'm here and can straighten it out. If the pianist for the ball is here, I can sing for your guests."

Fran! One of the world's great mezzo-sopranos would sing without any rehearsing? In a tent? Gratis?

"The pianist's here," Byron yelped. "He's been practicing. Said he didn't know enough about jazz beats for the dance part of the ball. Listen. You can hear him playing."

Our party, now numbering fourteen, raced inside the well-decorated tent that smelled sweetly from the bowls of roses on each table. Waiters, without their jackets, bent in shirtsleeves to finish with the table settings.

Hal, who hadn't earned his nickname MONEYBAGS idly, rushed to the pianist and asked, "How much will you charge to start playing, right now?"

This pianist understood money. And he understood that he was to play NOW. His knowledge of English was also excellent. "One thousand pounds sterling."

"Done." Hal pulled out his usual fat roll of bills, separated pounds from pesetas, and paid up front.

The five hundred charity-write off guests were streaming into the tent and ogling place cards for the seating arrangements.

Fran asked the pianist, "Can you play Musetta's aria from Boheme? Carmen's song when she boasts of her sexy prowess? Susuki's lament from Butterfly? How about Zerbinetta's fun-filled aria?"

"All of those. I know them all by heart. And I was the pianist at the Teatro Real for the first performance of Ariadne auf Nexus that was such a success. You, countess, I heard you sing that aria last night. You were sublime."

Once the entire five hundred were seated an expectant hush had come over them, lights were dimmed as if in a concert hall, and Fran took a position leaning against the piano. Unknown to her, the whale boned hoop skirt that had given such a Gone With The Wind style to her gown now ballooned outward, exposing her legs all the way up to the thighs.

Didn't matter. Nobody giggled. Fran was wearing tights which hid the important bits. She sang well, and when intermission was signaled, the applause was deafening.

While Fran had a moment of repose in the waiters' smaller tent, watching as the drinks van arrived and bottles began to be distributed, a man approached her whom none of us knew.

"I'm one of the Ten Tenors," he introduced himself. "I'd be pleased to sing a few duets with you, if you'd permit."

"We could do the duet in the tomb from Aida," she said, accepting his offer. White wine was served to the waiting audiences, and that enlivened the mood. God, I certainly felt relieved that the drinks van had appeared.

The duets were fantastic. Fran bonded with this tenor immediately. I said to Hal, "Oh! Oh! I'm afraid our Fran is going to add this guy to her string."

Hal laughed. "Not on your nelly. She isn't aboot to trade a red-blooded Marquis for a pansy boy."

"You sure he's homosexual?"

"Not aboot to try him oot. Of that you can be sure. But come on, let's ask for champagne. Enough of this white wine shit. Tastes like horse pee!"

When the dinner part of the evening began I felt relieved to see that I wasn't seated next to Mafalda. By some quirk of fate I landed the very young and palatable Madame Galé. As I know damn-all about the silk industry, I left her subject alone and talked about what I do know: horses.

"Do you ride, Madame?" I asked after learning she had no interest in racehorses.

"Yes, certainly, I do. I'm from Normandy, and we have some of the finest horses in the world in my area. I ride to hounds, chasing the deer. I don't kill them. I leave the hunt before the kill, but I adore the excitement of following those exquisite creatures in their haunts. Do you hunt?"

"Not any more. I did go foxhunting when I was a teenager because everyone in my pony club did that. At present I'm too busy riding out for morning and evening stables to chase foxes. Do you still go hunting?"

"Certainly. In fact, tomorrow my husband and I are going to try out a new region for enjoying this sport. There's a futuristic hotel in Spain's premiere wine-growing region. Totally unexpected delights are promised for those of us who enjoy riding. That, in addition to the fun of wine-tasting at many of the vineries. Why don't you join our party?"

Madrid's Mocking Murders

I wondered if this ingenuous young woman had any idea of my precarious finances. Back at my establishment in Epsom, there are employees in the stables and in the house, gardeners, and stable lads who work the horses. If I should lose even one more owner I might have to declare bankruptcy. This jaunt to Spain to pacify Fran had been disastrous in so many ways. The worst of which was the death of our adorable Irish!

M. Galé encouraged me by leaning across the table from where he sat sandwiched between Happy and Giselle Pont, and echoing his wife. "Yes, do join us. All expenses paid, of course. And we could discuss the possibility of my buying a racehorse for you to train."

An additional owner. Wouldn't that be good news after so much tragedy!

I calculated how simple it would be for the Galés to fly from Nice Airport direct to Heathrow and attend Ascot races. Easy. They could be from their home in Lyon to Heathrow inside of two hours.

Quickly I reached across the table and stuck out my right hand. "Let's shake on that," I said. "I've got one extremely fine yearling. I believe he'll win some very good races. Never know what ailments or accidents might come his way, but all things being equal he should be a great buy for you. Diessis for a sire. Dam won two races."

A roar of protest came from Fran from the far end of our rectangular table. "I heard that! Why are you offering a great yearling to a stranger, instead of *to me?*"

No reply to that. But seated next to Fran was dear Hal, and he also roared out, "Why haven't you told me about this colt?"

I could foresee I was going to have a lot of trouble with those two owners. Would it be worth chancing their wrath to get one more? Yes. I was THAT desperate.

The evening wore on. Giselle danced with M. Galé, so I had no further opportunity to get him to repeat his offer. Fran danced with her tenor. Maybe he was a homosexual, because he certainly excelled on the dance floor, and that sometimes hints at that inclination. The other dancers left a wide circle for those two, and he showed off partnering famous Fran. Talleyrand stormed out of the party and out of our lives.

What a relief when I could go back to our hotel and hold Happy in my arms. She had trouble concentrating on our lovemaking. Every few minutes she'd interrupt that with a query about Maheen.

"When do y'all reckon we'll hear from her?"

I accepted those interruptions because her ardor was so fantastic when she did concentrate that anything was worth enduring.

Chapter 22

When we did hear from Maheen it was to land us with a huge dilemma.

"Where-all are y'all?" Happy asked when she recognized Maheen's voice on a telephone call that came early next morning.

"London."

"Wut y'all doin' there? We'all been worried sick that the noospaper would be describin' how po-lice found another girl with a screwdriver in her throat, and thet girl be y'all."

"Luca's been sent on another mission by his superiors to study terrorism on trains. I decided to use the allowance money Hal gave me and take a flight to London. I'm checking up on Lord Hogan. Listen up."

"Ah's listenin'."

"I thought there was something wrong about him. Thought the title must be phony. He's such a dork, but no, when Blair was Prime Minister he got Hogan into the Lords, all right. But Hogan didn't go to Spain to be a tax exile. He had to leave Britain. He's on every council list as a pedophile."

"Naw!"

"Wait, there's more. I guessed that Sadie wasn't his daughter. He couldn't adopt a child, so he bought one. Sadie. There are countries where you can do that. Former Soviet Russia has so many ex-satellites there's no one to control the money-grabbing goings-on. Lord Hogan had no trouble getting exactly what he wanted. White, pretty, and very young. She wasn't sixteen months old."

"Naw! Disgustin'."

"He abused her from almost the first year. Gruesome. That crap about giving a debut party for her to meet boys? How cruel that suggestion was! To better control her, Lord Hogan encouraged her love for horses. Nerdy, or what?"

"Where she be, NOW?"

"Heaven only knows. Heaven, and maybe the MI6. Luca's on to MI6 now. He's already clawed through the Interpol files. But he's awfully busy with the terrorism on trains thing."

"Rick has a great pal who be an ex-MI6 person. Believe it or not, the man's Fran's husband, Lord Cabrach." Happy turned to me and handed me the telephone receiver. "Talk some, Rick. Please?"

I said to Maheen, "You're a brave darling, to take this on by yourself. I recall you did something similar in Milan and almost got yourself killed."

"Me? I'll be fine. But for closure, I know I have to rely on Happy. I've been thinking, this horror of a beast, this yuk Lord Hogan, he may not be a killer. A pervert, sure. One of the worst. But murder young girls with a screwdriver? I doubt it. I'm on the track of somebody else who originated here."

"Come back to Madrid, Maheen. Your mother will be frantic."

"You must be kidding! My mother doesn't give a damn what happens to me, as long as it doesn't embarrass her."

"Hal cares."

"I guess so. He's a really good step-father. Don't hurry me, though. I've a feeling there's a lot more I can unearth here in London."

Happy retrieved the telephone. "Maheen, honey. Come stay with us'n at ourn ho-tel. Soon's y'all can. Do what y'all must, but be quick about it. Take care."

No sooner had Happy said her goodbye than the telephone rang again. This time I heard the cultured voice of Monsieur Galé. "*Bon Jour.* My wife and I want to invite you most formally to join our little romp to a Spanish vineyard. In the Rioja Alavesa region. Not far from the ancient town of El Viejo. Wine tasting, horse riding, fishing and there's a Festival of Flamenco Dancing in the area. We'll take it all in stride."

Should I ask him if he'd like to buy my yearling? Yes!

"Monsieur Galé, have you given any thought to purchasing the yearling I told you about?" I wanted an affirmative response before I committed Happy and myself to venturing into the vineyards' region, leaving Fran's filly's care to the groom.

"Rick, may I call you that, Rick if you'll have your staff at the Epsom stable FAX me photos of the yearling and more about his sire's and dam's wins, I may be interested. But I do want to mix more with you, Rick, personally before I decide to spend at least two years going to racecourses with you."

Trapped! I had to agree to wait on his response and give mine immediately. I did. "Thank you. Happy and I will be delighted to join you both."

"I'll send my helicopter for you two. There may be other passengers, I've invited Hal and Mafalda Murphy, the Ponts and their daughter, and Norman.

I'm considering having Norman paint our portraits, mine and my wife's, and I need to learn more about how these other people truly feel about the portraits Norman did of them. On the Q T, of course."

Helicopter? I wondered about how large that could be, and I took notice that Lord Hogan had not been included among the guests. I figured he wasn't Galé's class. I doubted that Galé had any suspicions he was a pervert. But Hal wasn't his class, either. Yet he'd invited my rough diamond Canadian owner. I was beginning to understand that Monsieur Galé was very astute, and I resolved not to underestimate him in the future.

Monsieur Galé added, "My helicopter can land in the center of the field at the Zarzuela racecourse. It will be there this afternoon at three. Bring clothes for riding, and for formal dining. *Au revoir.*"

Promptly at three p.m. a large helicopter whisked down on to the grass centerfield. I'd seen other helicopters use the space to bring jockeys and other trainers here. But this helicopter was way beyond their size. This was a Sikorsky model, capable of transporting twelve passengers and three crew in comfort.

Dodging the whirling blades and their brisk tails of wind, Happy and I carried our overnight bags with us and were helped aboard.

Mafalda and Hal were already quite tipsy, having emptied one bottle of champagne. The Ponts and their daughter were munching on sandwiches, the host and hostess were sharing the contents of an elegant silver coffee pot.

Norman was sipping Pellagrino. I guessed he didn't want to make any faux pas in front of the Galés and thereby lose a potential goldmine. In the seat next to his he'd propped two full-size canvases on which he could portray each Galé from head to toe.

The helicopter had not cut its blades. It was able to take off immediately after we boarded. Champagne flutes were pressed into our hands by Madame Galé, and we accepted hors d'oeuvres passed by a stewardess.

Within very few minutes we were skimming the mountainous terrain that is so typical of most of Spain. I envisioned in my mind the captains of Castille and Aragon crossing these hills on horseback in full armor, ready to defend them against Moors. I imagined the early conquistadors riding towards Cartagena to sail to the Indies. I was reminded of how Napoleon's army had wasted this land after occupying it, and having his brother placed here as a usurping king. I thought of the bloodbaths between Republicans and General Franco's monarchists during the 1930s Civil War.

Now all was peaceful below. Wide highways crisscrossed the valleys. Neat farms were perched on hilltops. Eventually these gave way to striped acres of vines, their long pathways like the teeth of a comb.

Down we went to a helipad fashioned close to an extremely modernistic hotel. Not my style. So futuristic that its windows had no curtains, this hotel inside had practically no furniture and certainly no carpets. It was painted all in one color: white.

There was no garden, we drove up to a front door and entered its hall where there were no porters in sight. We carried our overnight bags with us, and an employee wearing no uniform pointed our way to the lifts, that Happy calls "el-e-va-tors."

The saving grace was an exceptionally huge king-size bed in our room. But I worried about the soundproofing, because exactly as in that big uncurtained hallway, the noise from other guests was terrific. How could we make love in that inviting bed when Happy gives so many ecstatic yelps?

I wasn't to find out for some hours. Monsieur Galé had scheduled our stay to the minute. First we were to visit the stables for saddle horses. They were okay, but the horses were nothing special. We weren't to go on a wine tasting bash until the following day. According to Monsieur Galé, we'd ruined our palates by drinking champagne on the helicopter ride.

The first evening was spent at a local bistro that featured Flamenco dancing. "Not a local art form," Monsieur Galé elaborated. "This dance comes from Seville's gypsies."

Happy and Giselle tried to emulate the dancers, but they were woefully deficient in knowledge of its intricate steps.

"Ah cain't arch mah back like them dancers do," Happy moaned. "Ain't wut kind o' dancin' we'all does in mah Kentucky hills."

The following morning the lady guests were all invited to participate in a cookery class provided by the hotel's chef. His kitchen had all the latest appliances, and wonderful smells came out of it, but I know Happy was glad to escape it after two hours. "Ah ain't no good at cookin' anyhow."

Ghislaine fell in love with the recipes, and tried them all. There were tapas, a tortilla de patata, chorizos, jamon de Serrano, and arequipe. Nothing that my grooms at home in Epsom would eat on a bet. Maybe the ham with the potato cake, but they'd turn up their noses and demand raises if I fed them on that stuff for any length of time.

Rain pelted down. Monsieur Galé suggested we go fishing. I don't mind fishing in the rain, but I need the appropriate clothes. The hotel furnished them. We were kitted out with waders, rubber boots, plastic capes and plastic southwesters. A jeep took us high into the rolling hills to a stream.

I looked into the limpid waters and saw nothing but pebbles. Then the pebbles moved. I spied a fat elderly trout, who knew these waters better than I did. He nosed up to my hook, that I'd plopped unskillfully. At the next beat was Monsieur Galé, whose line had been masterfully arched behind and then in front of him to sail far into the middle of the stream. He winked at me, encouraging me. I watched the old trout think about this unfamiliar item in his water. He touched the hook repeatedly, then swallowed it. Away he sped, pulling out my line, burning my index finger where I was trying to control the amount of spin. No way was I going to best this trout. I thought how similar his tactics were to the killer of those girls with screwdrivers in their necks. This trout had studied the hook, and yet had taken it. I wished the screwdriver killer would take a hook!

A ghillie approached me with a readied net. After some minutes of reeling in and then letting the line play out, I managed to bring our trout close to shore, where the ghillie expertly netted him.

"Release the trout," I said.

"But very good to eat," the ghillie countered. He had some use of the English language, having worked with tourists who fished.

I released the trout myself, after removing the hook as gently as possible and easing him back into the stream. My trout sedately swam away toward the far bank.

"No bites for me," Monsieur Galé called. He sent for the jeep and we returned to the hotel. I couldn't gauge from his polite expression whether or not he would have wanted to eat my trout.

Having cleansed our palates by joining our ladies and duly tasted their recipes, we were finally permitted to venture to various vineries to judge their individual brews. Wonderful! Personally I preferred one that came mixed with fruits and other goodies called sangria. It went down as a special treat. Better still, Happy got a little drunk, just enough to add additional zest to our love making that night.

The next morning we never got to test those nothing-special horses. Heavy rain continued to douse any hopes of that. Monsieur Galé apologized. "The trails go up into higher hills, where the horses couldn't hope to get any purchase in the mud."

Reduced to sheltering in that blandly decorated hotel, we crouched around a blaze in its circular fireplace. That's where Norman made his pitch.

"Monsieur Galé, have you decided whether you'd like head to foot portraits of yourself and your charming wife, or just head and shoulders."

Kind Monsieur Galé, a considerate host, was gentle as he dashed Norman's hopes of a lucrative commission. "Sorry, Norman, but my darling wife has decided against having portraits done, of any size. No space in either our Paris apartment or our home in Lyon. But we'd be happy to pay for you to do a charcoal sketch of Ghislaine, which I know the Ponts want and cannot afford."

A charcoal sketch! Usually Norman gave those away for free to prospective sitters who'd given a down payment for a portrait in oils.

Norman disguised his disappointment. We heard no gnashing of teeth nor saw any down turned lips. He forced a smile, and said, "In that case, Monsieur Galé, I won't overburden you with my company. I'll return tonight to Madrid."

He bowed pleasantly enough and thanked Madame Galé for the visit to the wine country, left us, and a half hour later we watched as he crossed the great bare hall with his overnight bag to wait for a taxi. I assumed he'd find his own way back to Madrid. Cheapest by bus. For that he'd have to overnight locally.

We were driven by limos to another local Bistro, where instead of Flamenco dancers, we were introduced to a local artist who proceeded to make agreeable sketches of each of us, charging Monsieur a few pesetas. I liked mine.

Happy whispered to me, "Ah doesn't think much o' these here por-traits. But they sho turned out to be cheaper than Norman's. Lucky he left heah befo'e this evenin', Ah thinks he might have had a heart at-tack to see por-traits sellin' fo' a pittance."

When we returned to the hotel, there were three portraits in charcoal left behind on the hall's single table. Norman had sketched Monsieur and Madame Galé cartoon-style, exaggerating their less attractive features. Monsieur Galé had Dumbo ears. Madame Galé's nose was longer than Pinocchio's.

Far ruder was the portrait of Dr. Pont, not done in a cartoon style so that there would be no mistake about whom the sketch portrayed. Dr. Pont had horns sprouting from his head.

Horns of a devil, or horns of a cuckold! Who was to know?

Later that night Happy's lovemaking was subdued. I'd done my best to arouse her, with small success.

Next morning a smaller helicopter awaited us, having over-nighted on the hotel's helipad. This helicopter carried only six passengers, because our party had slimmed to six.

Not only had Norman left, but little Ghislaine had said she'd decided to stay behind at the hotel and pursue her fascination with Spanish recipes. Monsieur Galé had agreed to foot the bill for cookery classes and two additional nights at the hotel.

I wasn't sad or nostalgic at leaving the wine country. Our little EC-155 helicopter was neat, with its rotors gleaming.

There was a well-stocked bar to complement the fresh sandwiches on board.

Monsieur Galé insisted all passengers wear parachutes, though. He didn't own this helicopter. He wasn't familiar with either the aircraft nor with the pilot, he explained. "I hope you don't think I'm acting paranoid, but to humor me, please I ask everyone to put on their parachutes before they buckle themselves into their seats. Uncomfortable? Not familiar with the use of a parachute? Forget it. That's better than DEAD."

Monsieur Galé, in tour operator mode, described the scene below. "Those are the Campo Viejo vineyards. Only forty years old. But already they produce some of the finest wines of Rioja. Look at that seemingly crazy architecture beyond, it's a gravity-fed facility designed by one of our leading Spanish architects, Ignacio Quemada."

Not to my taste, that building. Looked like some of the horrors I'd disliked in Dubai. But what I DID admire were the amazing triple tiers of bare cliffs that edged the area. I wouldn't want to be in a helicopter that crashed into THOSE.

We'd left the Rioja area and were grazing even higher mountains when I sensed rather than heard a dangerous gasping from the rotors of our helicopter.

Everyone, except the stewardess, had strapped on their parachutes. The stewardess, not a standard addition to this type of aircraft, had to crouch on a bench in the middle.

We'd started out well enough, leaving the gentle hills of the vineyards going towards those sheer cliffs. But now we'd reached the high mountains that are more typical of Spain's general landscape.

Happy was the first to notice that there was serious trouble. "Listen up, them two rotors ain't makin' no noise. Them's shut down."

She was right. The next thing I knew our host had pushed open an emergency door and instructed his wife and all of his guests to jump. He jumped. His wife jumped.

I'd never made a leap into the sky before. I stared down below and felt relieved to see that we'd skirted a mountain and had therefore reached a high spot in the sky which gave an advantageous drop to the low valley deep below us. But the aircraft's plunge gave me the feeling of a very tricky rollercoaster, and I knew I had to be quick on the ball. I speedily unfastened my seat belt, stood up, completed buckling my parachute, made certain Happy's was strapped on carefully then I took the blast of air from the emergency door, and jumped.

Happy jumped next. I imagine she'd thought if we were to be killed at least it would be together.

The two Ponts jumped. The pilot had remained on board to attempt to maintain the aircraft's RPM, but without thrust from the two failed engines the blades rotated ever more slowly. Finally, he jumped. He went last, like the captain of a ship.

The very young stewardess, hysterical, refused to jump. She hadn't bothered to collect her parachute. Now it was too late for her.

We watched in horror as she remained inside the fast descending helicopter that bypassed our opened parachutes to crash like a meteor to the valley below.

Strapped into my harness, by manipulating my lines, I attempted to veer closer to Happy. "Stop that!" The pilot yelled from above me. "You'll entangle the chutes."

I veered away. The stream of air rushing up at me was damp and warm from yesterday's rain. That had softened the ground where I hit, and although I became covered in revolting mud, I was alive.

Happy seemed to understand this mode of transportation. She manipulated her lines as if they were the reins of a galloping horse, and came safely down to be cushioned by a hay stack. Hay sprouted from her hair, clothes, and mouth. She removed it from her lips and yelled to me, "Ah's right used to hay, ain't I?"

Our group assembled near where the pilot landed. None of us had suffered serious injuries. Pont limped painfully, but he didn't have a real break in either leg.

"Where are we?" Monsieur Galé queried the pilot.

"Sir, we're near a resort fishing village. I know this area. Have flown foreign fishermen to take their luck in that river over there."

We all stared at the fast moving river and its lethal rapids. I, for one, felt very content not to have landed in its killing waters.

The huge blaze from the helicopter had alerted authorities to our arrival. Also I imagine several fishermen might have seen us in our leisurely descent in our parachutes, and used their cell phones to call for help for us.

An ambulance and its siren soon made its loud arrival. Medics jumped out to cut us free from our parachutes.

Happy was one of the first to be able to accept a cup of coffee from their ready thermoses. She asked the medics, "Could y'all please hurry over to thet there hel-i-copter to see if'n there be any chance a girl stewardess on boa'd could have survived?"

"No chance of that," an ambulance driver said in forced high-school English. "Too bad wreck."

Together, my two arms around Happy's quivering shoulders, we gazed at that horrific blaze. Happy said a prayer.

Chapter 23

Aravac looked wonderful to us when we reached it hours later. We decided to take a taxi there, yes, expensive, but we were in a rush to get to our hotel.

Happy was desperate to check on our 'chillun.' I too, but also I needed to see how Fran's filly had responded to her treatment.

* * *

The Ponts had wanted to alert Ghislaine that they had survived the helicopter crash, but that futuristic hotel had very poor telephone service and they hadn't reached her. The Ponts e-mailed Ghislaine to urge her to come home by train immediately.

We didn't see The Ponts again that day.

I learned from the Ponts that their friends, our hosts, had hurried to return to Lyon. No more was said about my chance to train a horse for them. Maybe after that helicopter crash Monsieur Galé felt I was unlucky for him.

Our 'chillun' were fine. Amazingly, Maheen had arrived from London and had been caring for them. After generous hugs, Maheen said, "Happy dear, I'll give you all the info I've collected once you've settled your kids."

I went to the stables. The most important thing I noted there was that Fran's filly was in astonishingly good form.

We checked with the Ponts. They'd had no word from Ghislaine, but weren't worried. They expected all was well and she'd arrive by train on schedule tomorrow.

She didn't.

Instead, as had happened on various other fraught occasions, before she could fill us in on what more she'd learned in London, Maheen received a frantic call from Giselle Pont.

She'd returned to Madrid, had separated from Dr. Pont after a row that followed his discovering that Norman's sketch of him was correct, and that Giselle had a lover. Giselle gasped, "You've been close to Ghislaine. Tell me. Have you heard from her? I'm in hell with worry."

Maheen had replied truthfully, "I've been in London, then went to take care of the Harrow children. I haven't been in touch with Ghislaine."

Then she'd turned to my Happy.

Before Maheen could say a word, Happy asked, "Ghislaine? She be a victim, too? Disappeared, like them other girls? Could what y'all learned in London have any con-nec-tion?"

"Very possibly. What I stumbled on makes this disappearance more unsavory. It was Norman I researched. Not a pedophile, our Norman. A crook. With a criminal record for stiffing wealthy sitters. Jail time. More worrisome, he'd been giving away the portraits he'd made of old ladies in exchange for choosing him as their stock broker. He'd been selling them dicey hedge funds."

Happy astonished me by asking Maheen, "Same hedge funds wut Lord Hogan sells?"

"How did you guess?"

"Ah's figured thet Lord Hogan made his big money about the time he left England. Sadie said a pile of money, wut he didn't want taxed. How did he get a fortune? The fash-ion-able way, with them hedge funds. He done told us he'd started bus'ness life as a 'barrow boy' so we know he were clever at sellin' things. We'all knew he'd met up with Norman. He told usn Norman did his po'trait in England, soon after he got himself sent to the Lords."

Maheen had nodded at each of Happy's statements. She added, "And incidentally, I checked up and learned Norman's title was a fake."

I asked, "Never knighted? He added the Sir title here in Spain. Phoney. I thought so. Norman would never have been a Baronet, and even Tony Blair wouldn't have asked the Queen to knight someone like Norman."

"Correct. Norman also added a huge jump in fees. While in England, he earned two hundred pounds a picture, never thousands. He did much better offering to give them as gifts to the old ladies who bought his hedge fund." Maheen interrupted herself to take a call from her cell phone. She listened. A heavy male voice gave instructions.

"Wut be it darlin'?" Happy was jumpy. Even having Richard nuzzle her nose with his head didn't calm her.

"That was a police officer pal of Luca's. Wants us all to come to the station in Madrid."

"Not before tomorrow morning. I'm on strike," I complained. "We've only just arrived, after surviving a terrible crash."

"Luca's pal said tomorrow would be fine. The Madrid police are waiting on the arrival of crash experts to examine the helicopter. People from the helicopter's manufacturer. And other people who specialize in tracking sabotage."

"Yeah man! Ah sho hopes them do a good job at findin' out wut happened to thet there hel-i-copter. Don't usn forget thet sweet little steward-ess thet died."

I said gravely, "Sabotage. I thought as much. But how. And who did it?"

We found out the answer to my first question in the morning at the main Madrid police station. Experts had arrived from the E C-115's manufacturers. They'd already flown to the crash site and made extensive discoveries. They'd learned that rags had been put into the compartment next to the shaft where they would have come loose eventually to get entangled and stop the motors.

A tall Texan, wearing his cowboy hat and high-heeled boots, explained to me, "In California we know how that could work. A helicopter works off a shaft of engines which produce the forward thrust. With no horsepower from the two engines, the blades slow to naught."

I nodded, without total understanding. I was still intrigued to learn the answer to WHO?

Again, Happy astonished me. She turned to the cowboy engineer and asked, "Did y'all find any parts of the rags? Did they have oil paint on them?"

"Yes, M'am. They sure did. Lots of flesh colored paint. The paints bein' analyzed by Forensic right now."

Happy turned to me, as if I was saddling a horse for her to race in a Derby. "Rick, honey! We'all got to make tracks fo' Lord Hogan's house. We ain't got no time to fritter."

The Madrid police are so efficient at commandeering taxis. We were seated in one within seconds, and hurtling towards the barrio containing Lord Hogan's mansion.

It was locked up. No answer to the front door bell. After Happy banged on the door as if it led to a fire in a stable, she abandoned that ploy and darted to the back terrace which we'd viewed on that previous visit when shown into Lord Hogan's study. The terrace had French windows. My Baptist wife proceeded to commit 'breaking and entering' by using a shoe to smash the window pane nearest an inside handle. She entered with me following, just as an alarm began to bellow like a banshee. Undeterred, Happy rushed around Lord Hogan's library, looking for something. What?

She found a button over the bar, pushed it, and disclosed a hidden stairway. We ducked through its mini entrance, to fling ourselves down, down, down to a murky cellar below.

There were no windows here. A single low-wattage bulb hung from a damp ceiling dripping moisture. It took us a while to be able to accustom ourselves to the gloom.

We heard her voice before we saw Ghislaine. "*Dieu merci*, you've come to save me!"

The girl crouching on a bed of loose straw, was naked. Ghislaine! I looked away while Happy tore off her own dress to pull it over Ghislaine's head. Left in a cotton slip, Happy asked, "Can y'all walk, Ghislaine? Ah'd loan mah shoes but mah feet be so small."

Behind me there was girl talk. But my attention had been drawn to an open tool box. It contained an expensive set of screwdrivers. Two of the largest were missing. I guessed that the Madrid police would be very enthralled by it, and ready to test Norman's fingerprints and DNA against the two they'd found imbedded in the murdered girls' throats: little Miss Hernandez Aza, and the child prostitute.

I turned back to see Ghislaine jump up from the straw, and stride toward us. "Hurry. Please, we must get out of here. Norman will come. He'll have heard the alarm go off. I did."

Norman! We heard his steps sounding their downward tread on the stairs. I took off a shoe and broke the one bulb. Pushing both girls ahead of me, I drove them toward a dim ray of light emanating from a coal bin.

Ghislaine whispered "Hogan moved the coal with a shovel to use it to cover Sadie's body. Yes, Hogan boasted to me that Sadie had got too rebellious and Norman had been told to eliminate her."

I examined the coal bin, and its approach from outside.

It was empty. But coal had been delivered into the bin at an earlier time and there remained a wide chute leading to a barrier made of ancient, rotting wood. I pushed Ghislaine up the chute, then gave Happy a shove up, before I finally heaved myself against the rotten barrier and gave a giant heave to splinter it and permit our exit.

We exited into the rear garden. A group of wrought iron chairs circled a round matching table. I lifted one of the chairs and waited for Norman to follow us up the chute then crashed the chair onto his head.

He crumbled like a spent balloon. We left Norman, unconscious, and sped to the road below.

Unbelievably, we saw a cruising taxi. I hailed it, and we stumbled inside.

"Where to?" I asked Ghislaine.

"To the police," Ghislaine gasped. "We must have the police arrest Norman. Stop him from committing any more murders. Collect poor Sadie's body."

Chapter 24

Lord Hogan was at the main police station by the time we arrived. We'd had to stop at a dress shop to supply another outfit for Ghislaine that included bra, panties, and shoes. All three of us used the shop's facilities to wash off the coal dust we'd been baptized with in the chute.

Hogan glared at Happy, and me, pointed at us and simultaneously declared, "They are the two people who broke into our house. Arrest them."

Hogan ignored Ghislaine, as if she was too young a person to even be in a police station.

But Ghislaine didn't ignore Hogan. She marched up to the police sergeant at the arraignment desk, shook her fist at Hogan and spoke up like an officer addressing his troops. "That man has kept me kidnapped in the cellar of his mansion. Go to the address and you will find a man unconscious there. His name is Norman Steele. He chloroformed me while I was in the Rioja region after the cookery class I was taking at a hotel. When I came to, I was in a car arriving at the outskirts of Madrid. Lord Hogan helped Norman drag me into the Hogan house, where I was locked up in his cellar. Lord Hogan, he . . . He abused . . . He abused me . . . ."

Finally, Ghislaine wept. Her tears didn't flow easily. They dripped, one by one, down her shivering cheeks.

The sergeant yelled for assistance. He came out from behind his desk, manacled Lord Hogan and gestured to me to help restrain him. A third officer asked for Lord Hogan's address. Shortly after, we heard motorcycles revving and then leaving. No doubt other officers left in the direction of Lord Hogan's home to arrest Norman.

Luca's friend appeared from an inner office. He had with him the tall Texan, still wearing his cowboy hat and his figured-leather highheeled boots.

The Texan said, "Howdy, you' all. What's up?"

I raised a shoulder toward my wife. "Happy figured out who in our circle had rags with oil paint on them. Who had placed them on the shaft of that EC-115 helicopter. Norman Steele! She believed he was in cahoots with Lord Hogan, and insisted that if we'd go to Hogan's house we'd know why this portrait painter had wanted to down the helicopter. Which caused the death of its stewardess."

The Texan drawled, "My company knew our helicopter wasn't at fault. Now, tell me why this Norman person brought it down."

Happy answered the query. "Norman and Hogan work together. Prey together. They got them a business sellin' them Hedge Funds. Sadie, she be gettin' too old to sat-is-fy Hogan sex-u-ally. Also gettin' too rebel-lious about workin' fo' him. Hogan and Norman had trained her to set up meetin's with very rich folks. She'd tell them folks thet Norman could do a po'trait, take them to see Lord Hogan's, then Hogan would sell them the Hedge Funds. But Hogan, he got him a real evil taste for girls thet still be chillun. He wanted Ghislaine. He told Norman to sabotage thet hel-i-copt-er. Because he guessed thet Ah was on their track, and also he were hopin' to kill the Ponts so's they wouldn't be alive to make a fuss when Ghislaine disappeared. Thet Norman, he done managed to stay ahead of usn, mockin' usn and the Madrid police." Lucas' friend gave a raging snarl at that. Happy continued: "Mockin', mockin', they-uns felt too sure we all were i-diots they-uns could go on foolin'. But thet first day at the Hogan man-sion Ah done noticed how Lord Hogan's eyes shifted from our faces to see if we'd had a look at a strange button on the wall. Ah guessed it opened up a hidin' place fo' somethin' terrible."

I crossed the room and placed my arms around Happy. "My darling wife, let's go to our hotel, to our children." I gave a nod to Maheen, and she joined us. Outside, heavy rain was falling. We were drenched, waiting for a taxi. Eventually, on cue, the police managed to commandeer an available taxi. The three of us took the taxi to the train station. There, we got some astonished looks because Happy's cotton slip had become transparent from the rain.

Cove Creek and son

Chapter 25

Fran's filly was due to run her race the following day.

Happy and I didn't have much sleep that night before the race. We needed lovemaking to cleanse the horror we'd lived through that afternoon.

The next morning we decided to take our two older children to the Zarzuela racecourse to watch the race. Baby Richard we left with that ever-patient wife of our hotel's manager.

"Wow, we sho got to find us a real nice present fo' thet woman," Happy said. "Cho-co-lates? A silk scarf?"

Silk! That reminded me that I hadn't heard from Monsieur Galé. My Dad had often said, "No answer is an answer." I hoped that in this case the answer might still be in the affirmative.

With Maheen in tow we walked the short distance to the racecourse, located the Owners and Trainers entrance, showed our passes, winkled Maheen in with the excuse she was the kids' nanny, and went in search of Fran.

Surprise! It was Dad who met us in the Owner's section. He looked hale and hearty. There was no sign of Nashville-Mary.

"What happened to your girlfriend?" I asked with a grin.

"I have no girlfriend," Dad replied stiffly. "If you are referring to that lady from Nashville, she has returned to her husband."

Husbands were getting their wives back! In the paddock, who should appear with tardy Fran, but Jeremy Cabrach. He was beaming, with the look of a man who has spent a satisfying night of sex with his wife.

Soviet Heiress dominated the paddock. She pricked her ears, danced on her toes, tossed her mane and generally showed off as the most promising contender there.

And she didn't disappoint.

On perfect ground, neither too soft nor too hard rather like a teenager's vulva, with a sweet breeze to ruffle her mane and add air to her flaring nostrils, our Soviet Heiress responded instantly to our English jockey's commands.

She zipped from a comfortable sixth place at the half to be even with the two leaders. She inched ahead. She certainly possessed enough speed to do the job, but I had lingering doubts. She ran a terrific race, then she began to ease back farther than I'd want. Oh God! Suddenly, like lightning, she surged forward through a bit of space between the leaders and took the front. Would she be disqualified for interference?

English punters on hand began to cheer. Some threw up hats to signal a British victory. I held my breath. The Stewards' word could go either way. We could have won, or be placed last for interference. Or taking another horse's ground.

Fran hustled into the winners' circle to stand by the First pole. But would Soviet Heiress keep that placing?

Jeremy Cabrach lurked back with the paying Members, too diplomatic to assume the Cabrachs had won.

Happy and I were obliged to take a position next to Fran. The suspense was painful. Three other horses had entered the winners' circle. None of their jockeys led them to any of the poles. Waiting. We all paused for the Stewards' decision. Would the other three horses soon take First, Second and Third?

The racecourse's loudspeaker began to crackle. We heard a Steward clear his throat. Then, finally, the decision was announced.

Soviet Heiress had won!

Happy hugged me, she hugged Fran, and she hugged our jockey. Hal and Mafalda pushed into the winners' circle and congratulated Fran.

Spanish and British racing journalists asked us for interviews. I spoke to the RACING POST man, but could say nothing to the Spanish scriveners. I hadn't learned any Spanish except Por Favor, and Gracias.

I said Gracias a lot.

Giselle Pont, looking sheepish because her affair had been revealed, approached with Ghislaine, who beamed with joy for us.

Dr. Pont was nowhere to be seen. He'd disappeared. I began to suspect that he wasn't as nice a man as I'd assumed.

After the "Horses away" barked in Spanish, we marched like the victors we were to find drinks.

Miserly Fran opted not to offer champagne, but her elegant husband behaved better. He had entry to the Jockey Club's premises due to his membership in the Jockey Club Rooms of Newmarket and wearing its yellow and black badge in his lapel he had the right to give drinks to our party. Believe me, I needed one.

Late, because she'd left us to go wait at the gate for her Luca, Maheen found us in the Jockey Club, and we celebrated more good news. "We're going to be married next week in London. I'm eighteen in six days. Legally no longer a minor."

Happy kissed her, I did the shoulder clapping thing to Luca, and we agreed to serve as witnesses because Happy and I would be well settled in England by then.

Many tax exile Brits came forward to shake hands and rave over a win for Britain. It was heart warming to hear the tones of Ole Blimey voiced by so many on this foreign soil. I reflected that if I hadn't been so homesick to hear the English language spoken, I might not have got involved with Lord Hogan and Norman Steele.

Before we returned home, Happy bought an entire box of chorizos to present as a gift to the hotel manager's kind wife. The box was heavy and leaked grease, but I didn't care. That woman had been wonderful.

We were packing to catch an evening flight when the manager knocked at our door. To thank us? For once his usually surly face was wreathed in smiles. I guessed he was more than pleased with the hefty tip in pesetas I'd given his wife in addition to Happy's awful chorizos.

No. He'd come with a letter. It had a French stamp. It was addressed to Richard Harrow, Trainer.

The letter contained a large check as a down payment from Monsieur Galé for that unnamed colt I'd offered him. The colt was still available because neither Fran nor Hal had soiled our relationship by fighting for it while we were still recovering from the recent horrific events.

I handed the letter and check to Happy. "Hallelujah! Ah just knows them two—hoss and Galé—would go t'gether like grits and bacon. But he sho has lots o' conditions. Wants to know the name of ourn Vet. Wants to know how often he can come to Epsom to judge the colt's im-prove-ment. Wants usn to write him a letter each week. But don't matter. Ah just loves the fact usn will see mo'e of them Galés."

We hugged each other. But then came a sad moment. Happy took the small vase containing Irish's ashes and placed it inside a specially padded traveling container, then handed that to Tim.

"Y'all can carry this, son. Y'all be a big boy now."

I restrained my own tears. Staring at that container I blamed myself for bringing all our children here to Spain. What had been in my mind? Bring Tim, yes. Because after the trauma of his kidnapping in Kentucky, we always kept him near us. But, Dorothy, Irish, and baby Richard? The last two had suffered so greatly. I recalled my old school books with their tales of the Black Prince's great battles, and how he'd been brought down in northern Spain by a wasting disease when he came there to help stop the Moors' invasion. And how the Black Prince had never left his sick bed, suffering for many years until he died. What in Heaven had prompted me to bring my infants to Spain?

But in my heart of hearts I know the answer. It wasn't only Tim who needed us. All our children needed not only our love, but our caring presence. They wanted Happy and me to be there for them, wherever "there" should be.

Gathering Dorothy in my arms, I tucked her little legs around my neck so that she could sit tall above my head and lead us away from this hotel which had brought us a lot of sorrow albeit we'd found kindness there too. Happy took tiny Richard in his carrycot and we went downstairs to a waiting taxi.

Chapter 26

Maheen and Luca's London wedding was a true delight. It took place in the Chelsea Registry Office, where a bouquet of other brides waited their turns. Some of the brides were in full wedding dress, wearing tiaras on their heads or mere sprigs of late blooming ivy. Several of the brides were heavily pregnant, with bumps as big as Maheen's.

We stood as witnesses, as promised, and underwrote a reception at the Turf Club after. That venerable club offered us their glass-roofed room where the walls were plastered with marvelous old paintings by the greatest of equine artists: Stubbs, Munnings, and Herring. There were two contemporary paintings of club officers. Not a Norman Steele portrait among these!

Mafalda and Hal had refrained from appearing at the Registry Office. But hearty Hal wasn't going to miss the party.

Fran and Jeremy Cabrach were in jolly moods. Fran's bump had begun to show, and both Cabrachs were elated to announce that ultrasound had confirmed that they were going to be parents of a boy: heir to the Cabrach earldom.

None of Fran's former boyfriends had the gall to show up. But tactless Fran just had to go on and on about babies. Not a great idea considering the bride had a bump as large as a suitcase.

"My Soviet Heiress will have a baby next year," Fran blared. "I've paid for a nomination to Diesis. You know, champion two-year-old of England in his year. He's sire of 1,064 foals, 816 starters, 77 stakes winners, 7 champions, 510 winners of 1,499 races earning $45,795,661 in prize money. How about that? You two Harrows can sit in on the birth."

I grinned. "I'd rather be standing."

Happy said, more to the point, "Sho thing. Ah's known she be wantin' to breed. She done told me, plenty times. No mo'e racin' just wants babies. Real broody, yourn Soviet Heiress."

When it was time for us to go back to our cottage in Epsom, I whispered to my darling wife, "Are you in the mood for breeding?"

"Naw. But fo' lovemakin' yeah. Thankee."

THE END

Mexico's Movieland Murders

CHARACTERS Mexico's Movieland Murders

Rick Harrow, narrator, who is a British trainer of racehorses
Happy Riley Harrow his wife, born in the Kentucky hills country, an apprentice jockey who moonlights as a sleuth
Gonzi Gonzalez, Mexico's most famous comedian who has earned $27,500,000 as an actor-comedian
Himelda Gonzalez Balthazar, Gonzi's ugly eldest daughter
Julio Balthazar, Himelda's husband, a small role actor
Soledad Gonzalez Jimenez, Gonzi's youngest daughter, mother of five
Marco Jimenez, Soledad's husband, an actor with important roles
Guadalupe Gonzalez, Gonzi's fifteen year old illegitimate much-beloved daughter, nicknamed Lupe
Giselle Pont, a French vineyard owner, buying bloodstock from Gonzi Gonzalez
Ghislaine Pont, Giselle's fifteen year old daughter, raped and almost murdered in Madrid, has put her traumas behind her
Hal Murphy, Rick's richest and most generous owner
Mafalda Murphy, Hal's Egyptian wife, formerly an international courtesan
Maheen Palacio, Mafalda's eighteen-year-old daughter, a close pal of Happy's
Luca Palacio, Maheen's Sherlock Holmes-type sleuthing husband, an Italian police officer
Tony Farinas, popular Mexican polo player
Mae Ellen Farinas, Tony's wayward wife, proud of her Georgia, USA background
The Marques Salvador de Arroyo Largo, a "walker" falls for rich fifteen year old Guadalupe
Alberto Lopez, Gonzi's lawyer
Edouard Bonvouloir, a vet whose wife was held hostage by El Jefe
El Jefe, a Mexican killer for hire who had millions

Chapter 1

It's tough trying to solve a murder when the victim's fans, family, and friends don't want your input. Gonzi Gonzalez, Mexico's greatest comedian since Cantinflas, had been found in a hotel closet with his hands and genitals tied with the same cord that had hanged him. His fans didn't want his body cut up by an autopsy. His family didn't want any snooping in case it was alleged to be a suicide and his life insurance wouldn't be paid. His friends were embarrassed at the similarity between his death and movie star David Carridine's in Thailand, and would have preferred no unfavorable publicity.

Only his illegitimate fifteen-year-old daughter Guadalupe Gonzalez wanted to know the truth and pleaded with my sleuth wife, Happy, to find his killer. We'd met Gonzi Gonzalez with her a week before his murder.

"Mrs. Harrow, you've been so kind to me specially when you were in England. Help me now. My father's been murdered, and I want to know who did this."

I'm Rick Harrow, a British racehorse trainer who had brought my wife with me to Mexico City at the request of one of my new owners, Giselle Pont. Her fifteen-year-old daughter, Ghislaine, had met Guadalupe Gonzalez at the school I'd recommended in England, St.Mary's Burford. "Just call her Lupe, she's my best friend. Please help, Mrs. Harrow," she'd said.

Ghislaine Pont's life had been saved by Happy in Madrid, after Ghislaine had been abducted by a pedophile and his murderous accomplice. Ghislaine had good reason to appreciate Happy's moonlighting as a sleuth.

Happy Harrow, my wife, is a licensed jockey and a great help to me in my business. Giselle had bought, sight unseen, a three-year-old gelding from Gonzi Gonzalez shortly before his murder. Gonzi had wanted to emulate Maria Felix, Mexico's earliest movie star, who had devoted the entire latter end of her life to horse racing. But Gonzi's racing know-how wasn't on a par with his jokes or Maria Felix's talent. This particular gelding, called

MIST, had been a *mistake*. He'd unloaded it, a dicey thing to do, on Giselle figuring she lived far away across the Atlantic and might never discover just how bad MIST was.

By now thoroughly magnetized by racing, Giselle had e-mailed me at my Epsom stables and suggested that Happy and I fly to Keeneland with her to buy additional bloodstock, then head southwest to New Mexico to test MIST.

When we accepted her invite, ecstatic that Giselle wanted additional bloodstock and that from Keeneland, an oasis of good horses in a world of phonies, Happy packed up our gear and we kissed our three children goodbye. Their faithful Chinese Amah waved us off down our manure-strewn driveway, only too glad to have the children all to herself.

Keeneland didn't disappoint. We bought a colt sired by a descendant of top stallion STORM CAT, and a filly by a sire with NUREYEV blood. We rubbed shoulders with Kentucky owners like John and Marylou Whitney Hendrickson, who'd won the 2006 Belmont with a STORM CAT colt. We were introduced to a new friend, Dr. Kendall Hanson, who had ten horses in training and had won with all of them. There were no demanding orders from our new owner, because she'd left it to us to choose her new bloodstock on our own. Giselle got her jollies by watching her winners cross the Finish Line, not by attending auctions of untried yearlings.

Meeting us at the Ruidoso Downs Track, Giselle cheered MIST in a stakes race at the New Mexico course, and suffered her first racing downer when the gelding lost.

"Mon Dieu, ce n'est pas possible!" Giselle had exclaimed to us in the Turf Club, and promptly began to weep like an infant whose toy had been grabbed by an older child. She wept without shame in front of the racecourse Stewards, the other owners, and Gonzi. Losing a race was just too much following the attempt to rape and murder Ghislaine.

Gonzi's advice was that Giselle should have MIST "put down" and sent to a knacker's. "You can get money from the sale of his meat." Giselle, who had never lost a race in the two outings she'd enjoyed at Longchamp in Paris with the horse I'd bought for her late husband, was adamant that she'd *never* have MIST or any other horse sold for meat.

She'd moved to Mexico City, asked me to help, and I'd found a complaisant farmer who'd been only too glad to give MIST grazing room for a fair price. In Ruidoso, I'd bought a two year old colt from Gonzi, called EL MILAGRO, for Giselle. He proceeded to live up to his name, winning his first race in New Mexico.

New Mexico's now-famous Ruidoso Downs track, famous thanks to MINE THAT BIRD going on to win the 2009 Kentucky Derby after breaking his maiden at Ruidoso, had magnetized Giselle.

AND SHE WON THERE WITH EL MILAGRO.

Happy and I were present for that win, with Giselle, her daughter and Gonzi's Guadalupe. To our amazement, Gonzi Gonzalez had shown up for the Ruidoso season, expecting to best EL MILAGRO with a second class gelding he'd brought from Chihuahua's track across the border. Yes, he'd sold EL MILAGRO to Giselle. But stealthily he didn't sign El Miraglo's papers correctly, leaving Giselle's ownership in limbo.

When EL MILAGRO had entered the stalls for his maiden race, he bellowed like a stallion who smells a mare in season, tossed his mane and tail as if there was a high wind, and generally misbehaved. My jockey controlled him well so that EL MILAGRO wouldn't miss the Up of the starting gate. Loving the going, EL MILAGRO tore down the track managing to reach the rail ahead of the charging contenders. EL MILAGRO had kept to the rail, blocking any interference there, and maintained his lead all the way to the Finish Line.

Success!

Gonzi unaware that he was about to die, and present as the owner of a contender, had flashed his famous teeth in that huge smile so-well known to his millions of fans. *"Mejor que MIST,"* he'd said, laughing.

My Happy, who's an amateur psychologist, whispered in her Kentucky Hills accent, "Sho nuf, thet act-or, he don't really mean one word he says."

Seconds later Happy had more reason to distrust Gonzi, or his sanity. Gonzi turned his back on the race's Stewards and proceeded to perform his signature trick, he'd shown them the bare patches on the rear of his trousers that exposed his caramel colored flesh. Like two ripe mangoes his famous buttocks flashed at the Stewards.

"Don't be surprised," I'd whispered in turn, "Gonzi does that in all his movies. Those bare patches have endeared him to Mexico's poor. I'm told that many a peon removes his trousers at home, to save them from wear and tear. He's done Cantinflas one better: Cantinflas used to dip his trousers very near to where EVERYTHING would show."

Happy whispered again, "Ah sho remembers thet Cantinflas. He were the Passe-par-tout character in Mike Todd's AROUND THE WORLD IN 80 DAYS."

"Spot on, my darling. But Cantinflas belonged to an earlier generation, when stars didn't go as far as they do today. Gonzi's established a new record for semi-nudity. Which, when you recall that Sacha Baron Cohen displayed his entire nude body on the cover of GQ lately, Gonzi's ploy isn't all that terrible."

A racetrack security guard collected Gonzi from the Owners' stand and led him to the main gate to ask him to leave. Grinning widely, knowing he'd been on national TV by pulling his trick when the winning horses had been featured, Gonzi entered his limo with aplomb.

Happy shook her head. "This ain't the place to play them shenanigans. Not after MINE THAT BIRD started his winning career here, to go on to take the Kentucky Derby and thet Preakness. Wut's thet Gonzi got makes him think he can be-have like thet?"

"Fame. A huge fortune."

"Well, Ah de-clare. Ifn he didn't be Dad to thet sweet Guadalupe, Ah'd ignore him in future. It be my habit to reserve opinion on somebody wut mis-be-haves. Won't reserve my opinion of Gonzi. Ah reckons he's past acceptin' not even fo' Lupe's sake."

"Did you know that Gonzi had two other daughters?"

"Nah. Never seen *them* at the racetrack."

"And you won't! The eldest, Himelda, she feels she's far too superior to her father. She doesn't want to be reminded Gonzi's her father, what with his 'mooning' in the movies and at racetracks."

"Yeah man, like the Aunt Jemeima character's daughter in IMITATION OF LIFE."

"The younger sister Soledad, married into high society. She doesn't want her country club friends to connect her to Gonzi, who always plays the poorest of peons."

"Them sisters be snobs."

"I think it would be fair to say so. Yes, snobs. Too good for the father who earned the money and fame that launched them into the big world."

Giselle had been listening to us. She added, "Guadalupe's worth ten of her half-sisters, illegit or not. Watch her now, she's left the Winners' Circle to rush to her father and join him in his limo. We won't see her for a time."

But we did. At Gonzi's funeral. We'd been invited by Guadalupe to come to the funeral in Mexico City. She'd been very specific in her note to Happy. "Please come to my father's *funerales*. And then, dear Happy, please *please concentrate all your talent on unmasking his murderer."*

Chapter 2

Giselle Pont financed our stay in Mexico City. She was ultra generous, offering to pay for our children and Amah to travel from England to be with us.

Again as when our Canadian owner, Hal Murphy, had paid for our children to come to Milan, Happy felt overjoyed to be back in the role of a mother. Her deepseated motherly instincts had been put on hold when a murder hit our circle, but once our three babes were in her arms being hugged, she went all out to oversee their comfort, safety, and fun times.

Because our youngest daughter, Irish, had died of meningitis during our sojourn in Madrid, Happy took particular care with the feeding and bathing of our youngsters. In our four star hotel, she cautioned:

"Careful, Amah, when y'all wraps the chillun in towels. Ah's heard of a tourist in Mexico City bein' stung by a sc-or-pion wut hid in a towel."

I pooh-poohed that caution, but had nothing to add when later at our first meal together, Happy advised Amah, "Cain't be too careful with raw fruits or ve-ge-tables. Ah's heard tell thet on some Mexican farms the peons use human poop fo' fert-i-lizer."

Giselle interrupted our meal with an hysterical phone call.

"*Mon Dieu! Ce n'est pas possible.* Guadalupe and her mother have been shot at by drive-past assassins. Lupe's mother is dead. Lupe is in the ABC Hospital. Tell your radio taxi to take you to ABC, the hospital's real name is American British Cowdray. Don't take just any taxi, particularly not a minicab. The VW ones are dangerous. You'll be stripped of your cash, and maybe even your clothes. Get your hotel to call for a radio taxi. I'll meet you in an ABC waiting room outside the Third Floor *Emergencia* desk. Hurry!"

Happy took the receiver from me. "We'all will be at thet there hospital in no time." She turned over the children to Amah, and we fled to the hotel lobby to ask for a radio taxi.

Not the time for sightseeing! We scarcely took notice of the pushing crowds on the narrow streets or the grander boulevards leading to museums or government offices. Our target was the ABC hospital, which loomed next to our curb sooner than expected. I paid the driver, tipped well, and we entered to ask for directions for lifts to the Third Floor.

"Lifts? You mean the elevators," a Mexican security officer sneered at my British term. But he cocked a brown finger toward a bank of lifts and we could read the number 3 easily enough. I didn't need to push the 3 button, *that* had already been done by a woman dressed all in black, including the shawl over her head and her thick stockings. A security guard, in the dark blue uniform of the *Policia Auxiliar*, who protect shops and restaurants, was on duty on the Third Floor. As we approached the Emergencia desk two more police, undercover men with the Policia Judicial Federal, arrived ahead of us asking for Lupe Gonzalez's room. Tailing them, we had a long walk down a corridor with ugly unrelieved tan paint not offering the solace of a cheerful landscape picture as would have been the case in Britain.

Guadalupe lay suffering under a web of tubes in a not-too-clean bed. We'd gained admittance to her room on the heels of those two *judiciales,* otherwise Happy and I would have been banished to be with Giselle in the waiting room outside.

Happy quickly pushed forward to take Lupe's left hand and press it. Lupe's eyelids flickered. Opening her eyes she recognized Happy, attempted a feeble smile, then pressed back.

"We'all's here. Tell usn wut to do for y'all."

Guadalupe whispered hoarsely, "Find Mama's killer."

"Did y'all see him?"

Very weak whisper, "No."

"Y'all gettin' enuf food?"

"Need apples. Bring apples."

Now Happy nodded. She 'd wanted apples when pregnant, and knew about cravings.

A busybody nurse rustled her starched apron entering the room, pushing Happy away from Lupe's bed, and smiling coyly at the two *judiciales. She put on a huge officious act to impress them, bringing out a dirty thermometer from an unsanitized pocket where a dirty Kleenex peeked, then poked Lupe's mouth with a finger to get her to open up for a dicey dirty thermometer.*

The two *juidiciales* had no intention of being outdone by this nurse. One bellowed to me: *"Largase."* When I shook my head as if not understanding this Spanish expression, he added in fractured English, "Get out."

His buddy, a short brown man whose blue uniform contrasted with tobacco smoke reddened eyes, spoke more courteously to Happy, *"Por favor, señora, salga del cuarto."*

Both *judiciales* had taken notes of everything that had been said between Happy and Guadalupe.

I wasn't leaving Guadalupe to their mercies without a word. I said, "This young lady has been shot. She needs rest."

The short brown *judicial* spoke up in American High School English. "We know all about her and that *puta* of a mother she had. We specialize in homicides, and drug pushing. Maybe no drugs are involved here. But her mother was the querida of a rich and powerful recently murdered actor, Gonzi Gonzalez, cousin of Consuelo Velasquez, who was in our legislature. There will be hell to pay for *his murder,* and the *querida's* death from a shoot out is probably related."

His two brown hands were placed on the backs of my shoulders and I was forcibly ejected from Guadalupe's room.

Happy accepted that with a strange smile. In the waiting room accompanying Giselle, she explained, "Thet little brown off-i-cer, he done give us some real good hints."

Chapter 3

We brought a dozen Washington State apples to Guadalupe on our next visit, later that evening.

She was crouched in the cranked hospital bed, a bandage swathed around her temples like a Muslim's turban. Guadalupe had regained her verve.

"Have you got a knife? I'd like to slice up an apple. My front teeth are capped and I'm afraid I'll dislodge them if I take a big bite."

I carry a Swiss army knife with me. I opened it and handed it to Lupe.

Happy placed a Kleenex under Lupe's chin in lieu of a plate.

Lupe, apparently more concerned about the insulting word used to describe her mother by the brown skinned *judicial* earlier, added: "My mother was not a puta. That would suggest she slept with many men. She only slept with Gonzi. Before and after I was born. She truly loved only him. And he loved her, I'm sure of that."

Happy stroked the hand that was paring an apple. "Usn don't know them Mexican words. Ah's sho she been a real nice lady to have brought up a girl like y'all. Rick and I want to offer con-do-lences for her death."

Lupe, like a dog with a bone, wasn't about to drop the subject of that *judiciale*'s raw comment. She said, "My mother never slept with my father until after his wife died. She respected his marriage. That's more than his other *queridas* did. He had many before my mother. But none of those women had a child by him. He adored my mother for giving him another daughter."

Very gently, Happy changed the subject. "Tell me about yourn two sisters."

"*Half*-sisters. They would never accept that I was their sister. My eldest sister, Himelda, is *wild. Really cool.* She flits around all levels of Mexico's Bohemian crowd. The most famous actors, the bit players, the call girls who want to be movie stars. Anybody who will hire mariachis to play for her and pay for her tequila. And she *did* help one call girl to get into the movies, by introducing her to Father's agent. I guess he slept with her for free, then passed her on to a movie director for more of the same. Himelda's married to an actor who's famous for being killed in every movie role. In atrocious ways. He lets Himelda sleep around as long as she shuts up about all the girls AND BOYS he pays for sex."

"Wow! Ah do believe it should be y'all who *snubs her!*"

"Soledad, my youngest sister, is so different. She has five children by her husband, Marco Jimenez. You must have heard of him. His films are distributed in England and America. He's a very serious actor, and expects that one day soon he'll be tagged for an American movie where he can win an Oscar."

"Yeah man, Ah sho has heard of thet Marco Jimenez. He were real fine in thet Mexican remake of WAR AND PEACE."

I asked a question. "Soledad and Marco are very social?"

"That's their end-all: High Society. Soledad has to be a member of the top clubs, send her children to the best and most elegant schools, and she wants to be known as the greatest society hostess in all Mexico. Everywhere she drops the name of our great-aunt Consuelo Velasquez, a famous composer who came from a distinguished family and was a member of congress. Of course, she never mentions that when her biggest hit, BESAME MUCHO, first came out and was so popular, the family wanted to disown Consuelo Velasquez for being a composer of love songs."

Happy's voice changed. She'd stopped thinking MOVIE STAR and started thinking *murderer.* "Would Marco have killed yourn mother?"

"*Carambas!* What a question! Marco's known all over Mexico as the most loving husband and father, who would never hurt anyone."

I asked, "What about Soledad? Could she have wanted your mother's share of Gonzi's estate?"

"We don't know what was in his latest will. That should be read tomorrow. He gave me an old will to see, once. Long ago. I was mentioned, getting a third. I believe my mother was listed under the bequests permitted after family members had got their shares. Why?"

Happy mumbled, "Greed's wut mot-i-vates most killers."

Guadalupe's eyes filled with tears. She'd managed the pain of her wounds, but she couldn't handle the idea that her mother had been murdered for money. When she could speak again, she said quietly, "I won't be able to go to Mama's funeral, nor the reading of the will. Happy dear, will you represent me?"

"Sho thing! Now, eat them apples. Y'all will feel better." Happy kissed Lupe on her cheek, found a plate for her apple's core and seeds, and we left the room. The *judiciales gave us dirty looks when we passed them in the corridor, but they didn't stop us exiting from the hospital.*

Chapter 4

Back at our four star hotel after Lupe's mother's funeral, Happy took off her clothes and lay on the bed. She didn't hold out her arms, inviting me for lovemaking. She stared at the ceiling. "Y'all notice how much thet there fun-er-al copied the openin' scene in EVITA for the funeral of Evita's father? Only, my friend Guadalupe weren't there to be snubbed like Evita was."

"Yes. All the mourners in total black. Must have been a huge change for all those movie stars to put aside outfits suitable for Premieres to wear what any wealthy Mexican traditionally wears for a funeral. I'll bet there were several actresses who regretted going for unbecoming black because they didn't guess there would be so many paparazzi there."

"Ah weren't lookin' at them bit actresses. Ah were mo'e int-er-ested in seein' Guadalupe's elder sister, Himelda. Ugly gal. One wut she called 'wild.' Thet weren't *all* she vo-lun-teered about Himelda. The sister wut goes bar crawlin' to drink and hear mariachi music. Maybe find some lowlife macho who be willin' to kill off Guadalupe's mother for a few thousand pesos."

"You think Himelda would have also paid to have her father murdered?"

"Ah ain't said thet. Ah's reservin' my opinion of Himelda until Ah gets mo'e in-form-a-tion about her. Ah wants to *see* mo'e of her, too."

"How about we put the Gonzi murder problem on hold?" I lay down beside my darling wife and caressed her nipples in the way that usually sends her ballistic. Making my pitch, I said, "You know how I love to make love to you in a new bed. And particularly in the afternoon."

Afternoons at home in Epsom were perfect because there was just enough time for lovemaking before evening stables.

Happy wiggled away from my hands and sat up.

"Ah's sho to *see* Himelda later, after the studios close for the day and Gonzi's will may be read in his lawyer's office. Rick, honey, don't ask me to put Gonzi's murder on hold. Y'all knows Ah's been asked by Guadalupe to help find his murderer."

No lovemaking that afternoon!

Happy dressed very carefully for the reading of Gonzi's will. Like the members of his family at Gonzi's funeral, she chose a knee-length simple black silk dress with a matching hat. No gloves, I don't think she owns a pair except for the knitted mittens she has for when it snows in Epsom.

The lawyer's office was very pretentious. Gonzi had selected for his attorney a pompous fat Santa Claus look alike, except that this Santa had crafty eyes. His office was the penthouse of an entire building in El Centro, with a fabled view of the Museo de Antropologia. As soon as we entered the holy of holies, the lawyer's den, Happy crossed to its enormous plate glass window to stare inquisitively at the great museum. Señor Alberto Lopez, Gonzi's lawyer, had correctly interpreted Happy's fascination for the place and whispered in Oxfordian English, "That fine edifice houses our nation's Anthropology Museum."

"Wut be an *anthropology museum?*" she whispered to me, already guessing the answer.

"The study of mankind as it developed over the ages. But here, it would be a museum devoted to artifacts left by the various tribes that inhabited the very varied terrain of Mexico."

Oh, oh. Instantly a gleam brightened Happy's beautiful pool blue eyes. I know what that gleam signifies. It means we will spend many hours wandering around that museum and then exploring ways and byways of this country to learn more about Aztecs, Toltecs, Mayans and others from more distant ages. Oh God! And maybe my Happy will trek alone to see more than I can stomach, just as she did going to Karnak in Egypt, to Alice Springs in Australia, and almost fatally to the Carnoso Castle in Italy. My wonderful wife has few flaws, but her craving to visit ancient stones has been a thorn in my side.

Soledad, educated at St. Mary's Ascot in England, spoke out irritably with a cut-glass accent. "What's all that whispering about? I thought we'd got together here to have my father's will read."

Happy left the plate glass window with a sigh, and took a seat close to Himelda. She proceeded to study Himelda with as acutely an eye as if Himelda was a priceless artifact.

This sister wasn't merely ugly, she was hideous. She had open sores on her face, pus in her eyes, and a gaping purple mouth.

Himelda didn't like Happy's probing glances. Himelda tossed her waist-long black hair, which was already knotted like a witch's, and I thought she might stick out her tongue or spit at Happy any minute now. Himelda didn't. The reading of the will began, and Himelda applied all her attention to every word the lawyer said.

The more Señor Lopez read, the more furious Himelda became. Her name and Soledad's had been mentioned first as receiving eleven million dollars each. To my surprise that sum didn't satisfy Himelda. She'd started by pouting and then her mouth turned as lethal as the tip of a tornado. As he read out bequests to twelve of Gonzi's former mistresses, plus five thousand pesos each to his chauffeur, housekeeper and favorite auto mechanic, the tension in the room rose as if villagers were watching for a tornado's tip to hit their homes. There were two final bequests, one hundred thousand to Gonzi's agent, Miguel Aguas, as well as five and a half million dollars for Guadalupe.

The tornado hit!

Both Himelda and Soledad rose from their seats with a roar that anyone who'd ever experienced a tornado would recognize.

Simultaneously, like twins congenitally joined sharing one heart and stomach, they shrieked: "Five and a half million dollars! That money belongs to us!"

Señor Lopez, who evidently had been expecting the outburst, tapped his desk with the embossed cover of Gonzi's will. In Spanish he declared, *"No hay nada que decir. Gonzi ha decidido."*

Both Happy and I understood what he'd said. We'd picked up enough kitchen Spanish during our dicey trip to Madrid, a trip that had lengthened into many weeks and had cost the life of our precious baby daughter, Irish.

Solemnly, Happy now took notes. Her spelling was absurdly bad, but she *would* be able to transmit the gist of this evening's news to Guadalupe.

Like Kruschev's famed shoe act at the United Nations, also dictated by fury, Soledad removed a five-inch-heel Manolo Blahnik and banged it on Sr. Lopez's desk. "We'll sue for our rights. Himelda and I are the *legitimate* daughters."

Growling, spit bubbling in the corners of his beard-encased mouth, Sr. Lopez didn't look up to meet Soledad's flaming eyes. "Gonzi has done this will in the full knowledge of Mexican law. His agent served him well. Worth every centavo of one hundred thousand dollars. As for Lupe, an illegitimate child receives half of what legitimate children get."

With that habitual toss of her mane of waist length hair, Himelda said more carefully, "We will not dispute the bequest to Aguas. He represents both of our husbands. We know he has earned his right to be in the will. A great agent for all the men of our family. But why not give Lupe's mother a share which would go to Lupe? The same amount as what went to all the other mistresses?"

"Because *I* advised Gonzi that with five and a half million dollars for Guadalupe he didn't need to place her mother on the level of his other mistresses. Guadalupe would have been well able to provide for her mother, poor woman. God rest her soul." He made the sign of the cross, and pocketing his copy of the will left the room.

Evidently there was no love lost between Sr. Lopez and the two legitimate Gonzalez daughters. I guessed there had been earlier altercations. What I couldn't guess was what the outcome of this one would be.

Chapter 5

We returned to our hotel bedroom. It seemed too late for a hospital visit this evening. Instead of telephoning Guadalupe right away, first Happy called Giselle Pont, who had a single room on another floor.

"Giselle?" Happy had been on a first name basis ever since saving Giselle's daughter, Ghislaine, from being murdered by a psychopath in Madrid. "When do the Easter vacation end at Ghislaine's school?"

"Oh, hello, Happy. The Easter vacation? It's been a long one, hasn't it? In another fortnight, I believe."

"Ah's thinkin' it be a good idée for Ghislaine to return earlier, and take Guadalupe with her. They met o-rig-i-nally in school. Why not have them go back together? But soon's can be. Tomorrow, if thet's possible. We needs to know ifn Guadalupe can leave thet hospital by tomorrow. Ah sho hopes so! Ghislaine and Lupe can stay at ourn house in Epsom until school starts again. Ride ourn saddle ponies. Ride out with ourn string. Get Guadalupe out of Mexico."

Astutely, very aware as to the importance of the bequests in wills since her husband had died and left her his vineyards, Giselle said, "You've been to the reading of Gonzi Gonzalez's will! You think Lupe's in danger."

"Yeah. Mighty sho she be in danger."

"I'll have to ask Ghislaine if she's found all the Mexican recipes she wanted. It *is* her long vacation too. I'm doing my best to bond with her, and I don't want to upset our improving relationship. And, Lupe? Maybe she wants to finish out her vacation in Mexico."

"Don't mater what Guadalupe prefers to do. She won't be alive in two weeks if she don't leave Mexico. Ah's got to talk to thet there Sr.Lopez, Gonzi's lawyer. Ah could see he ain't no fool. Lupe tole me he were her legal guard-i-an. If he gives his OK, and he *must*, Ah figures Ah cain convince Guadalupe to fly out of here soon's she can travel."

We didn't go far. Giselle met us in our hotel lobby. She said, "I'll call down to the kitchens and ask for Ghislaine. The hotel chef has been sharing his recipes. Do you think it's too late for us to go to see Lupe in the hospital? We four should go together."

We did. Ghislaine joined us in the hotel lobby, her dress covered in flour with spots of tomato sauce. With Happy and Giselle we crossed the city again to the ABC Hospital. Mexican visiting hours were like Spain's, late and later.

Happy was suffering, I could see, as we hurried through the nighttime quiet of empty corridors so alike those in Madrid to which she had become so horribly familiar when baby Richard was sick. That didn't stop her from noticing that the security guards were gone from in front of Guadalupe's door. No more *judiciales* either.

We found Guadalupe eating another of the apples we'd brought. She looked brighter, sitting upright, her hair nicely combed and her face alight with makeup. Like any teenager, she wanted to look her best, and had expected us to come to tell her news about Gonzi's will. She'd *checked as to visiting hours*.

"Darlin' Guadalupe, y'all seems much improved. Thet turban y'all had been wearin' got re-moved."

"Yes. And aren't I glad it's gone. Gave me a terrible headache, anyway that's what I told the doctor. What really cured me was I've heard from Sr. Lopez that I've inherited five and a half million dollars from Papacito. You were present, Happy. Were my two sisters very upset about that?"

Happy and I exchanged glances. It wasn't for us to fuel family feuds. I mumbled, "Just let us say they weren't best pleased. But Guadalupe, you're looking so improved, surely you can be fit enough to travel. Happy wants you to go to our home in England for the remainder of your Easter vacation. What say you to that?"

There! I'd done the spade work for Happy, and she took the hint. She stormed right into the expected battle. "Y'all ain't safe here, darlin' girl. England be better for y'all at the moment."

Surprising us, Ghislaine put in a suggestion. "There are cookery classes in a manor house outside Epsom. I've seen them advertised. Just like for the ones in castles in France and Italy. It would be great fun to take those classes." No stranger to a life threatening experience, had Ghislaine guessed that Lupe was in imminent danger? I think so!

Guadalupe continued to eat the apple, leaving us in suspense. Then her smile erupted like sunshine from behind clouds. "Yes. I'd enjoy taking cookery classes. But don't I have to stay in Mexico while the will is probated?"

I spluttered, "Probate takes months, even years when a will is contested. No, Guadalupe, it would be wise for you to leave Mexico soonest. How about tomorrow?"

"Cool! I love doing things on the spur of the moment. When Papacito suggested I go with him to England to look at boarding schools, we left the next day."

"Oh? And didn't your mother have to agree to that?"

"My poor Mamacita never argued with anything Papacito suggested. In private she'd always told me that comedians have a right to be outrageous, do and say things other people would be criticized for. When he chose St.Mary's Burford for me, she went along with the decision. Although I knew she wanted to keep me close to her in Mexico."

Ghislaine interrupted again. "We both ended up there because St.Mary's Ascot wouldn't take either of us. Me, because I'd been raped. And darling Lupe, because your father hadn't married your mother, as D.H.Lawrence so famously remarked about his own background."

Guadalupe looked dismayed for a moment, then sweetly said, "I imagine that my two brothers-in-law weren't very happy about the money Papacito left me."

Happy paused a long minute before remarking, "Ah's reserved my opinion of them two. They sho got dif'cult names, Marco Jimenez, and Julio Balthazar. Ah knows somewut about thet second one from my Bible. Both husbands are clever. Ah don't know how pro-fess-ion-al they be as actors. Ah did see Marco Jimenez in WAR AND PEACE. Ah's seen Julio Balthazar dyin' in two Amer'can movies. Ah guess Amer'can agents gits him hired fo' them death scenes because he done so many in Mexico. He didn't play act at dyin' in thet there Sr.Lopez's office. No siree. Very active. He got his noisy wife to shut up. Both husbands were good at thet."

"Papacito's LEAVING one hundred thousand pesos to his agent can't have made them very pleased."

I put in a word. "Personally, I noticed that both the husbands were sucking up to that agent. I surmised that the agent's important to their continuing to get movie roles."

"Papacito introduced them to his agent. I've always believed that was one reason the brothers-in-law got married into the Gonzalez family. They'd figured the girls would be heiresses, but also they needed an introduction from them into the movie world that Papacito could provide for them." Guadalupe finished her apple, and threw the core towards a waste paper basket hitting her target with a bullseye. "The movie world's one I've never wanted to enter. Too much graft, too much envy and dirty business. I'm going to be as famous as Frida Kahlo, painting my primitives. Someday there might be a museum for *my* work just as there is for Frida Kahlo's. And I DON'T MEAN THE DIEGO RIVERA MUSEUM. Frida Kahlo's work is in its own place."

Museums! Oh, God. That gleam returned to Happy's beautiful turquoise eyes that meant she planned to visit all the places that stored old stones. And

I'd read there were very many such museums spread all over the country here.

Yes, Happy spoke up quickly. "Darlin' Lupe, you fly off to England tomorrow. Rick and I, we uns got to stay on here until Sr. Lopez works out what will happen to EL MILAGRO. There was no mention of the colt in your Papacito's will."

"Sr. Lopez has to deal with EL MILAGRO. He's the Executor of Papacito's estate, and has the last word."

I grumbled, "EL MILAGRO has to be fed, watered, groomed and exercised every day. If he isn't transferred properly into Giselle's ownership, who's going to pay for all that?"

Guadalupe smiled. "I'd love to. I've always wanted a horse of my own. Neither of my sisters would go to the horse races with Papacito. I was the one who kept him company at the races, not only for the joy of being with Papacito but to learn about racehorses."

"But you're a minor. Thanks, but you can't pay the bills. The horse can run in the time-honored fashion under the banner of In The Estate Of, and he'd best run soon or he'll miss out on the best races for two-year-olds."

Giselle, who hadn't participated in the conversation once it became established that Lupe would travel to England with Ghislaine, now became heated. "Mon Dieu, this horse has been trouble from the start. I've paid for him, yet he'll run under the banner of In The Estate Of?"

"Sorry, Giselle. Happy and I would dearly love for things to be otherwise. You mustn't give up on EL MILAGRO. He *is* a very good horse. I am delighted to be training him. I have a very soft spot for him ever since he won for you at Ruidoso, in *New* Mexico. But his transfer into your ownership hadn't been properly completed. Not by Wetherby's standards."

"Mon Dieu, don't let us argue. I value having you as my trainer." Giselle fluttered her Revlon-enhanced eyelashes. She added in a whisper, "I have something to say to you once we are outside this room."

Taking that hint, I hurried the Ponts to say their goodnights to Guadalupe. Then Happy kissed her goodbye, judging she might not see her until we too returned to England. I retrieved my Swiss army knife, tucked in a loose corner of Lupe's sheet, and added my goodbye.

On cue, outside in the corridor, Giselle made a sweeping gesture, and complained, "There are no security guards here. Who would have the power to order that the guards be sent away?"

"Maman," Ghislaine had her experience with the police in Madrid to give weight to her comment, "Only Sr. Lopez, the lawyer who is the executor of the Gonzalez will."

With those words ringing in her ears, Happy made a downturned upsidedown U of her gorgeous mouth that I treasure for kissing. She sighed. "Ah sho don't like his eyes. Thet Sr. Lopez done give me the creeps."

Chapter 6

This time, when we returned to our bedroom, Happy wanted to make love. She needed the comfort of our two bodies melding. She didn't calm down, she *turned on* and that certainly helped to change the black mood thrown over her like a sodden blanket in Lupe's sick room.

We did see Lupe again when she caught a flight for England. We turned up at the airport in time to watch Lupe and Ghislaine leave the Duty Free and go through Security. We waved. The two girls returned our waves, and then disappeared in the mass of passengers that followed them.

That museums' gleam came into Happy's sparkling eyes when we returned to the taxi stand outside the airport. "Where usn goin' now? Ain't no res-o-lu-tion yet to thet there EL MILAGRO ownership problem. Ah sez we go to thet Antho-po-logical place."

No escape. As is written in the Bible, I 'girded my loins,' and prepared for hours looking at old stones.

To gather strength for the hours of touring I knew would follow, I said, "Let's find a bistro. You can't run a car without gasoline and you can't walk a husband through a museum on an empty stomach."

We found a bistro that featured Mexican specialties. I burned my mouth with a too large helping of peppery chili over quesadillas: goat cheese with a corn fritter wrapped around the white mess. Awful! Happy was luckier. She'd ordered guacamole, and went easy on the Picante sauce because as she adores avocados she'd had plenty of experience with salsas that were too fiery.

Time passed more pleasantly than I could have imagined. The Mexican government's curators knew well that tourists lap up a country's early history and had these artifacts displayed at their best and at great expense. Not like in Olde England, where we permit our wonderful Druid Stonehenge pillars be exposed to the elements.

It's so nice to see Happy exulting in her favorite interest. That is favorite after our children, the movies and movie stars, and *me,* in more or less that order. I'd accepted years ago that my place on Happy's Totem Pole of interests was near the bottom except when we're making love.

Finally we started our exploration of the museum. Its first three galleries very wisely introduced Mexico's earliest cultures, starting with Olmec, which flourished around 1700 B.C. Just what the doctor ordered for my Happy. I had a difficult time to draw her away from a representation of "jaguar boy" because the Olmec art featured filed teeth. "Just like wut the fake vampire used in Morocco," Happy squealed, causing at least ten tourists to stare at her in shock.

No way will I attempt to list all the wearisome galleries we visited, Happy glowing with joy from satisfying her hobby.

Personally I found all those skulls and torn open bodies absolutely horrible. I admit the immense size of these early statues stunned me, and I was impressed with the height of the temples built by Mayans, Toltecs, and Aztecs as well as some of the other peoples who populated this region of Central America. But my toes hurt, because I'm accustomed to wearing riding boots, not shoes. My eyes could hardly focus on yet another ceramic warrior or huge stela. Then Happy dropped the bombshell: "Ah's just *got* to visit some of them temples pictured here."

Oh, oh. I should have seen that coming. I hadn't.

All the way during our return bus trip, with us crowded among locals in clothes varying from T-shirts and shorts to authentic china poblana outfits, embroidered in sequins, possibly worn for a Viva Mexico party, my Happy slogged on about how she wanted to visit those damn temples.

I was plagued by the thought of the many hundreds, or thousands, of victims sacrificed on their altars, some steps still stained today with their blood.

My mood was distinctly gloomy as I entered our bedroom and went to the telephone, where its red light announced a message.

"Yes?" I barked.

Giselle's cultured voice was as unruffled as always. She'd not taken offense at the way I'd barked. "Rick, I think you should be among the first to know that Soledad's husband, Mario Jimenez, was shot down in the street this afternoon. He was rushed to the ABC Hospital, but died on arrival. Thank God we sent Guadalupe out of the country."

Chapter 7

"Do Lupe need to return to Mexico for her brother-in-law's funeral?" Happy asked me. She'd used the children's bedroom extension to listen to Giselle.

I said hurriedly, "You'll have to convince her otherwise, if Guadalupe suggests that. Anyway, I doubt her snobbish sister Soledad would want her at the funeral."

"Any idée who would have shot down thet Mario?"

"Doesn't matter who the hit man was. I'll bet all three murders were authored by the same person."

"Ah sho won't take thet bet. Ah agrees. Same person."

"Happy, put on your thinking cap. These murders are likely to continue until there isn't a Gonzalez family member left."

With Timmy climbing into my lap to demand we take him to a McDonald's and Dorothy pleading to go shopping for a *china poblana* doll she'd seen in a shop in the hotel's lobby, I couldn't develop that thought of a Gonzalez family wipe-out.

The telephone rang again. I hesitated to answer.

Happy picked up the receiver. "Who'all?" She sounded astounded. "Thet mean eyed lawyer, Sr. Lopez? He done got shot down enterin' his office?"

I asked, "Lopez, too? He wasn't in line to inherit. He'd have got a hefty sum for being Gonzi's executor, but not enough to provoke his murder! I tell you, Happy, put on your thinking cap."

Happy sat down on Dorothy's bed to give her a cuddle.

Our toddler, Richard, who had only recently taken to standing on his two legs, now showed off his newly developed skill and rocked to the bedside to pull at Happy's skirt.

"Time we'all stayed in with our chillun. Cain't do much while these gangstyle killin's go on at this rate. Four murders. A hangin', and now shootin' from cars. Looks like someone seen too many Mexican gangster movies."

Heavy knockings at the door of our bedroom announced the arrival of police.

Happy's eyebrows shot up. "Wut all do them po-lice want? Seems like they could do mo'e good combin' the streets for them murderers." She took Richard into her arms, and leading Dorothy, she returned to our bedroom to face two burly brown-uniformed policemen. Not *judiciales*.

I shushed Timmy. "Son, we'll try to find a McDonald's a little later." I followed Happy, determined to spare her from being grilled by these newcomers.

She'd opened the door to them and ushered them to two upholstered chairs facing away from the window. With the light streaming in, it became difficult to read their facial expressions while our features were illuminated only too well. I restrained my anger, and tried to put on an agreeable expression.

"Do you speak English?" I asked for openers. "What can we do for you?"

Like the American comedians, Laurel and Hardy, one policeman was tall and thin, while the other was shorter and fat, bursting out of his khaki uniform. Both looked as strong as bulls. The shorter man had an excuse of a mustache, Hitler-like, a blur under his nose.

Mustache said, "I speak English." He did, American high school level English. I doubt he'd ever read a play by Shakespeare. "We haven't come here to be grilled as to our knowledge of your language. We want facts."

"Yes, facts," the Stan Laurel character echoed.

"My boss has looked up Happy Harrow on his computer. She's been involved in nine murders."

"Ten," Happy corrected quietly.

"Ten," the Stan Laurel fellow squeaked.

Mustache gave his sidekick a glare. "*I'm* conducting this investigation," he bellowed. "Senora, you came to Mexico just when four of our citizens have been murdered. We find that suspicious."

"Suspicious," came the echo.

"You have been known to deal with strange people. A Chechen terrorist. A fake vampire in Morocco. A pedophile in Madrid. A fiend in Milan. My boss wants to know what people you have associated with in Mexico?"

Happy didn't flinch. Sweetly, taking this interrogation in her stride, she said, "Horsemen, folks wut love racehosses. And movieland people. Friends and fam'ly of Gonzi Gonzalez's."

A silly laugh came with the echo, "Gonzi Gonzalez."

Roaring now, fatso boomed, "And you haven't seen any blood yourself here in Mexico."

Happy nodded. "Sho thing, seen a lot of blood in pictures at thet there Anthro-po-logy Museum. Victims wut had their blood run down the steps when them hearts wuz torn out."

No echo after that comment. Both policemen looked at each other. They stood up. Fatso declared, "I will report to my boss that you were uncooperative, and made fun of our national history."

The Stan Laurel-type repeated scornfully, "Our history."

Slamming our bedroom door they disappeared toward the hotel's banks of elevators. As they entered one, a startled Giselle stepped out of another.

She rushed to Happy, who was standing at our open door with two of our children still hanging on to her skirt. "Mon Dieu! What on earth? Those pavement-beat patrolmen came here to grill you? What a nerve! What could you possibly contribute to this case?"

What, indeed.

It would take another Gonzalez family murder for Happy to begin to clue into what was going on.

Chapter 8

I'd been firm with Happy about not visiting any gory temples. But I did offer to give her and the children a day in the gardens of Xochimilco. A true Brit, the word GARDEN always drew up my antenna. What I hadn't known was that this garden consisted of floating vegetable and flower *chinampas*, plots built up over roots and soil.

As the village of Xochimilco had flourished in the time of the Aztecs, being lakeside connected to the old Tenochtitlan by one of it causeways as described in the museum we'd visited, these plots had provided since that era flowers and vegetables to the nearby city. I loved that concept. I loved even more the fact that there were rows of flower-decked boats waiting to take tourists for rides down Xochimilco's canals, that still exist since the days of the Aztecs. We chose one called LUPITA, no prizes for guessing why.

The LUPITA had wooden chairs on a tiny deck, a Roman arch leading inside to its salon that was comfortably protected by a roof, and over its arch there was a most unusual wooden sculpture that was as contemporary as any in the Museum of Modern Art. It also contained a hint of the Aztec symbols that had inspired it.

We took seats on the deck, and listened to mariachis playing in boats that glided by, their caroling like sailors singing in gondolas in Venice. I tipped several of them. But I didn't concede to Happy's suggestion that we buy ice creams for our chillun. I'd heard both good and bad about the local treats, "they taste swell" but also: "they'll give you the worst belly ache you've ever had."

Richard wasn't looking well anyway. He'd burped up some of the lunch he'd had at our hotel. I decided we should head for home.

Oh, no. Happy's motherly instincts were smothered by the sight of a Sixteenth Century pink Church in the main square. She put on hold any rush back to the hotel. She'd seen Richard puke many more times than I had, and was almost immune to the problem.

There was nothing for it but to hire a guide who would show us around the rose colored church.

"Its name is Iglesia de San Bernardino. This was built by Franciscans when Aztecs still fought them, that is why it is fortified. See its crenellated façade? But also notice the classical style of the surround of its main door, almost Baroque. Now we go inside." He stretched out his palm for a tip before the next phase. Happy paid him and rushed inside the church.

It smelled musty. Like from a ghost's mantle there was a gloom. But a burst of glory came from its high altar where incredible early paintings were displayed without any fear of robbery.

Our guide pointed them out. "Those paintings on the altarpiece are by the great colonial artists, Cristobal de Villalpando and Juan Correa." Again the palm was extended for another tip.

Happy complied, but when Richard threw up again adding the smell of vomit to the odor of unwashed peons who had assisted at the latest service, Happy decided it was time to go home to our hotel.

Entering our bedroom I saw the red light blinking on our telephone that announced a message.

I hated to go listen to it.

Chapter 9

Giselle again. She had news of another murder. "Soledad's been killed. Shot dead. So it wouldn't have mattered if Lupe hadn't returned for Marco's funeral. Soledad won't be counting heads for her to be missed. Rick! Should we stay here in Mexico City? Waiting to see who is next? When it could be one of us?"

I took a deep breath before answering. "Giselle, that's up to you. We came here to unravel the situation concerning EL MILAGRO's ownership. If you say leave, we leave. The local racing authorities can work it out with Wetherby's about EL MILAGRO."

A silence.

Finally, Giselle spoke. "My daughter's safe in England. She called to say that she was at your house and the weather was fine. She is enrolling in the cookery classes today with Guadalupe. I'll give this El MILAGRO problem a few more days here. Then I think we should join the girls in England."

She hung up.

Happy had listened again on the extension in the children's room.

"Ah's thinkin' we'uns will be mighty glad to get back to Epsom. Meanwhile, Ah's goin' to see thet py-ra-mid near the city. Ah wants to climb it while y'all deals with the racin' au-thor-i-ties."

No retort to that. But what did change our plans somewhat was an e-mail from my friendly Canadian owner, Hal Murphy. He announced he was arriving in Mexico City in the morning and would be grateful if we'd book him into our hotel with a suite for him and his bride Mafalda and her daughter Maheen.

That news brought a huge grin to Happy's lovely face. "Maheen, here! Now we'uns *will* git to the root of these Gonzalez family-and-friend murders. She sho helped me in thet there Milan, Madrid, and Morocco. She'll help me here!"

Chapter 10

On arrival at Mexico City's airport the entire Murphy family came down with altitude sickness. Neither of the Egyptians, Mafalda and Maheen, had ever been to a city located at seven thousand feet. Hal Murphy had visited several, but had forgotten how badly he'd reacted to the altitude.

We'd both been at the airport to welcome the Murphy family. Happy's immune to altitude sickness because she was raised in Kentucky's highest hills. I 'd spent my youth climbing Scotland's Buck, where once I'd disturbed a spate of hornets on its peak.

Hal had been the first to faint. He slid to the floor while his porter did nothing to catch him before he hit the tiles. Mafalda went next, and her newly added weight had made it next to impossible for me to lift her up. When Maheen tried to help, she passed out, with Happy holding her head from cracking against a nearby wall.

This phenomena, not being new to Mexico City's airport personnel, brought out a bevy of helpers. The Murphy family members were propped up in chairs, oxygen masks were applied, and within minutes all three had revived.

"Let's get oot of here," Hal yelled. "I need a drink. How far away is your hotel?"

I'd booked the taxi ahead of time so we were able to go straight to their suite. I checked out that the living room had a bar. Hal wanted to add ice to his whisky from an ice bucket brought by a chambermaid, but I cautioned against that and found there were trays of ice in the suite's refrigerator where the ice had been made from bottled water.

With iced whiskys in hand, we settled down for a talk. Hal had experienced altitude sickness, I didn't want him to add Montezuma's Revenge with belly trouble from dirty ice as another welcome to Mexico.

I said. "It's great to see you here, Hal. But I do hope you'll stay close to the hotel, not take too much exercise, and watch the ice for your drinks, could be contaminated."

"Great to see you, Rick. I've come to help Giselle Pont. I'd be willing to buy EL MILAGRO from her so that she can avoid all the hassle here, and also perhaps ending up a victim of this serial killer."

"Hal, El Milagro isn't for sale."

"Giselle may change her mind aboot that when time runs on, and the *horse* don't run."

My rough diamond of an owner certainly had his heart in the right place. My words of caution to keep it healthy hadn't registered. Hal served a second whisky while still downing the first, and added ice from the bucket. He chuckled, sucking on the ice cube, "Rick, I'm a toughie. I doubt Giselle's a toughie. Let me see what I can do aboot this mess. Clue me in to where we are."

"EL MILAGRO's in limbo. He CAN'T RUN BECAUSE THERE WAS MISSING A VITAL PAPER WHEN GISELLE PAID FOR HIM, and now Gonzi's estate is claiming him. With Gonzi killed, his lawyer killed, his youngest daughter and her husband killed, believe me this is not an easy one."

Happy left Maheen's room to join us at Hal's pull-out bar. She said, "Ah's heard most of thet. No, it ain't easy. Ah's read online that the JOURNAL OF ZOOLOGY printed thet the great white sharks are like serial killers, they stalk their victims. They come in close enough to see their prey but not so close as to be seen. They like the victim to be alone. And them sharks gets better at killin' mo'e they does. The po-lice in England told me they find crim-i-nals by lookin' for *patterns* of how they strike. Ah's beginin' to get me a pic-ture of this murderer's pattern. Shark-like."

"Well done, Happy. But hurry solving it before there's another victim." Hal said decisively, "I'm buying EL MILAGRO. No disputing that, then no more murders."

Maheen had followed Happy to the minibar. She dug deep into the bar's refrigerator for a coca cola. There was no bottle opener available. Hal grinned, took the bottle and went to the door, propped the bottle's metal top against the lock's groove and PRESTO the top went flying.

Maheen served her drink without ice. She played with it, didn't take a sip, and said, "Happy, I recollect that it was you who suggested Ghislaine would be better off in England after her rape. Ghislaine's name meant nothing there, the British newspapers hadn't run the story, and Rick got her into that St.Mary's School. Then *Ghislaine became friends with Lupe, another girl far away from home. You took both of them out to tea and movies.* You could approach Lupe now and ask her to telephone her sister Himelda with the idea that she go to England too. With what I've heard of the Gonzalez family saga, I think she'll be killed next."

"Maheen-girl, Ah's not so sho." Happy's voice had dipped an octave, as it often did when she was thinking deeply. "Ah's reservin' my opi-nion. But Lupe could still *ask Himelda.*"

Mafalda Murphy appeared in the doorway of the suite's master bedroom. She wasn't dressed. Her hair hung loose, unbecomingly, aging her body that had opened like an accordion. Over a baby doll nightgown she had pulled a loose fitting negligée that revealed her newly added rolls of fat. I guessed that Hal Murphy had given her many a seven course meal in five star restaurants.

In a cranky tone, Mafalda complained to Maheen, "You shouldn't be talking so much when your poor mother is trying to rest."

Maheen tried a smile. It came out as damp as a new born kitten. She'd heard that particular complaint over and over the rare times she'd been permitted in her mother's presence.

Before the appearance on scene of kind Hal Murphy, all through her lonesome childhood Maheen had been hidden behind doors while Mafalda entertained paying "guests."

Unscarred by her mother's courtesan era, Maheen had retained a monumental desire to please. It contributed to her successes in solving murders with Happy. Maheen swallowed a quick retort to her mother, as she had so many times before. Maheen said to Happy, "Let's go back into my little room. We can talk there without disturbing anybody. Happy, I haven't met Himelda. I'd like to meet her. Could you manage that?"

Chapter 11

Happy managed. We had received a formal invitation to attend the double funeral for Soledad and Mario Jimenez. Happy included Maheen, thanks to one brief telephone call.

This was *no* Vice Presidente—EVITA funeral. Himelda, the last surviving legitimate Gonzalez family member, produced a show like no other. Her harridan side was represented by dozens of lowlife barflies. Her father's actor associates turned out in satisfying clusters, some of them well-known movie stars. Her mother's so-called aristocratic background had surprisingly caused the city's Old Guard to surface.

Himelda, no actress herself, had been brought up in show business and knew the value of great props. She chose the Basilica of The Virgin of Guadalupe for the funeral. In addition, she paid a pop band to play there to contrast with a traditional choir selected from a high society school under the patronage of Himelda's snooty Dona Magdalena de Fuentes Calientes.

"Wow! Ain't she the *GRAND* one, though!" Happy had whispered when we entered the Basilica and we were shown to privileged seats in the third row as family friends. Doña Magdalena had pride of place in the front pew, her huge hat blocking out our view of the magnificent gold encrusted altar.

The biggest surprise was Lupe. She'd flown over from England without warning, and proceeded down the main aisle with Himelda as chief mourners. Clothed entirely in black by outfitters for Britain's Royal Family who knew perfectly how to dress for these occasions, Lupe looked older and very dignified.

Happy was engrossed studying this ancient Basilica with its unique cape said to have been filled by the Virgin Mary with roses for a Mexican Indian called Juan Diego. She read every word of the Basilica's brochure describing the meeting in 1531 between the lonely local peon and the Virgin Mary. My Baptist wife had never *heard* a story of such a visitation before. The lady in the visitation, who was believed to have appeared four tmes to Juan Diego, is actually named after the Virgin de Guadalupe in Extramadura, Spain.

I'd traveled there as a student and knew that as a fact.

My darling wife missed what was going on two rows ahead. A dashing, too dapper thirty-ish man had appeared in the Basilica alongside Dona Magdalena. I guessed he was her walker. Lupe hadn't taken her eyes off him. In any event she had DRY eyes. She didn't weep a tear for Soledad or Mario. Tears might have made her mascara run, and Lupe had gone to great lengths to make herself bloom on this day. She had determined that no matter what outlandish outfit Himelda chose for the funeral *she* would not be bested in the makeup stakes.

We had to wait until the end of the service, when all the vast congregation was filing past Himelda, to learn the walker's name.

"I'm the Marques Salvador de Arroyo," he introduced himself, when we were crushed against one another in the slow-moving Condolences line. "And you are?"

No need to stretch out a hand. This wasn't the right occasion for that sort of courtesy. In a whisper, I said, "Rick Harrow. Racehorse trainer for Madame Giselle Pont, who bought the late Gonzi Gonzalez's horse, EL MILAGRO. And this lovely lady with me is my darling wife, Hillary. Her nickname is Happy, she answers to that."

Happy *did push out a hand. For a moment I was afraid she would curtsy as if to The Monarch.*

Lupe wasn't receiving condolences. Breathless, she pushed herself next to Happy, then also shoved out a hand to the Marques, and said. "I'm Guadalupe Gonzalez. Gonzi was my father. He loved that horse. I wanted to run EL MILAGRO in my name, but Rick says it has to run as In The Estate Of."

In Britain I'd often heard it said that many a romance starts at weddings. But I'd never thought that a funeral would make that claim. That day, it did. The intensity of a teenager's first affair and a middle-aged sophisticate's money-hungry love! What a potent combination!

The Marques bowed to Lupe. His eyes took in the British cut of her clothes and London haircut. "Mucho gusto, señorita." he murmured, and kissed her outstretched hand.

I thought Guadalupe would swoon like a Victorian-era spinster.

She didn't waste any time with Victorian-era niceties. Raising her voice, causing mourners' heads to turn and eyes to stare, she declared, "Cool! I've seen gentlemen kiss the hands of ladies in old movies. But this is a prima first for me." Guadalupe than responded with a kiss on his cheek.

Doña Magdalena's sharp antenna had caught the scene. She didn't like it. She barked, "Guadalupe you have no right to be here. You are from the wrong side of the blanket as regards Gonzi's paternity. Go back to that school which I'd heard was willing to accept you." Giving the Marques no time for regret, she used one hand to place it like a vise on his near arm, then used her cane to strike Guadalupe's legs two painful blows like Britain's Queen Alexandra was reputed to have done to her ladies in waiting.

Sweeping out of the Basilica's main door, Doña Magdalena pulled the Marques into the stretch limo waiting past the plaza. A stretch limo was her one concession to the modern world, she liked its bar and opened a bottle of champagne to share bubbly with the now reluctant Marques. The last I saw of that limo was the Marques with neck twisted to permit him to get one last look at Lupe.

Romance had flourished, in the square of the Basilica!

Chapter 12

I'd hurried Guadalupe to our own rented car. I hadn't taken any chances for my Happy to be gunned down while we waited hopelessly for a taxi. I'd found a rental car agency, flashed my British driving license, and used my credit card to make the high deposit. It didn't seem cricket to me to ask Giselle to pay for a car to take us to that funeral.

Maheen had shared the back seat with Happy on the ride out. Those two fast friends had caught up on girl talk, compared their babies' progress, and probably would have had lots to say about their husbands' ability in bed if I hadn't been driving.

It being a cheap little four seater, Maheen had to share the rear with Guadalupe on the return trip. She hadn't met Guadalupe, although she'd been concerned for her safety after hearing the saga of the Gonzalez family deaths. Now she tried to make up for lost time.

"Hello, I'm Maheen Palacio. I'm not much older than you are, eighteen to be exact. Awesome how a few years can make such a difference in life. I was barely seventeen when I met my husband, Luca Palacio. Still a school girl in Italy. Now we've been married almost a year and we have a lovely little girl. You'll meet her, he's bringing our baby to Mexico tomorrow. She'd had a cold and couldn't fly yesterday."

Guadalupe, who had been drooping like a flower that hadn't been watered, now brightened at Maheen's story. "Married at eighteen? Here in Mexico a girl becomes a woman as a *quinceañera*, and I am fifteen. Maybe I could marry soon."

Marry! She'd only just met the guy!

I took the Avenida de Insurgentes to head for our hotel. I asked Lupe, "Where are you spending the night? Not in your mother's apartment!"

"No. Not in her apartment. It's up for sale. Sr. Lopez put it on the market the day after she died. I hope you don't mind, Rick, but I've dropped off my luggage at your hotel and told Reception I was your guest."

Oh, Oh. With Giselle Pont picking up the Harrow family's tab, I could hardly ask her to extend that generosity to include Guadalupe. More dent to my finances!

Maheen saved the situation. She offered to share her room, "I'd love for you to come to the Murphy suite. We have three rooms, and mine has twin beds. Luca and our baby won't arrive until tomorrow. And tomorrow's another day, or so the song from ANNIE goes."

Chapter 13

Happy spent the remainder of the day with Maheen and Guadalupe. I was left to keep vigil over Amah and our three children. Not lonely! I had a great time watching Tim giving orders to our toddler Richard, telling him to walk. Dorothy glued herself into my lap, and the two of us had ended asleep from the warmth and comfort of each other's bodies. When Happy returned from visiting with Maheen, I was still groggy with sleep and we didn't make love.

By morning I was Gung Ho to get Guadalupe on the next plane back to England, for security's sake and so I could have Happy to myself.

It was an early flight. But Guadalupe had taken great care again with her makeup and hair. She looked stunning as we crossed the airport's Aztec-art-decorated hall to check in her luggage. And who was also there checking in? The Marques Salvador de Arroyo! A coincidence, or what?

He, too, had taken great care with his appearance. Too much so. The suit he wore was made by Lanvin of Paris, tailored to perfection for him. To an Englishman's taste, the points of the lapels were too high and exaggerated. I thought I'd check his ankles to see if he could possibly be wearing *spats* to complete his Grande de España image.

No spats, but his shoes were highly waxed, his fingernails manicured with a hint of transparent nail polish, and his grey hat was an exaggerated version of what is appropriate for races at Royal Ascot. Honestly, a top hat early in the morning, and worn with a business suit! Hardly correct, even if the suit did come from Lanvin.

The Marques flashed his tobacco-stained teeth with a smile as warm as Guadalupe's. Those two ignored the rest of us until they were through Security, and Guadalupe felt an obligation to wave. Her rib-to-rib escort didn't bother to acknowledge we were in the airport.

No wave from him. Not even a brief goodbye-nod.

Returning to the taxi stand queue, Happy turned to me, grinning: "Maheen said she'd be willin' to go see Mexico's Templo Mayor with me. Luca and their bambina don't arrive until tonight. Wut'all are yourn plans for today?"

"I thought I should go check on EL MILAGRO. I need to know if he's eating properly, his manure looks healthy, and he's being exercised."

"Good idée. But y'all got yourn ipod? Ah may want to text y'all."

Happy's comments were flushed away by a shriek from Maheen. She was staring in disbelief at her cell phone's screen. "C-ah-rist! Take a look!" She handed the cell phone to Happy, who also shrieked, then handed the cell phone to me, admonishing, "Y'all mebbe best not look too long. Ain't right for y'all to see Guadalupe naked."

On the screen, totally nude, was fifteen-year-old Guadalupe. She must have rushed to the Ladies Toilets in the Departures lounge, set up the camera of her cell phone, stripped, and clicked. Now she'd e-mailed the picture to Maheen.

Happy groaned, "Wut'all she be thinkin' of?"

"Easy answer," Maheen grunted too. "This picture was taken for that Marques to look at on his cell phone."

I agreed. "Maheen, you were only an additional audience."

"Naw! Maheen be one in the millions who can look. Thet there pic-ture is in cyberspace now. Rick honey, y'all got to get clued in to this Twenty-first Cent-u-ry. Y'all still be stuck in yourn Eton years. Long time ago."

Admitted. "Yes, I'm forty-six. But that Marques—*if he's a genuine Marques*—isn't that much younger. I'll bet he doesn't know much about cyberspace."

Maheen laughed. "He WILL. His family and friends will all be keen to describe his new love's body. He'll learn about cyberspace soon enough, I promise you. And Rick, you need not go on about men who choose younger women to love. My Luca was thirty-one when I was seventeen. You, Rick, are certainly twenty-two years older than Happy. And I doubt that the Marques is more than thirty, which makes him barely fifteen years older than Guadalupe."

Happy chimed in, with a lyrical up-the-corners-of-her-lips smile. "Ro-meo were older than Ju-li-et. Dante was *much* older than Be-a-trice, she were but twelve. And how about Nabokov's Lolita?"

"My darling wife, you are mixing fictional characters with real life ones. Of all the people you've mentioned, only Dante himself really lived."

My educating Happy was interrupted by a snarling taxi driver. *"Quien sigue?"* I took that to mean that one of us had to take his taxi and leave the other on the pavement. With a nod to Sir Walter Raleigh's legendary gesture, I handed my jacket to Happy, and said, "I'll wait for the next taxi. "Bye, you two." And I waved.

Chapter 14

Thank God I waved. It would be fraught days before I'd see my Happy again, or have news of Maheen and Guadalupe.

Entering the next taxi, I'd given the address of the stables, then followed my customary habit tucking my cell phone into my sunglasses' CASE, and put on the glasses. I settled down for the drive. At least I figured I could charge this drive to Giselle. Happy's taxi, I knew from my conscience, I would pay for out of our savings.

Arriving at the stables, I'd found EL MILAGRO's stall *empty*.

"Ejercisios?" I asked a passing groom.

He shrugged, but then hurried away with a *guilty* look. As movies-fan Happy would have described it: 'like in GODFATHER when a henchman runs away from the bomb he'd placed in the car which killed the Sicilian bride.'

What was going on?

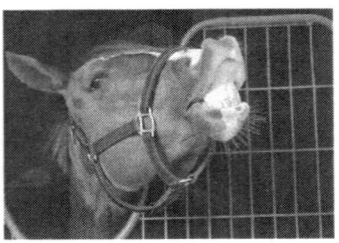

Chapter 15

I didn't wait long to find out. A garlic-smelling hand was clamped over my mouth. I felt a hard blow to my head. Seconds later I barely managed to realize that my feet were dragging on the stables' soft dirt floor, then I was tossed into the back of a pick-up truck.

It sped away. I was barely conscious.

I could make out the sides of the pick-up but not focus on anything on either side of the road. My abductors were not the best of drivers. They alternated who was at the wheel. I could tell that because the one erratic style was totally different from the next crazy one. We took every bump, and there were plenty of those. We cannon-balled around corners, and thankfully I wasn't aware of the steep canyons where the pick-up could have fallen.

When many hours later I was pulled, extremely stiff, from the pickup and dumped on the gravel of a sculptured driveway, believe me, I was disorientated.

A rough voice said in acceptable English, "You okay? Don't need a doctor!"

"Yes, okay. But maybe a doctor, just to check up on my skull. No fracture."

My response was ignored. Rough Voice gave various orders to the drivers of the van. They melted away. Rough Voice was some sort of local *jefe*. He had four bodyguards. They formed a phalanx around him, rather like the sort of box British soldiers used until the nineteenth century when under siege. I was going to attack Rough Voice?

Hardly likely. I was unarmed, groggy from being hit on the head, and with wobbly knees. In this deserted place, a dirt road with no houses in sight, what was I supposed to do to this guy?

A stretch limo came bouncing down the lane, hitting every rock and fallen branch. It stopped in front of Rough Voice, a fancy-capped chauffeur jumped out from the front and held open a rear door for Rough Voice as if he were about to be driven to Buckingham Palace.

Rough Voice entered the limo, arranged himself comfortably on scattered cushions, and regally gestured that I was to sit in the rear with him. I obeyed. What else? I watched as the four bodyguards took possession of the abandoned pick-up, which they used to follow the limousine in close tandem.

A large mansion appeared after a curve in the trail. It was surrounded by many out-buildings, some suitable for a farm, others more reminiscent of a military camp. As twilight was approaching, lights came on. Some lights illuminated a large plaza in front of the mansion, a center for all the other buildings. All of these lights flared simultaneously when Rough Voice stepped from the stretch limo. He gestured again, signaling I should follow him.

We crossed this large plaza, which was expensively paved with antique ballast stones. As we reached the mansion, a set of imposing ten foot high double doors swung open. Inside, a vast hall twinkled with candles. There was a huge fireplace, big enough to roast a deer. And who was standing in front of it, warming her legs? Mafalda Murphy!

SHE STARED AT MY AMAZED EXPRESSION. I MUST HAVE LOOKED AS IF I WAS A CHILD WHO HAD ENTERED THE WRONG BIRTHDAY PARTY. SHE PROCEEDED TO EXPLAIN WHY SHE WAS STARING. "Oh, hello Rick, you shouldn't be so surprised to see me here. Hal bought EL MILAGRO this morning, and this gentleman wants the horse. He thought if I came along to his place, Hal would trade."

God almighty! Mafalda was handling her abduction as seamlessly as if Rough Voice was one of her more dangerous customers in her era as a courtesan. Well done, Mafalda. I wouldn't have thought she was capable of handling such a situation with so much expertise.

Verbally putting the ball back into her court, I left the next move up to her experienced ways. "Oh, hello, Mafalda. Yes, I understand. And, by the way, where is the horse? Here?" I must have sounded like a lover caught with his pants down when the husband had walked into the bedroom.

Rough Voice interrupted. "I have the horse. This lady's husband has *her* back when we get all his papers."

Smoothly, oh so smoothly, Mafalda smiled crookedly and said, "It's lovely here. I'm enjoying your beautiful home."

How many times before had Mafalda repeated something similar after a knife had been put to her fat throat?

I said, "I'd like to see EL MILAGRO."

"*Carachos*. Of course you're going to 'see' that damned horse. Why else would I have brought *you* here? YOU have no money. Nobody would pay millions for YOUR return. In my business, I don't waste my talents. Follow me. I'll take you personally to *my* stables."

We left Mafalda, still with her crooked smile, as she turned her backside to the fire and raised her skirt to warm her huge tush. No doubt she'd learned that trick at British houseparties. She remarked, "Awfully cold here, at this altitude. It's eight thousand feet up, here."

The stable was at a distance of a thousand meters from the mansion. I could recognize EL MILAGRO's furious bellow. No mare for him, just incarceration.

Oh, Oh. I recalled that when the Aga Khan's syndicate's SHERGAR was abducted, *the racehorse behaved so badly* that his kidnappers had to put him down. And, possibly, had eaten him when February's hard ground had made it impossible to dig a hole deep enough to bury him out of sight of searching helicopters. Would EL MILAGRO be shot! And, *eaten*?

That memory brought one consoling thought. I remembered that the Aga Khan's stable manager had also been kidnapped in order to handle that valuable horse, and released, alive. As a stallion, SHERGAR would have earned millions. But kidnappers couldn't have hoped to use him as a stallion at the figure he could command in an open market. Perhaps they meant to send him to Japan or Russia by airplane to serve mares secretly. What emboldened **me** was that the stable manager had been released alive.

I said firmly, "EL MILAGRO needs exercising. Proper meals. The water he's accustomed to. Friendly grooms." I pointed at the unkempt barbaric-looking stablehands that guarded his stall.

EL MILAGRO recognized me. Immediately he calmed down, and like a spoiled child whose indulgent Nanny had arrived, he pushed his sweating carcass next to my body as I slipped into his stall. Seeing me, he expected proper oats, good water, and a gallop.

Rough Voice commanded, "*Rapido, muchachos. Haga salir el animal.*" El MILAGRO was brought out of the stall. Reins and a bit, a saddle and stirrups were all familiar to EL MILAGRO. He settled, and waited for the pats and the caress on the soft nose he knew I'd give him.

With his reins in hand I leaped into the saddle. Rough Voice yelled, "Don't think you can ride him out of here. You'd be gunned down. My men are experts at that. There's no place to go for miles around that doesn't belong to me and is not guarded with army-like precision. But, you may give him a gallop. I do know he needs one."

A stable lad called out, "*Jefe, el animal sufre un mal. Diarrhea.*"

I understood the last word. Diarrhea is a very common complaint for humans in Mexico. Why not horses? I turned EL MILAGRO so that I could examine his stall. Yes, his manure was watery.

Dismounting, I said to Rough Voice, "No good giving him a canter. He'll be *weak* from diarrhea. You'd better call in a vet."

Rough Voice gave a short, nasty laugh. "Don't try that one on me. I know your game. You think a vet would help *you* to escape. Forget it. I don't need to 'call in' a vet. We have our own. One of the best in all Mexico. As my colleagues in America say, I MADE HIM AN OFFER HE COULDN'T REFUSE."

I shrugged, and tried a grin. No good. There was nothing here to grin about. But the *jefe had* given me an idea. I WOULD find a reason to call for a doctor, a specialist, and then maybe he'd help me *and Mafalda* to escape.

Much as I cared for EL MILAGRO, I was keenly aware that my primary aim must be to bring Mafalda safely back to Hal. Her excellent act, feigning indifference, had not hidden from me a truly desperate need to return to Mexico City. I've never been a patron of brothels, but I recognized deep trouble when a whore plays calm. It's like the glassy surface of the sea just before a terrible storm. God knows how many whores have had their throats cut, their vulvas burned, their toenails pulled out. Mafalda knew she was in grave danger. Would she let me help?

With EL MILAGRO back in his stall that was slippery from liquified manure, I said, "That's up to you. But be very sure you get in that vet. Your groom here was right, the animal is sick. I could prescribe a change of water and hay. Oats. But I'm no medico, and I'm sure EL MILAGRO needs more. Needs medicine."

"I know all that. This is a $4 million horse. I'm not going to screw up on his care. But, meanwhile, I've got good use for you. This estate has everything, except an English butler. You just got the job." The laugh that followed was more like a growl, but I followed the *jefe* to his huge kitchen and accepted the striped apron that was handed to me.

Play at being a butler? Certainly, if that was what was needed for the moment.

When I was ten and Dad in his prime, we *had* a butler. His name was Ronald Chivers, and I remember him well. He went by his surname, Chivers. He'd been employed for many years by a London gents' club that went broke. It had been located on Eaton Square, and when many of its members gave up on London to concentrate on saving their country estates and petrol became too expensive for jaunts up for an afternoon's bridge, the club closed down and Chivers came to us. Dad had been a member of that club, and was among those who no longer could afford weekly jaunts to London for bridge plus a visit to a brothel, as was my father's choice.

Chivers had remonstrated with me when I failed to place knife and fork together on my plate "like two soldiers on parade." On the few occasions when Dad entertained and I was recruited to serve the vegetables while Chivers poured the wine, Chivers had taught me to serve from the left. And to take away used plates from the right.

At eleven I left home to board at Mr. St. Adwyn's at Eton. Dad decided he could make do with trays of food served to him by his 'daily', Mrs. Wrench, in front of the television set. When Dad decided that, he found a job as a waiter for Chivers at the local hotel. But I'd learned to serve at table, and now I hoped those lessons might save my life in the coming days.

Mafalda reigned over *jefe's* dining room. When the evening meal was announced, by me wearing a butler's tails with black tie, Mafalda swept in to take unbidden the armchair at the head of the table.

She played the Lady Of The Manor to perfection. Mafalda demanded that each course be passed twice. This was a rich household, and she wasn't going to go on a reducing diet here.

Her gluttony gave me an idea. In the Butlers' Pantry I'd noticed a piece of rotten meat left to accumulate mold. I chopped up that meat, very fine, and mixed it with the next course which happened to be lamb stew.

Mafalda wolfed down the lamb stew, and asked for seconds. Oh, I was only too glad to pass the lamb again. She cleaned her plate.

I wasn't surprised when Mafalda gave a sharp scream when I was serving coffee. She dropped her Limoges demi tasse cup, and grabbed her stomach as if it was a dying baby.

In the vast sitting room, beside yet another great fire, Mafalda howled like the winds of a hurricane.

She cried out for a doctor. "Appendicitis," she yelped, "I know I have appendicitis. Here, in the middle of nowhere. I'm going to die. There can't be a hospital for miles. I need to be operated on, *now*. Tonight."

Jefe responded with alacrity. Mafalda's survival could mean $4 million to him. She had to remain in good health if Hal would give up the horse in a trade. "I'll get in a specialist," he offered. It occurred to me that *jefe* must be feeling sick too, by now.

Right! On time, *jefe* grabbed his stomach and fell to the floor, writhing in pain. "Call for the *medico*," he ordered. "Call for a *priest*."

Clearing away the demitasse cups, I grabbed my stomach too, letting the valuable Limoges china crash to the tiles. I, too, slipped to the floor writhing as if suffering intolerable pain. I moaned out, "Not a medico. The vet! This is a germ brought by EL MILAGRO. Like the Swine Flu, but a stomach influenza that can be equally fatal."

"The vet! Si, *señor*. You, Englishman, get off the floor and send for my vet. You English beat the Nazis, can a little germ keep you down?"

I pretended to try retching. When *jefe* rose to dash for the nearest toilet, I snaked along the floor to the pantry. There, I stood up, called through the swinging door to the kitchen in a voice supposedly altered by pain, "*Rapido, el veterinario. El sacerdote!*"

A village priest arrived. He took command of the *jefe's* spiritual need, he heard his confession after the *jefe* emerged from using the toilet. The *jefe's* confession sounded long and complicated, giving me time for the vet.

Within minutes, a dapper Frenchman appeared. He was neatly shaved, his shirt had been recently washed and wife-ironed, his shoes were clear of manure or dog shit. I looked at his hands, they were clean with short clipped nails. I liked him. In my desperate Spanish, I asked, *"Usted, el veterinario?"*

He replied in the excellent English that French gentlemen acquire from British nannies. "Yes, indeed I am. What's the trouble?"

"There IS trouble. Listen, I'm Rick Harrow, a racehorse trainer. I've added rotten meat to the dinner I served and the *jefe* thinks he's dying, along with a hostage. One of my owners is Hal Murphy, a billionaire. It's his wife who's being held hostage by the *jefe* until Hal Murphy releases the papers of a recent acquisition called EL MILAGRO. That horse is *here*. Have you been to see EL MILAGRO in the last hour? Checked his manure?"

"Yes, indeed I have. That horse needs clean water, oats, exercise. Then his manure will be normal. But, what do you plan to do with the *jefe*?"

"Tell me your name. Tell me what you're doing in this godforsaken place. And tell me if you would be willing to act out for us that EL MILAGRO is suffering from a Swine Flu-like intestinal germ that could kill the *jefe*."

"Ah, bon. I understand. Yes, indeed. All right, my name is Eduoard Bonvouloir. I came to Mexico with my dear wife under the auspices of a Veterinaires Sans Frontières program to help save animals here. I was kidnapped by the *jefe*, and kept hostage while he threatened to kill my wife. Indeed, I understand your plan. Yes, I *will* play along. I can say that my wife has been exposed to EL MILAGRO's germ. As I will have been, of course. And perhaps we will all get safely to a hospital. Later I'll collect my wife and leave Mexico."

"What about EL MILAGRO? Is there any way we can save him from being slaughtered?"

"Yes, that too. Indeed, I can have a sick old mare buried after a switch that will save EL MILAGRO. The mare will be buried, not EL MILAGRO. I'll give orders the grave must not be examined because the horse died of a contagious disease. Can you ride?"

"That's part of my job."

"Indeed. But you'd never find your way safely out of this area in the dark. Many crevasses and drops into canyons. No beacon to follow. But if you can manage to bring out EL MILAGRO when I load up your victims for the ride to a hospital, you can follow my van."

That was agreed. I added more rotten meat to the stew to be served as a late dinner to the stable boys and the *jefe's* bodyguards. They ate it with gusto on long rectory-tables in an enclosed room beside the kitchen.

We could still hear the *jefe* at his confession. "No, I did not trade in drugs. No prostitution. I sent men, and women, to their deaths for money. I was paid to organize murders. Shoot-by, and more complicated ones. I sent a trapeze artist to kill Gonzi Gonzalez."

When I heard groans from the stable boys and heard the bodyguards rushing to the available toilets, I slipped into the *jefe's* wine cellar, from where I'd collected the Beaujolais for dinner, and collected a crate of Malvern water for EL MILAGRO. Then I changed out of my butler's garb to pull on my old jeans and manure-caked boots.

Inching into my woolen sweater, I hurried down to the stables.

EL MILAGRO was asleep.

Opening his huge, limpid eyes he gave me a horse smile. He licked the top of my head, and watched with anticipation while I filled his bucket with Malvern water. With massive gulps he drained the bucket and pawed the stable floor asking for more of that water. I obliged.

I kept a watchful eye on the mansion's front doors.

Edouard Bonvouloir had parked a van in front of them. It was not the same van that had brought me, captive, from Mexico City. I could hear *jefe's* strangled voice, "Has EL MILAGRO been in this van? I will not travel in any van he used."

Soothingly, Edouard answered, "Indeed, no. You must not. But do you not recall that EL MILAGRO arrived here in a special windowless horse box? You will be fine in this van."

Edouard arranged cushions brought from the living room sofa. Gingerly he positioned *jefe* on to the cushions, speaking comforting words so low that I couldn't hear them. Next came Mafalda. *She* wasn't acting now. Poor Mafalda, my victim for the greater good, barked out complaints like bullets from a machine gun.

"This mode of transport is disgusting. I should have a proper ambulance!"

As I observed that scene from a hundred meters away, I was suddenly made to remember that my cell phone was in the eyeglass case inside my trousers. I'd turned off the ring mode, but it was pulsating.

Alone in the stable while EL MILAGRO drank up that second bucketful of water, I looked at its text box. "Hal desperate. Find Mafalda."

I texted back, "Sequestered with Mafalda."

New text, "Where r u?"

My reply, "Hospital circumference 2 hours from city."

But I wasn't in a hospital, not yet. After I'd replaced my cell phone in the sunglasses' case. I was galloping behind Eduoard's van, with an ill horse under me and a pitted trail injuring his poor hooves.

In consideration of EL MILAGRO's poor condition, Eduoard drove slowly. I could hear the *jefe's* rough voice, "Faster, faster."

And Eduoard's professional tones, "Must not go too fast. Bad for you."

We must have traveled for an hour. I could sense that EL MILAGRO's two bucketfuls of Malvern water weren't going to get him much farther.

Once, feebly, he tripped and I had to pull hard on the reins to stop him from going down to the rocky road.

One hour into this disastrous ride, we turned a hill and suddenly before us twinkled the lights of a village like on a Christmas crèche. The outlying parts consisted of peons' huts, but as we approached its center I recognized residential neighborhoods featuring two storied homes and then the horizontal block of a hospital.

Edouard made straight for the hospital. I didn't.

Watching my "victims' being unloaded, I kept a respectable distance while searching for any building that might pass for a hotel. WITH STABLES. I found one, that had a sign inviting *"parientes de los enfermos."* Just like in the UK and the USA, relatives of the sick would need rooms near a hospital. In Mexico, at this village level, they would need stabling for their donkeys or mules.

Even at this late hour I was welcomed, and so was EL MIRAGLO. No doubt the sick who used this local hospital weren't stuck in time frames. When a heart attack hit, a leg was broken, an appendix came close to bursting then the relatives trundled their patients here whether the sun shone or the moon.

In my saddlebags I'd carried six bottles of Malvern water and a handful of oats. Not enough. I didn't like the look of the stable's one bucket, so I'm afraid I was guilty of "borrowing" twin pots that held decorative carnations. I threw away the carnations, used my shirttails to rub clean those pots, poured the water into one and the few oats into the other. EL MIRAGLO, gentleman that he was, gave me a grateful nod before he tore into the oats and then the water. Oh, I do know that it's not the greatest way to care for a racehorse, giving drinking water after a challenging ride, but my desperately dehydrated EL MILAGRO had to be treated as an exception.

I didn't sleep in the bed I'd paid for at the so-called hotel. When I thought of all the sick people who'd slept in it or their about-to-be-sick relatives, I decided I'd be better off stretching out near EL MIRAGLO and using his saddle for my pillow.

A helicopter overhead was my alarm call. Dawn, and a police helicopter hovering over the hospital were both extremely welcome.

Dashing outside the stables, I pulled off my shirt and used it as a flag. Did the pilot see me? I wasn't to know. The pilot kept circling to locate a safe pad on which to land. I tried to help, but my little hotel was built on a hillside. Useless area.

Edouard sallied from the hospital, made urgent gestures with his arms denoting a flat space suitable for a helicopter landing. It was the hospital's partially unused parking lot. In it there were no cars except his van, because patients and doctors arrived by donkey or on a horse. I suppose the nurses walked.

Chapter 16

The helicopter landed. Police ventured out first. Then came Hal Murphy and his bodyguards.

I watched from my hillside, and waited.

Hal Murphy! Here! The police entered the hospital, following Edouard's lead. When Hal and his bodyguards also disappeared inside the insignificant door, I secured EL MILAGRO's reins and scooted down to join the new arrivals.

What a hospital! It was neither clean, nor furnished with any recognizable medical necessities, nor were there any private rooms. The place was more like a barracks, or a prison.

Mafalda was in the fetal position on an iron bed in the Womens' Ward. There was no sheet on top of the bed's bloodied mattress. The hospital's one doctor was arguing with Hal's English-speaking bodyguard.

I caught the words *"Cholera"* and *"Typhoidea."*

Hal was shaking his head. I'd never seen him look so desperate, not even when his son had run off with a pre-teen girl. Stepping out of the shadows from the main unlit corridor, I spoke to Hal where he stood in front of the one window.

"Thanks for coming." We exchanged hearty back slaps. But Hal pulled away to hang his head. I decided to tell him the truth about putting rotten meat in the *jefe's* lamb stew. "Hal, please don't worry about Mafalda. She doesn't have any kind of fatal disease."

"Rick! Wonderful we were able to find you. I'd been about to contact my Canadian Ambassador for help. I can't live without my Mafalda. Not since she took me to Paradise. Rick, don't play games with me. What do you mean she hasn't any serious condition! Look at my poor darling writhing in pain."

I took a long look at Mafalda. Even with her stomach cramps at the manor house, she'd managed to spirit her lipstick into a pocket. Now, with

Hal present, she'd applied it skillfully. I noticed she'd combed her hair, and that the cramps weren't coming as frequently as last night.

"Mafalda, I apologize most sincerely. But there was putrid meat in that lamb stew. Once you've eliminated that from your system, you'll be as good as new. Just chalk it up as Montezuma's Revenge."

Hal gave a great joyous yelp. "Poop! That's all she needs to do. Go to it, honey. And we'll hold the helicopter until you're done."

Mafalda knew well where the toilet was. She managed to lift her heavy frame, and skirted away to do what she had to do.

In this Womens' Ward there were two other patients, a teenage first—time expectant mother, and an old wrinkled crone who labored for breath. Although the girl's pains had started, she didn't want to miss any of the scene playing out here. The wrinkled crone, whose face looked like a walnut from last year's Thanksgiving decorations, sat up on her two pillows to reach for oxygen and enjoy the show.

Hal had brought provisions. He had a basket of fruits, a box of pastries, and a bottle of wine. Mafalda returned from the toilet, emptied the glass on her bedside table of a tired toothbrush, and poured out a hefty drink.

When she'd finished it, down to the last drop, Mafalda declared, "Get me out of here."

I was looking for Mafalda's shoes when we all heard the sound of a single gun shot. The sound came from the Mens' Ward, a corridor away. I hadn't seen Eduoard during the charade in the Womens' Ward, and hoped that he hadn't come to any harm.

Within seconds Hal and I'd arrived in the Mens' Ward, alongside two of his bodyguards. On an iron bed, similar to the one Mafalda had, lay *jefe*, his *rough voice* forever silenced. His mattress had *fresh* blood, and most of *jefe's* brains spilled on to its striped ticking. Next to the bed, with a smoking regulation pistol in his hand, stood one of the four policemen who had made the helicopter trip. His light brown uniform was spattered with more of *jefe's* brains and blood. "*Quizo escapar*," he commented blandly, tucking the pistol into its holster.

Eduoard, alerted by the pistol shot, joined us to stare at the policeman. Hal said, "I know the police in Mexico expect bribes, I learned they are called *mordidas*. Or to be given tips, like for a headwaiter. But I didn't offer this policeman any money. Not to kill this man, even though he *did* abduct my wife."

"AND your horse," Eduoard shoved out a courteous hand. "How do you do? I am Eduoard Bonvouloir, a veterinarian who has been looking after EL MILAGRO and other horses the *jefe* had at his hacienda. Your horse has not been well, but Rick has ridden him here and he's outside if you wish to see him before you take off."

Hal had known many vets in various countries around the world, but he hadn't come across one who could write a book on etiquette. "Pleased to meet you, I'm sure. But my primary concern will always be my Mafalda. Once she's comfortable in the helicopter, I'll come take a quick look."

While Mafalda, with her ever-increasing girth was being helped, squeezed and laterally pushed through the helicopter's narrow door, I tried to text Happy. No response. I scribbled a note for her and handed it to Hal, as he rushed to join Mafalda. "I can't go with you and abandon EL MILAGRO. Eduoard will help me get him back to you."

Hal followed through with his promise to take a look at EL MILAGRO, but he did so through the mud-spattered window of the departing helicopter. His four bodyguards and the four Mexican policemen seemed far more interested in viewing a $4 million horse.

I breathed a sigh of relief that Mafalda was "in the saddle" again, although I knew that for the next twenty-four hours she'd be making many visits to her "throne."

"Eduoard, what is our next move?" I asked, chasing a butterfly away from EL MILAGRO's unkempt mane.

"You, Rick, must indeed *make* a move. Ride as far as you can, away from the *jefe's* territory. His household help will be alerting the *jefe's* day shift bodyguards that he'd been taken by me to this hospital. They aren't sick from putrid meat. They could arrive at any moment. I want to try to free my wife before all hell breaks out here."

"Of course, you must get to your wife before these gorillas know the *jefe* is dead. You have the van, you two can drive to the nearest big city and ask help from the French Consul."

"Spot on, Rick. I will indeed go to my nearest Consulate, and then leave this country. Your problem is magnified by this horse's value. You can't ride him again as hard as you did last night. He'll break down. Perhaps, permanently. I suggest you walk him to the nearest town and telephone your Mr. Murphy to send a horse box for transport."

I pointed to EL MILAGRO's hardened coils of manure. "Now his poop looks healthy enough. But, I agree. Walk him. He's undernourished. Lost too much condition. There's one hitch, the *jefe's* gorillas know me. Know what I look like, and will be keeping an eye out for this horse. They know what EL MILAGRO looks like too."

"Disguise yourself. And the horse. Buy a large sombrero and a bolero style jacket. Use the same black hair dye, Mrs. Murphy uses, to alter EL MILAGRO's chestnut coat. There is a small shop in this village that doubles as a *farmacia*. I've often come here to get gasoline, hay for the horses, makeup for my wife. They will have typical Mexican clothes, and hair dye.

The shop also sells maps, next to the gasoline pump. Get one. Today, indeed, I'm buying nothing. I'm hurrying to free *mon amour*."

"Wait. One more word. What do you reckon happened in the *jefe's* ward? He couldn't have been trying to escape, he was too weak from pooping all night. What made the policeman pull the pistol from its holster?"

"He executed the *jefe*. Gangland style, one single shot to the back of the head. Someone wanted him silenced. Not a question of 'What" but *who!*" Eduoard didn't embroider his comment. He revved the motor of the van, waved, and drove off.

Would he be able to free his wife, and the two of them get to the nearest French Consulate? I wasn't to know.

Chapter 17

My feet hurt. I'd walked miles along the dirt road that led to high mountains in the far distance. Oh, how I hoped that one of the ranges ahead had The Sleeping Lady Iztaccihuatl, or its companion Popocatepetl, The Smoking Mountain. Both topped altitudes over 17,000 feet, and I knew it was possible to view them from the capital.

No way would I have wanted to climb those mountains, even if Popocatepetl wasn't issuing clouds of soot threatening to erupt. Oh, that would be just what I needed, a volcano in eruption. Next on my schedule? A real one, and not just Mafalda's *temper tantrums* when she learns I planted that putrid meat. I stared more kindly at Popocatepetl. Volcano or no, I'd be glad of it because I could imagine my darling Happy putting our children to sleep on the far side of it.

I felt dizzy, probably from hunger and lack of water. The bottles of water I'd bought at the village *farmacia* were downed hours ago by loyal, but now faltering, EL MILAGRO.

My huge Mexican sombrero, lavishly embroidered and decorated with silver thread, weighed me down. I certainly didn't feel full of music like the Mariachi I was supposed to represent.

Rain had hindered our progress. Worse, it had washed away most of the black dye I'd managed to put on EL MILAGRO. I could have used more rain just to raise my parched face to it, and cool poor EL MILAGRO.

Night was lurking behind high clouds, blotting out the sunset's amazing display of colors that could have diverted me from my misery. That partial sunset was beyond belief beautiful.

We were on a highway, with expensive cars speeding past, when Lady Luck smiled. I heard horses neighing. I smelled good hay, and my favorite of all smells, clean groomed horse.

EL MILAGRO and I had arrived at the environs of the Tecamac Polo Club. Even in England I'd heard of this club, famous for furthering a campaign to save unwanted horses. This club had sent out to the world the Gracida family of players, ten goalers, topped by Carlos and Memo Gracida. In the fading evening light, I looked at the map I'd bought to check. Yes. We were on Carretera 39. We'd reached an oasis of lovers of horseflesh, sport, and fair play. Tecamac!

I had the devil of a time finding the right entrance. When your feet will barely move, and you are leading an exhausted horse, every step is agony. I tried one entrance, closed because there was no game that day and these doors were for paparazzi. Another pair of gates were closed, because that entrance was for members only.

"*Hola, necesita ayuda?*" I heard a friendly voice call out.

AYUDA. Help. Yes, I certainly did. The voice belonged to a rider completely outfitted in white except for the dark leather protective pads on his knees and elbows. His white helmet gave him the air of a jousting knight.

I took off the ridiculous sombrero and sent a thank you gesture. "*Ayuda, si.*" That word prompted another from my short vocabulary. "*Agua?*"

"You're Rick Harrow. We know each other. I met you at Windsor Great Park at a polo game after Gold Cup Day at Royal Ascot," he said in lightly-accented correct English. The Rider dismounted and took my arm. I must have seemed about to faint. I looked closely at him. Yes, I vaguely recalled joining a group to drive into Windsor Great Park to watch polo. And, I also remembered that his team had lost. At the time I thought he'd taken losing with the good will of an Etonian, who has been taught that the game is *all*, win or lose. Taking EL Milagro's reins to join them to *his* pony's, he added, "What in God's name are you doing in this Mariachi costume, with a racehorse at our polo club?"

I caught my breath. "Any chance of a whisky? Maybe some sandwiches. I can pay. I've been abducted, but the gorillas didn't take my money, my credit cards, or my driver's license. First though, I'd be deeply grateful if my horse could have water and some of that sweet fresh hay I smell."

"Whisky, certainly. Oats and hay for your horse? You don't need to ask." He swung open a pair of heavy gates, releasing the reins of the horses to a tidy peon, who patted EL MILAGRO's nose. "Was this the horse that was stolen from Hal Murphy? Hal was in the party you brought to Windsor Great Park. There's been a lot about his horse in the local newspapers. London's DAILY MAIL even gave it a spread. By the way, in case my name escapes you, I'm Tony Farinas."

Good God! Tony Farinas was a legendary name among Sloane Rangers when ex-debs prowled looking for fun sportsmen. Polo player, cricket champs. Whatever, think Jemeima Goldsmith marrying her Pakistan cricket-star husband.

I didn't get my whisky right away. After accompanying EL MILAGRO to his well-appointed stall, seen the hay net filled, the water bucket overflowing and the efficient groom cutting the nettles out of El MIRAGLO's mane, I made straight for a landline telephone. No texting. I dialed our hotel, asked for my room, and – bliss! – heard Happy's Kentucky hills "Hiya."

"My darling, are you and the children okay?"

"Yeah man, except for Timmy. He done got the sniffles. Cold here at night, but he don't want to put on no jacket. And you? Where y'all been? Ah's been feared Ah's got me a husband wut had flown to Argentina or some such place to see a woman, like thet Governor of South Ca-ro-lina."

"My darling wife, for me there's no other woman. Couldn't be. But I do want to ask after Mafalda. Does she still have stomach cramps? Mad as a wet hen?"

"Oh, thet Mafalda, she sho somethin' else. Ain't mad at the little trip she done took out into the countryside. No man. She done lost ten pounds. De-lighted! Ah guess as she went to some sort of spa. Leastways thet's wut Hal said to tell the noospapers."

SOME SPA! What Happy said about Mafalda losing ten pounds I could certainly believe but I wouldn't recommend visiting the jefe, and then being in the next ward while he was murdered. I wanted to tell Happy all the nitty gritty details of my odyssey, but I didn't.

"Did you and Maheen have a great day at the Templo Mayor pyramid?"

"Sho nuf. But Luca and their baby are in Mexico now, so I won't see so much of her. Rick, y'all cain't get away with changin' the subject. Ah done asked where y'all been?"

"I went to take a look at EL MILAGRO. Planned to give him a gallop. He'd been taken away by some thugs. Same sort took me to the compound where he was being held. He'd got sick."

"Where he be now?"

"I think it's wiser if I don't say. He's very tired, but not so sick. He's in the last place you'd look for a racehorse. I'll be with you tomorrow. I don't want to talk any longer, in case this call is traced."

How I hated to end the conversation, relinquishing the sweetest sound in the world.

I joined Tony at the club's bar. My whisky tasted great. I didn't worry about the ice cubes. I sucked on them as if they were brown sugar in the coffee at my London club. Tony offered to give me a bed for the night. I just hoped that would include a shower.

Chapter 18

Tony's home was magnificent. It wasn't a *copy* of a colonial era house, it *did* date from the colonial era. It had an intricately designed baroque façade that set the tone. Lattice work screens hung above tiles forming intricate designs. The furnishings were of the same era, but in extraordinarily good condition, having been maintained through the centuries and restored when necessary. In all its patios there was an abundance of flowering shrubs and potted palms in Versailles boxes. The climate was perfect, at its altitude neither too hot nor cold.

In this elegant other-worldly atmosphere I had to appear there in my filthy jeans, the ridiculous Mariachi jacket that was too small for me, and carrying the awful hat. I met with officers of the club to discuss whether or not EL MILAGRO could stay at Tecamac until his papers had been cleared.

Tony was truly helpful, pushing for keeping him where he was. EL MILAGRO had settled in well, accepting the attentions of the many curious grooms, and exulting in the quantity of good oats and water.

I arranged a conference call for the club's officers with Hal Murphy, who explained the position. He underlined how dangerous it had been for Giselle Pont to continue on as owner. He reiterated that he was a toughie and could handle whatever threats arose.

The most interesting part of the morning happened when Tony's wife made her appearance. She was an American Southern belle from Georgia. Her accent was thicker than Happy's but she didn't use ain't or double negatives. Instead of Happy's y'all, I heard a clearer yo'all.

"Ah's from south of the Mason Dixon line," she laughed. "Way south!"

Her name came out slowly, like molasses from a jug. "Ah'm Mae Ellen, and Ah hears as yo'all married a sweet girl jockey from Kentucky! True?"

I brought Mae Ellen up to date, I related how we had accumulated four children but lost one last year in Madrid.

I studied Mae Ellen. I liked the sad sweet look of condolence she gave me when I SPOKE OF BABY IRISH'S passing. I thought, "This was a good woman." I related her to a polo pony, and thought how she must respond well to any innovation suggested by Tony, enjoy being ridden, and like his sport as much as he did.

She was taller than Tony, with broad hips and a well-developed bust. She carried her figure well, with no stooping from her heavy breasts. Her voice was soft, as befitted her Southern Belle image, but she added a lilting quality, particularly when she told jokes. Today's jokes were not barbs, but I guessed others could have worked like a knife to cut meat.

When the club officers left us, Mae Ellen ordered two parlor maids to bring lunch to a monks' table set up on the terrace. Seated comfortably, very at ease as the hostess of an imposing mansion, she said, "How'd yo'all like to go with me to the capital? Ah buys all mah clothes from American catalogues. Cheapos like Chadwicks, and Roamans, and fo' best Nieman Marcus. They arrives nice and easy by mail, then Ah takes, what Ah wants to keep, up to a dressmaker in the capital to make them fit proper-like."

"Thank you, I'm desperate to see my wife and children."

"Fine. Ah knows yo'all don't have any packin' to do. So, after the coffee let's usn go to mah car. Poor Tony has to stay put here, to oversee a plumber. Another pipe done broke in our home!"

I thanked Tony, and followed Mae Ellen to a superb Mercedes roadster. She pushed buttons making the convertible top lower, and we boarded. To bucket seats.

The highway was ablaze with blossoms. We entered a section of some two miles where on both sides of the cement dual carriage way there were Jacaranda trees. These were just past their prime, and with a slight breeze blowing they cast their mauve petals to fly like butterflies and land all over us in the Mercedes' open seats. Magnificent!

Lady Luck disappeared somewhere between the club and the capital. I hadn't been talking. I'd been watching the traffic getting heavier. We reached where the Aztecs had built causeways to cross the rounded lake that created a natural moat for their city. Worse traffic. No conversation. I decided I should let Mae Ellen concentrate on driving.

She didn't. Near a bridge, she stopped the car at a long low building with a sign understood in many languages. It read MOTEL, in flashing colors, a different one for each letter of the word, MOTEL. Red for the M, yellow for the O, green for the T, orange for the E, and purple for the L.

"Why are we stopping?" I asked.

"Ask me a stupid question, get yo'all a stupid answer. We's goin' inside, and yo'all will fuck me." Mae Ellen spoke as calmly as if she'd needed to go to the toilet. Perhaps in her mind she equated sex with nothing more THAN going to the toilet. When needed, do it.

Not me.

My lovemaking with Happy was on a plain that defies comparison to lust or an animal need. I opened the door next to my bucket seat, and strode away.

There was a bus stop not too far from the Motel. I suppose not all the Motel's customers had cars. I waited next to a fat peon woman who held two live chickens, heads down. They squawked, and tried to nip at her skirt. When she smiled at me I saw she had need of a dentist. She was missing two front teeth the others were dyed tobacco brown.

The peon woman was smiling because she'd watched the scene in Mae Ellen's car and guessed what had happened. I believe she didn't think much of Mae Ellen.

Her invite turned down, Mae Ellen had sped away. Not a word from me, thank God. What was there to say? I love my wife, I like your husband, and I think you are a crude unfaithful bitch?

Hardly.

Chapter 19

Happy had Richard carried on a hip as I swung into our bedroom. No smile from HER! She closed the door to the adjoining room, intimating she didn't want the older children to hear what she was going to say.

"Y'all told me there weren't no other woman. But thet Mae Ellen Farinas just called me, in-tro-duced herself and said y'all had spent the night in her house. Made love, but she don't think much o' wut y'all call lovemakin' and she done feel right sorry for me."

Oh, the green-eyed monster was surfacing. Happy, jealous! That's a first.

I was right about Mae Ellen being a bitch. What a revenge for being turned down!

"Honey, that woman's a liar. A nasty, vengeful bitch. All right, I spent the night in the Farinas family home, but I hadn't even met her until breakfast. She came in with the coffee, told me she was a Southern gal from Georgia, and I'd thought she could make a nice new friend for you! Then she said she was going up to the capital to see her dressmaker, and did I want a ride?"

"So you gave HER a ride."

"No way. I swear that I didn't. Sure, she stopped her car at a motel and made her intentions clear. I acted like a no-manners Cockney, just opened her car door and walked to the nearest bus stop. Took one of those beetle shaped buses painted in gawdy colors. No sex with that woman."

"Thet's wut the President Clinton, done said. Not e-xactly ac-cu-rate."

"Darling Happy, there's no other woman in the world I want sex with. Only you." I took Richard from off her hip and lay him down on the too-empty bed. I drew Happy into my desperate arms and gave her a very long, hungry kiss.

She responded, opened her mouth and did that tantalizing dance with her tongue I so enjoy. "Ah believes y'all. In thet filthy sweater and broken boots, wut gal would have sex with such a dork? Only me!" Happy picked up Richard and carried him into the next room, where he had a crib. When she shut the door again, returning, this time she locked it.

After heart-warming sex, I lay in her arms thinking about the incredible days I'd just endured. Tell Happy all the particulars? I decided against that. As for Mae Ellen, I gave her one last entry into my mind: I recalled how when we'd first met I'd compared her to a polo pony. I'd thought Tony had a satisfactory one. Ha! Poor guy. She was more like an unpredictable filly I'd had as an assistant trainer, and how that filly had bit me and bucked me to the stable floor.

Kissing, kissing and also licking my darling wife, I cleaned all other thoughts from my mind.

As so often happened to us during our afterglows, the telephone rang. Neither Happy nor I can ignore a telephone call. Even if the caller wants to sell us something, by habit we're courteous.

This caller wasn't courteous.

A man's voice, but with a tinge of the female. As an Englishman, an Etonian, and a Cambridge graduate I'm familiar with the sound of a bull homosexual. That was the tone I heard. "You have the horse we want. You know where he is. You tell us, or we'll finish off the girl."

"You haven't got a girl from our circle. We haven't missed anyone."

"Lupe Gonzalez, and her boyfriend the Marques, flew in yesterday night from London. We were at the airport to meet them. We HAVE them."

"Who's 'we?'"

"YOU won't find out. Now do exactly what I say, or you won't see either the girl or the Marques alive again."

"Say away. I'm listening." I tried not to groan, not to show any weakness although my bowels had just given a lurch. Lupe, in Mexico! With her boyfriend, and both held by abductors who could be a lot harder on them than the ones who had held Mafalda and me. Little Lupe, a budding woman who had a big loving heart. Oh, God! Why hadn't Happy and I returned to England to protect her! I didn't doubt that it was her Marques who'd convinced Lupe to return to Mexico City to claim her inheritance. Like a terrier chewing on a golden slipper, Salvador hadn't wanted to miss out on the big deal.

"You, Rick Harrow, will bring the horse, EL MILAGRO, from wherever he is and deliver him to the stable from which he was taken several days ago. Then you walk away from the Gonzalez family and return to your country. Go HOME, Rick Harrow. You're not wanted here."

Not by you, and your bosses, I thought. But I waited before giving a reply. For some reason my mind skipped back to Mae Ellen, and how fortunate that I'd turned down the sex and hadn't been driven up to my Mexico City hotel by her. The Mercedes had a distinctive license plate featuring the TF of her husband's name. It would have been noticed. No doubt this gang had my hotel staked out 24/7. Mae Ellen's car, with its distinctive license plate, could have led them to the polo club and EL MILAGRO. I took a deep breath and said firmly,

"Go to hell. You'll be going there anyway without any help from me. If you persist in these threats I'll have the police go to the *jefe's* hacienda."

The homosexual's voice disappeared. Instead I heard raucous laughter from several throats. Some belonged to more feminine homosexuals. I hung up.

What made them laugh? What was so funny?

Happy had been listening on the extension in the children's room. She joined me, gave me a hug, and read my mind. "Ah's goin' to tell y'all what them goons thinks is so funny. Like in a poker game, them goons hold the cards so yourn threats meant nothin'. The po-lice? Don't y'all recalls how thet po-lice-man shot 'n killed a man in the hos-pi-tal where y'all had took him? Or so y'all just told me, in thet re-duced ver-sion o' wut went on durin' them two days y'all dis-a-ppeared. The po-lice works fo' THEM."

I nodded. "Call Maheen. Ask her to come to our rooms, and to bring Luca. I've heard it said it takes a thief to catch a thief. How about it takes a policeman to catch crooked policemen?"

"Yeah man, 'n Ah wants to see thet baby o' theirn."

Happy used the phone while I showered and changed into clean jeans, sweater and shirt. She reached Luca.

He said, "Happy, I've heard Rick's back. Id like to see him. Can I come to your rooms?"

"If y'all brings Maheen 'n yourn baby," Happy was delighted. She hadn't needed to ask, he'd offered to come before she'd had a chance to ask.

Luca appeared in his uniform, that was the same light blue as that of the *judiciales* uniforms. Those officious jerks who'd been such pests when Lupe had been hospitalized!

We gave each other Italian-style bear hugs while Happy cooed over Maheen and their baby.

Settling down to a bottle of wine from our bar, Luca's expression became extremely serious. "I imagine you've heard that Lupe and her boyfriend have been grabbed by the thugs."

"Welcome to the party, Luca. How did YOU hear?"

"Maheen had gone to the airport to collect Lupe and her man. Never got to see her. The two of them had been collected by a group of actors, and left in a convoy of Mercedes. At least that's what Maheen learned from an airport official, when she complained she'd wasted a trip out to the airport. Maheen KNEW that Guadalupe wouldn't have gone voluntarily."

"No. Of course not. She'd have waited for Maheen, after asking to be collected by her. But Maheen hasn't wasted her trip. At least now we know that ACTORS are involved in this. Gonzi Gonzalez was an actor. His daughters were married to actors. Luca, we're getting somewhere on the case."

"But EL MILAGRO has been sold to Hal Murphy. The paperwork has gone through. Why would a bunch of actors want to get the horse?"

"That's one of the questions for which we need answers," I said glumly. Turning to Happy, I asked, "Any thoughts?"

"Ah ain't made up my mind. Ah's reservin' my opinion fo' the moment. If y'all would at least TELL me where'all thet horse be, Ah'd tell Hal to send some transport there, collect EL MILAGRO and take him back to the Ruidoso track in New Mexico. Get him out of this country. The Lupe problem? Ah hopes to deal with thet. Soon. Ah doesn't want her killed. Once the horse gets away, Lupe ain't goin' to sur-vive this."

Maheen, who'd been busy with her baby, put in her two cents. "We should call Lupe's half-sister. Ask for her help. Maybe we should go see her, that would add some punch to our request." Maheen had always come up with practical ideas. This one I was afraid was a bit far out. Himelda had never shown any fondness for Lupe. Quite the contrary, I'd seen her snub Lupe at the funeral. I'd had no other personal experiences with the woman, but she certainly hadn't bothered to accompany Guadalupe to the airport any of the times she'd flown to England.

I could understand that Himelda wasn't pleased that Guadalupe had inherited five and a half million, nevertheless she WAS the only blood relation left to her, and she could have demonstrated some human kindness to a younger half-sister.

Happy giggled. "Maheen, thet be yourn idée. Y'all call Himelda."

Maheen did. She asked Reception to get Himelda's telephone number, and dialed it.

She had a long wait, while Himelda's servants passed the call on from one to another. Finally, Himelda designed to take the call.

Himelda had a voice that had been trained by professionals. Gonzi had wanted an actress in the family. Himelda proved too undisciplined to memorize lines, or take on a character's role. She was always the hedonist. The wild girl who did what she damned pleased.

"I know who you are," she said unpleasantly. No hello, no 'nice to hear from you.' "This is about Guadalupe, I suppose."

Taken aback by Himelda's crassness, my little Egyptian friend, educated in old-fashioned European schools, countered gently, "Yes. How do you do? Yes, it's about Guadalupe. I went to the airport to meet her plane coming in from London. But I never saw her. She'd been hurried away by a group of men. She hasn't contacted me."

Happy took over the receiver. "This be Happy Harrow, a friend of yourn late father's who asked fo' my help."

"Help with a horse, I believe," Himelda interrupted, sneering.

"Yes. But also he made a request regardin' Lupe, suggestin' as Ah help with her too. *Ah* WAS contacted. To-day, regardin' both thet horse and yourn little sister."

Interruption again. "Half-sister. A little bastard, born on the wrong side of the blanket."

"Ah was told to give over EL MILAGRO, or yourn half-sister would be killed."

"Oh, but that's terrible." Himelda's remark rang as false as the curves in her bra, stuffed with styrofoam.

"Himelda, Ah's just about—"

New interruption, "Mrs. Balthazar to *you*, and don't you forget that!"

"Okay, Mrs. But Ah wants to meet up with y'all. This same afternoon. Where at?"

"I'm terribly busy. Maybe next week I could find a moment."

"Y'all knows as we'uns won't be in Mexico next week. Not if I can help it. I said THIS AFTERNOON. Y'all come here. Or we'uns goes to yourn house."

"I won't be at home."

"Us, or the po-lice. Which y'all pre-fer?"

"The police, of course. They are my friends. Most of the local ones are. My latest boyfriend is a commissioner of the capital's police. If they want to keep their jobs, the policemen do as he tells them."

"We'uns guessed that. But there be OTHER po-lice what work fo' the national government. They'uns will call on you this afternoon. Ah mean po-lice from your Procuradoria General de Justicia."

"Oh, all right. You can see me at home at three. I have guests for lunch, and can't possibly expect them to leave before three." The telephone conversation ended with a determined click. No goodbye. Himelda had hung up. So rude!

Chapter 20

It was a good thing that the girls stopped talking, because Hal burst into our bedroom as wild as the winds of a typhoon. ""Look at this!" Livid, his hands shook the early edition of the evening newspaper. "I was downstairs at the bar, and the concierge came to find me with THIS. My picture twelve inches on the front page. He translated the accompanying article. Says where EL MILAGRO is stabled. At a polo club. Gives the address of the polo club, and even tells its readers that my horse is in a stall leased by Tony Farinas. And the article must be authentic, because the source for this article was MRS.TONY FARINAS."

God Almighty. I was right about Mae Ellen being a bitch.

"What can I do to help?" I asked briskly.

"Go with me to those stables. I'll hire private detectives, proper transport for the horse, and we'll try to get there before those kidnappers can abduct him again."

I said to Happy, "My darling, if you'll deal with Lupe's capture by those thugs, then I can go with Hal and try to get the horse."

Luca spoke up. "I'll go with Happy, and Maheen. I've got a license to use my gun. We may need it." He tapped his holster.

Thanks to our babysitter, we were able to leave our children and get going. Hal asked the hotel's concierge to rent a limousine to take us to a helicopter. Transport for the horse could have been very daunting until I recalled that polo ponies were shipped from Mexico to compete at Wellington, in Florida. That meant we could get proper transport for EL MILAGRO from the polo club.

Of course, Hal being Hal, he had to lease an enormous helicopter with rotors the size of the wings on a DC-9. Or almost!

The pilot knew well where the Tecamac Polo Plub was located, because he'd transported ponies from there. We could have arrived before the thugs, except that Mafalda made a scene when she heard where Hal was headed.

Like an express train, Himelda roared through the hotel lobby. "My dear wonderful husband, I positively forbid you to go anywhere near the dreadful men who abducted me. They are not like the waiters in five star restaurants. Those men will slit your throat easier than cutting jello."

"Mafalda, darling. I thought you said you hadn't had a hard time, until that tummy upset."

"I didn't want to worry you, my precious. But I tell you, don't go anywhere near those people. Forget the horse."

"No. Mafalda, angel, I don't want us to have our first argument. I'm a tough guy. I can take care of myself, and get the better of those people. Just kiss me, and wish me luck."

They kissed in that lobby full of tourists, who stared, and some even applauded. After all, it isn't every day you see an old man embracing with such zest a 200-pound woman.

Hal's bodyguards and four *federales* came with us. We piled inside with the bodyguards. They checked their weapons. They'd brought rifles and a machine gun as well as pistols. At the heliport we hurried aboard, our transport's rotors swirling like the waters of a whirlpool.

My return to the polo club was spectacular, arriving in that huge helicopter. I'd pointed out to the pilot where we should land. My choice had been on the polo field that was nearest EL MILAGRO's stable.

Impossible. Below us swarmed all the ponies of the polo club. They'd been released to conceal EL MILAGRO in the crowd.

Why, released? Because there were six thugs with Kalashnikovs placed strategically around that field. They had aimed their AK-47s at the ponies' grooms, and were shouting orders to them to clear the field of their charges.

What a scene! Below us on the green grass were magnificent polo ponies shoulder to shoulder, barely able to sway because the swarm was so large. I recalled an old Western movie about rustlers at the turn of the century and how the hero cowboys had a hard job herding the herds because they were packed so closely.

Up in the helicopter, we had the high ground. Hals' bodyguards had no hesitation to shoot at these rustlers. They aimed, they fired, and they downed four of them. The remaining two fled to a Mercedes and sped away. Gleefully we landed on the polo field. I thanked the grooms and weaved through the charges to locate EL MILAGRO. He came to me immediately with very little difficulty. I helped the pilot position a ramp that led into the helicopter's interior. EL MILAGRO went straight in, like a kid to a birthday party.

We were airborne. But any jubilation turned sour as we approached the outskirts of Mexico City and recognized Himelda's stretch limousine below us just when it was broad-sided by one of the *jefe's* vans. The crash tore off a side of the limo and out fell the cadavers of Soledad's five children. Earlier, they had been on route to their Flamenco dancing class: it was a trek always taken at the same hour on the same day of the week. The children had been killed before the limo collected them! Like Freda Kahlo's trolley, their transport brought on the tragedy. I recognized the van as the one that had taken me as a hostage. Those poor dead kids! They'd been in line to inherit their mother's eleven million pesos. Wouldn't happen now. How could I alert Happy from Hal's helicopter? My cell phone had no signal.

The whole operation hadn't taken ten minutes.

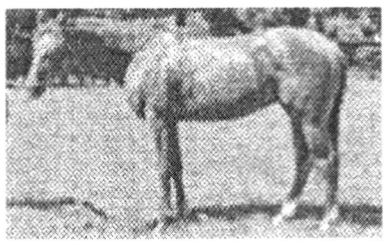

Chapter 21

My Happy, Maheen and Luca couldn't find an available radio taxi. They took a bus to Himelda's classy neighborhood. Their mode of transport had a psychological effect, making them feel inferior to the chatelaine of the very grand mansion they approached.

They had left behind in the bus a group of passengers dressed in servants' uniforms, all of them heading for work in the neighborhood's elegant houses. Most of the women were maids wearing black uniforms with white aprons that had frilly lace hems.

The servant who opened Himelda's front door was a step above those they'd traveled with: a po-faced butler. This butler, in black tails and black tie, frowned at them. He was accustomed to receiving ladies in couture outfits. If Luca hadn't been with Happy and Maheen, both in T-shirts and jeans, the butler would have refused them admittance. But he mistook Luca's light blue Italian policeman's uniform for a *judiciales*'s.

There were no signs of a recent lunch party. No fresh flowers, centerpieces, or lipstick-stained demi tasse cups.

The threesome had barely crossed Himelda's threshold when they heard shots. Himelda was screaming. Happy and Maheen recognized another distraught voice: Guadalupe's.

Himelda's fancy butler didn't hesitate. He darted through the open door and ran down the street. He wasn't too fancy to ride a bicycle, and stole one with the lettering PIZZA, that was parked outside a neighbor's gate. He disappeared down the opposite boulevard. There were no other servants in Himelda's house.

Luca sped toward the sound of the women's screams. Drawing his revolver, he loaded it as he ran. Happy and Maheen followed, close on his heels.

All three arrived together at the source of the screams. They entered a huge living room, over-decorated with Spanish antiques, and too many flowering plants. The Marques lay, shot, on the Aubusson carpet. Guadalupe was bent over him, applying CPR, her mouth pressed to his. A scarlet rivulet of blood stained the Aubusson carpet. Himelda was busily trying to mop up his blood before it ruined her valuable French antique. She was still yelling, "Stop, stop." As if that could STOP the Marques's blood from flowing.

Luca hurried toward the Marques's body. He knelt and pressed fingers to the Marques's throat artery. There was no pulse. "He's dead," he said as gently as possible while urging Guadalupe to stand.

"Her husband Julio Balthazar!" Guadalupe cried out. She pointed with deep revulsion at Himelda, as if a leper was kneeling beside the bloodied rug. "My God, Julio killed my Salvadorcito." Her fury was so great that she couldn't weep. "Find him. Kill HIM."

Himelda tossed away the bloodied rag that was now useless because Salvador's intestines had spilled out from a huge hole in his stomach. She stood up and slapped Lupe, hard. "Don't you dare say such things. My husband hasn't killed anybody. He's in Acapulco, waterskiing."

Guadalupe recoiled, rubbed her reddening cheek, and said without complaint, "I KNOW THAT BROTHER-IN-LAW OF MINE WHEN I SEE HIM. And I recognized the guns he used too. They were the ones that were always in a gun case in Papacito's study. Dueling pistols. Antique ones. He fired from one and then the other. Point blank at Salvadorcito."

A smooth voice, honed by professionals who had worked to improve its original blandness, came at them from hidden stereo boxes. "Not point blank at the Marques. Point blank at YOU, Guadalupe. I don't usually miss, but those guns *are a*ntiques."

Himelda swung around from staring at the rug's blood stains. She knew exactly where the stereo boxes were placed. She spoke towards the nearest one. "My darling, run! Catch a plane for Brazil. No extradition there. One of these visitors is a policeman. I'll hold him here as long as possible." She thrust herself toward a far wall, where a rifle had the place of honor over a fireplace. She pulled down the rifle, loaded it with bullets stored in a nearby cigar box, and pointed it at Luca.

Happy went into action. She grabbed two cushions from the sofa and threw them into the air, each cushion in an opposite direction. Distracted, Himelda went wild and her shots were misdirected. One hit the cushion to her right, but she wasn't able to deal with the other. The speed with which Happy had thrown the cushions had caused Himelda to take her eye off her target, Luca. Himelda's plan was to kill Luca, Maheen, Happy and Lupe.

With Himelda's aim thrown off balance, Happy took a chance and gave a karate chop to Himelda's wrist, sending the rifle flying. Happy scooped up the rifle, and called out to Maheen. "Tie up Himelda. Y'all has a belt. Use it."

Maheen didn't hesitate. She ripped off her belt and pulled it tight around Himelda's wrists, using the buckle as a lock. She shoved Himelda to a wall next to the sofa, and left her there to cross to Lupe. She took Lupe in her arms, and soothed her as best she could. She muttered, "It's awfully hard to lose the man you love."

Happy added her words of comfort. "Let's usn pray t'gether fo' Salvador. Luca, y'all get busy and call yourn colleagues in the po-lice, but also call fo' an ambulance. Salvador should leave this house in dig-ni-ty." Happy and Maheen lowered their heads. Happy prayed with the words of the Twenty-third psalm, "The Lord is my shepherd, I shall not want, He maketh me to lie down in green pastures, He leadeth me beside the still waters, He restoreth my soul."

Seething against the wall, Himelda made rude noises. "'Restoreth'! What balls. Lucky I don't believe in any of that superstitious crap, otherwise I'd have been loaded with Soledad's five brats when she got killed. Aunt Magdalena said I was barred from taking Soledad's kids. Lucky, because Julio hates kids."

Guadalupe, who had been crouching next to the Marques's cadaver, now stood up and glared at Himelda. "You're a demon. Inviting Salvadorcito and me to come after lunch, when there was no lunch, no cook in the house, only that sinister butler, you'd paid to help you and Julio to kill us and dispose of our bodies."

"I heard that. Very naughty. You should be more choosy with your accusations." Julio Balthazar strode into the room carrying a Kalashnikov. An ugly man, he could have been Himelda's twin. His face was pockmarked, as well as covered with Herpes sores. His eyes were filled with pus. His stride was like a woman's, his frame rocking from side to side, as he positioned one small foot to curl around the other. He was as cool as if he was going to a concert. "Hello, everybody," he said, in his schooled actor's voice. He made a Sir Walter Raleigh bow to Guadalupe, removing his jacket and placing it before her as a rug. Did he plan to shoot her there and roll up her body in that rug?

Happy wasn't accepting his ploy. She flew like a lance at him, butting him as hard as she could, striking his left shoulder. He released the Kalashnikov and plunged to the ground, screaming. Julio screamed like a terrified woman. "You've killed me," he yelled. "My heart's exploding."

Guadalupe scooped up the Kalashnikov, and placed it on the sofa. She said, "Oh, do shut up. You're wasting your time, looking for pity from us."

Julio stopped screaming. He went into convulsions. Spit foamed at the corners of his mouth. His breathing became erratic, then stopped. His eyes rolled up toward his forehead, showing pinkish whites at the bottom lids. His mouth hung open, the jaw loose.

"Dear Lord, Ah's killed him," Happy cried. She had brought four babies into the world, and had never caused a death. Giving life was her forte, not taking it. She knelt beside Julio, and placed a hand on his cold forehead. "Like ice. Like mar-ble," she moaned.

Himelda shouted, "You could be a murderer. Get him up off the floor. Put him on the sofa. Try to make him comfortable, if there's any breath left in him."

Luca shook his head. "No. He shouldn't be moved. My police training has taught me you leave such cases on the floor. Could be a cardiac thrombosis. You remember all the trouble that was made over Dr. Murray leaving Michael Jackson in his bed, when he should have been put on the floor."

"Do as you're told. This is my house, and Julio's my husband. Put him on the sofa."

Luca shrugged. He had considerable difficulty raising Julio, whose arms and legs flopped like a marionette's.

When finally Luca was able to cross with him to the sofa, Himelda rushed over from the wall and with her manacled hands managed to thrust the Kalashnikov next to Julio.

The dead man sat up and rose quicker than the biblical Lazarus. Back into place went the whites of his eyes. Gone was the erratic breathing. Julio bounded from the sofa with the Kalashnikov, aimed it, and fired. No dead man, he! We'd forgotten Julio's specialty was playing dead. He shot straight at Herminia.

Herminia's head exploded. Her brains showered over the sofa's silk damask and the Aubusson carpet.

Next, he aimed at Guadalupe. But just as Salvador had done earlier when Salvador had shielded her body, now Luca placed his body over Lupe. Julio shot straight at him.

Julio didn't wait to see if Luca had been fatally hit. He bolted from the room, went to the hall's grand staircase and rushed to the upper landings with the speed of an Olympic runner.

"He's got a helicopter on the roof," Guadalupe called. She'd emerged from under Luca was unhurt.

He had a grin on his face. "You didn't think I'd come into this nest of vipers without my bullet proof vest, Cara," Luca explained. He called the National police and for an ambulance. He turned to Happy. "What is Hal Murphy's cell phone number? Do you know it? Or do you, Maheen darling?"

Maheen shook her head. She was too relieved to speak.

Happy said, "Try 416-428-4424. That's a Toronto number. Ah thinks as Ah got it right."

Within seconds Hal's efficient voice boomed through Luca's cell phone. "That you, Luca? I see your name on my cell phone. Tell Happy we've got EL MILAGRO. We're in a huge helicopter flying over Mexico City."

"Hal, there have been two murders at the Balthazar home. Ask your pilot if he knows Calle Moroni, in Barrio Laguna. I've called for the police, and an ambulance. But I need your help to stop the killer from leaving this house in his helicopter."

"My pilot says he knows Calle Moroni, he knows the Balthazar house. Says as he's a fan of Julio Balthazar, the actor who plays death scenes so well. That we're within minutes of the place. Over and oot."

Happy was the first to hear helicopter rotors. "Ah thinks as Julio has taken off. Guadalupe, he be a GOOD pilot? Ah sho don't want him crashin' into Rick and Hal."

"Yes, I suppose he's good enough. He got his pilot's license. Special one. If you two want to go up on the roof, go ahead. I'm staying with Salvadorcito until the ambulance arrives. Then I guess the police will want to move Salvadorcito's body to the morgue. Forensics will take him." She began to cry.

"We'all will stay down here. Cain't leave y'all alone with yourn Salvador." Happy crouched next to Guadalupe, who had returned to kneel beside her Marques.

"Julio, that monster. He ordered all the killings," Guadalupe moaned, cradling Salvador's blood-soaked head, not caring that she'd painted her clothes, stockings, and hands with the goo. She took a finger and lovingly dipped it first into his oozing blood and then slowly, adoringly placed the bloodied finger in her mouth. Her other hand cradled parts of his intestines.

Maheen thrust herself next to Luca's strong chest. With tears for the lovers who'd never enjoyed lovemaking, Maheen whispered, "Poor Salvador, poor Guadalupe. So much money in the Gonzalez family, and so much death."

Guadalupe sighed deeply. She stuttered, "I needed love, not money."

Luca used his jacket to cover Himelda's open head. His jacket instantly became sodden with what remained of her brains mixed with her blood. He sighed, "What a husband, Himelda's Julio! Mowed Himelda down as if she was a metal duck at a shooting gallery you'd aim at to get a prize."

Happy mumbled, "His prize? Himelda's eleven and a half million pesos, if he could have killed her without usn bein' witnesses. I supposes as Julio intended to put in a claim for Guadalupe's five and a half million, had he killed her too."

"Yes," Guadalupe agreed, her tears drying up when she got her teeth into the subject. "If I'd died first, Herminia would have inherited from me. I'd no one else. What with Soledad dead. She'd already got Soledad's money."

"Do you think he killed Soledad?"

"I've no doubt he did, *and* her husband too. Also their five children. Needed to get them out of the way. Just as he'd killed Papacito's lawyer."

"Forgive me, for bringing up that painful subject, but did he kill your father?"

"I'd had my suspicions. Now I'm certain Julio hired one of his homosexual henchmen to fake all that *crazy* stuff. I'm sure the pathologists will find Papacito was drugged, before being hung in that closet with cords around his wrists and his genitals."

"You think it was always about money?"

"Of course. Or, maybe money AND envy. My father was such a success, but all the acting jobs that Julio could get were death scenes. And to think, we almost fell for one!"

Chapter 22

A roar of rotors interrupted Guadalupe. She left Salvador's cadaver to rush to a window. Outside, low on the horizon, two helicopters were vieing for space to manoeuvre. Hal's huge helicopter, like a giant hornet, dominated the scene buzzing Julio's helicopter like a hornet might a wasp.

Happy, Maheen and Luca joined her, staring at the air duel.

It didn't last long. When the two aircraft reached the sky over a gasoline station, Julio's helicopter attempted a daring escape. He cut the rotors. That didn't work.

An unexpected wind downed Julio's helicopter to plunge to earth like a bug that was swatted, without hope of survival. And Julio didn't survive. This wasp had crashed into a gasoline pump that exploded. His helicopter burst into fire. Acrid black smoke, scarlet flames and hideous body parts fouled the air.

I managed to convince Hal to order his pilot to land on the rooftop heliport of Himelda's house, in spite of the ashes and thunderous noise.

Within minutes of the rotors slowing, I'd pounded down the marble stairway to find Happy and take her into my arms. "My darling, you're safe!" Then I groaned out, "But we've just seen all five of Soledad's children dead in Himelda's limo. I'm guessing that Julio was the serial killer."

"He were." Happy used her fingers to tick off the dead, "He murdered Gonzi, his lawyer, Guadalupe's mother, Soledad, Marco Jimenez, Salvador, and Himelda. Julio also ordered all five children killed to inherit all the millions."

"Don't forget that Himelda was responsible for the *jefe's* death. It was Himelda who asked her boyfriend-police supremo to order him silenced. Sorry, to cast Himelda as a murderer too. Not just Julio's accomplice. A murderer. She'd been determined to have EL MILAGRO. She'd lied that she wasn't interested in owning the horse. She WAS after she'd learned EL MILAGRO was worth $4 million."

"And how is EL MILAGRO?" Happy asked, her lips wet, shining with my saliva.

"Oh, he's fine. With Julio and Himelda dead, their pay-as-you-go thugs will melt away out of our lives. We'll fly EL MILAGRO to the Ruidoso track. Weeks ago I'd entered him for a race there next week. You can ride him in that race. How about it?"

"Ah thinks as how Ah'd rather find usn a kingsize bed and make love." Happy snuggled up close.

Maheen took a hint, and she placed Luca's hand on a breast as an invitation to him. But there would be no foursome for us. We don't do foursomes, or threesomes.

Happy and I take our lovemaking *à deux*. Frankly, she makes too much noise to expose anyone else to it.

Later that night, waiting to initiate lovemaking, I said, "I know you want to go to see that Mayan pyramid, El Castillo, at Chichen Itza. I've read that twice yearly, at sunrise, you get an optical illusion on the north stairway. We're at the right time of the year for that. Wasn't there something like it at Karnak that excited you? We'll go."

"Yeah man. Thankee."

The lovemaking that followed was very, very special.

Chapter 23

The following week Lupe joined us in the Owners and Trainers stand at New Mexico's Ruidoso track. What a difference these past few days had made in Lupe's life. From a half-child half-woman adolescent, full of joy and fun, a girl who had large breasts but an untouched vagina, she'd matured into a grieving beauty whose doe eyes brimmed constantly with tears for her murdered love, Salvador.

"Cheer up, gal," Happy said, meaning well, and trying to lighten the atmosphere. "Y'all's a multi-millionaire. Y'all got twenty-seven million five hundred thousand dollars!"

"Money! My family wiped out and Salvador killed, all for money. I don't want the $27,500,000. I would give that and both my arms and legs if I could get back my father, my mother, my Salvadorcito, Soledad, and those five little children."

Oh, yeah? I wondered. Maybe now, with the illusions and tenderness of some teenagers, Lupe would feel that way. But would her millions corrupt even our little friend, Lupe? I hoped not.

For Lupe, I wanted what Happy and I have in great abundance, a lasting love and great sex.

THE END

Books by Beatrice Fairbanks Cayzer

TALES OF PALM BEACH
THE PRINCES AND PRINCESSES OF WALES
ROYAL LOVERS (with Barbara Cartland)
THE ROYAL WORLD OF ANIMALS
DIANE, PRINCESS DE POLIGNAC
MURDER BY MEDICINE
THE HAPPY HARROW MURDER TRILOGY
VAMPIRE MURDERS IN MOROCCO
LOVE LOVE IN DARFUR

Cover from painting by French Impressionist Jean de Botton

CPSIA information can be obtained at www.ICGtesting.com
Printed in the USA
269653BV00003B/84/P